Jailed by Lust - Released by Love

by

Gerard C. Cole Sr.

Sheila's missing something

Wandering through her teenage years
Trying to be
The girl of somebody's dreams
To the detriment of her own.

Her stars cross in Chicago
A tumultuous whirlwind
Rumbles through the Midwest
And leaves her humbled

Able to see herself
Clearly now
She truly starts to blossom
As a release of love waters her
She is nourished to the core.
pharess marie

Ponderings

*J*ailed *by Lust – Released by Love* is an amazing and wonderful book because of its powerful inspirational messages of love, faith, hope, and renewal. I found myself growing spiritually as I co-edited this sincere book that reminds us all of the power of love to heal, to help us grow and to transcend. As an ordained interfaith minister, I believe that we are here to evolve, and this is the message that comes across so very clearly through the pages of this book as the characters grapple with many of the most pressing issues facing us today and choose love as the path to healing, reconciliation, and transformation. What I love about this book is that it not only tackles powerful spiritual themes, it is also entertaining with a clever plot twist! I am pleased to have been a part of the bringing forth of this work, and I expect that it will have a profoundly positive impact on all who read it.

– Rev. Andrea Payne,
minister, artist, Earth champion

About The Author

Gerard C. Cole was born in the Bronx, New York and currently resides in Boston, Massachusetts.

As a child, Gerard was being raised at home with his 10 siblings when suddenly, at the age of nine, he and all his siblings were taken from their home, separated into pairs, and sent to foster and group homes.

On Gerard's 18th birthday, without any direction or guidance, Nassau County Social Services dropped Gerard from the foster system, leaving him out on the street to literally fend for himself. In a world where people throw blame around like a baseball, Gerard never blamed anyone, not even his parents, for any of the misfortunes in his life.

Gerard has always relied on his faith and has made it his life mission to be the best person he can be while also sharing love and knowledge with young adults, so that they too, can become the best version of themselves that they can possibly be.

Jailed by Lust - Released by Love is Gerard's first book. He is also known for his work as a talent consultant and manager of young and older adults. His client list includes *America's Got Talent* phenomenon "Voices of Glory."

"The definition of self-worth and success should not be defined by the guidelines that have been written for you, but by the guidelines that you have written for yourself."

- Gerard C. Cole Sr.

Dedication

This book is dedicated to young adults and families everywhere!

This book speaks about faith, love, family, and the importance of being sexually responsible, and it illustrates how not doing so can come with some serious consequences.

If you haven't heard or have forgotten, let me remind you that HIV is real, STIs are real, unwanted pregnancy is real. Abortion and having to make life or death decisions is real.

However, remaining abstinent is also a very real and safe choice that you can also make.

Choose to keep you and your partner safe, either by using protection or remaining abstinent.

The Centers for Disease Control and Prevention have information for teens and young adults: Staying Healthy and Preventing STDs—for more information, call 800-232-4636.

Acknowledgements

I'd like to thank God for giving me the health, strength, and experiences to write this book. To You, I give all the glory.

Many thanks to my beautiful wife, Geraldine V. Cole. You have given me so much love and supported me throughout the publication of not only this book, but throughout many of my endeavors.

To my sister and close friend, Mary Cole Watson, for encouraging me to write my book by giving me an opportunity to work on her essential book *Wisdom Warriors.*

A very special thanks to Pharess Marie for the marvelous job she has done editing my book and bringing the characters to life, and to Rev. Andrea Payne, and Jordan Sahley who provided the copy editing for my book. You all are amazing and I couldn't have completed this book without you.

To Marcos Palacious, thank you for the illustration! You are a very talented artist; I am so honored to have had you do the artwork for my book.

To my children, grandchildren, and siblings, each one of you are precious to me! I thank God for you and will always love you!

Table of Contents

Chapter 1

A Beautiful, Hot Summer Morning in Chicago

It's a beautiful, hot summer morning in Chicago, and seventeen-year-old Damien Jackson is suddenly awakened by the smell of his mother's freshly baked biscuits. Still groggy from yesterday's hours-long football practice with his popular high school football team, the Morgan Park Stallions, Damien creeps out of bed. Stretching his arms to the ceiling, he says, "Yes! It must be Saturday! Other than special occasions like Thanksgiving, Christmas, and my birthday, the only other times Mom makes her famous biscuits is on Saturdays."

Taking his phone off its charger, Damien begins checking his messages. Realizing there's nothing requiring his immediate attention, he places his phone on the dresser, walks over to his closet, and selects a casual outfit for the day consisting of a gray Polo T-shirt, gray sweatpants, his special gray chain that holds a picture of his late dad, and a pair of gray and black Air Jordans.

Neatly placing the selected items on his bed, Damien heads straight for the shower. Once showered and dressed, he makes his way downstairs to the kitchen, where surely enough, he finds his mother preparing a breakfast feast that includes smoked bacon, corn beef hash, grits with cheese, a fruit bowl, and yes, her famous homemade biscuits that Damien loves so much.

Feeling playful, Damien quietly sneaks up behind his mother, Sharon Jackson, who is standing at the kitchen sink. He says a goofy good morning while giving her a big, wet kiss on the cheek.

"Damien!" she shouts, "Didn't I tell you to never sneak up on me like that? You scared the crap out of me."

"My bad," Damien responds while reaching for a biscuit.

While facing the sink, Sharon shouts playfully, "Damien, don't you touch those biscuits!"

Damien's mouth drops in awe, "Mom, how did you know I was reaching for a biscuit?"

"Because ever since you could reach the stove, you've tried that same move every Saturday morning."

Damien laughs, and after practicing some basketball moves around his busy mother, he jokes, "Well, Mom, I guess I'm going to have to change-up my biscuit moves."

Smiling sweetly, Sharon swats her son with a kitchen towel and dries her hands before turning over a sizzling piece of bacon. "You most definitely will," she says, glancing at Damien as he reaches into the fridge, "but for now, would you mind passing me the eggs from the fridge please?"

"No problem," says Damien. He searches the fridge but doesn't see any eggs, "Mom, it looks like we're out of eggs."

"Oh no!" she exclaims, "I had written eggs on the top of my shopping list, and I must have forgotten to buy them. Can you please run to the corner store and pick me up two dozen eggs and some orange juice before your sister wakes up?"

"Yes, Mom," Damien replies with a smile.

Sharon reaches into her purse sitting on the kitchen chair, takes out a twenty-dollar bill, and hands it to Damien. "That should be enough."

"Yes, I think so. By the way, you don't have to worry about Tanya. She's not getting up for another couple of hours. You know how she likes to sleep late whenever she can."

Sharon smiles, "Son, you are so right. What was I thinking?"

She shakes her head as Damien takes the money, puts it in his pocket, and runs back upstairs to retrieve his Chicago Bears hat. On his way out, Damien sneaks back into the kitchen and steals a biscuit. "I got you, Mom!" He gives his mother a quick kiss before dodging his way out of the kitchen, barely missing a flick from her dish towel.

Looking to the heavens, Sharon shakes her head, "Sometimes, just sometimes, I wish I could knock him out!" She laughs to herself, "Lord, you know I'm just kidding. Thank you for blessing me with such wonderful children." She continues preparing breakfast and humming as a song plays quietly in the background.

Walking to the store with a biscuit in hand, Damien hears someone calling his name. He looks around, confused, until his eyes fall on Mrs. Vivian Johnson, his neighbor and family friend, who is waving to him from her porch. He brushes the lingering biscuit crumbs from his face as he waves back.

"Can you please come here for a moment?" Vivian shouts, waving him over, "I'd like you to meet someone."

"Good morning, Mrs. Johnson!" Damien shouts back, "I'll stop by on the way back! I have to run to the store for my mom."

"Okay," Vivian shouts, "please don't forget!"

"I won't," Damien promises.

He continues walking to the corner store to fulfill his mother's wishes. Knowing the store like the back of his hand, he grabs the items in ten seconds flat, a new record for him. As he approaches the register, Mr. Davis, the store owner, smiles at him, "Hello, young man. How's the family?"

"We are all fine," Damien answers with a smile as he turns the volume down on his headphones.

Mr. Davis nods, smiling warmly, "That's good news."

Mr. Davis bags Damien's purchases, and Damien hands him the twenty-dollar bill that his mother gave him. Mr. Davis politely brushes Damien's hand away and slides him the bag, "This one is on me. Please stay safe, and tell that beautiful mother of yours that I said hello."

Damien pockets the bill and nods at Mr. Davis, "I will, and thank you so much for the groceries."

"You are so welcome," Mr. Davis grins widely as Damien exits the store and heads home.

Damien arrives home and places the groceries on the kitchen table, he then hands the grocery money back to his mother. Catching his breath, Damien says, "Mr. Davis would not take the money, and he said, 'This one is on the store, and please tell your beautiful mother that I said hello.' Mom, I think he likes you," Damien shakes his head.

Blushing, Sharon says, "Maybe, son, but either way, that man is so sweet and kind. I'll have to remember to buy him a card." She then gives the twenty-dollar bill back to Damien and smiles.

"Thanks, Mom." putting the money in his pocket, Damien pats it happily.

"No, thank you, for going to the store." Sitting down, Sharon picks up a magazine. Excusing himself, Damien heads for the door.

"Where are you heading?" Sharon questions disappointedly, "Are you not staying for breakfast?"

"Mrs. Johnson wants me to stop by and meet someone," Damien replies.

"I wonder who it is? Well, hurry back. Breakfast will be ready in thirty minutes. Oh, and please ask Vivian if she will be attending church tomorrow."

Eyeing up the biscuits one last time, Damien smiles, "Okay, Mom." He marches out the door and up the street to Vivian's house.

Vivian is still sitting on her front porch, reading the morning paper when Damien arrives.

"Good morning, Mrs. Johnson. How are you feeling?"

She glances at him before casually flipping a page, "With my hands."

"That's a good one, Mrs. Johnson," says Damien, rolling his eyes as they both laugh, "What's new in the morning papers today?"

"Actually, I'm considering not reading the morning paper any longer," Vivian replies, tossing it down in disgust.

"Why?" Damien inquires.

"Well, for starters, there's really nothing new in the papers. It seems like every time I pick up the morning paper, it's either someone is dying from these drugs or another young person is getting shot." She closes her eyes and clasps her hands fervently.

"God, I pray that the city of Chicago can solve these problems. Oh, the state of this world is unbelievable," Vivian shakes her head.

Damien's face grows somber, "I hear you loud and clear. Two days ago, a classmate of mine was shot just because he was trying to stop someone from literally stealing his Jordans right off his feet."

Clutching her chest, Vivian gasps, "Oh no, Damien! Please be careful. My heart could never recover if anything ever happened to you."

He nods, "It's rough out here. But I always follow my mother's advice."

Vivian's eyebrows raise in curiosity, "And what is that?"

"My mom always says to choose my friends wisely, keep my enemies close, and to always stay vigilant."

Vivian chuckles to herself, "Well, Damien, that's some excellent advice. Speaking of your mother, how are she and your sister?"

"They are both doing fine. And you know, before I forget, my mom wanted me to ask you if you will be attending church tomorrow?"

Vivian flashes a smirk, "Please tell your mother that if that fine Pastor Chisholm is preaching, I'll definitely be there."

Damien laughs, "You are so funny. I'll definitely let her know."

"So, Damien, the reason why I wanted you to come over was to meet my beautiful niece, who is visiting me from New York. She'll be living with me for most of the summer, and she doesn't really know anyone here in Chicago. Considering that I've known your family for decades and that you are a truly respectable and responsible young man, I was hoping that you could show her around Chicago for me today."

Damien's eyes light up. "You did say that your niece was beautiful, right?"

"Yes, Damien." Vivian chuckles, "She's both beautiful and smart."

Damien stands back as his face gets hot with embarrassment, "I was just joking."

Vivian waves him off, "I knew you were. But is that a yes?"

Damien shrugs, "Well, I really don't have any special plans for today, and you did mention your niece's beauty and brains. So yes, I can definitely do that for you, Mrs. Johnson."

"Oh, thank you so much Damien," Vivian beams, "I know my niece doesn't want to just hang around old people all summer."

"Oh, you're not old, Mrs. Johnson. You're the same age as my mother."

Vivian lets out a hearty laugh, "You're absolutely right, Damien. I am the same age as your mother, and regardless of what she says, we are both old! I am definitely too old to be running my niece around Chicago."

They both laugh hysterically, and Damien asks, "Where is your niece now?"

Vivian looks toward the house, "She's upstairs straightening up her room. I'll go inside and ask her to come out to meet you."

"Oh, Mrs. Johnson, not now. I am heading home for breakfast, so how about after that?" Damien figures that this will also allow him more time to put on some different threads to really impress Mrs. Johnson's niece.

Vivian relaxes back into her seat, "That sounds great. I'll tell her that you will be stopping by later this morning."

"Great!" Damien exclaims as he turns to head home. As he starts to walk, Damien suddenly realizes that he forgot to ask Vivian for her niece's name. Turning around, Damien says, "Excuse me Mrs. Johnson, what's your niece's name?"

"Sheila," Vivian replies.

"Cool," Damien says, "That's a very easy name to remember." Closing the gate, he heads home with some extra pep in his step as he braces himself for the beautiful day unfolding before him.

Despite being preoccupied, Sharon hears Damien when he enters the house. "Damien, we've been waiting for you!" she shouts.

His little sister, Tanya, chimes in, "Yeah, Damien, we've been here waiting for you and we are starving!"

"I'll be right down. I'm going upstairs to wash my hands," Damien says as he scrambles up the stairs. After frantically washing his hands, Damien rushes to his room to change into a black muscle shirt. Spraying on a little too much Bond No. 9, Damien checks himself out in the mirror to ensure that he looks extra smooth for when he meets Sheila. Satisfied with his outfit, Damien heads downstairs and goes into the kitchen, where he finds his mother and sister already at the table eating. ·

Savoring her food, Sharon looks her son up and down, "I see you changed into your muscle shirt." She sniffs the air curiously, then coughs slightly, waving at the air in front of her, "And it sure smells as if you put on your special cologne. Who are you trying to impress?" She eyes him coolly and takes another bite of food.

Damien flashes a pearly grin, "No one, Mom."

Rolling her eyes, Sharon says, "Okay, son, if you say so. Now come make yourself a plate before the food gets colder."

Rubbing his hands together in anticipation, Damien says, "You don't have to tell me twice." He eagerly sits at the table after preparing a heaping plate for himself. Damien looks at his mom gratefully as he savors every bite, "This breakfast is so delicious, Mom."

She beams, "Thanks, son."

Tanya can't help but chime in, "Yo! Big brother, you need to slow down! The food isn't going anywhere."

Damien shakes his head, unable to stop himself from demolishing the food, "I know, little sis, but I have someplace to go."

She looks at him curiously, "And where are you going with that big head today?"

Ignoring her jabs, Damien says, "I promised Mrs. Johnson that I would show her niece, Sheila, around Chicago."

His mom scoops another forkful of sticky, buttery grits into her mouth, "I never knew she had a niece."

"Me neither," Tanya adds.

"Well, Mom, according to Mrs. Johnson, she does, and she said that her niece, Sheila, is visiting until early August and she doesn't know anyone here in Chicago." He continues to eat, "And she said that she's too old to be running around Chicago."

Raising an eyebrow, Sharon says, "She's not old. She's the same age as me."

"That's exactly what I told her, Mom!" Damien exclaims as he wipes the crumbs from his face, "But she said that you are both old."

They all laugh before Sharon responds, "Well, okay. You have a great time. Just promise me you'll both be extremely careful."

"Yes, Mom. I will," he promises.

Digging into her grits, Tanya mutters slyly, teasing her brother in her sing-song way, "Shoot, Sheila's the one who needs to be careful. Damien may try to kiss her!" Laughing, Tanya throws a crumpled-up napkin at her big brother.

Looking at Tanya softly while rubbing her son's hand, Sharon says, "Your brother is a very responsible person. Right, Damien?"

"Yes, very responsible," Damien assures her. Narrowing his eyes at his sister, Damien tosses the napkin right back at her, hitting her nose.

Mrs. Jackson smiles. Turning to Damien, she says, "By the way, son, I'm sure that Sheila will be very impressed with your muscles and your cologne." Sharon and Tanya burst into laughter. Even Damien can't help but chuckle.

Shaking his head, Damien mutters, "You two really have jokes." Remembering his conversation with Mrs. Johnson, he exclaims, "Oh, Mom, I almost forgot to tell you that Mrs. Johnson said, and I quote, 'As long as that fine Pastor Chisholm is preaching, then I'll definitely be in church on Sunday.'" He impersonates Mrs. Johnson's soulful voice. Sharon laughs again, shaking her head knowingly, "That woman will never change."

"That's too funny," Tanya replies as she wipes crumbs from her face.

Rubbing his six-pack, Damien says, "Thanks, Mom. May I be excused from the table?"

"Yes. Just don't forget to take some dishes with you, and rinse them off at least," she replies.

Damien gets up, and as he reaches to grab the last biscuit in the basket, his sister beats him to it as they both knew there won't be another batch of their mother's delicious biscuits until the following Saturday. Damien pulls out a five-dollar bill, dangling it before his sister's nose as a bribe for the biscuit. She readily accepts it.

Sharon finishes the last few bites of her breakfast and quickly glances at her daughter, "Are you really going to keep your brother's money?"

Finishing her orange juice, Tanya replies matter-of-factly. "Is Chicago cold in the winter?"

Raising her eyebrows, Sharon almost feels the Chicago chill in that moment, "Yes, indeed."

Flashing a look of satisfaction, Damien takes a soulful bite out of the biscuit, "No problem, Mom, I made out big time. These biscuits are so delicious, I was ready to offer her ten dollars!" All three members of the Jackson family laugh and together begin cleaning up the kitchen.

Finished helping his mom and sister, Damien rushes out of the kitchen. Checking his appearance one last time in the mirror by the front door, he shouts, "I'm heading to Mrs. Johnson's house to meet Sheila!"

"Okay, son," Sharon replies, "If you'd like, you can invite Sheila to the house tonight for dinner."

Damien pauses, "You know, that sounds like a great idea." As he exits the house, Damien declares, "I love you, Mom. I love you, sis."

"We love you, too, Damien. Be safe," Sharon says.

"I will," Damien chirps as he shuts the door behind him.

Damien is excited as he makes his way to Vivian's house. He swings open the gate and charges up the stairs to ring the bell. A few seconds pass before Damien is greeted by a gorgeous young woman with a beautiful smile. Through the screen door, Sheila looks at Damien, liking what she sees, "Are you Damien?"

"Yes, I am," Damien replies with a radiant smile. The young woman opens the door, wearing a huge smile of her own.

"Please come in. I'm Sheila. My aunt told me to expect you." Damien enters the house, and Sheila asks, "How's your day going?"

Not hearing Sheila's question, Damien just stares at her. He notices that Sheila is looking absolutely stunning in her low-cut blouse and pink fitted jeans that accentuate her figure masterfully.

"Hello?" Sheila waves her hand in front of his face with a quizzical look, "Damien? Are you okay?"

Quickly composing himself, Damien replies with a goofy smile, "Oh, yes, I'm very okay! Why do you ask?"

Rolling her eyes, Sheila responds, "Because I asked you how was your day, and you remained speechless while staring at me."

"My bad," Damien apologizes with that same goofy smile. Trying to redeem himself, he says, "I was looking at your fly braids."

Pointing at her head, Sheila says, "My braids are up here."

Damien laughs, putting his hands up in the air, "Well, I guess you got me. But to answer your question, my day is going fine, and believe it or not, it just got one hundred percent better."

"Well, I'm happy to hear that 'cause so did mine," Sheila says, eyeing him lustfully.

Just then, Vivian walks into the room, "Well, hello again, Damien. I see that you've met my niece, Sheila."

Damien replies, "Well, not officially, Mrs. Johnson." Reaching out his sweaty hand to Sheila, he clears his throat. Remembering his dad's instructions, he says, "Hello, Sheila, I'm Damien. It's very nice to meet you."

This time, Sheila smiles shyly. Shaking his hand, she replies in a very low but pleasant voice, "The pleasure is all mine." She turns to her aunt, whispering, "Auntie, you were right. He is handsome."

Vivian smiles and invites Damien to follow them outside to the backyard. As Damien follows Vivian and Sheila outside, he catches himself, again, staring at Sheila's shapely figure. Sheila, feeling Damien's vibes as he observes her, knows that her aunt is just out of earshot. She turns around with an excited smirk of her own and whispers playfully, "Do you like what you see?"

Sheila's teasing is so unexpected that Damien has no answer for her, and at this point he has no idea how his encounter with Sheila on this hot summer day in Chicago will change both of their lives forever.

Chapter 2

Chilling in the Backyard

Immediately upon entering the backyard, Damien, who is very familiar with the space, notices that Vivian has purchased new patio furniture. He reminisces about the many hours he has spent in this backyard. Damien's mother and Vivian have been best friends for decades. They both taught at the local elementary school for many years and have always enjoyed having the entire summer off. During their summer break, Sharon and Vivian loved entertaining at their homes, and the pair took turns hosting bi-weekly cookouts for their community to enjoy.

As if reading his mind, Vivian asks, "So how do you like the new patio furniture?"

"It's fire, Mrs. Johnson." Damien sinks into the soft, blue cushioned loveseat that sits underneath a beautifully shaded tree. But remembering where he is, Damien quickly corrects himself and sits upright in the loveseat, "I mean, it looks wonderful!"

Vivian laughs, "I know I told you that I was old, but I actually knew what you meant when you said fire. Sheila's been teaching me a lot of the new words that you young folks are using today."

Looking at Sheila, Damien can't help but think that she must be quite the teacher. Smirking, he asks, "How long have you been in Chicago?"

"Just two weeks," Sheila says. Looking around the backyard, she kicks at the grass. Damien can tell she is ready to get moving.

"Sheila, baby, please ask this young man if he would like something to eat or drink. I still have some grits and honey-glazed ham on the stove," says Vivian.

Sheila, sitting across from Damien, looks straight into Damien's eyes, "Would you like something to eat, Damien?"

"No thanks. I just had a pretty big breakfast. But I would love something cold to drink if you don't mind."

Sheila shoots Damien an annoyed look as Vivian chimes in eagerly, "Go 'head, Sheila, and give the nice young man something to drink. I have some fresh-squeezed lemonade and that sweet iced tea that he loves."

"Yes, Sheila, if you don't mind, I would love some of that sweet iced tea," Damien teases.

Groaning, Sheila gets up and walks slowly to the house. Aware that Vivian is watching him, Damien tries his hardest to restrain himself from watching Sheila's every move.

The screen door shuts behind Sheila as she enters the house. Vivian looks at Damien with a knowing smile, "So how do you like my niece?"

Damien pauses, "Well, Mrs. Johnson, I really haven't had the chance to speak with her. I just met her."

Laughing, Vivian says, "I know, Damien, but do you think she's pretty?"

After hesitating for a few seconds, Damien says, "No, ma'am."

Shocked by Damien's answer, Vivian is just about to ask the question again when Damien bursts out laughing, "No, ma'am, I think she's fire!"

Vivian and Damien laugh heartily just as Sheila returns carrying Damien's cold beverage. "And what are you two laughing about?" Sheila inquires with a raised eyebrow.

"Nothing really. Damien is just being silly," Vivian replies as she gets up and walks toward the door, "I'm going to leave you two out here to talk. I've got so many things to do in the house, but if you need me, you know where to find me."

"Okay, Auntie," Sheila replies as she gestures for Damien to come sit beside her. Damien smiles flirtatiously.

"There's too much sun where you're sitting," Damien says and gestures for Sheila to come sit beside him on the comfortable loveseat that's placed perfectly in the shade. Sheila obliges.

"So, how do you like Chicago?" Damien asks.

"I haven't seen too much of it," says Sheila, "I was hoping that you could show me around today."

"Yes, I would love to," Damien excitedly replies.

"Are you sure your girlfriend won't get upset?" Sheila asks.

Damien replies honestly, shrugging slightly, "I don't have time for a girlfriend because of my job and school. But don't get it twisted, I date. I just don't have time for that girlfriend thing. It gets too complicated."

"That's what's up," Sheila says, rolling her eyes playfully. "So where do you work?"

"I work a couple of days a week at the Nike store on Cottage Grove Ave."

"Wow, that's cool," Sheila says.

"Yeah, I like it," Damien replies. "I work there mainly for the discounts, and of course the cash," he says with a wide smile as he rubs his hands together.

Sheila leans in toward him, "So… you can get me a discount on some sneakers?"

"Sure," Damien responds with a slight shrug.

Sheila waves him off, "I was just joking. But maybe before I head back to New York, I'll take you up on that."

"No problem," Damien says. "Well, how about you?" he asks as he leans forward to get his tea.

"What do you mean 'how about me'?" Sheila asks with a side eye.

"Do you have a boyfriend that I should be worried about?" Damien asks. "Oh, and how old are you?"

"Well, how old do you think I am?"

Damien responds with a hint of a question in his voice, "Eighteen?"

Sheila shakes her head, "Nah, I'm just 16, but I'll be 17 in December. And no, I don't have a boyfriend. We broke up last year."

"I'm sorry to hear that," Damien offers.

"Oh please, it's nothing to be sorry about. Shoot, I'm sorry I even gave him the time of day," Sheila responds with a wave of her hand. Damien chuckles to himself as Sheila sips her lemonade. "And how old are you?"

"Seventeen, and I'll be 18 in December."

"When in December?" Sheila asks.

"December 15," Damien replies.

Sheila looks at Damien in amazement, "No way. That's my birthday!"

Laughing, they high-five each other. Just then Vivian looks out the living room window and sees that Sheila and Damien are getting along just fine. She smiles, shakes her head, and looks up to the heavens, feeling thankful and remembering the puppy-love she had with her own late husband, Mr. Johnson.

"So, where are we going today?" Sheila asks standing up and stretching her body.

Leaning back comfortably, Damien answers, "I thought we would go down to North State Street first, so we could hit the thirty-seven Block Mall."

"What is a Block Mall?" Sheila wonders.

"It's similar to the malls in most cities, but instead of being long and very spacious, it's floors upon floors of stores that just go straight up." Gesturing up to the sky, Damien says, "That's the best way I can explain it."

"That sounds pretty weird. But I will never turn down an opportunity to go to a mall of any kind," Sheila smiles. "I can't wait to go."

"Well, we can leave now if you want," Damien replies, finishing his tea. "Let's just go inside and let your aunt know that we'll be leaving."

"Sounds like a plan," says Sheila. Damien gets up to go inside when Sheila suddenly gasps, "Wait, hold up. Do I look okay? Should I go and change?"

Damien looks Sheila over, and with a passionate gaze, gives his answer, "Trust me, Sheila, you look fire."

Sheila spins around as if she's on a runway, which makes them both laugh.

"Now, can we go inside and tell your aunt that we'll be leaving?"

"Yeah, let's go," Sheila agrees, clearing the empty glasses from the table. Damien and Sheila head inside the house as Sheila calls out, "Auntie?"

"I'm down here in the basement, sweetie," Vivian replies.

"And what are you doing in the basement by yourself, Auntie? I told you, as long as I'm here, I will handle all of the extra chores."

Vivian ignores her niece's offer, "Well, if you must know, sweetie, I'm just doing some laundry. I appreciate your willingness to help, but go have some fun. You've been helping me since you got here."

Sheila smiles, feeling grateful for her favorite aunt, "Thank you, Auntie. I just wanted to let you know that we're leaving now."

"Hold on sweetie, I'll be right up," Vivian fills the washing machine before climbing the stairs.

"Okay," Sheila excuses herself as she heads upstairs to get her mini backpack and her phone, leaving Damien in the kitchen, alone.

While he waits for Sheila to return, Vivian appears in the kitchen, "There you are, Damien. Where's Sheila?"

"She went upstairs to get her phone and backpack," Damien replies.

"So where are you and Sheila going today?" Vivian inquires.

"I thought I'd take her to Millennium Park and then to the thirty-seven Block Mall on North State Street."

Her aunt nods approvingly, "That sounds like an excellent idea. Do you need a ride?"

"No thanks. It's nice out so I thought we would take the CTA. Give her the full Chicago experience, you know?"

"Well, okay, just please be careful. I'm just a phone call away. And please have Sheila back home before dark."

Damien nods, "Yes, Mrs. Johnson, I hear you loud and clear."

Just in time, Sheila walks into the kitchen, popping a piece of gum. "I'm ready."

"You look absolutely beautiful, sweetie," Vivian says. "But if you button up that blouse, you'd look even better. Don't you think so, Damien?"

Knowing this was a battle he couldn't win; Damien chuckles and shrugs his shoulders nonchalantly.

"But Auntie, that's how all the girls wear their blouses," Sheila protests. "Plus, it's very hot outside. You wouldn't want your favorite niece to have heat stroke, would you!? Or melt!" she adds dramatically.

Sighing, her aunt gives in, "All right, Sheila, but remember what I told you. You don't have to do what everyone else is doing. Be a trendsetter, an independent thinker, a leader, not a follower. Do you understand?"

Sheila nods, "I do."

"Besides, how would you feel if I started walking around in low-cut blouses like that, huh?" Vivian teases, strutting around the kitchen, making Damien and Sheila turn away, laughing in embarrassment.

"Okay, Auntie, I see your point! Now put that away before you hurt somebody!" Sheila jokes.

Still laughing, Vivian walks over to her purse before asking, "Do you need any money, Sheila?"

Sheila's eyes light up, "Oh yes, Auntie, I always need money."

She hands a wad of cash to Sheila, "Well, how's two-hundred dollars for you? With all the work you've helped me do around here, baby, you deserve it." Sheila accepts the money with a loving embrace for her sweet and silly aunt. "And Damien, here's some money for you, too, son. Thank you so much for showing Sheila around Chicago for me."

Smiling sweetly, Damien pauses before accepting the cash, "Thanks, Mrs. Johnson, but you don't have to give me anything for showing Sheila around today." She looks at him unmoving, prompting him to gingerly extend his hand for the folded cash. Sheila looks at Damien and quickly reaches out her hand. Laughing, she says, "Well, you can always give the money to me."

Damien playfully pushes Sheila's hand away and puts the money in his pocket.

Looking at the clock, Vivian waves them off, "Well, you two go ahead and have a great time. I think I'm gonna take me a nap."

26

Sheila walks up to her aunt and kisses her, exclaiming, "Thanks for everything, Auntie."

"You're so welcome, sweetie," Vivian replies. "I love you, and I'll see you later."

Damien also thanks Mrs. Johnson for her generosity with a hug, "Have a good nap and a great day."

"And you have lots of fun," Vivian says, following Damien and Sheila as they walk out the door. "How about you two call me when you arrive at the park?"

"I'll make sure that Sheila calls you," Damien promises as he and Sheila exit the gate and begin their journey to Millennium Park and the 37 Block Mall.

Chapter 3

The Trip to Millennium Park

The two teens walk toward the closest CTA stop, feeling the hot sun beat down on their beautiful, brown skin. Sweat beads roll down their faces, prompting Sheila to get a tissue from her bag and blot herself. She should've worn shorts with all the walking they were about to do, Sheila thinks to herself. "So, what park was my aunt talking about?" she asks, hoping that some conversation can help her take her mind off the boiling afternoon heat.

"Well, I was hoping to surprise you. But since you ask, we are going to Millennium Park first."

"That sounds like a plan," Sheila reaches for the water bottle and takes a sip.

Damien glances at her and teases, "You like saying that, huh? Is that your catchphrase?"

"I like saying what?" Sheila asks.

"You like saying, 'It sounds like a plan,'" Damien comments.

"I guess so," says Sheila, laughing, "I never really thought about it." They remain silent for some time. "Are we walking to the park?" Sheila tries not to sound too worried. Feeling the sweat pouring down her back, she says, "You know, heat stroke is no joke, man."

Damien shakes his head, "Nah, we're taking the CTA."

"What's the CTA?" Sheila asks curiously.

"That's the Chicago Transit Authority," Damien answers proudly.

Sheila nods, "Oh, we have the Transit Authority back home in NYC. Why didn't you just say the bus or train?"

Damien shrugs, "I guess I could have said that, but doesn't the CTA sound so much cooler?"

Damien points in the direction of a local mini-mart, "That's where we'll be catching the bus."

Sheila finishes her water and tosses the bottle into a recycling bin, commenting, "Oh great, there's a bodega."

Damien raises an eyebrow, trying to follow her gaze, "No, that's a convenience store. What's a bodega?"

"That is what we call a convenience store in New York."

"Oh, word," Damien nods.

"Well, I'm going to buy another water from the convenience store," Sheila says mockingly, "You want one?"

"You're funny. But no thanks. I would love an orange Gatorade," Damien answers graciously.

"You got it," Sheila walks toward the entrance of the mini mart and goes inside.

Damien gazes at her in her entirety without any shame. Once she's out of sight, he takes out his phone to call his mom and let her know where he and Sheila are heading. The phone rings, but there's no answer, so Damien leaves a voice message and decides to join Sheila in the mini mart.

Entering the store, Damien sees a group of young men surrounding Sheila as she stands in line. One of them has what looks like Sheila's phone in his hands. His suspicions are confirmed once he recognizes the bright pink case with large NYC lettering on the back, it belongs to Sheila. He walks up to discover that one of the young men is plugging his number into her phone. Damien glances at Sheila and sees the discomfort in her face and body language. In an attempt to defuse the situation, Damien puts his arm around her shoulder. He whispers a deep, "Hey," in a voice that sends a tingle up Sheila's spine. Before she can reply, Damien says, "We have to go. Our bus will be here shortly."

The young man quickly hands Sheila her phone and looks at Damien before backing up and getting a last look at Sheila, "My bad, bro. Is this your girl?"

Damien coolly replies, "Yeah, man."

"My bad, she's just so beautiful. I didn't mean any trouble," the young man replies.

"All good," Damien waves him off.

As Damien and Sheila exit the store, they can still hear the boys laughing and talking about how lucky Damien is to have a girl like Sheila. Sheila shakes her head, feeling somewhat embarrassed yet flattered by the attention. She looks over at Damien, whose arm is still around her shoulders. Sheila realizes that for the first time since they met, Damien is upset, "Are you all right?" she asks.

"Yeah, I'm good," Damien quickly answers.

The two walk outside where they see the bus arriving and before Sheila can reply, they bolt to catch it.

"Whew! We just made it," Sheila exclaims as she flops down in an empty seat. "This air conditioning is giving me life!" Other passengers nod in agreement.

"Yeah," replies Damien coolly. "We would have had more time if you weren't flirting with those boys," he says, visibly disgruntled.

"I wasn't flirting with them," Sheila retorts, "They were flirting with me."

She looks out the window at the passing scenery and realizes that she hasn't seen much of Chicago other than her aunt's front and back yards. Not giving much thought to the matter at the convenience store, Sheila enjoys the bus ride. As a New Yorker, Sheila is used to, and even fond of, riding the buses and trains. Seeing the busyness and the sprawling city makes her feel alive. Amid her reverie, Sheila realizes that Damien is talking and is seemingly concerned.

"Well, why did one of them have your phone?" Damien grumbles. He is mostly curious but also a little annoyed.

Sheila can see that Damien is pretty on edge. Calmly turning to face him, she explains, "Look, this is what happened. The guys asked me for my number and because I didn't want to give my number to them, I thought that the quickest and most polite way to get rid of all the boys was to allow one of them to put his number into my contacts. Don't be jealous, I'm never going to call him."

Damien can see the innocence in her face as he remembers she wasn't really engaging with those weirdos. "Well, why didn't you just say no?" he asks curiously.

Sheila smiles slyly, "Yeah, I could have done that, but I just wanted to be nice. Besides, he was pretty cute anyway." Sheila looks at Damien and says, "Oh no, you aren't really jealous, are you?" She jabs at him with her elbow.

"No," Damien replies, sitting up a little taller in his seat, a calm expression on his face, "You just need to be more careful. Those guys could have run off with your phone. They do that all the time here in Chicago. Or what if they were into gang banging or something and I had to deal with that?"

"My bad," Sheila says. The smile is long gone from her face, replaced with a more serious expression. Putting a hand on Damien's shoulder, she says, "You're absolutely right. It happens a lot in New York, too."

Sheila then reaches over and kisses Damien on his cheek. She looks into his shocked eyes, "Do you forgive me?"

"Yes, you're forgiven." Damien smiles, feeling as if he is melting into the seat.

"So, I'm your girl now?" Sheila chuckles, attempting to lighten the mood again, "I mean, I just met you."

"No, at least not now anyway," Damien says as he glances over at her and smiles, "I just said that so those guys would leave you alone."

"Oh, really? Well, tell me the truth," she says, adjusting herself as if she's holding a mic up to Damien's lips, "Mr. Damien, weren't you a little jealous? Just a teeny, tiny bit?"

"No, Sheila," Damien speaks into the imaginary microphone with a flashy smile, "And please stop asking me if I am jealous. It's just that I take the safety of women very seriously. I was taught that a man is supposed to protect and provide."

"Well, okay Black Panther," Sheila jokes, nudging Damien again as they both laugh and playfully shove each other. Older folks on the bus look over at the teens, shake their heads, and smile at the blossoming buds before them.

"Well, I guess this is a good time for us to exchange numbers," Damien interjects. He pulls out his phone and hands it to Sheila.

Sheila looks away from the window back at Damien and laughs. "Oh, so now you also want my number?"

"Yes," laughs Damien, "In case you get lost or something. I mean, it is your first day out on the town in Chicago. I can't lose Mrs. Johnson's precious niece."

"You right, you right," Sheila flashes a charming smile. "After all, I *am* precious. I was wondering when you were going to ask me for my number," she says, handing Damien her phone before plugging her number into his.

Damien laughs as he finishes putting his number in Sheila's phone. He looks for some silly emojis to add and finds a crown and a heart to accentuate his name. He glances over at Sheila, who has added a heart, a peach, and a sparkle to her name. Just as he shuts off Sheila's screen and prepares to hand her the phone back, Damien sees an awestruck look overcome her face. Sheila gasps, "Wow, look at that body!"

Damien leans over to see what Sheila is talking about and notices that Sheila has clicked into his photo app and is looking at a picture of him working out while shirtless. Damien smirks. He is happy to know that she likes what she sees. He considers trying to get his phone back but, deciding it would be better to let her browse, Damien relaxes in his seat.

"Man, is that you?" Sheila asks.

"Why yes, yes, it is me," Damien states proudly as he lifts his shirt, flashing his rock-solid abs.

"You have a *great* physique. I wouldn't mind seeing the rest of you." Damien looks at Sheila, who has a sultry look on her face, and shakes his head.

"Girl, you're so bad. Hand me my phone," he demands with an outstretched hand.

Sheila slaps his hand instead of giving him the phone at first then, finally, she waits a minute and hands it to him. Damien, seeing that she isn't as innocent as she seems, asks her, "Are you always this bad?"

"What do you mean?" Sheila inquires, batting her eyelashes dramatically.

Damien chuckles, "You know what I'm talking about."

Sheila gives him an innocent smile. Placing a hand on his leg, she says, "How about we make some plans for you to see for yourself?"

Dumbfounded, Damien realizes that he has never encountered someone as bold as Sheila. Unsure of what to say, he tries changing the subject. Realizing that the next stop is theirs, Damien says, "Make sure that you grab your backpack."

Sheila gathers her things as she mumbles, "I'd sure like to grab something else."

"All right, Sheila. Enough," Damien grumbles. Having just met her, he prefers to get to know her better before diving into that type of talk.

"I'm just kidding," Sheila responds, sounding a little embarrassed. Usually, guys like that kind of stuff, or so she thought.

Damien looks at Sheila as they step off the bus. Glancing at her body again, Damien tries not to be overpowered by the feelings rolling through him. Tugging at one of Sheila's braids, he says, "You play too much." Sheila swats at him as they walk toward Millennium Park.

Upon arrival, Sheila notices that there are a ton of people at the park doing so many different things. It sort of reminds her of New York's Central Park. "This place looks so cool!" Sheila exclaims. She tries to take it all in at once, but there's something happening on every side of them.

"Yeah, there's a lot to do here. I try to visit the park whenever I can. It gives me a good chance to be alone with my thoughts," Damien comments.

Sheila looks to her left at a group of kids performing dance moves, then she turns to the right and sees a long line of people outside various food trucks that are parked on the sidewalk. She catches the intoxicating scent of grilled onions and seared chicken floating on a welcomed breeze in the hot sun. Now that she is no longer in the air-conditioned bus, she is quickly reminded of how hot it truly is.

Damien suddenly taps her on the shoulder. "Hey, Sheila, check that out," he says.

"What's that?" Sheila asks as she turns toward Damien. Without saying another word, he takes her hand and guides her over to their next destination.

Sweat beads roll down their faces as they stand in the center of the park. Taking out tissues for each of them, Sheila dabs at her own face as she hands the other tissue to Damien. They both take some sips of their cool beverages before continuing their excursion. Sheila looks up to see a giant, bean-shaped object. Damien stands and smiles at Sheila as she stands there gaping at everything sprawled before her. He explains, "This exhibit is called the 'Cloud Gate,' aka the 'Bean.' Lots of tourists like to take selfies here."

Turning back toward him, her phone already in hand, she replies. "Sounds like a plan!" Sheila starts taking selfies beside the metallic bean-shaped exhibit which acts as a mirror, showing everything around her in a panoramic view. "This is so dope," Sheila says to herself. She waves for Damien to join her in the selfies. They take several pictures together and find a bench to sit on so they can review them. Sheila looks over the photos and remarks, "We look so good together." She hands her phone to Damien so he can view them.

Damien views the selfies and jokingly comments, "Yeah, I really make you look good."

Sheila laughs and pokes Damien's stomach, "Now you're the one that plays too much."

While touring Millennium Park, the two go back and forth about who makes who look good.

"Okay, you win. We make *each other* look good."

Sheila looks at Damien with a smirk, "That's something you will learn about me."

"And what's that?" asks Damien curiously.

"It's that I always win," Sheila says.

"Okay, if you say so."

Checking the time on his phone, Damien reminds Sheila that they need to check in with their loved ones. Damien suggests making the calls at Louie Garden, a beautiful and much quieter area of Millennium Park. Enjoying the playful competition between the two of them, Damien tries to race Sheila to the garden, but she takes off much faster than he does.

"I gave you a head start!" he shouts. Sheila's only reply is a hearty laugh as she makes it to another bench, upon which she sits. Taking out her phone, Sheila calls her aunt. Stopping just short of the bench Sheila rested on, Damien attempts to call his mom again. This time around, he reaches her and fills her in on their plans. Sheila also confirms with her aunt that she has arrived at Millennium Park. Letting Auntie know that she is having a great time, Sheila assures her that she will indeed be home before dark.

"Thanks for updating me on your whereabouts, Sheila," Vivian says, "I love you, and please stay safe, baby."

"Okay, and I love you, too, Auntie," Sheila says before ending the call.

Noticing that Sheila is off the phone, Damien walks up to her. "Were you able to reach your aunt?"

"Yes," Sheila replies, giving him the thumbs up sign, "How about you, were you able to reach your mom?"

"Yeah," says Damien, his stomach growling noisily. Sheila looks back at the spot where they entered. The lines near the food trucks are much smaller.

"Race ya to those food trucks over there," Sheila suggests excitedly.

"Do I get the head start this time?" Damien teases.

"Nah, let's see how this goes," Sheila challenges. Squinting her eyes, gripping her bag and crouching slightly lower, Sheila is planning on winning. Damien stands next to Sheila, unfazed by her intimidating stance.

"Ready?" he says, glancing her way.

"Set." She looks at him, makes a silly face, and shouts, "Go!"

The pair race to the food trucks. Sheila is in the lead. Damien sprints past her and nearly trips. Sheila passes him, wearing a giant smile upon her face as she gets closer to the trucks. A group of pigeons flutter out of their way as Damien regains momentum. The two of them are now neck and neck. Sheila stays slightly ahead of Damien, but he catches up to her as he bears down on the nearest truck, which serves authentic Mexican cuisine.

The teens stand panting in the heat. Sheila bends over to catch her breath. Damien stands with his hands on his hips, feeling his heart pounding under his black shirt which is now decorated with sweat spots. "That was definitely a tie," Damien says, "I see you, Sheila! You play sports or something?"

"Not for school, but I love to run, walk, and dance whenever I can. It just feels so good."

"That's really dope," Damien says. Taking out his water, he finishes it before continuing, "You know what would really feel good right now, though?"

Sheila looks at him as she finishes her water. "Some food?" she asks, hearing her stomach grumble.

"You guessed right!" Damien announces. The two stand closer to the food truck, scanning the menu and discussing options. They take a moment to decide, then they each place their order. To their surprise, being the 100 and 101st customers of the day, they receive two free large lemonades. Sticking the straw in his cup, Damien takes a sip and smiles. He gestures for Sheila to hold his drink as he fishes for his wallet. Sheila starts to protest, but Damien quickly takes out twenty-five dollars and hands it to the cashier.

"Keep the change, man. I can see you're working hard," Damien tells the cashier, who flashes a warm smile and points at Damien.

"My man, let me hook you two up right now."

"Thank you for paying. What a gentleman," Sheila remarks.

"Well, you paid for our drinks earlier. It was only right," Damien chimes, "and it's my honor. You're really cool."

"You, too," she blushes. Teasingly, Sheila asks, "Is this a date?"

Damien looks at her and shakes his head with a small laugh as he goes to get their burritos. He hands Sheila her food before tearing into his own bag.

"Wow, Damien, slow down! Down, boy!" she laughs, "Who am I kidding, I'm feeling rather peckish myself." Sheila tears into her own bag, unwraps the burrito, and takes a huge bite.

"Girl, what is peckish?" Damien asks.

"It means ravenously hungry. I like to study the dictionary, and when I found that word, it made me laugh for a week."

Damien shakes his head as they both continue enjoying their burritos and each other's company while watching the passersby in satisfied silence.

After their feast, Sheila wipes her mouth before finishing her lemonade. Damien cleans his face and uses hand sanitizer before offering some to Sheila. He casually mentions to Sheila his mom's dinner invitation.

"Seriously?" Sheila asks, her eyes beaming.

"Yeah," Damien casually replies.

Sheila moves closer to Damien. The toes of their shoes almost touch. Smiling beautifully, in a very soft-spoken voice, she makes a request, "Please ask me to come over to your house tonight for dinner."

"I just did," Damien replies.

"Seriously," Sheila says, "invite me to your house tonight for dinner."

Damien looks straight into Sheila's dazzling brown eyes and sighs, "My mom invited you to dinner at my house tonight."

Sheila rolls her eyes and grabs his arm, "No, I want you to ask me as if it's *you* personally inviting me."

Damien laughs and sighs again. "Okay, Sheila. Will you join my mom, my sister, and me at my house tonight for dinner tonight?"

"Yes, I will. I thought you'd never ask." Without thinking, Sheila leans in and plants a kiss on Damien's lips. Drawn to her, Damien kisses her back. Seconds later, Damien collects himself and checks the time on his phone.

Looking at Sheila, Damien tries to conceal the pounding of his heart and tries to change the subject, "If we are going to hit the Block 37 Mall and be back home before sundown, we should be on our way."

"Okay," Sheila replies, feeling her heart beating in time with Damien's own growing passion. "I need to find a bathroom before we do that, though," she says, looking around frantically for a public bathroom.

"This way," Damien says as he extends a hand to Sheila and guides her to the nearest store with a public restroom.

Walking back from their bathroom break, Sheila recalls that Damien was pretty shy after they kissed. Making sure he wouldn't forget what had just happened, she asks, "So did you like kissing me?"

Damien glances at her and tries to play cool, saying, "It happened so fast that I really don't even remember kissing you."

Sheila smiles knowingly, "Well then, I guess we will have to do it again soon. And next time, we should take our time so we both can remember."

"Oh, really?" Damien feels excited but also concerned, "But we just met, Sheila. I really think you need to slow your engines a bit. Let's just see where today takes us."

"Okay," Sheila says, "I just feel really good about this."

"About what?" asks Damien.

Sheila grabs Damien's hand and replies, "About us."

Shaking his head, Damien whispers, "Okay, Sheila. Whatever you say."

"See. I win again!" Sheila declares.

Damien smiles at Sheila. "You are mad funny," he says.

Suddenly Damien notices that the 146 bus that will take them to the Block 37 Mall is heading toward them, and they need to get across the street fast to catch it. Damien grabs Sheila's hand, and they run across the street.

Chapter 4

Fun at the Mall

Once on the bus, Sheila sighs. "That was fun." Walking slowly, she catches her breath as she feels the cool air conditioning circulate over her hot body.

"What was fun?" Damien inquires, following closely behind her as he scans the aisles for some seats. "Running for the bus?"

"No, you holding my hand while we were running," she teases.

Damien shakes his head and continues walking toward the center of the bus, where they find two empty seats. Sheila sits down gracefully and scoots toward the window as Damien swings himself down next to her.

After some silence, Sheila looks out the window and asks, "So how long before we get to the mall?"

"About fifteen minutes," Damien replies while glued to his phone.

"Great," says Sheila as she takes out her own phone and begins checking her text messages and posting the selfies she took at Millennium Park. There are pictures of her alone and a few with Damien. As Sheila begins posting, she asks Damien for his Instagram.

"It's @DamienMorganParkStallions."

"Morgan Park Stallions?" Incredulous, Sheila asks, "You belong to a gang?"

Damien chuckles, "Sort of. It's the name of my high school football team."

"You didn't tell me you're on the football team," Sheila says, continuing to eye him.

"In fact, there's a lot of things I haven't told you about me. Besides that, I don't have a girlfriend."

"I know," Sheila replies, rubbing Damien's shoulder and gazing into his eyes. "I'm looking forward to getting to know you a whole lot better before I leave to go back to New York."

Gulping, Damien tries to remain composed as he inhales the lingering scent of Sheila's minty gum. "I figured that," he says in that deep voice Sheila likes. The two of them try to laugh off their growing hormones as Sheila places her head on his shoulder. Damien realizes he likes it there and settles comfortably into his seat for the remainder of the ride.

Sheila pops her head up and asks, "Do you want mine?"

"Do I want your what?"

"My Instagram," Sheila responds.

"Oh, yeah," Damien says, "Just follow my page, and I'll follow you back."

Sheila immediately scrolls from her page and types his username into the search bar, she finds Damien's Instagram and follows him. Glancing over his profile, she is awestruck. "Wow, you sure have a lot of followers. And it looks like most of, if not all of them, are girls."

Damien looks at Sheila, leans over as if he's about to kiss her ear, and asks, "Are you jealous?"

Sheila smiles warmly and replies, "No, I'm just saying though!"

"You're just saying what?" Damien teases, nudging Sheila's rib playfully.

Moving out of his reach, Sheila replies, "I'm just saying that you have a lot of girl followers."

"And I'm sure once I look at your page, I will see that you have a lot more boys following you than girls."

"Maybe," says Sheila with a shrug. "But I don't have half the followers you have."

"Well, I guess that just means I'm more popular than you!" Damien jokes and sticks his tongue out at Sheila.

"Hmm, maybe," says Sheila, nudging him playfully in the chest. "But I doubt it!" She sticks her tongue back out at him.

While playing with Sheila, Damien catches a glance of the scenery outside and realizes that they have arrived at the mall. "Time to get off," he says, scrambling out of his seat.

"That was quick," says Sheila as she grabs her belongings and checks behind herself before hopping off the bus.

Immediately upon entering the busy Block 37 Mall, Damien runs into a group of his high school football teammates. He greets them with the popular Morgan Park Stallions' handshake. One teammate, Chris, asks, "Dude, where have you been hiding this fly girl?" He looks Sheila up and down with no shame.

Sheila doesn't notice because she has her head down, texting one of her New York friends. Damien smiles and taps Sheila's arm so he can officially introduce her to his friends. Damien explains that Sheila is visiting family for the summer and he's showing her around Chicago.

Thomas, another one of Damien's teammates, asks, "How can I get a summer job like that? Sign me up right now!" Everyone bursts into laughter, including Sheila.

Sensing the growing attraction to his new friend, Damien says, "Well, guys, it was great to see you! I'll catch you at the gym sometime this week. We got to keep moving. You know, we've got things to do and places to be."

"Yeah, I bet," Thomas mutters before they come together for a group handshake.

As they walk away, the teammates look over Sheila one by one, mumbling a variety of compliments and corny pickup lines. Sheila shakes her head and rolls her eyes, embarrassed by the thirst these boys display. Thomas, however, squeezed her hand and says, "It was great meeting you, Sheila. Maybe before you leave for the summer, Damien can bring you to one of our awesome summer parties."

"That sounds dope. I'd love that," Sheila says, shaken by the now loosening grasp of Thomas' large hand. The flecks of gold in her brown eyes sparkle as she turns away from Thomas and back to Damien.

"Yeah, we'll see about that," says Damien as he waves goodbye to his teammates, who file into the food court.

"And what exactly did you mean by 'We'll see' about me going to one of your summer parties? You don't want to take me with you?" Sheila chides as they continue their stroll.

"What I meant was that it depends on whether or not I'd even be available to go myself. This summer, I haven't even gone to one of those parties! I do have a job, you know. But you know, if I'm able to go, I'd definitely want you to come with me."

"That's what's up. You really are a very responsible young man," Sheila observes. Feeling reassured by Damien's response to her question, she adds, "And if you have the time to go, you win the grand prize of seeing me and my fly dance moves." Sheila shakes her shoulders to the rhythm of a distant song playing in the bustling mall hallway.

Damien joins in the shoulder bouncing as he recognizes the old school song playing overhead. Laughing and enjoying themselves, they approach the mall directory. "We've got about two hours to spare," Damien informs Sheila. Looking back at his goofy teammates filling the food court excitedly, he asks, "Are you hungry?"

"Nah," says Sheila. "I'm still pretty full off that burrito, so I think I can wait until dinner at your house."

"Me, too," says Damien, looking over the directory. Sheila joins him, and Damien asks, "Which one of these stores would you like to visit first?"

Sheila barely lets him finish before blurting out, "Let's see." She pauses and scans the directory intently. "Oh! Yes! Sephora and Zara." She hums as she continues looking over the directory, hoping to see a Victoria's Secret. When she doesn't see one, Sheila sucks her teeth and shouts out emphatically, "Aw, man, they don't have a Victoria's Secret here? What kind of mall is this you got out here?"

"If you don't see it in the directory then they don't have one in this mall. However, I actually know where they do have one."

"Where?" she asks, her eyes wide with anticipation.

"At the Water Tower Place up the road on Michigan Ave," Damien responds.

"And is that supposed to be a mall, too?" asks Sheila, a finger twirling around one of her long, neat braids.

"Yeah. Now stop hating on my city, girl," Damien retorts, swatting Sheila's twirling finger.

Laughing and swatting back at Damien, she assures him, "I'm not hating. You've been redeemed with this new mall you're talking about. How do you know that there's a Victoria Secret there anyway?"

"Because I've been there several times with some of my female friends."

Sheila smiles and says, "I'm sure you have, but first of all, please don't refer to us as 'females.' It makes my skin crawl, dude. How about young women friends, ladies, or Sista friends? Anything other than females."

"Sorry," Damien mutters as Sheila continues.

"And let me guess, did these lady friends of yours model their outfits for you too?"

"Actually, they did," Damien replies proudly. She glances back at him to see yet another one of those dazzling smiles lighting up his mahogany face.

Unfazed by his honesty, Sheila stops and turns to him. They lock eyes again. "I bet I'll look way better in my lingerie than they did." Her face fills with a proud smile.

"Maybe," says Damien with a larger-than-life grin. "I can only know if I get to see you in an outfit, too."

"Oh, word?" Sheila says, feeling herself taken aback by Damien's growing attraction. "Then what are we waiting for? Let's go!" She grabs his hand and heads for the exit sign before remembering the other stores she wanted to hit first. "I mean, well, let's go to Sephora and Zara right quick, so I can pick up some items that I need. And it won't hurt to see if Zara could be having a sale. Then after that, if you don't mind, I'd love to head to Victoria's Secret."

"No problem," replies Damien. "Then, by the time we're done at Victoria's Secret, it will be about four-thirty, which is a good time for us to begin heading home," he suggests.

"Sounds like a plan," says Sheila as she points at him.

"There you go again with that 'sounds like a plan,'" Damien notes.

Sheila smiles as she makes her way toward Sephora. "I'll just wait out here," Damien informs her, "I want to check my text messages."

"All right, I won't be long," Sheila replies as she walks through the doors and makes a beeline to her favorite store.

Standing outside Sephora, Damien receives a text from his sister.

Tanya: Mom wants to know if Sheila's coming over to the house tonight for dinner?

Damien: Yes, she's down, however, Sheila still has to ask her aunt. What time should I tell her to be at the house?

Tanya: 7:00.

Damien: Kool, I'll let her know so she can check in with her aunt.

Tanya: What time are you returning?

Damien: No later than 5:30.

Tanya: Ok, big bro, I'll let mom know.

Damien smiles at the heart emoji his sister sends before going to update their mother. Damien then checks his last unanswered text and sees it was from his teammate, Chris, who he saw earlier.

Chris: What's up, bro? Sheila is on fire. I just know you are going to get with her.

Damien: Yeah, bro I definitely think she wants me too.

<He sends a smirking emoji and a strong arm.>

Chris: Why do u think that?

Damien: Trust me I have my reasons.

Before he can elaborate, Damien sees Sheila checking out at the register, and he wraps up his conversation with Chris.

Damien: I gtg bro. I'll hit you up later.

Chris: Kool

<Chris sends a thumbs up and peace symbol emoji.>

Sheila exits the store, swinging her bag happily and asks, "Now, may you please point me in the direction of Zara?"

Damien points behind Sheila and says, "I've been seeing a lot of girls coming from that direction with Zara bags."

"Then we'll head in that direction," Sheila declares as she marches forward. She proudly holds her small Sephora bag.

After a few moments of walking, she points up ahead and exclaims excitedly, "Yes, there's Zara! I'll just step in here for a few minutes."

She heads off by herself, looking back at Damien who is standing a few feet from the store and looking around for a place to sit. Sheila walks back to him, lightly touching his hands and asks, "Why don't you come in here with me?"

"All right," Damien says.

They walk into the store, but after just a few minutes of perusing the aisles for sales, Sheila realizes there are no special discounts going on. She turns to Damien, who looks pretty bored and says, "Well, I'm ready to go to Victoria's Secret."

Relieved, Damien replies, "Cool. But before we go, can you please call your aunt to make sure that you'll be able to come to my house for dinner?"

"Shoot, you're right!" Sheila reaches for her phone, calls her aunt, and when her aunt picks up, Sheila confirms that she's having a great time. "Auntie, will it be okay if I have dinner with Damien and his family tonight?"

"If it's okay with Sharon, it's okay with me, honey," Vivian replies. "Just make sure you stop home first."

"I will, Auntie. I love you."

"I love you more."

"Everything's all set for dinner at your house," Sheila tells Damien, who nods and proceeds to text his sister.

Stuffing his phone back in his pocket, Damien and Sheila make their way to the doors from which they entered. Hearts aflutter, the two teens pass by the crowd of young people roaming the mall on that hot summer day as they use shopping as an excuse to get out of the heat. Every eye glances at the two of them. People are unwittingly captivated by something seemingly magical left lingering in the air wherever the pair goes together. Some of his remaining teammates nod at Damien as they pass the food court on the way out into the thick summer air.

Chapter 5

Sheila's Sultry Secret

Damien and Sheila stroll to the Water Tower Place Mall. Sheila walks confidently, feeling right at home with the bustling urban life around them. The teens take their time enjoying the silence as they check each other out and tease each other's senses. Some call it a vibe, some say it's magic, and there are even some that doubt it altogether. But oh, is it something.

Arriving at the new mall, Sheila notices that all the stores that she likes, such as Forever 21 and Nike, are there. Realizing that she'll only have time for Victoria's Secret, she turns to Damien. "We have got to come back here before I leave!"

This time, Damien cleverly replies, "It sounds like a plan."

Sheila laughs. "I guess that phrase is becoming contagious."

Damien joins in her laughing. "Oh, I truly hope not." He looks around and points toward the elevator. "Victoria's Secret is on the third floor."

Sheila replies coyly, "Oh, that's right. You've been there many times." She rolls her eyes and bounces in front of him, heading toward the elevator.

"Yes, I have!" Damien announces with a triumphant smile.

They enter the elevator and are transported to Victoria's Secret. Sheila walks in as though she is on a mission. Scanning over the aisles, she suddenly spots the perfect outfit. Flipping through the items to find her size, she spends a few moments combing over the tags. She gets to the last garment before successfully finding her size, which she triumphantly holds in front of her. Looking over the garment, she asks Damien what he thinks. Damien cranes his neck to get a better view. Enticed by the visuals racing through his mind, he says, "I love the color. But again, I'll have to see it on you."

Sheila smiles to herself as her own naughty thoughts course through her mind. Overjoyed by his teasing, she says, "Okay, then follow me to the fitting room."

Damien follows Sheila to the fitting room and stands by the door where he can hear Sheila singing, "Sex with Me" by Rihanna. She steps out of the fitting room, looking dazzling in the lingerie she's selected. Damien's mouth drops open as he shoves Sheila back into the fitting room.

"How do I look?" Sheila inquires, knowing the answer to her own question.

Gawking at her, Damien is unable to hold back. "You look absolutely amazing," he says, caressing her tanned skin. Goosebumps rise up on both of their exposed arms as they stand consumed by each other in the hottest moment of their day together.

Sheila breathes into his neck, her lips barely touching his skin. "Do I look better than the other girls you've seen in their Victoria's Secret outfits?"

Without hesitation, he nods excitedly. "No doubt, Sheila. Way better. So, I'ma need you to take some pictures and send them to me ASAP," he demands.

Sheila replies quietly, looking over her own curvaceous body in the tantalizing outfit she's chosen, "I can do better than that. I can wear it for you whenever you want me to."

Damien looks at the two of them in the mirror before wrapping his arms around her waist. He squeezes Sheila before turning to leave, and just as he's about to shut the door, he reaches in and pinches her butt. Damien's chest pounds as he braces himself against a wall just outside of the fitting area.

After spending several more minutes inside the dressing room, Sheila exits and heads toward the cash register. While Sheila pays for her purchase, Damien suddenly receives several text messages back-to-back. The constant buzzing getting to him, Damien reaches in his pocket and opens his messages to see a series of revealing photos of Sheila in her Victoria's Secret outfit. Sheila looks back over her shoulder as the cashier bags her items and sees Damien observing her photos. Their eyes lock before Sheila turns back to the cashier to finish her purchase. She gives Damien a huge smile.

The cashier hands Sheila her bag, "Thank you for shopping at Victoria's Secret." Then looking in Damien's direction, the cashier lowers her voice, "He's pretty handsome. You two make such a cute couple. I'm sure he will love this, honey."

"You know that's right!" Sheila laughs, fist-bumping the cashier. "Thank you so much!" Sheila takes her bag and walks over to Damien, who's still looking over the photos.

Once she's in front of him, Damien looks at Sheila and laughs, "Sheila, you're mad crazy." He follows behind her as they walk out of the dimly lit store into the vibrancy of the mall hallway. Damien can't help but notice the sway of Sheila's hips, then focuses on her braids to not overwhelm himself.

"What? You don't like the pictures?" her voice heavy with concern.

"Nah, I love the pictures," he assures her, "But you really caught me by surprise."

"Well, I thought that it would be special to give you something to look at until I am able to wear it for you in person," Sheila says coyly.

Damien's mind is blown. "That's mad cool, and I'd like to take you up on that. But I mean, are you always this quick with boys?"

Offended, Sheila stops in her tracks and turns back to Damien, "What do you mean?"

"Well, I mean we just met today, and you've been flirting with me real heavy," he thinks over the day before continuing, "And now these pictures, it just seems like too much, too soon. Don't get me wrong, I definitely have no problem with it. I'm just trying to figure you out."

Unfamiliar with guys commenting on her outright nature, Sheila replies coolly while continuing toward the exit, "It's just pictures of me in a sexy outfit. Didn't you say that you *wanted* me to send you some pictures?"

Thinking to himself, Damien gives in, "You're right. I did say that."

"So, what's the problem?" she snaps, "Do I make you feel uncomfortable?"

Aware that she may have been hurt by his question, Damien puts his hand on Sheila's shoulder and assures her, "Not at all, it's just the opposite. I really think you're mad cool, and I really like chilling with you."

Sheila sighs. "Then let's continue to have fun. I'm only here for the summer, so I'm not trying to have a long-distance relationship with you. And to answer your question earlier, no I'm not like this with all the guys. I've flirted with other guys, but I have never sent pictures of me like the ones I just sent you. Cause even though we've just met today, I feel that we're becoming mad close," Sheila explains as they pass a vending machine. She puts in a five-dollar bill and puts in the code for two waters. Retrieving them, she hands one to Damien, and they proceed to exit the Water Tower Place Mall. "And you better not share them with anyone," Sheila warns.

Looking up at a display across the street with the time listed, Sheila notes that it is four-twenty-five in the afternoon. They've made some good time.

Damien looks at Sheila, taps her arm, and pulls her in for a hug. They stand there engulfed in each other's presence before he whispers, "Thank you, I feel the same way, too." His gravelly voice sends tingles up her spine as she squeezes a little tighter.

Unraveling from each other's grasp, the summer heat kicks in around them as they stand outside, preparing to catch the bus back home.

"I really like the pictures, and don't worry I won't share them with anyone," Damien says.

"You promise?" Sheila asks, extending her pinky to him.

"You have my word," Damien says, locking pinkies with Sheila. "I promise."

Damien takes Sheila's hand and says, "Now, let's head home. I'm getting hungry again."

"It sounds like a plan. I wouldn't want to hear that angry stomach again," Sheila jokes. The two laugh as they head up the avenue hand in hand to catch their bus.

As the two teens stroll back down Michigan Ave. toward the bus stop, the setting sun allows for cooler breezes to caress the sticky skin of the passersby. Damien looks at Sheila and catches the shining sun glinting off her glittery eyes. He is about to compliment her beautiful eyes when Sheila suddenly asks, "What should I wear to your house tonight for dinner?"

Damien looks at her sideways and quickly replies, "I know what you *shouldn't* wear."

Sheila slaps Damien on his shoulder and says, "That's not funny!" They both burst into laughter.

"No really, what you have on is fine, though," Damien says assuredly.

"No, Damien, I've been sweating in these clothes all day. I need to shower and change my clothes. So, I guess I'll just have to surprise you," Sheila states with a flirtatious smile.

"I hope not the same way you surprised me at the mall," Damien laughs.

"You know what? You keep cracking jokes and I will wear the Victoria's Secret outfit to your house tonight," Sheila threatens.

"No, you wouldn't," Damien looks to make sure she's joking, but with the expression on her face paired with her behavior that day, he can't really tell. Never has he met someone so straightforward and yet so mysterious.

"You're the one who keeps cracking jokes," laughs Sheila. "So, keep it up and see what happens," she shrugs innocently. Her braids swing as she puts some more pep in her step.

"Okay, you win," Damien declares, admitting his defeat.

"Aye, that's three wins to uh… zero!" Sheila teases, "But who's counting?"

Damien and Sheila finally reach the bus stop where they wait for the bus. More passengers arrive within the few minutes that they stand waiting. Within five minutes, the bus arrives and, unfortunately, there is standing room only. Sheila isn't too happy on the crowded bus. "Man, I didn't even think about rush hour," she mutters to herself. She is all too familiar with the crowded trains and buses that plague cities everywhere during rush hour.

Damien notices Sheila giving the death glare to ignorant passengers bumping into her as they get on and off the bus. Damien touches her hand and assures her, "We only have two more stops before we get off."

"Thank God!" Sheila exclaims, releasing the tension that has built up in her arms and shoulders with her aggravation.

Satisfied with Sheila's ability to remain calm for the remainder of the ride, Damien steadies himself and reaches into his pocket to pull out his phone. He's about to text Chris back when he realizes that he has a missed text. He looks at it and realizes it is from Celeste, one of his closest lady friends. Damien opens the text.

Celeste: I heard you were at Victoria's Secret with some fine honey.
<She includes the side eye and detective emojis.>
Damien: That's Mad Crazy, Celeste. Word really travels fast 'round here. I'll call you later.
Celeste: Kool, but be aware, I have friends everywhere.
<She adds two eyes, two ears, a smile, and a heart emoji.>

Damien shakes his head and puts his phone back into his pocket, happy to look up and see Sheila beside him. He nudges her shoulder, and she looks at him as he makes his way to the doors, saying, "Looks like this is our stop." The bus comes to a halt, and they both exit from the rear. The shining sun greets them again, reminding Damien to tell Sheila something else he noticed about her.

"Sheila, you really have some beautiful eyes, by the way."

"Thank you," she replies, batting them dramatically. They both crack up. "I can see the future with them, and it looks like you're in it."

"Sounds like a plan," Damien points at her coolly, and they laugh at the thought.

Chapter 6

Winding Down in Chicago

D amien escorts Sheila back to her aunt's house. They step up onto the classic Chicago style porch. Feeling the weight of their legs after all their activity that day, Sheila lets out a sigh as she reaches for her key. Just as she's about to put the key in the door, Vivian emerges.

"Oh, my Lord! You two scared me half to death!" Vivian gasps, "I was just about to check the mailbox, but seeing that you're here just in time, can you please do it for me?"

"Yes, Auntie," Sheila replies. While she drags her tired legs to the mailbox, Vivian looks over at Damien, who has just finished sipping the last of his water.

"So, Damien, did you all have a good time?" Vivian asks.

Damien adjusts his posture. "Oh yes, Mrs. Johnson," he says pleasantly and attempts to elaborate just as Sheila walks up to her aunt and informs her that there is no mail in the box.

Her aunt jokingly replies with her hands on her hips, "I've been waiting and waiting for a love letter from an old friend for more than 10 years now." She looks at Damien and teases, "Do you think he was too cheap to pay for a stamp and just chose to e-mail me instead?" The teens chuckle while she shrugs, "I guess I'll have to go check my spam later." They all laugh lightheartedly. Eager to freshen up and be on their way, Sheila and Damien are restless with anticipation.

"Did you have a good time?" Vivian asks.

Sheila looks at Damien and replies with a wide grin, "I had a fantastic time." Turning to Damien standing in the doorway, she says, "Thank you so much, Damien."

"You're welcome, Sheila," Damien responds while tipping an imaginary hat which makes Sheila giggle, "I'll be heading home now to freshen up, but I'll see you a little later at the house tonight for dinner." He gently takes Sheila's hand, giving it a little squeeze as he backs out the door, "Do you need my address or would you like me to pick you up?"

"Seeing that it's getting dark, I would feel more comfortable if you would pick me up," Sheila answers politely.

"You right. I got you. I'll bring you there and back, safe and sound," Damien replies. He walks down the stairs then looks back, "So, I'll be back to pick you up at six-forty-five."

Grinning, Sheila singsongs her famous phrase as she waves to her new friend, "Sounds like a plan!"

Damien shakes his head and smiles to himself as Sheila prepares herself to close the door. They steal one last glance at each other before Damien closes the gate and heads up the road to his house.

Vivian notices her niece carrying some packages. Eyeing the Victoria's Secret bag, she asks, "What do you have there, Sheila? Get anything nice?"

"I can show you my makeup purchase from Sephora, but my Victoria's Secret purchase… well, that's Sheila's secret now, Auntie."

Vivian eyes her niece candidly, unsure of how to reach out to this grown child in front of her. She shuffles back toward the chair she was sitting in and sighs, "I can respect that, sweetie."

Sheila lets out a sigh of relief. In an attempt to change the subject, she blurts out, "By the way, Auntie, I bought you something!"

Her aunt glances at her again, "What did you buy me, sweetie?"

Sheila pulls out a fresh tube of her aunt's favorite lipstick from her Sephora bag and hands it to her.

"Oh, sweetie, thank you so much. But you didn't have to do that."

Sheila stands near her aunt. She crouches to meet her aunt face to face as she rests in her favorite chair, "I know, Auntie. That's what makes it a gift. Maybe you can see it as a little something we call 'treating yourself.' And after all you've done for me, that's the least I can do for you, for now."

Appreciating the lovely gesture, Mrs. Johnson stands up to give her niece a great, big hug. She whispers, "Your mother taught you well." Sitting back down, she continues, "So tell me, how did you like Millennium Park?"

"I loved Millennium Park," Sheila confirms, "It was lots of fun, and the malls were fun too."

"Was Damien a gentleman?" her aunt asks and looks at her quizzically.

"Absolutely a gentleman, Auntie. He is so nice, and he's really funny. I really like him."

Vivian reaches to touch her niece, "All right Sheila, I see that look in your eyes. Be careful with your feelings, sweetie. You are only here for the summer."

"I know, Auntie, but I feel good about him," Sheila assures her aunt.

"Yes, I know you do. But baby, you just met him today. Do you even know if he feels the same way about you?"

Remembering the scandalous pictures she texted Damien, Sheila smiles knowingly to herself, "I'm pretty sure he does."

"What makes you so sure?" growingly curious, her aunt turns slightly to face her niece, who is still standing by her side.

"I have my reasons," Sheila replies with an enticing look on her face.

"Chile, what have you done?" shaking her head, Vivian can't even fathom what is transpiring between the two kids.

"If you really want to know, Auntie, I did something very nice for Damien."

"And what was that?" The question lingers in the air, heavy with the weight of the infinite answers her aunt is too tired to even fathom.

"I gave him gifts," Sheila grins proudly.

"Should I even ask what those gifts were?"

"No," Sheila responds honestly, "But I'm very sure he will enjoy them."

Hoping her aunt is done prodding, Sheila looks at her phone. Noting it was nearly five-thirty, she gathers her things and heads toward the stairs. As her aunt reaches for her dog-eared book on the table beside her, a golden tassel dangling from where she left off, Sheila says, "Just checked the time, Auntie, and you know how I do when it comes to getting dolled up."

Opening the book, her aunt proceeds to find her place without looking up, "I know that's right, baby. Go right ahead. I'll be here finishing up my book." She holds it up for Sheila, who squints attentively to see.

"Is that Michelle Obama's book?" Sheila asks, taking a step up the stairs.

"You know it," Vivian replies.

"Can I borrow it when you're done?" Sheila looks at her aunt, who gazes at her before she answers.

"You got it, baby. Now go on and get dressed." They can feel the unspoken words lingering between them as they are both being called to other things.

"You don't have to tell me twice," Sheila says and races up the stairs. Tossing her bags filled with purchases on the bed, Sheila throws open her closet to find the perfect outfit.

Chapter 7

All Dolled Up

Vivian sits in her reading chair, scanning the page hungrily as she devours the deep and passionate words of her favorite First Lady. She only manages to finish one page before the phone rings. Somewhat irritated, she sighs before she looks up and recognizes that it's her best friend, Sharon Jackson, Damien's mom. She picks up the phone excitedly.

Sharon greets her warmly, wrapping her dear friend Vivian Johnson in the joyful embrace of sisterhood. The book can wait.

"Good evening, Vivian baby. How are you doing this evening?"

"Good evening to you, Sharon, love. I'm doing well today. I'm a little sore, but I'm here, and I'm grateful. How are you?"

"I'm just finishing up this dinner. I hope I didn't outdo myself this time."

"Well, we know you like to cook up a storm, Sharon. There's no telling how you'll blow this child away in true Chicago fashion with all that loving flavor you put into your food."

"Now you know that's right, honey," Sharon laughs, looking over at her daughter, Tanya, who lies sprawled all over the couch, scrolling through her phone while the TV murmurs in the background. Her eyes fall on a family picture perched on the table beside her. Holding it for a moment, Sharon lingers over the image of her late love and father of her dear children, Brian Jackson. She resumes her conversation, smiling mournfully, "The reason I'm calling is to invite you over to the house for dinner. I was sure that I had asked Damien to invite you both."

"I guess they've been too caught up in the rapture of love," Vivian jokes, singing loudly as she impersonates Anita Baker. The two friends laugh heartily. She continues, "But that's okay. Besides, I had planned to stay home and finish Michelle Obama's book tonight. If you have enough left over for a plate, you can just send that along with Sheila and Damien when he drops her off."

"You know I got you, Viv. I'll send you two heaping plates because I tell you, I really think I outdid myself tonight." She gets up to turn off a remaining pot on the stove, lifting a spoon to stir the collard greens. "And oh yes, honey that's a great book! I read it myself." Sharon puts the spoon down and walks back over to relax after standing up cooking for the last two hours.

"Yes, honey," Vivian replies, "I'm really enjoying it. She is truly a phenomenal woman."

After sharing their sentiments on Michelle Obama, Sharon goes on to say, "I'm really looking forward to meeting your niece tonight, though. Her name's Sheila, right?"

"That's her," Vivian replies candidly.

"I must say, Vivian, in all the years I've known you, I've never once heard you mention Sheila."

"Yes, I know. It's a complicated story. I'll need more time to explain it to you," Vivian responds, looking toward the stairs to gauge where Sheila is.

"Oh, I understand," Sharon remarks, "We look forward to meeting her tonight."

"Well, she's getting ready now. You will meet her soon enough," says Vivian as she flips impatiently through the pages of her book.

"Oh, Sheila doesn't need to dress up," Sharon declares emphatically.

"Well, we both know that. I think she's probably trying to impress Damien, though, girl," Vivian whispers, "But many moons ago, we were teenagers, too." They both erupt with laughter,

Looking at the whirlwind of a mess in her kitchen, Sharon clears her throat, causing Tanya to pop up from the couch. Sharon points at the kitchen, and without a word, Tanya switches her phone and the TV off and proceeds to help clean up. Sharon sits back in the chair, removes her slippers, and attempts to bring the conversation to a close, "Well, I'll see you at church tomorrow, Viv."

"Oh yes, especially now that I know for sure that fine Pastor Chisholm is preaching. Maybe I can get all dressed up and impress him," Vivian jokes.

"Oh, Lord! Damien told me what you said earlier. You are a whole mess!" Sharon chuckles, "I'll save you a seat right in the front next to Jesus himself," she says.

They laugh together before bidding each other good night. Sharon goes over to the couch and decides to put her feet up for a bit while Vivian finally gets a chance to read Michelle Obama's book.

Damien turns off the shower and opens the curtain to a steam-filled room. He wraps himself in his towel before turning on the fan to clear some of the hot, misty air surrounding him. He dries his skin and opens the bathroom door.

Tanya, standing in front of a mountain of dishes downstairs, hears her brother plodding around upstairs. "I hope you washed those big old feet you got flopping around up there, Damien!" Tanya yells before turning on the water.

Tanya feels her mother's piercing gaze all the way from the living room. Sure enough, Sharon is looking right at her and shaking her head at her wise-cracking daughter. She soon reclines on the couch and closes her eyes again to resume her rest.

Upstairs, Damien puts some shea butter on his deeply tanned skin. He sprays some more Bond No. 9 over his body. This time he uses it a little more sparingly. Damien scans his closet for a pair of dark blue jeans, a hot pink graphic tee and his customized, hot pink Nikes. After considering a matching hat, Damien pulls together another outfit. He pulls out a yellow polo, some light-wash jeans, and his white Air Forces. Shifting his eyes back and forth between each option, he finally decides on the yellow polo outfit, complete with his father's necklace.

Damien checks out his image in the full-length mirror that hangs on the back of his door and grabs a brush to slick down his hair which enhances the ripple of waves swirling around his head. "Tsunami Time," Damien smiles as he poses and reviews the finished look in the mirror. He takes his phone off the charger to take a couple of selfies. Noting that it's approaching six-fifteen and feeling satisfied with his look, Damien folds his towel neatly and drapes it over his shoulder before turning off his bedroom light. He returns his towel to the bathroom, dusts off his freshly cleaned Air Force Ones, and jogs down the stairs. Damien can hear his sister washing the dishes, pots, and pans downstairs, he laughs to himself because she's stuck cleaning up. Remembering her slick comments, Damien sneaks up on her, flicking her quickly in the back of the head with a towel.

"Ow, man! Dang, Damien! I'm going to get you, man," Tanya threatens her brother while rubbing the back of her head with a soapy hand.

Sharon, who had dozed off, awakens quickly from her sleep. "Excuse me? You two better not be cursing in this house."

"No, ma'am," Damien and Tanya insist as they poke at each other while Damien makes his way to the door. "I'm about to get Sheila, Ma. Be right back."

"Okay, son," Sharon says. She sits up and puts her slippers back on as she prepares to freshen up. "Tanya, if you aren't done in there yet, just try to make it look neat so we can start getting ready for dinner."

"Okay, Mom. I'm almost done," Tanya answers calmly while she plots ways of getting revenge on Damien. Just as something crosses her mind, she hears him shut and lock the door behind him.

After finally making it through to the last chapter, Vivian looks at the time, "It's six-thirty, baby. Remember Damien said that he would arrive at six-forty-five. You almost done up there?"

"Yes, Auntie," Sheila replies, smoothing down her baby hairs in the mirror and giving herself one last look, "I'll be right down."

Her aunt has an old school vanity in Sheila's bedroom. Looking in the mirror, Sheila stands back a few feet to gauge the full effect of her outfit. The yellow patterned A-line dress that hangs off the shoulders accentuates her curves in a tasteful way. She runs her hands down the front of her dress and considers adding a light denim jacket that lies sprawled in a chair. Sheila looks over herself one last time before stepping back in front of the mirror to apply another layer of lip gloss over her plump lips. Finishing up her look, she adorns herself with gold hoop earrings, a gold necklace her mom gave her when she was five, and several gold clasps to bedazzle her braids.

A few moments later, the doorbell rings, and of course it's Damien. Sheila puts on some eyeliner and bats her eyes in the mirror before looking at the time on her phone. "If that's Damien, he's ten minutes early," she shouts out to her aunt.

"He must be hungry," Vivian replies and laughs to herself, "I'll tell him you'll be down soon." Vivian shuffles over to the door where Damien is standing in his new outfit.

Sheila continues taking her time getting ready. She inhales deeply with her eyes closed then exhales slowly as she opens her eyes. Sheila smiles and hugs and squeezes herself. Suddenly, tears appear out of nowhere. She quickly grabs a crumpled tissue on her vanity and dabs at the corners of her eyes to calm her nerves. She breathes again, relaxing into her body before standing up to put on some chunky, pristine white wedges. Instantaneously, she decides to grab the denim jacket after all before heading to the bathroom one last time.

"Hello again, Damien," Vivian says as she opens the door, "You're pretty early, young man. But you look so good. Aww. I remember when you were just a little boy and now look at you sprouting up right before our eyes. Watch out, Chicago!"

"Thank you, Mrs. Johnson," Damien chuckles charmingly, "And yes, I believe I'm ten minutes early." The setting sun shines in through the doorway, covering Vivian and Damien in a magnificent glow as their melinated skin absorbs the sun's rays.

"Now, you got your mother and sister living with you, and *still* don't understand that we women need all the time we can when we get dolled up, child?" They laugh as she adds, "Sheila's still upstairs, baby. She'll be right down."

Damien sits in the same chair Vivian was sitting in when he saw her that morning. He closes his eyes and feels the setting sun beaming down on his skin. Damien smiles to himself as he remembers his father. An image of his dad putting his strong arm around his own smaller, youthful shoulders flashes across Damien's mind. Deep feelings of nostalgia well up within him. Damien sighs loudly to keep from sobbing. Taking another deep breath, he opens his eyes and exhales.

Vivian looks out at the horizon and feels a cool breeze sweep over her body. With a sigh, she says, "You have always been such a gentleman, Damien. That's what I like most about you." He looks at her graciously as she asks, "Would you like to come in? Sheila should be finishing up now."

Damien declines before proceeding to apologize to Vivian for forgetting that his mom had also invited her to dinner. She stops him modestly, "No need to apologize, baby. You've had a very busy day today keeping my niece safe, and I had already made plans to stay home tonight." They look at each other and smile before sharing a hug.

Sheila comes downstairs to find her aunt and Damien sitting on the front porch. She quickly returns to her room to retrieve her phone and looks herself over one last time in the mirror. She adds one more gold clasp to her braids, turns off the bedroom light, and walks downstairs.

When Sheila goes outside, Damien turns to see her looking perfectly made up with the Sephora products that she purchased earlier that day. She looks elegant in her sleek A-line dress. Sheila notices that her outfit matches perfectly with Damien's. Damien notices Sheila's hot pink Yves Saint Laurent clutch bag into which she slid her phone. Closing her purse, she flashes a bright grin, "Well, how do I look?"

"You look absolutely beautiful," Damien answers plainly. Damien, entranced by Sheila's near-perfection, barely registers Sheila's "thank you." His eyes are locked on Sheila as he takes in her every move, making him completely helpless against the tide of his own thoughts, feelings, and fantasies rolling through his active mind.

"Yes, you look like a model, honey. Let me spin you around! Oh wait, pass me my phone and open up the camera. Let me get some pictures," Vivian readies herself to assume the photographer role. She walks inside, beckoning for Sheila and Damien to follow.

"Oh, Auntie. I don't want to be late. What type of impression will I be making on Damien and his family?" Sheila protests.

Reluctantly, she reaches for her aunt's phone on the table in the kitchen and opens the camera for her.

"It'll only be a minute, baby," Vivian assures her. "Now let me see you in a few different poses. Then I want some of Damien by himself. And oh, I've got to get some pictures of you lovebirds together," Vivian teases while snapping away.

Sheila rolls her eyes before she naturally jumps into several model-like poses by the stairs for her aunt. Damien steps in to take some casual, macho-man photos himself. Then he beckons for Sheila to come over, and he puts his arm around her waist, pulling her in close. They smile effortlessly, and Vivian beams proudly at the teenagers as she snaps her final picture. Suddenly, she sniffs the air curiously.

"You smell wonderful, too! Girl, is that my Chanel No. 5 you have on?"

"Yes, ma'am," Sheila declares without shame. The two of them laugh as her Auntie swats at her playfully.

"So, since you up and used my Chanel No. 5 without asking, you're going to do my makeup tomorrow before church. How about that? Who taught you how to put makeup on so well, anyhow? I know your mother doesn't even go near it." Vivian caresses her niece's freshly made-up face, which looks marvelous in the setting sunlight.

Sheila laughs and starts to explain, "Okay, Auntie, that's fair. And when it comes to makeup, I like to say it all starts with the products, and a little something nowadays called YouTube."

"Well sign me up for that YouTube, baby," Vivian say, "They teach yoga on there? I was thinking of taking up some lessons to help with these aches. I heard it helps to balance and strengthen your mind, body, and spirit. Can you believe that?"

"Yes, I'll look into that, Auntie," Sheila responds, looking at Damien and then toward the door.

"Thanks, sweetie," Vivian replies. She looks back at her book waiting to be finished, "But it looks like it's about time for the two of you to be heading on now. Don't want dinner to be cold."

The teens head for the door. Sheila takes the lead, and Damien follows closely behind her. He takes in the scent of her perfume and gently touches her fingers as she walks out the door. Her heart flutters again, catching her off guard as she steps onto the porch.

Vivian shuffles toward the doorway to lock up tight, "You two enjoy yourselves! Sheila, Damien's mom said she'll be sending me some plates, so don't you go forgetting about me."

"Thanks, Auntie, and I won't forget," Sheila promises as she scurries over to her aunt to give her a peck on the cheek.

"Good night, Mrs. Johnson. I'll have Sheila home before nine," Damien says.

"Thank you so much, Damien," Vivian beams at the respectful young man and closes the door as the kids make their way out the gate and to Damien's house. She locks the door and turns on the porch light before returning to her Michelle Obama book. She revels in the thickness of the comfortable silence of her home. She tunes in to the open window, hearing the beautiful chirping of birds and humming of bees as they finish up their busy little day. A chorus of cicadas join the symphony, which she loves. Vivian Johnson rises out of her chair once more to get a bottle of water and to open the living room window. There's nothing like a front row seat to nature's own enchanting choir.

Chapter 8

Dinner with Damien's Family

Damien and Sheila are heading up the road to his house when Sheila turns to Damien and nervously asks, "Are you sure I look okay?"

"Yes, Sheila," he assures her. Sheila, still feeling a bit nervous, adjusts her dress and checks her reflection in a random car's side view mirror.

Flattered that Sheila is so concerned about making a good impression on his family, Damien smiles at her. "Sheila, you look absolutely beautiful," he says.

Sheila smiles back and regains her composure. She stops for a moment, watching Damien walk up the stairs to his house. Admiring the beautiful architecture, Sheila asks, "Did your mom or dad grow up here?"

"Yeah, my mother's mother grew up here. Actually, the house goes back to about the 1920s," Damien replies.

"Wow, this house is so beautiful."

"Thanks," Damien says while fumbling with his keys to open the door. He finally hears the lock click, opens the door, and looks back at Sheila. He gestures for her to lead the way, "Welcome to our crib."

Sharon hears the door open and brushes off her apron before making her way to the living room. She walks up to the young lady with Damien. Extending a hand, she says, "Aren't you a doll! You must be Sheila."

"Yes, I am," Sheila replies, shaking Mrs. Jackson's hand.

"Well, I am Mrs. Jackson, Damien's mom. Welcome to our home and please make yourself comfortable. Dinner will be served shortly."

"Nice to meet you, Mrs. Jackson. Thank you so much for inviting me to your beautiful home tonight for dinner."

Smiling warmly, Mrs. Jackson says, "You are so welcome, sweetheart."

Damien then introduces Sheila to Tanya, who has just entered the room, "Sheila, meet my sister, Tanya. Tanya, meet Mrs. Johnson's niece, Sheila."

"Nice to meet you, Sheila. I love your outfit, especially that YSL bag. That is such a nice color," Tanya raves.

Flattered, Sheila says, "Thank you so much, Tanya. I love your outfit, too. Are those Balenciaga sneakers you have on?"

"Yeah, girl."

Sheila high-fives her, "I love them. I really need to get myself a pair."

Damien excuses himself, "Well, I'm going to leave you two here to talk fashion and go check in with Mom in the kitchen." Both Sheila and Tanya smile and continue their conversation.

Damien walks into the kitchen, "Ma, it smells so good in here. Need any help?"

"Thanks, son," Sharon replies, "Dinner is ready. Do you mind setting up the table in the dining room? And please ask your sister to come in here."

"Yes, Mom," Damien says as he reaches for the silverware and plates, "Mom, is there anything else I can help you with? It seems as though Tanya and Sheila are kicking things off pretty well in there, so if it's okay with you, I want to let them talk while I help you in here."

Awestruck by her son's gesture, Sharon says, "Well, that's really thoughtful, Damien. If you want to help then by all means, please do." Putting a plate on the table, Sharon continues, "And by the way, son, Sheila is absolutely stunning. I look forward to getting to know her myself."

Flipping her hair lavishly, Sharon teases her son, "Now I can see that you've inherited your father's good taste." They laugh as Damien rolls his eyes and walks to the dining room carrying dinnerware.

Tonight was special to Damien, so he decided to include a space for his late father.

Damien looks over to where Sheila and his sister are sitting in the living room and smiles. Sheila looks up just as Damien smiles. "Hey, what if we go help Damien set up the table?" she suggests to Tanya.

"Oh, our mom is just gonna love you, Sheila. You're a guest and you're offering to help set up the table? Whew."

Sheila giggles. "You're funny, Tanya. But that's just how I was raised."

Tanya stands up. "Well, let's go help that big head in the dining room," she jokes.

Sheila follows Tanya into the dining room where Damien is still setting the table. "Oh hey, you decided to come help after all? Thanks a lot. I forgot the napkins. Be right back," Damien says as he rushes back to the kitchen to get some napkins.

Tanya looks at the layout on the table and notices an extra plate. She pauses before placing forks at each place setting. Knowing her brother, Tanya realizes the extra plate was for their late father, and she makes sure to tend to that space with extra care.

Sheila stands admiring various pictures adorning the living room. Before making her way to the table to assist in setting it, she notices a framed picture with a fine, older gentleman wearing a military uniform in what appears to be a family photo. Damien returns, and she asks him about it, "Is this your dad?"

Without looking at the picture, Damien quickly answers, "Yeah." He lays out the napkins and the glasses. Damien is very familiar with the picture to which Sheila is referring. Sheila puts the photograph back in its place, brushing over it tenderly. Damien prays that she doesn't ask anything more about him.

"I see where you get your looks from, especially that charming smile," Sheila continues, "Your father is handsome. Will he be joining us tonight?"

"No," Damien replies in a low, monotone voice, "Our father passed away last year from a heart attack."

Sheila pauses, unable to bear the weight of the information. She puts a hand on Damien's shoulder. Damien, overcome with emotion, takes a break from setting up the table to gather himself. "I'm very sorry to hear that," Sheila replies.

"Thanks. He was wounded while serving in Iraq and was getting pretty sick prior to the heart attack. I've found peace in the fact that he was asleep, so at least there was no pain," Damien responds, staring absently at the same picture Sheila was holding.

Tanya, standing by the door, overhears the conversation between Damien and Sheila. She knows how hard it has been for her brother since their dad passed. Seeing how well he and Sheila are getting along, Tanya, feeling that the pair were having a very private moment, backs out the room and finds something else to do in the kitchen.

"Were you very close to him?" Sheila asks, unsure of how to relate.

"Yes, very close," Damien affirms. Sheila places the glassware on the table just as Sharon walks into the dining room with a large pan of her delectable pot roast. Damien assists his mom as she lays the steaming pan at the center of the dining room table.

"Oh, Sheila. You did not have to lift a finger, baby. But I see you were raised with some good manners, and I appreciate your help," Sharon says lovingly.

"You are so welcome, Mrs. Johnson. I can only imagine how much work it took for you to put all of this together. Thank you," Sheila beams. The two of them smile at each other before Sharon returns to the kitchen. Sheila looks over at Damien, who has become noticeably flustered. She touches his arm gently, "You were very blessed."

"How am I very blessed?" he snaps, "My dad is dead, Sheila."

Sheila moves her hand back as if she was burned. In a low tone of her own, she says, "At least you knew your dad. I never had the opportunity to meet mine."

The tension drops from Damien's shoulders as he looks at Sheila. They stand with an arm around each other as she finishes, "My mom said that he left her when she was pregnant with me. She thinks he lives somewhere in Atlanta or, believe it or not, somewhere around here in Chicago."

Damien is better able to realize where Sheila's comment came from. Though his dad's death had arguably been harder for him than anyone, he is gracious enough to acknowledge that comforting someone in a position like his is a challenge in itself. At least she is trying.

"Yeah, I guess since you put it that way, I was very blessed to have at least known him, and I'm very sorry to hear about you not knowing your dad. I really miss mine," Damien wipes his face quickly as Tanya brings out more food from the kitchen. While Sheila heads down the hall to wash her hands, Damien turns to go in the kitchen and help his mother and sister.

Returning from the bathroom, Sheila is amazed by the tantalizing feast laid out before her. Dinner consists of a fresh salad; a succulent, fall-off-the-bone pot roast; classic dirty rice; perfectly baked mac & cheese; collard greens; and warm cornbread. Sheila is awestruck as she peers at the love-filled feast. Damien emerges with a tall pitcher of homemade iced tea and gestures for Sheila to come to the table as his mom and Tanya position themselves to say grace.

Damien, standing on the left side of the table, motions for Sheila to stand just to his left, Damien's mom stands at the head of the table, and Tanya stands to the left of her mother across from Sheila. The extra plate for his father sits at the other end of the table. Damien notices that his mom has placed a candle there to honor his presence as well. A tear just barely escapes Damien's watering eyes as he tries to take in everything around him. Overflowing with gratitude, he looks at his family and his new friend, Sheila, and suddenly realizes that she was right. He really is blessed.

Looking at Sheila, Sharon says, "Well, once again, Sheila, welcome to our home. I'm not sure if Damien told you, but it's a tradition in our home that anytime a new guest joins us for dinner, we stand, join hands, and allow the guest to bless the food. So, Sheila, will you do us the honor of blessing the meal?"

Without hesitation, Sheila eagerly replies, "Yes, ma'am."

One by one, Damien, Sheila, Sharon, and Tanya all join hands. Tanya blurts out, "Sheila, I'm hungry. Please don't tell me you're going to give us a sermon here." Sharon nudges her daughter before bowing her head, signaling for Sheila to begin her prayer.

As she finishes chuckling to herself, Sheila prays, "Dear Creator, we come to you today to thank you for not only bringing us together here, but for the hands that grew, harvested, and prepared this food. We thank you for our ability to stand together in the name of love and togetherness. Here's to much more time to get to know each other and share more loving family meals like this. Amen."

"Short and sweet, now let's eat!" Tanya says. Everyone laughs as they sit in their chairs. Damien scrambles to pull Sheila's chair out for her, making Tanya roll her eyes dramatically.

Damien decides to serve Sheila before making a plate for himself. Stretching across the table, he makes sure there's nothing on the table that she wouldn't want on her plate.

Sheila replies with a smile, "Oh no, I'm definitely going to start with a little bit of everything." Damien prepares Sheila's plate and hands it to her. "Oh, thank you!" Sheila says, looking at all the mouth-watering food before her.

"You're welcome," Damien replies, looking over at his mom, who stood up to go into the kitchen. "You want me to start your plate, too, Mom?" he shouts.

"I'll get it, son. Thank you for being so thoughtful, baby," she hollers back. Sharon hustles back into the room with one last decorative dish. A joyous gasp escapes from Tanya and Damien as they see another fresh batch of her famous biscuits!

"Oh, you're really special," Tanya says, glancing in Sheila's direction.

"What makes you say that?" Sheila asks and takes a hefty bite of the roast. Some juice rolls down her chin, and she quickly uses her napkin to clean it off before continuing to enjoy her meal.

"Well, Mama only makes her biscuits on Saturdays and for special occasions. So clearly, we've all come to agree that you're pretty special, Sheila," Tanya says with a smile.

"You look like a chipmunk," Damien tells his sister.

"If I wasn't busy stuffing my face like one, you know I'd be on you in a minute," Tanya warns, "You just wait, big bro. I've got my master plan for you."

Pretending to feel frightened, Damien waves his hands, and Tanya waves back just as Sharon sits down.

"I don't even want to know," Sharon says as she shakes her head, reaching for food to put on her own plate.

Laughing between bites, Sheila reaches into the heaping platter of flaky, buttery, soft biscuits. Her eyes pop open as she takes her first bite of Sharon's famous biscuits. She turns and looks at Sharon, who has just taken a bite of her own cooking, "This dinner is absolutely delicious."

Between chews, Sharon looks up at Sheila with a charming smile of her own, "Thank you, sweetie. My mama started teaching me how to cook well before I was your age, and I took off and ran with it ever since."

Damien wipes his mouth. A completely empty plate sits before him as he debates a second helping. "Basically, what my mom is saying is that her mom was an excellent cook, and now she's an excellent cook." He looks at Sheila, who has long since resumed tending to her own plate and says, "She also makes some killer pies."

Tanya nods her head in quiet agreement. She's too content with her meal to utter another word. Damien continues. "My friends at school who have all visited our home at least once, always ask, 'What's your mom cooking tonight?'" He pauses as everyone giggles.

Still focused on their plates, Sheila and Tanya also consider seconds as they close in on their final bites. Damien continues, "Our mom never lets anyone visit our home without feeding them right, Mom?"

"You got it, son," she says, "No one ever leaves my house hungry." Sharon smiles and nudges Tanya. "Well, I guess when it comes to cooking, I got it like that!" She high-fives her daughter.

"Also, Mom, that's why my teammates always want to come to our house after practice. I'm no fool. It's because of your awesome cooking and not my video game collection," Damien says. Suddenly, Tanya, Damien, and Sheila all reach for another helping of food at the same time, prompting snickers and giggles around the table.

As everyone lounges around, Sharon throws her napkin on her plate and reclines in her seat. She looks at Sheila with a warmth in her eyes that only a mother could have. "So, Sheila, where in New York are you from?"

Sheila answers proudly, "Harlem!"

Tanya's face beams with excitement, "Really!? That's where the Apollo Theater is, right?"

"Yes, it's not too far from my house. I've been to a few shows there with my mom."

"I've always wanted to perform there," Tanya says dreamily.

"Ooh, do you sing?"

Damien doesn't give his sister a chance to answer, "Oh yes, she does! She's an excellent singer. In fact, she's my favorite." Tanya looks at her brother lovingly, and they high-five each other across the table. He continues confidently, "I think that if she got on *The Voice*, she could win it all."

"That would be so big! Have you auditioned yet? I love that show!" Sheila asks.

Tanya rattles on excitedly, "Yes! I auditioned last month, and I'm waiting to hear back from them!"

"That's cool! I sure hope you make it, but before then, you know you're going to have to let me hear you sing something!" Sheila says happily.

"Maybe after we excuse ourselves from the table, you can come to my room," Tanya suggests.

Damien looks at Sheila knowingly before she answers, "Sounds like a plan."

"Okay everyone, that is probably the tenth time Sheila has said that phrase today," Damien announces, "Now, let's see how many more times we hear it tonight. It's clearly her catchphrase, and allegedly it's contagious, so watch out!"

Another course of laughter ensues before Sharon redirects the conversation back to Sheila, "So, Sheila, how old are you?"

"Well, right now I'm 16, but I'll be 17 on December 15th."

With an incredulous look, Sharon sits up slightly in her chair. "Is that so?" Mrs. Jackson looks at Damien, who's sitting upright with a large grin on his face. "Did you know that's Damien's birthday as well?"

"Yes, we discovered that earlier. Isn't it wild!?" Sheila asks.

"What a coincidence," Sharon shakes her head.

Tanya intercepts, "So, Sheila, I'm guessing you don't have a boyfriend if you're here with my big-headed brother?" Damien tosses a napkin at Tanya. It hits Tanya in her head and falls into the empty plate in front of her. Even their mom laughs at that one.

Sheila squeezes Damien's hand under the table and meets Tanya's gaze, "No, I don't have a boyfriend. How about you, Tanya? Do you have a boyfriend?"

Sharon looks at her daughter, "Yes, Tanya, do you have a boyfriend?"

Tanya takes a nervous gulp, "Mom and I have discussed that I'm too young to have a boyfriend. Besides, I'm concentrating on school and my music career."

Turning to Sheila, Mrs. Jackson asks, "Well, what do your parents do for work?"

"Well, I never knew my dad, so I can't answer that. But my mom is a nurse at Harlem City Hospital. She's been working there for the last twenty years," Sheila responds.

"Oh, I'm so sorry to hear that about your dad, baby. But that's great news about your mom being a nurse. I wonder how she likes it. I've always wanted to be a nurse."

"Yes, she mentioned to me that she loves her job, but it definitely keeps her busy, sometimes too busy. That's part of the reason my mom sent me to spend the summer with my aunt. Being that I was home alone often, she started to worry someone would try to break in or something."

Sharon sighs, "Well, Chicago has its violence too, baby. You've got to keep your head on a swivel no matter where you go. Young women especially have to be careful." Tanya takes a sip of her iced tea and nods in agreement as Sharon continues, "Luckily, there's plenty to do and see in Chicago, and I'm sure you will have a great summer here."

Sheila smiles at Damien, who walks into the room carrying another decorative tray.

"Yes, Mrs. Jackson. I'm sure I will."

"Sorry to interrupt you, Mom, is this the dessert?" Damien asks excitedly.

"Oh yes, son. I wasn't sure if you all were too stuffed from all those biscuits and the two servings of food each of you had," Sharon teases and smirks. "It's apple pie, and you can serve it if anyone would like some." Without a word, everyone sits up eagerly, prompting Damien to get the serving utensils and four small dessert plates.

"I'll go get the whipped cream. It's in the back of the fridge so it could set faster," Mrs. Jackson announces as she stands up and follows Damien.

"You mean, you made the whipped cream from scratch?" Sheila asks in disbelief.

"Yes, I did!" Sharon answers on her way to the kitchen.

Sheila is taking a liking to Damien's whole family. However, in the back of her mind, she knew no one else's opinion of her will ever define her. Still, she hopes they like her too.

Chapter 9

Sweet as Pie

As Tanya and Damien clear the remaining dishes from the table, Sheila asks if she can help. Both Tanya and Damien decline. Nevertheless, Sheila picks up the lingering forks, spoons, and other utensils from the table and follows behind the two siblings. Just before stepping into the kitchen, she overhears Sharon raving about her to Tanya and Damien. Tanya chimes in, "Do you see the way Sheila looks at Damien?"

Before anyone can answer, Sheila pops into the kitchen and says, "I thought I would bring these last few utensils. Where can I put them?"

"Oh, thank you, sweetheart. You really didn't have to," Sharon replies, "You can just hand them to me. Go ahead and make yourself comfortable. The remote should be on the couch somewhere." Sharon places the items that Sheila handed her into the soap-filled sink.

Sheila goes to the bathroom to wash her hands. When she returns, she finds the family sitting around the TV preparing to watch *Wheel of Fortune*. They decide to divide into teams. It's Tanya and Sharon against Damien and Sheila. Each team takes turns guessing the words until the show goes off. Sharon gives Tanya a high-five. Smiling, Sharon says, "We crushed them." Glancing at the small clock sitting on the coffee table, she exclaims, "Wow, where did the time go? Time for me to call it a night."

Sheila looks over at Sharon, who stands stretching before them. Remembering her manners, Sheila thanks her, "Dinner was phenomenal, Mrs. Jackson. Thank you so much."

"You're so welcome, sweetie," Sharon smiles, "And you are always welcome in our home." Sheila eagerly stands up as Sharon reaches out to her for a hug. They squeeze each other warmly.

Bidding everyone goodnight, Sharon reminds Damien and Sheila about the plates of food she has made up for Vivian. "I have the plates wrapped up right by the door," Damien assures his mother.

Tanya yawns, "I think I'm going to bed, too." Turning to Sheila, she says, "It was great meeting you. I really hope to see you again soon."

Sheila and Tanya hug. "Me too, good luck with your call back! I know we didn't have time tonight, but I still wanna hear you sing sometime before you're famous," Sheila says lovingly. They smile at each other as Tanya makes her way toward the stairs.

Damien stands up and pecks his mom and sister on their cheeks. "I'll be dropping Sheila and these plates off shortly, and I should be back in about thirty minutes."

"Okay, baby. Don't forget to lock up when you come back in," Sharon says.

Damien stretches as Sheila reaches for her purse. They smile at each other before going over their day together. Sheila sits back down on the couch and turns the TV off so that they can talk in the silence of the cooling summer night.

Twenty minutes later, Damien opens the door to leave the house. Just then, Tanya comes downstairs and hands Sheila one of her CDs. Sheila, very grateful for the gesture, thanks Tanya and gives her another big hug.

Damien and Sheila head back to Vivian's house carrying the plates from Sharon.

"Oh, hey! I almost forgot my denim jacket! I can feel that Chicago wind y'all are known for," Sheila exclaims. Damien goes back inside, grabs the jacket, then closes and locks the door behind them as they embark on the very short journey to Sheila's house.

They walk in silence, strolling hand in hand and taking in the fresh breeze coming off the Great Lakes. They reach the house in less than five minutes. Sheila reaches for Damien's other hand as they stand on her aunt's porch, "Thank you so much for such an awesome day. I've had so much fun with you. And your family is so sweet."

Damien squeezes her hands and gives her another charming smile, "You're welcome, Sheila. I really enjoy chilling with you, and I'm looking forward to doing more of that."

Sheila leans in toward Damien and kisses him. Damien, swept away by the natural flow of their encounter, wraps his arms around Sheila's waist, pulling her toward him hungrily. They continue to kiss intimately as they stand outside Vivian's house. Damien can't help but let his hands slowly slide down Sheila's back. Sheila smiles mid-kiss and teases him, "Have you lost your mind? My aunt could come popping up in that window any second."

Damien smiles back and adjusts himself. "You're so right. I was getting caught up in the moment."

Sheila taunts Damien. Flattered by his unbridled passion for her, she asks, "Wow, are you this quick with other girls?"

He swats at her playfully, "Hush up."

Raising an eyebrow, Sheila looks at Damien as she fumbles for her keys, "Make me."

Knowing where this is headed, Damien presses up against Sheila as she turns to unlock the door to her aunt's house. Damien whispers in her ear, "Talking to me like that, I'm not sure what I plan to do to keep you quiet." Breathing in deeply to calm his nerves, he asks, "What have you got planned for tomorrow?"

Sheila stands frozen in front of the door. Feeling the feather-light kiss of his breath caress her neck, she responds, "I'm not sure. My aunt is going to church tomorrow, and I will be here all alone. Do you want to stop by and keep me company?" Sheila asks dramatically. "I'll make it worth your while," she promises. Turning to give him a wink, she feels his rising anticipation.

"Well, if you say it that way, I guess I have no choice," Damien responds. "Text me in the morning, and I'll let you know for sure. We may have to come up with an alibi," he says.

Damien reaches in and kisses Sheila on the cheek. She turns around for another kiss on the lips before going inside. Damien watches until Sheila closes the door behind her before heading back home.

Arriving at his house, Damien accidently slams the front door, startling his sleeping mother. Looking to the closet where she keeps her mace and baseball bat, Sharon yells, "Damien, is that you?"

"Yeah, Mom. My bad!" Damien shouts.

Sharon lets out a deep sigh of relief, "Oh, thank God. Please make sure you lock all the doors, son."

"I will," Damien promises as he makes his way toward the back of the house to double check if there are any doors that may still be open.

Damien then heads upstairs to take a cold shower. His therapist told him that cold water showers have many benefits for the mind, body, and spirit. Damien stands in the cold water, listening to it run and feeling it drip over his body before it goes down the drain. Standing with his eyes closed, Damien reviews the fun day he had with Sheila. He smiles to himself, anticipating the fun they'll have tomorrow.

Finished showering, Damien heads to his room to get some well-deserved sleep. After moisturizing his skin and brushing his hair a few times before tying his favorite red do-rag, he hops into his well-made bed and reaches for his laptop. As he scrolls to find something worthwhile on Netflix, he remembers that he promised Celeste that he would text her back later that day. He reaches for his phone, and as he unlocks it, he notes that it's only ten-thirty. Celeste is usually up until midnight, so he texts her.

Damien: Are u available to talk now?

Celeste: No, my mom and I are watching Netflix. Can I call you tomorrow?

Damien: No problem.

<He inserts the thumbs up emoji.>

Damien: Well, good night.

Celeste: Night!

Damien opens up Instagram on his phone to scroll through his feed when Sheila texts him.

Sheila: Are you sleeping or are you up looking at my pictures?

<She inserts an emoji sticking its tongue out.>

Damien: Neither. I was just about to go to sleep though. I'm beat.

Sheila: Me too. I just wanted to thank you again for an awesome day. Sweet dreams.

<She adds a kissy face emoji.>

Damien: I look forward to seeing u tomorrow. Get some rest.

<He finishes with a winking emoji.>

Chapter 10

Easy Like Sunday Morning

I t's early Sunday morning, and Vivian is grateful to wake up to another bright, sunny day. To show her gratitude, she pulls herself up and out of bed and kneels down slowly. Praying, she thanks God for the gift of being able to see another day and asks God to please guide her, Sheila, and all of their loved ones safely through the day. Vivian spends a few more moments absorbed in the Word as she reads over some of her favorite scriptures before making her way to Sheila's room.

Assuming her niece is still asleep after such a long day yesterday, Vivian is very surprised to find that Sheila is not in her room. Worried, she recalls hearing Sheila come in last night. Clutching her chest, she tries not to assume the worst. Considering that Sheila is likely just in the house somewhere, Vivian calls Sheila's name only to find that there's no response other than the sound of a dozen birds chirping just outside the open window. Hoping that Damien is with her niece, Vivian decides to call Sharon. Looking out the window, she sees Sheila sitting on the comfortable loveseat. Laughing to herself, Vivian quickly hangs up the phone and gets herself a cup of coffee as she views the backyard, she sees several cardinals in all of their vibrant splendor. Topping off her coffee with some of this new almond milk creamer Sheila's been carrying on about, Vivian makes her way outside onto the patio to join Sheila.

Sheila looks up and smiles at her aunt, "Hey, Auntie. You were knocked out last night! I didn't want to disturb you."

"Good morning, young lady. You had me worried sick in there! I checked your room, then called out for you with no reply. And don't you ever worry about disturbing my sleep if I'm waiting for you to come home." She sits down across from Sheila, who leans forward for a kiss before plopping back down in the loveseat.

"I didn't mean to scare you, Auntie. I apologize. I promised my mom that I would call her before she headed off to work, and I thought that out here on the patio would be the best place for me to talk to her without waking you up."

Taking a sip of her steaming coffee, Vivian looks at her charming niece. "Well, now that you put it that way, it was very considerate of you. I'm just glad you're safe!" She takes another sip, "Hey, baby, you mind getting me a couple of ice cubes for this coffee, please?"

"You got it, Auntie," Sheila says. Standing up, Sheila skips to the kitchen to get a cupful of ice for her aunt. Returning shortly, she hands her aunt the ice and returns to the loveseat she adores so much. Lying down, Sheila puts her feet up and looks to the sky before closing her eyes and breathing deeply.

After a few moments of silence, the two very different generations of women bask in the serenity of that gracious new day. Sheila's aunt breaks the silence, "How is your mom? I've got to make sure to call her sometime this week."

Sheila answers without moving from her restful position. Feeling a bit tired and sore from all the walking yesterday, she says, "She's doing fine, Auntie. She says that she's very tired from working so many hours at the hospital, but she plans on taking a few days off soon to relax. I really hope she does. I can't wait to apply for some jobs so I can help out and possibly take some of the load off my mom."

"Yes, Sheila, your mom is a very hard worker, and every time I talk with her, I tell her to slow down. She always says that she wants the best schools for you and the best schools cost money. But dear, that is so noble for you to want to help. If you focus on those books harder than on boys," Vivian responds, "then you will be able to apply for some scholarships, and that'll help both of you out." Seeing that Sheila has grown somewhat uncomfortable with their conversation, Vivian changes the subject, "Do you have any idea of what careers you would like to pursue?"

Sheila pauses for a moment. She opens her eyes and looks to the nearly perfect blue sky, except for a few clouds sprinkled here and there. "Yes, Auntie, I always wanted to pursue boys!"

Her aunt gasps, spilling a bit of coffee onto her house dress. Before she has a chance to chastise her niece for being fresh, Sheila, moving her head slightly to look at her aunt, reassures her, "Oh, Auntie, I'm just kidding! I really would like to attend Spelman College and major in politics and then attend Harvard University for my masters and PhD."

After wiping up the coffee, Vivian looks at her beaming niece. She takes another sip of her remaining coffee. "That sounds like a really good plan, baby. I can really see you making a big difference in our beautiful and strange world."

"Yes, Auntie, that's my plan." Sheila rests her head against a pillow and continues to stare into the deep blue sky as a fluffy white cloud morphs before her eyes until it simply disappears.

Reiterating her original bit of advice, her aunt continues, "So, sweetie, you know that your plans will take a lot of commitment, and that includes putting your study ahead of boys."

"Trust me. I will," Sheila responds with her eyes closed.

"Well, while we are on the topic of boys, from the looks of things, you and Damien are getting along just fine. Is that true?"

"Yes, Auntie. And oh, his mother and sister are so nice, too."

"Oh yes. Aren't they all so wonderful? And to think, still teetering on the edge of a devastating loss and everyone is still so warm and open. God bless them," she waves a solitary hand in the air as if to signal to her Lord that she is feeling his presence and is so grateful. She lets out a deep sigh and takes a final sip of her coffee. "How did you enjoy dinner last night?"

"I had a great time. Everyone made me feel right at home. And I even got to see Damien and Tanya go at it. They're hilarious," Sheila recalls.

"And isn't my girl, Mrs. Sharon Jackson, an incredible cook? Oh, and her pies are to die for," Sheila's aunt swoons, as if tasting a bit of Sharon's sweet potato pie right then.

"Yes," says Sheila, "Can you believe she made a pie and her famous biscuits just for me!?"

"Wow, really? What kind of pie did she make this time?"

"Apple. I don't know how she could have possibly known that's my favorite type of pie," says Sheila, "And now, I'm gonna have to come back and forth to Chicago just for a taste of her delicious pie!"

Sheila and Vivian laugh as Sheila sits up slowly, "You know, Auntie, I'm going to go and check to see if any pie was put into your little goodie bag last night." Sheila stands up and takes her aunt's empty cup. Opening the fridge, she sees the bag of food for her aunt sitting right on the top shelf. Opening it, she smiles when she sees a heaping plate of pie wrapped up for them to share. Sheila smiles and exclaims, "Yes!"

When Sheila returns, her aunt continues, "I'm very happy that you had the opportunity to experience Sharon's cooking and her wonderful family."

Remembering Tanya's conversation, Sheila looks at her aunt excitedly, "Oh! That reminds me. Did you know that Tanya auditioned to be on *The Voice?*"

"Wow! No, I didn't know, but that's some great news. I'm not surprised, though. Whenever I hear Tanya sing at church, she just gives me goose bumps. I think she can win it all."

Nodding in agreement, Sheila adds, "That's exactly what Damien said."

Vivian smiles joyously, "Well, we both can't be wrong now, can we?"

After another half hour of small talk and silence, Vivian stands up slowly and stretches. "Okay, sweetie, I'm going in the house to make breakfast. How hungry are you?"

Thinking for a moment, Sheila replies, "Hmm, I'm not that hungry."

"Well, are you hungry enough for my award-winning pancakes and some scrambled eggs?"

"I mean, if you put it that way, then yes, ma'am," Sheila states. Shooting her aunt a curious look, Sheila says, "Auntie, when did you win an award for your pancakes?"

"The church had a breakfast fundraiser a few months ago to raise money for single mothers struggling financially, and I unanimously won the award for best pancakes," she responds with a satisfied smile and her hands on her hips. Sheila laughs and shakes her head. She's still reclining in the loveseat. Vivian starts to shuffle toward the door before looking back at her niece, "You coming in, baby?"

"Not yet, Auntie. Thank you," Sheila replies, "I think I'll stay out here and catch up on my emails and social network stuff. We both know I was too busy yesterday to pay attention to much else."

Laughing lightheartedly, Vivian shakes her head and turns toward the door again. "Okay, honey. I'll call you when breakfast is ready." She closes the door and goes to her stereo to put on her favorite gospel CD, *The Best of Shirley Caesar*. She starts singing so loudly that Sheila sits up in her seat, startled at first before realizing it's only her aunt belting out some prayerful notes. Sheila laughs to herself while inside, her aunt begins making breakfast with a joyous noise.

Sheila texts her friends back home and tells them everything. She even shares some of her sexy photos in the group chat, and all of her friends proceed to gas her up. Smiling to herself, she reclines for a few minutes before her phone rings. She looks and sees that it's her best friend, Melanie. Picking up right away, they greet each other in their special way. "Girlllllll!" Sheila squeals.

"Girlllllll!" Melanie replies as she dangles off the side of her bed in Harlem. Two of her younger siblings jump around in the next room, prompting Melanie to roll her eyes after warning them about the jump several times that day. The loud sounds of car horns and busy bodies echo throughout the apartment. "You've been in Chicago for less than a week, and I see you're already getting in the mix."

Sheila starts laughing, lying back in the loveseat happily, "You know how we do, Melanie."

"And I've seen your posting on Instagram these last few days. Damien is fine! Does he have a brother?" Melanie inquires eagerly.

Sheila laughs again, "Yes, I've seen your comments, you're just as bad as me. But no, he only has a little sister, and she's pretty dope."

"You know how we do. That's why we are BFFs," Melanie reminds her friend, "And that's cool about his sister and all but, he got a friend, though?" The two friends laugh before Melanie continues, "So what's up with you and Damien for real? I mean, you just met each other recently, right?"

Infatuated, Sheila responds, "He's so fine, and so nice. He's pretty funny and smart, too. I mean, I have only met him yesterday, but I feel really good about him."

Melanie grabs a nail file and works on her hands before replying sternly, "Sheila, remember the last time you felt good about someone? We both know how that turned out."

"Yeah, yeah. You don't have to remind me, Melanie. Tory was such a jerk, and after all these months, I still regret the decision he forced on me. I should've listened to my gut. I can almost feel my dislike for him rattling around in my stomach. But Damien is nothing like him," Sheila declares, unsure if she's trying to convince her friend or herself about Damien's character.

Melanie sighs and shakes her head, "Okay, girl, I hear you. But I have to go. My dad is calling me." Melanie puts the nail file down as she gets ready to leave her room. "You stay safe and keep me updated, Boo."

"Okay, you know I love you, girl," Sheila sing-songs.

"I love you, too," Melanie says, drawing out the "too" before they both hang up.

Right on time, Vivian calls her for breakfast. Sheila stands up and hears her aunt saying something else, "I was thinking, it's such a beautiful day and it's not too muggy yet. Do you want to eat inside or out?"

Sheila plops down into her favorite loveseat. "If it's okay with you, I would love to eat outdoors."

"Okay. Can you come in and help me bring out the food?"

Sheila stands up, "Yes, Auntie, I'll be right there." Sheila enters the house and proceeds to help her aunt bring out their breakfast. They go back and forth for juice, syrup, and napkins until they finally feel ready to sit together for breakfast on the patio. Sheila rushes in to get two cups when her aunt calls out to her again.

"Sheila, can you please bring me my glasses off the kitchen counter when you come out?"

"I got you, Auntie," Sheila replies, scanning the counter for her aunt's glasses before returning outside with their cups.

Vivian dons her glasses, opens her Bible, and reads from Psalm 1:18 verse 24. "This is the day the Lord has made, let us rejoice and be glad in it." She proceeds to say a quick prayer over the food then says, "Now, let's eat!"

Sheila drizzles some syrup over her pancakes and eggs, then takes a bite of her aunt's award-winning pancakes. "Now I see what that hype was all about at the church! These award-winning pancakes are awesome. Hey, you and Mrs. Jackson need to get together and open up a restaurant! You could do breakfast or brunch, and she could do lunch or dinner," Sheila suggests excitedly as she enjoys her delicious breakfast.

Vivian lets out a deep belly laugh and shakes her head, "You know what, sweetie? That's extra hilarious because every member of the church says the same thing." Sheila smiles warmly.

"Well, Auntie, we can't all be wrong now, can we?"

Vivian returns the smile and wipes her mouth, "Speaking about church, I need to finish my breakfast so I can start getting ready. You're still doing my makeup, sweetie?"

Dabbing her mouth and tossing her napkin into her empty plate, Sheila says, "Of course I am. Let me go get the supplies now before I help you clean up the kitchen."

"Oh, thank you so much! I'm going to look even better than usual." Teasingly, Sheila's aunt does her infamous strut around the patio. "Watch out, Pastor Chisholm, you're about to meet your First Lady of the church today!"

Sheila laughs, and the pair hug before Vivian leaves to get dressed for her church service. Sheila's heart races as she dashes up the stairs to get ready for her plans with Damien.

Showered, moisturized, and having sprayed herself with some Chanel No. 5, Vivian emerges from the bathroom to pick out her clothes. After deciding on a bright orange outfit, complete with a stylish matching hat, she heads downstairs in her slip.

Sheila is just finishing up washing the dishes when her aunt comes downstairs. With a pair of large headphones blasting music into her ears, Sheila is unaware of her aunt, so she inevitably jumps when she hears her aunt's voice.

"I didn't mean to scare you, baby. So, what are your plans for today, Sheila?" Sheila laughs to herself.

"I can hear that music from here," Vivian says. "You better turn that stuff down before you end up with a hearing aid before you're twenty," Vivian warns, pulling out a chair to sit at the counter Sheila has just finished cleaning, "Are you planning on coming to church with me?"

Placing her headphones on the counter, Sheila starts organizing the makeup supplies. "No, Auntie, I was hoping to stay home today and catch up on some rest. My legs are pretty sore from all that walking around yesterday. I'll try to go next week!"

Eyeing her niece, Vivian replies, "Okay, as long as you promise you will come next week."

Sheila doesn't answer as she rummages through all of the makeup items in her professional looking kit. "Hey, Auntie. I have some orange eyeliner here and I saw your outfit hanging on the door. Would you like to go for a bold look today?"

Thinking to herself, Vivian replies, "Well, I'm not getting any younger, baby. Bring it on. I just don't want all that heavy foundation. I'm not knocking anyone who does, but I think a bold lip, some eyeliner, mascara and eyeshadow if you have it will do just fine."

Sheila gets the handful of items and decides to accent her aunt's orange eyeliner with some golden eyeshadow. Gently holding her aunt's face, Sheila applies the makeup. Her aunt closes her eyes and remarks, "You are so gentle, Sheila. I can't wait to see how this turns out."

Makeup applied, Vivian gives her niece a kiss and excuses herself to do her hair and carefully don her clothes. Successfully putting everything on without any of her makeup smearing, Vivian checks herself out in the mirror and yells out, "Sheila, you've got a magic touch baby. I look stunning! Thank you so much."

Coming downstairs, she is greeted by Sheila with her phone in hand, ready to take pictures, she teases, "Say Pastor Chisholm!"

Vivian bursts into uncontrollable laughter, making for some gorgeous pictures. Standing in the doorway, she looks at her niece while adjusting the purse strap on her shoulder, "Well, you have a set of keys. Keep me updated. And if you leave the house, please be sure to lock all the doors and close these windows up."

"I will, Auntie," Sheila promises. She shuts the door, locks it, and heads back to the patio to continue posting, texting, and making phone calls.

Chapter 11

If These Walls Could Talk

Damien is sitting in the living room watching ESPN when his phone rings. He looks around, and then remembers that he left his phone on the kitchen table where his mother and sister are seated.

Seeing the name displayed on the screen, Tanya smiles and calls Damien, "Hey big bro, your Boo is calling you."

"My Boo?" Damien remarks from the hallway, pretending to be oblivious.

Sharon laughs as Tanya continues, "Yes, your Boo, Sheila? She was here last night. You were with her all day? Is that ringing any bells for you?"

Damien enters the kitchen, where his mom and Tanya continue snickering. Shaking his head, Damien picks up his phone and heads back into the living room, where he sees he missed the call. Excited about the upcoming day, Damien calls Sheila back promptly.

Sheila answers readily with a hint of a smile decorating her voice, "Good morning. I figured you were still asleep."

"Nah, with a military dad, I've been primed to wake up no later than eight every morning," He chuckles, "What's up, though?"

"Did you sleep well?" Sheila inquires.

As if on cue, Damien yawns, "Not really, but it's all good. How about you?"

"I can't complain. I just got done sending my aunt off to church."

"Yeah, my mother and sister are about to head out now."

"Tell them I said hi!" Sheila says enthusiastically, "But back to more serious matters, we have some unfinished business to discuss."

Damien chuckles knowingly. "So did you decide if you wanted to come keep me company?" Sheila asks.

"Yeah, no doubt, I'll be there," he whispers, "What time were you thinking?"

Laying out the situation in her mind, Sheila rambles on, "Well, my aunt is sitting on the porch waiting for her ride, and I wanted to get myself ready for you, so you think you can be here around eleven-fifteen?"

"Sounds like a plan!" Damien says. Lowering his voice, he continues, "You're still going to make it worth my while, right?"

"No doubt," Sheila says.

"Then I'll see you for sure," Damien says, thinking to himself about whether he needs to buy new condoms or not. Chuckling, Sheila replies, "Oh, trust me, you won't be disappointed."

They hang up, and Damien punches the air excitedly, doing a happy dance as his thoughts and feelings muddle together in the summer heat. Back at her aunt's house, Sheila does a silly dance of her own before placing her Victoria's Secret outfit on the bed and heading for the shower. Plugging in her speaker, Sheila blasts her favorite songs in preparation for what is yet to come.

Damien goes to the kitchen and is greeted by Tanya's nosy questions, "So, big head, what did Sheila want?"

"She wanted to know when you'll start minding your own business!" Damien asserts.

Before she can pry any further, Damien and Tanya's sibling antics are interrupted by their mom's inquiries, "Are you coming to church with me and your sister?"

With a tired sigh, Damien reaches for a banana before answering, "Not today. I have to catch up on some school stuff, like going over my football play manual and finishing up my summer Black history assignment."

"I thought you told me you were finished reading that book for class. What was it? *Wisdom Warriors?*" Tanya says.

Glancing at his little sister, who is readying herself to get dressed for church, Damien bites into a banana. "I am. But being that I'll be a senior this year, I have a lot more on my plate. I have to do a book report on the '28 Lessons for African American Youth' that are included in the book."

"What is *Wisdom Warriors* about? And who's the author?" Sharon sounds pretty intrigued as she clears the table. "Before I forget, Damien, make sure you wash these dishes before you go about your day so Tanya and I can get ready. We barely have an hour before service starts!"

Damien notes his mother's request. "*Wisdom Warriors* was written by an educator named Mary Cole Watson. The book has twenty-two short stories that discuss issues African Americans face every day."

"Wow, that really sounds like a great book. When you're done with the assignment, I would love to read it, too," Tanya chimes in.

"No problem," Damien replies, tossing his banana peel into the compost bin his mother just started.

Looking at the clock, then looking at Tanya, Sharon says, "It's about time for us to start getting ready for church." As the two ladies head upstairs, Damien clears the rest of the table and prepares to wash the dishes. He figures that his mom and sister will be just about out the door by the time he's done. Glancing at the clock, Damien puts in his EarPods, puts on a random playlist, and busies himself with the dishes. He dances and sings out loud, causing his mom and sister to stop and laugh as they ready themselves upstairs.

After sharing hugs and kisses with Damien, Sharon and Tanya scramble out the door. Closing the door behind his mom and sister, Damien goes upstairs to pick out an outfit. Looking up on the top shelf where he keeps his various hats, Damien sees a box of condoms and remembers two years earlier when his dad knocked on his door and asked if he could talk with him for a moment. As if it were yesterday, Damien hears the knock.

"Yes? Come on in, Dad. What's in the CVS bag you have in your hand? Am I in some sort of trouble?" Damien began to panic, he thought over all of the things he'd gotten into that he had no business doing over the last year or so.

With a hearty laugh, his dad ruffled Damien's little afro. "No, son. In fact, what I have in this bag could possibly keep you out of trouble." Sitting down on the bed next to his curious son, his dad continued, "I would like to talk to you about sex and being a responsible young man. You're at the age where you may want to explore sex, and there is nothing wrong with being curious or interested in sex, just like there's nothing wrong with wanting to remain abstinent. As a matter of fact, son, abstinence is what I'd prefer for you, but I know I risk pushing you further away by forcing any decision on you for my sake."

"What's abstinence, Dad?"

Damien can see his dad clearly, as if he were in the room with him at that moment.

"Abstinence is the choice not to have sex. It's a method that is one-hundred percent effective in preventing pregnancy and infections, as long as all sexual contact is avoided. There's a large population of young men and woman who have decided not to have sex or even get intimate with anyone until they are married, and then only at that point do they choose to get 'down and dirty' if you will," Damien's dad said. He made a silly face, causing Damien to laugh at the memory.

Naturally, he wanted to test his father, "Were you abstinent 'til you were married to Mom?"

His dad chuckled to himself, realizing he may have just opened a can of worms. But he thought to himself, *Better to be honest with my son than to blindly hold him to a standard I hadn't maintained myself.* He sighed and answered, "Well, no, son. Sometimes, though, I think back and wish I were. So, if you decide that you are going to have sex and both parties have consented, it's an absolute must that you at least use protection." He handed Damien a bag containing a box of condoms, "See, son, these condoms will not only help protect you from unwanted pregnancy, but regardless of your preferences, they'll also protect you from sexually transmitted diseases."

Damien looked over the condoms and remembered opening one in health class and learning how to properly apply it. His dad continued, "Please understand me when I say that a condom will help, but anything other than abstinence can fall short of one-hundred percent protection. So, the least we can do is strive to be safe rather than sorry." Damien took in his dad's advice. He didn't have too many questions as he wasn't really into anything other than sports and video games at the time. His dad continued, "And don't go thinking that this conversation is my permission or approval for you to have sex. I've told you my wish; based on my experience and my newfound faith it is that you wait until you get married. But as I've come to learn as your dad, the choice is ultimately yours."

His dad smiled at his son and pulled him in for a hug. They continued to go back and forth as Damien's dad answered a few of his lingering questions. After thanking his dad for the talk and the box of condoms, Damien remembered one last thing to tell his dad, "I think I'm going to plan to wait until I am married to have sex. I don't want to risk the chance of getting a sexually transmitted disease or even worse, getting someone pregnant."

Beaming at his son, his dad replied, "I think that's some smart thinking. If you have any concerns or questions about anything we've discussed today, you can come talk to me or your mother. We both love you and your sister very much, and we are here to protect you." Damien smiled as his dad looked off into the distance. "The hardest thing for any parent is feeling like they can't help their child. And it's even harder to help if their child doesn't communicate with them," he said, eyeing his son to make sure he understood.

"I hear you, Dad." With a curious look on his face, Damien asked his father another question, "Did you have this same talk with Tanya yet?"

"Good question, but no son, not yet. Your mother and I will both have this talk with your sister when the time is right."

Damien can almost feel the strong hug that his dad shared with him after that long conversation. Tears well up in his eyes as he remembers his dad's final words in that moment.

"Son, I'm so proud of the young man you are turning out to be. Put your faith first, stay in school, eat healthy, remain focused, invest your time and money wisely, and you'll reach your goals."

Those last words fill Damien's mind as the remainder of the memory fades away, leaving Damien standing in front of his closet, looking at the box of condoms. Shortly after that conversation,

Damien became sexually active and had sexual intercourse several times. But he was proud that he had at least taken his father's advice to always use protection.

Damien takes the condoms from the top shelf and checks the date before putting the remaining few in his pocket. Then he reaches for his favorite cologne and splashes some over his body before taking out his phone to review the photos that Sheila sent him in her Victoria's Secret outfit. He smiles again and does another happy dance. Suddenly, Damien hears the door open again. Turning the screen off and tossing his phone on the bed, he tries to act casual as he can tell by the weight of the steps that it's his mom. He can hear her rush into her room to grab something before stopping in front of his door.

"Damien, are you in here?"

"Yes, Mom. I'm getting dressed."

"Okay baby, I almost forgot my Bible. Can you believe that?" She laughs at herself, "We should be home by three-thirty, baby. And if you get hungry before dinner, there's plenty of leftovers in the fridge."

Damien stands in the doorway, "Thanks, Mom. Where's Tanya?"

"She's in the car. Please remember to be safe today, and make sure you keep the doors locked."

Damien gives his mom a peck on the cheek, "I will, Mom. I love you."

"I love you too, son," Sharon hustles and descends the stairs, accidently slamming the door as she exits in a hurry. Damien fishes for his phone, which had bounced off the bed when he threw it in a panic. Thankful to see the screen wasn't cracked, Damien checks the time and realizes that it is already eleven. He takes a deep breath, feeling somewhat anxious and overexcited. Calming himself down and assuming his bravado, Damien texts Sheila.

Damien: Hey, we still on for 11:15?

Sheila: Without a doubt. I've been waiting.

Damien: Kool my mom & sister just left.

Sheila: Sounds like a plan.

<She adds a kissy face emoji.>

Damien breezes through the house, checking that all the lights are off and the house is secured. Once satisfied, he grabs his keys and heads out. He stands in front of his home for a moment, breathing in the somewhat fresh air. He smells the faint scent of the city drifting on the sticky wind. Damien enjoys the moment. He grins to himself, hearing the birds, watching the dragonflies zip around, and waving to some fellow neighbors before heading over to see Sheila.

As Damien heads up the road, he receives a text and pulls his phone out of his pocket rather quickly to check the message. Continuing to text as he walks, Damien's oblivious to the fact that the condoms he'd placed in his pocket have fallen out.

Dressed in a hot pink satin robe covering her special lingerie, Sheila looks over the various photographs on the mantle in her aunt's living room and is caught in a daydream. Suddenly, Sheila hears the gate close. She peeks out of the window once more to see Damien.

Damien reaches the door and rings the bell. Sheila quickly adjusts herself as she opens the door. Damien is mesmerized as Sheila grabs his arm and pulls him into the hallway as she locks the door.

As Damien enters the home, Sheila drops the robe to reveal her special outfit. Damien turns around in shock. He takes Sheila by the hand and spins her around delicately. Sheila smiles, feeling a flutter run through her chest.

"Oh, you look so fine," Damien says. He embraces Sheila with a tight hug and gives her a big kiss. While still embraced in Damien's arms, Sheila squeezes his waist. "You truly don't know how long I've been waiting for this moment. You can call it lusting." She kisses Damien again. "You smell so good," she whispers.

"So do you," Damien replies as they slowly unwind from each other. Sheila teases, "And it's not my aunt's Chanel this time. It's my favorite perfume."

"And what's that?" Damien asks curiously, standing back to admire her some more.

"It's from one of the African stores back home. It's an oil called *Thirsty*," Sheila says with a smirk. Her braids swing about her and jingle slightly as her beads clang together.

Rubbing his hands, Damien approaches Sheila and stands behind her with one hand on her waist. "Say no more. What time will your aunt be back?"

"My aunt won't be home until after three. So, relax and have a seat. I'll entertain you," Sheila reaches for the remote to her Bluetooth speaker and finds her favorite Beyoncé playlist. She begins dancing provocatively, much to Damien's delight. Reclining in the same seat where Sheila sat waiting for him earlier, Damien watches Sheila intently, taking in all that she is. His feelings go beyond lust, Sheila is funny, smart, caring, and completely mesmerizing. Damien fantasizes, as he smiles in anticipation, of the way that the afternoon could play out.

Sheila moves closer to Damien and begins giving him a lap dance, which he enjoys. Damien stands up to dance with Sheila, and they take turns kissing and showing off some of their best moves. Overflowing with life, they make each other laugh. Sheila turns the music down, takes Damien by the hand, and guides him toward the stairs, "Let's take this upstairs and get things popping."

Damien follows closely behind Sheila all the way up the stairs with the music thumping quietly from the portable speaker in her other hand. The pair are unable to keep their hands off of each other. Sheila backs into her room and pulls Damien's shirt over his head. Always finding the humor in things, Sheila teases him, "You do have a big head."

Damien smiles then kisses Sheila's cheek, and they start to play. Sheila manages to turn the volume back up on the speaker before carrying on with Damien. Things continue to get hot between them when Damien reaches into his pocket for the condoms. He pats frantically, and Sheila notices the look of frustration on his face.

Damien looks on the floor and approaches the door to go downstairs before Sheila touches his arm. She looks at him with concern, "What's wrong, Damien?"

"I brought some condoms with me, but now I can't find them. Now that I think about it, they had to fall out of my pocket on my way here. I know I had them."

Sheila, still caught up in the mood, closes the door and embraces Damien. Walking him back to her bed, she starts caressing and kissing him. In her sexiest of voices, she reassures him, "You won't need them. I'm on the pill."

In that moment, all of Damien's morals and values instilled by his parents and pastor become a distant memory. The feel of her skin, the sound of her voice, and the scent of her flowery perfume replace his careful guidance. With the power of their growing hormones edging them on, they kiss each other hungrily. In the heat of the moment, they proceed without the condom.

Damien and Sheila remain in the bedroom for some time. When they finally exit Sheila's bedroom, Damien, feeling rather anxious, turns to Sheila. "So, you're one hundred percent sure you've been taking your pill regularly?"

Sheila, donning her robe again and checking herself in the mirror, replies sarcastically, "No, not today."

Damien's eyes widen with intensity, "Sheila, what!?"

Looking startled, Sheila turns to face him, "Whoa, calm down, I'm just kidding. I've been taking the pill for sure."

Damien lets out a loud sigh of relief and kisses Sheila on her head, brushing over her braids with his hand, "Well, it's almost two o'clock. I have to head back. I'll text you in a few."

Sheila smiles widely and pecks his cheek before standing up again, "It sounds like a plan." Damien ruffles her hair before following her out the door and down the stairs. They kiss again before he leaves. The music is still playing as Sheila locks the door behind him and goes upstairs to shower.

Chapter 12

After Thoughts

Damien walks back home, and checks the ground to see where he may have lost the condoms, but there are no condoms to be found. Shaking his head in disbelief, Damien enters the house and secures the doors. He tosses his keys on the table in a little bowl by the door, where all of his family's keys go, and trudges upstairs to take a shower. He spends some time feeling the water wash over him as he comes to his senses. Damien recounts everything that just happened. He is grateful and very satisfied, but there is a deep-rooted sense of worry he can't quite shake. Not even his cool shower can wash away the muck of fear and uncertainty swirling about in his mind.

Once out of the shower, Damien dries off and lies on his bed. He stares at the ceiling for some time, feeling his nerves rattle inside him, and begins to chastise himself, "How could I let that happen? I know better and was taught better. How could I put my future at risk?" He feels tears well up in him as he kneels down to pray, "God, I know it's been a while, it's been pretty hard to talk to you since my dad's been gone. To be honest, I haven't really had much faith at all. But I come to you today, and I pray I didn't get Sheila pregnant or contract an STD."

Damien lets out a deep sigh of relief. Feeling the power of prayer, he starts to calm down again, thinking they'll be okay. After all, she said she's on the pill and seems to be honest. "I do trust her," he declares aloud. Damien reaches over and pulls out *Wisdom Warriors*. He lays it on the bed as he puts on some red and black basketball shorts, a simple black T-shirt, and of course, some slides.

He grabs his book and heads down to the kitchen table to complete his assignment on the '28 Lessons for African-American Youth.' Reading through the 28 lessons, he comes across lesson number 26, which reads: "We will demonstrate discipline and respect our sexuality to avert unwanted pregnancies, sexually transmitted disease, and emotional turmoil by engaging in behavior that requires adult maturity."

Damien is so astonished by what he has just read that he puts the book face down and rests his head in the palms of his hands. He tries to prevent his overthinking, and now realizes that his poor decision is haunting him. Damien gets up to get a cool bottle of water and sits back down to finish lessons 27 and 28. He goes upstairs to get his laptop and complete his report. Trying his best to concentrate on the assignment but placing the book down again, he zips upstairs to grabs his phone and immediately calls Sheila.

Sheila sits in her room drying her skin as her music continues playing. Sitting on her bed and wondering what to wear next, she sees her phone light up with Damien's name. She answers on the first ring, "You miss me already?"

In a bleak tone and feeling jittery, Damien stumbles over his response, "No. I mean yes, but that's not why I am calling you. I called to ask you if you're one-hundred percent sure that you've taken the pill regularly?"

Rolling her eyes, Sheila looks at herself in the mirror as she replies, "Oh my God, Damien. Please don't ruin the memories of us being together by asking me that question over and over. I wouldn't lie to you." Sheila, feeling her own sense of worry grow as she remembers her own predicament the year before, mutters, "I can't go through that crap again like with Tory."

Damien raises an eyebrow, "What crap?"

Sheila brushes it off, "That's a conversation for another day, but hey, I really miss you already. When will I see you again?"

With a deep sigh, Damien replies, "I'm not sure, probably on Friday 'cause I have a full week of football practice and work."

"Did you enjoy being with me today?" Sheila asks curiously. She continues to look over herself in the mirror.

Damien smiles to himself, remembering some of the better parts of their time together, "Yeah, you were incredible."

"You were too. You made a great first impression. I really don't think I can wait until Friday to see you again," Sheila says as she stands up to put on her house shorts before lying on the bed and staring up at the ceiling. She's thrilled by the thought of seeing Damien again.

"I'll see what I can do," Damien says, "But, right now, I'll have to finish working on my school report."

"All right, I'm going to continue watching Netflix since I finished my reports early," she teases.

"Yeah, yeah. Well, I'm going to get to it now, Sheila. Talk to you later."

"Bye, Damien," Sheila says with a hint of melancholy in her voice. She truly does miss him. Damien really seems like the whole package.

Damien lets out a sigh of relief, feeling a lot less worried after speaking with Sheila. He continues to work on his assignment at the kitchen table. Shortly afterward, Damien's mother and sister return from church.

He hears his mother's voice, "Damien, are you home?"

"Yes, Mom. I'm here in the kitchen," Damien replies, typing the final paragraphs of his report.

Tanya walks into the kitchen and reaches for an apple, "What's up, big brother?"

"All good over here, sis," Damien replies, "How was church?"

Tanya bites into her apple and leans against the counter, "It was great. I was asked to sing a selection by Pastor Chisholm, and when I was done, the whole congregation gave me a standing ovation for what seemed like five minutes!"

"That's expected," Damien says with a smile.

"Thank you, big head," Tanya smiles as she teases her brother. She heads upstairs to change her clothes.

Sharon goes to the kitchen where Damien is finishing up his report, "Were you home all day?"

Feeling nervous, he answers, "No, Mom. I got back home a couple of hours ago." Damien hopes his mother won't ask any more questions.

"Good to see you came back in time to finish up this report. Then you can really enjoy your summer, baby," she ruffles his hair, "Is that the '28 Lessons for African American Youth' report you're working on?" she asks, taking her shoes off.

"Yes. I'm almost done," Damien says proudly.

"Great! Don't forget to lend me the book when you're finished. I wonder if Tanya will read it with me. Hey, maybe we can all discuss it later?" his mother suggests as she walks over to the stairs.

"Good idea, Mom. It truly is an insightful book," Damien scrolls through his newly written document to review his assignment. Still staring at the screen, he continues, "How was church service?"

Beaming, his mom looks back at him, one hand on the railing, "It was great, your sister had the church rockin' with that anointed voice."

"Yeah, Tanya mentioned that they gave her a standing ovation."

"Indeed, they did," Sharon beams proudly, "Well, I'm going to get out of these clothes and start getting dinner ready. Did you eat?"

"I had some fruit a little while ago, but I can tell my stomach's about to start talking soon," Damien replies with a smile.

With a smile of her own, his mother turns toward the stairs. "Great, as I mentioned earlier, we have plenty of leftovers that we all can eat. Thank God for those leftovers. After I warm them up, I can relax for the rest of the day," she sighs peacefully and walks gracefully up the stairs to her room.

Meanwhile, back at Vivian's house, Sheila is lying on the couch in the living room, dressed in a white T-shirt and gray athletic shorts watching Netflix on her laptop. She sits up to get a drink when she sees her aunt coming through the gate. Sheila pauses her show and rushes to the door to greet her aunt, "Hey, Auntie, how was church?"

"Church was great, but before I say another word, let me get out of these shoes." She shuffles over to the couch with Sheila following close behind. They both sit on the couch. Vivian removes her shoes with a sigh of relief. "That feels much better," she notes. Sheila moves to rub her aunt's feet as her aunt eases onto the couch and continues her recount of the church service, "Church was great, sweetie. Pastor Chisholm, that handsome man, gave such an empowering sermon today. I think you would've loved it. He spoke about the youth and how social media is misleading the younger generations to chase ideals and values that don't amount to half of what God has in store for you all. Truly insightful. Oh yes, and my baby, Tanya had that church rockin' again."

"Oh, no. I missed Tanya's singing?" Sheila exclaims as she finishes massaging her aunt's feet and sits on the couch next to her.

With a sly look on her face, Sheila's aunt replies, "See, you could've heard her if you came. Sheila, Tanya truly has a powerful voice for such a small body. That girl sounds similar to Jennifer Hudson! Of course, she has her own unique sound, but that's the closest I can think of."

With a shocked expression on her face, Sheila comments, "That is amazing. She's definitely going to go far with that voice if she's serious about it. And I'm glad you enjoyed church, Auntie."

"Well, how was your day, baby? You look mighty comfortable."

Without skipping a beat, Sheila responds plainly, "I've just been laying here most of the day watching Netflix."

"Well, do you have plans for later?" Sheila's aunt asks, standing up with her shoes as she stretches her body slowly, "And did you ever find out about any yoga videos on, what's it called? The Boob Tube?"

Sheila lets out a loud cackle, "You mean YouTube, Auntie?"

Her aunt swats at her playfully, "You know what I mean, girl."

Sheila pretends to flinch, "I didn't find any videos for you, but I can definitely do that right now. I don't have any plans other than lounging here and enjoying this fine Sunday, though."

Making her way to the stairs, Vivian looks excitedly at her niece parked on the couch. "I've got a great idea, why don't I join you? We can make it a girl's night with pizza and some of that leftover vanilla ice cream. Then, once you find that yoga, we can wind down with that!"

"I would love that! And hey, there's some of that pie in the fridge, too!" Sheila flashes a warm smile at her aunt as she readies herself to search for some yoga tutorials.

Vivian reaches in her purse, finds her credit card, and hands it to Sheila. "There's a menu on the fridge for Giordano's, pick whatever you want," she goes up the stairs, "I'm gonna go get changed and I'll be right down."

Sheila hears her aunt thudding about upstairs as she looks over the menu and tries to remember the last time she had a pizza. Wanting to keep it simple, she looks over their pizza options, deciding that mushroom, onion, and peppers would be a tasty choice. Sheila calls upstairs to her aunt, "Auntie, did you want a sub or a pizza? I was thinking to get a pizza with a couple of toppings. We can do half and half if you don't like what I do."

Vivian pulls her slip off and searches for a decorated caftan to lounge in, "I'll eat whatever you order, baby. Right now, I'm just about hungry enough to eat a horse."

"Sounds like a plan," Sheila states as she dials Giordano's to place an order.

In the weeks that follow, Damien and Sheila continue to get together as often as they can. They alternate between each other's houses, carefully planning around everyone else's schedules so that they know for a fact that they'll be alone. Every time they are together, there is always a lot of laughing and playing which will somehow always lead to a sexual encounter, but never again without protection.

Chapter 13

The Moment of Truth

I t's now been seven weeks since Sheila arrived in Chicago and five weeks since she met Damien. Today is the last Thursday of the month, and that's when Vivian always does her grocery shopping for the upcoming month. Sheila heads downstairs and picks up her phone from the living room table to call Damien, not realizing how close her aunt is standing. Her aunt eyes Sheila steadily.

Sheila giggles with Damien as she updates him, "My aunt is going grocery shopping, so you wanna come over for a booty call?"

On the other end, Damien is also laughing to himself, scrolling aimlessly on his phone with his EarPods in, "You only have to ask once. What time?"

"Thirty minutes," Sheila says.

"Okay, cool, I'll be there," Damien promises.

"See you soon," Sheila says in a sing-song voice. The two teens hang up.

Fuming with rage and disappointment, Sheila's aunt composes herself before walking into the living room with a straight face, "Sheila, I need you to get dressed and come with me to go food shopping."

Sheila starts to feel anxious and tries to weasel her way out of going, "I'm not feeling well, Auntie."

Her aunt ignores her niece's manufactured pleas. She responds in a tone Sheila has never heard her take before, "Sheila, don't play with me. You're coming to the store with me. Get dressed." Sheila quickly texts Damien to cancel their little rendezvous.

Sheila: My aunt wants me to go shopping with her.

<She inserts an eye rolling emoji.>

Damien: Aw, ok.

<He inserts a sad face emoji>

Sheila: I'll text you later.

Damien: Got you.

Sheila gets dressed in a fury. She slams the doors shut before heading to the car where her aunt has been waiting. Once in the car, Vivian reminds Sheila to fasten her seat belt as she fastens her own, and the pair drive to her aunt's favorite supermarket, Peats Fresh Market on West Cermak Road. Although the market is miles away from the house, Vivian is not concerned about the drive. Peats always has the freshest meat and produce around. Plus, the employees are always so helpful and friendly. They even know her by name and hook her up with discounts any time they can.

Today, however, Vivian plans to use the long car ride to have a discussion with Sheila. After that conversation she overheard Sheila having, she is worried that the rumors her neighbors shared regarding Sheila are true. Though she knows better, she is hoping that what she overheard was some sort of foolish joking around between Sheila and Damien. And in the past, whenever she asked Sheila a direct question, she knew in her heart that Sheila never lied to her. And so, looking over at Sheila briefly before reverting her eyes back to the road, Vivian initiates the difficult conversation with her niece, "So, do you miss home?"

Looking up from her Instagram feed, Sheila gives a nonchalant reply, a hint of frustration lingering in her tone, "No, I mean, I miss my mom, but I don't miss New York, at least not yet. I'm really loving it here in Chicago."

With a knowing tone and another glance in Sheila's direction, her aunt abruptly transitions to the core of their conversation, "Do you love Chicago, or do you love being with Damien?"

Sheila gasps and feels her heart pounding in her chest. She tries to remain casual, "Oh, God, Auntie. I can't believe you're asking me that, but I'll be honest with you, I care about Damien a lot. I definitely don't love him, though."

Her aunt grips the wheel as she realizes her niece truly thought she did something with such a bogus statement. Remaining calm and exhaling deeply to maintain her composure, she musters up a response, "I'm glad you use the word 'honest,' Sheila, because honest is what I'm always looking for from you. But I've noticed the two of you are nearly inseparable. You're always on the phone into the wee hours of the morning, and I've been hearing from the neighbors that every time I leave the house Damien comes over and stays for hours at a time."

Still trying to play cool, Sheila looks out the window as she tries to divert the conversation away from her and Damien, "What neighbor told you that? It's probably that nasty old man, Mr. Peterson. He's always peeking out the window and staring at me. I can't stand him!"

Unwavering in her mission to get to the bottom of her niece's summer antics, Vivian continues, "At this point, Sheila, it doesn't even matter who told me. I just want you to be completely honest with me. Are you having sex with Damien in my house?"

Maintaining a solid front, Sheila looks over at her aunt. Her aunt glances back at her with a disappointed look on her face. Sheila is overcome with guilt, but she remains cool, "Auntie, please tell me why you keep asking me these questions."

Taking note that Sheila's lack of a direct answer is all the answer she needs, her aunt gives in to her feigned ignorance, "One reason, Sheila, is that nearly all of the neighbors on our block have expressed concern about y'all's behavior. The second reason is that I overheard your conversation this morning, talking about a booty call. Now, I'll admit I've had a few of them myself in my time, so I definitely know what a booty call is."

Sheila's face morphs from an expression of shock, to disgust and then ultimately, to shame. She lets out a deep sigh, unable to avoid coming clean any longer, "Okay, Auntie. Since we're being completely honest, yes, Damien and I have been having sex."

Glancing at her niece again, with no hint of malice in her face, she feels for the child sitting next to her, growing into an adult before her very eyes. She feels a well of tears bubble up, but proceeds to drive cautiously, hands gripping the steering wheel to help ease the flood of emotions rolling through her psyche.

"So, I ask you this question. Do you love Damien?"

Sheila shrugs with a roll of her eyes, "No, Auntie, I don't. It's just sex."

With a pleading look in her eyes, Sheila's aunt holds her gaze on her niece as they stop at another red light. Sheila fidgets uncomfortably, feeling judged by her aunt, who has known her and cared for her off and on since she was a baby. "Sheila, please answer me this question: How can you give yourself to someone you don't love? Because if it's not love, Sheila, then it's pure lust. Didn't your mother teach you to have any respect for your body, baby? And your heart?" Vivian pleads.

Staring forlornly out the window, Sheila jumps as raindrops fall on her sour face. The sprinkles turn into a heavier rain as they approach their destination. Sheila rolls up her window just before a thunderous downpour washes over them, "What is love, Auntie?"

"It's what God, your mother, and I show you every day."

Sheila's voice starts to get heavy with emotion, "I know that you and my mom love me, but we're talking about boys. I honestly feel that my body is the only reason I have ever heard the word 'love' from any of them. My own dad never even told me he loved me. I don't even know who he is." She starts to cry, "Besides, Auntie, you just said that you had a few booty calls back in your days. Did you respect your body?"

Myriad thoughts and feelings pass through Vivian's mind. She is shocked by her niece's audacity, yet she feels herself soften when she realizes the weight of Sheila's question. But that is for a later time. Vivian peeks at her niece while trying to maintain her gaze on the winding road.

"Have you lost your mind? I said what I said, but this isn't about me right now. It's about you. And my booty call days were well beyond my teenage years, sweetie. I will not tolerate that type of behavior in my house. I'm only going to say this once, Sheila, and if I have to say it again, I will send you packing back to New York, okay? Are we on the same page?" Vivian retorts.

Sheila cries quietly. Tears stream down her face, she is filled with embarrassment and frustration.

How do we learn when we aren't taught better? "Yes, Auntie, I apologize, and it won't ever happen again."

Vivian looks over at her crying niece. That growing young woman was once the sweet baby she knew and loved so much. A tear rolls down her own cheek as she extends her hand to her niece's knee. Sheila places her hand over her aunt's, and they remain there for the rest of the ride.

"Sheila, I'm so sorry that you never knew your dad. I truly need you to know that me, your mom, and God love you so very much. You don't ever need to use your body to get approval from anyone, male or female. You've got to learn to love and respect yourself more than anyone could ever love or respect you. Do you understand, baby?"

In a tired voice, her eyes puffy and red from the flow of long suppressed tears, Sheila answers quietly, "Yes Auntie, I'm really trying hard. And I see that I need to try a little harder."

Just then, Vivian pulls into the grocery store parking lot. She parks the car, and Sheila angrily unfastens her seatbelt and pushes the door open. Her aunt has other plans. Reaching for Sheila's arm, she says, "Wait, let's continue our talk." Looking at her niece's tear-stained face, she takes a hand and wipes the tears away. Gently holding Sheila's face, she continues their heavy conversation, "Is there anything else I need to know?"

Sheila pulls away and buries her face in her hands, bawling louder, "Auntie, I'm really scared. I haven't been feeling well. I've been vomiting, and I missed my period last month."

Her aunt's eyes widen fearfully, "Oh, my Lord, what are you saying? Please, please don't tell me what I think you are about to tell me."

Still crying, Sheila musters up a low, sorrowful answer, "Yes, Auntie, I'm not completely sure, but I think that I'm pregnant."

Vivian's voice becomes stiff, "Sheila, do you remember when we had our conversation about boys and sex? It was at that same time that you mentioned to me that you had been put on birth control pills." With her head hung low, Sheila nods slowly, remembering the conversation that she had previously put out of her memory. Her aunt tries to remain calm, hoping to find a ray of hope in this overwhelming situation for everyone involved, "I'm sure that Damien was smart enough to use protection."

"Yeah, but it's just that, one time, he didn't," Sheila sobs. The rain has steadied itself, but the thunder continues.

"Oh, my God," Vivian puts her head on the steering wheel and tries to calm herself down. She remains there for several moments, the two of them sitting in silence as Sheila sobs quietly, "What do you mean with 'all but one time'? How many times have you had sex with Damien?"

"I don't know. About six times," Sheila shrugs. Unable to look at her aunt, she continues to stare out the window.

"Doesn't he know that it just takes one time having unprotected sex to get a girl pregnant or to give and receive an STD?"

"Yes, Auntie, I'm sure he does. It just happened so fast. He had misplaced his condom, and because I was on the pill, I suggested to him that it would be all right," Sheila says, realizing the immensity and the carelessness of such a decision.

At a loss for words, Sheila's aunt just shakes her head. She tries to compose herself so as not to shame and ultimately push her niece away. She wonders how to reach someone who is missing the basic and vital love of a father in her life. "Unbelievable. I truly can't even believe what I'm hearing, Sheila. Who else knows?"

"No one other than Melanie, my best friend back home," with a sigh, she continues trying to find a solution to this pending crisis, "I don't know for sure if I'm actually pregnant. I need to purchase a pregnancy test."

"Well, as much as I love children, I truly hope you're not pregnant right now, Sheila. After we leave here, we'll go next door to CVS and purchase a couple of pregnancy tests."

They continue sitting there with Vivian staring out the front window and Sheila looking out her passenger side window, watching people go in and out of the store. Her aunt opens her door, and before Sheila can do the same, Vivian says, "Don't mention this to anyone until you are sure, and that includes Damien. You hear me?"

"Yes," Sheila groans, feeling drained by everything they've discussed, all the answers she doesn't have and the weight of wanting to have a little careless fun.

Looking at her niece, Vivian starts to cry quietly, "When were you going to tell me all of this?"

"I was planning on telling you in the next few days so I could see if maybe it was just a stomach bug or something. I was hoping that you could set me up with a doctor's appointment," Sheila says, sounding dejected and tired.

"I'll arrange for a doctor's appointment," says her aunt, "But you don't need one yet. The test that we will purchase is 99 percent accurate." Wiping her face, she touches her niece's leg, "Come on, let's go get these groceries, then I'll go next door and pick up the tests." She steps out of the car and goes to the trunk to grab some reusable bags for their groceries. Then she walks over and opens Sheila's door for her. She extends a hand for Sheila to take, "Sheila, I'm very disappointed in you, but I need you to know that no matter how this situation works out, I love you, and I want you to know that you can come and talk to me about anything."

"Thanks, Auntie. And please don't be mad at Damien. I was the one who suggested that we move forward without a condom." The rain slows to a fine mist as a few specks of sunshine make their way through the drifting clouds.

"Don't mention that boy's name to me now," her aunt replies, "I expected Damien to be smart enough to think for himself and not let his other head get in the way." Sheila steps out of the car. She's at a loss for words. She closes the car door, and her aunt locks it as they make their way into the store. Feeling sorry for herself, Sheila is thinking of who to turn to. She'll naturally call Melanie with the updates later tonight, but in this moment, she reaches for Damien and sends him a text.

Sheila: What are you doing later? I need to talk to you.

Damien: Not sure, I'll ask my mom & text u back.

Sheila: Sounds like a plan.

<She adds a heart emoji.>

Unsure of how to feel about it, Damien notices the heart emoji right away. Then he stuffs his phone in his pocket and heads downstairs where he finds his mom and sister sitting in the backyard.

Chapter 14

Coming to Light

Damien approaches the door, where he can hear the deep, baritone voice of a man. He eventually sees that his mother and sister are accompanied by Mr. Thomas, a friend of his mom's who, Damien is convinced, is trying to get with her. He rolls his eyes and proceeds to join them. "What's going on out here?" Damien asks as he emerges from the doorway.

Mr. Thomas stands in his short-sleeve shirt, two sizes too small, with his hair slicked back and shiny with product. He stands to reach his hand out to Damien, "How have you been, Damien?"

Extending his hand, Damien replies flatly. Eyeing Mr. Thomas suspiciously, he says, "I'm great, and how are you, Mr. Thomas?"

With a smile, Mr. Thomas reveals a gold tooth, "I'm doing just fine, son."

Feeling his blood boil and his skin prickle, Damien looks Mr. Thomas straight in his eyes. His muscles tighten as he fights to keep his cool, "Excuse me, Mr. Thomas, I know you don't mean nothing by it, but I've asked you several times not to call me 'son.' I only have one dad, and although he's deceased, he's still my dad."

Tanya looks up from her phone to see what's going on between Mr. Thomas and her brother. Sharon looks on as well, praying that they can handle this with dignity like Damien's father taught him. Taken aback, but completely understanding, Mr. Thomas looks at Damien with a softness in his gaze. He can only imagine how hard things are for Damien after losing his greatest mentor and friend, but he is hoping to do whatever he can to make up for his loss.

"Oh, I'm so sorry, Damien. As much as I'll never know or claim to know what you're feeling and going through, I truly understand and respect where you're coming from. Thank you for speaking up like the young man you are. Please accept my apology."

Feeling better, the tight muscles in Damien's shoulders loosen significantly, helping him to relax, "I do, thank you so much for understanding."

Changing the subject, Mr. Thomas continues making small talk with Damien as he sits back down in the seat across from Damien's mother, "So, I'm hearing good things about you from your football coach. He says that there have been a lot of scouts from big name schools looking at you, specifically."

"Yeah, I've heard from a few schools; however, I'm really waiting to hear from my number one choice though."

Mr. Thomas looks at Damien with an intrigued look, "Oh, really? Which school is that?"

With the most excited expression they've seen on Damien's face since he walked outside, he lights up with anticipation, knowing deep down that he is the perfect match for that school, "Ohio State!"

His mom, sitting calmly in the shade, takes a sip of some lemonade and says, "Wait no longer. Go look on the kitchen table, son. There's a letter there from Ohio State University that arrived today."

Damien runs into the kitchen, shouting back at his mother, "Mom!? Why didn't you say something sooner?"

Sitting peacefully, her bare feet wiggling in the grass, she says teasingly, "Well, I knew sooner than later you would walk into the kitchen. After all, it's your favorite place in the house."

Everyone chuckles as Damien retrieves the letter. His mom has her hand out when he comes back, "Can I see that letter for a moment, son?" Almost bouncing with excitement, he knows his mother's intentions, so he hands her the letter. She prays over it and hands it back to Damien. Looking around excitedly and brimming with anticipation, Damien says, "On a count of three I'll open it." Everyone joins in the countdown with him as they sit at the edge of their seat. Damien opens the letter and takes a moment to read it. With everyone's eyes on him, he reaches the bottom of the page and looks up with the sunken look of disappointment on his face. His mom tries to extend her hand to him, but he simply hangs his head down low and heads inside. Sharon and Tanya look around at each other with concern.

Just as Tanya starts to get up to check up on her brother, Damien starts laughing hysterically, "I got you! I was accepted on a full, four-year, football scholarship to Ohio State University with all expenses paid!" His mother and sister jump up and squeeze him in a tight hug.

Letting the Jackson family have their moment, Mr. Thomas sits back and smiles at the loving family they have. Still hugging Damien, his mom starts to cry as she sings her praises, "Hallelujah, oh my God. Thank you, Jesus!" Tanya has tears in her eyes, too, and she smiles at her big brother, who she admires so much.

With his own tears dotting his face, Damien looks up to the heavens, waving his letter, "Thank you, Dad, and thank you, God!"

Moments later, Tanya prepares everyone for an announcement of her own, "Okay, everyone. Sit down again, because I've got some good news for you too!"

Their mom, overcome with joy, finishes her lemonade. Sweat starts to roll down her face. "What is it, baby?" She fans herself while Mr. Thomas eyes her every move.

"Yeah, sis. What's the word?" Damien asks, taking a seat by the steps. He turns so that he's still facing everyone.

Tanya opens her laptop, and donning a large, glittery smile, she reads from her email:

Dear Tanya Jackson,

Congratulations! It's our pleasure to inform you that you have been selected to appear as a contestant on The Voice. Please confirm your participation along with the consent forms no later than August 1st.
Sincerely,
The Voice Talent Team

Everyone screams and hugs each other warmly. Damien jokingly blocks Mr. Thomas from hugging his mom. Mr. Thomas playfully locks Damien in a headlock, and they share a hearty laugh, hugging each other. Sharon looks around at her friend and her two incredible children, wiping away more tears, "This is a time for celebration. I'm going to plan a big party before the end of the summer so we can celebrate right. Tanya, please pass me my phone. I'm going to call Vivian to share the exciting news."

Vivian and Sheila stand in line as they finish up their grocery shopping. Sheila begins to place their items on the counter when suddenly, her aunt receives a call from Sharon, Damien's mom. Vivian Johnson stops short of the cashier to take her dear friend's call. Sheila continues to unload their items as the cashier scans the items with a dreary look on his face.

"I was just thinking about you, Sharon. But you caught me while I'm at Peats Market, girl. Yes, you know that's my store. And I was just about to pay for my groceries. Can I call you back later tonight? I have a few more errands to run before I can get settled."

Sensing the heaviness of stress weighing on her best friend's shoulders, Sharon sounds concerned, "Yes, is everything all right, Viv?"

Unsure of what to truly say to Sharon, Vivian sighs deeply, "I'm not sure, but I will know in a few hours. Is everything good on your end?"

"Yes, very. I just had some exciting news to share with you regarding both Damien and Tanya. But I can tell you need some time to gather yourself, baby. We'll talk later tonight, Vivian. Be well."

Happy to hear that things were going well with the Jackson family after such hard times, Vivian smiles, "Okay, Sharon. We'll talk then." Vivian pushes the shopping cart so that Sheila can start to load their bagged items. She inputs her card number for the discounts and proceeds to pay for the groceries.

As if there wasn't a thunderstorm just a half an hour earlier, Sheila and Vivian are greeted outside by beaming sunlight and clear skies. Sheila places the groceries in the car, while her aunt gathers herself to go to CVS, "So, Sheila, other than the pregnancy test, do you need any other items from CVS?"

Still feeling overwhelmed, Sheila closes the trunk and opens the passenger door to sit down. Her nausea is coming back, but she figures it is just from her nerves, "No, thank you, Auntie." She prays that her aunt won't make her go to the store with her.

Vivian rummages through her purse for her wallet and hands Sheila the keys, "Well, please stay with the groceries and lock the door. I'll be right back." Vivian enters CVS to purchase the pregnancy test. Resting her head hopelessly on the cool window, Sheila watches until her aunt disappears into the store.

Vivian walks up to the pharmacy window and waits for a pharmacist to come to her. She peeks over the counter to see if anyone is there. Just as she's about to go have someone page them at the front desk, she hears the scuffle of anxious feet and is promptly greeted by the pharmacist, a young woman not much older than Sheila. "Hey there, honey. Can you please help me?" Vivian asks.

Wiping her forehead, the young woman replies, "Yes, ma'am, how can I help you? My apologies for making you wait. We've been short-staffed and I just had to take a break to eat."

"Thank you for letting me know that, hon. I won't be too long. I just need to know which pregnancy test gives the most accurate reading."

The pharmacist walks from behind the counter and gestures for Vivian to follow her as she heads down aisle five where she hands Vivian a pregnancy test. "Although there are many tests, this seems to be the most popular brand. We also have the off-brand version so you can save a couple of bucks. The price doesn't affect the quality though," the pharmacist guarantees.

Determined to get to the bottom of her niece's summer fling, Vivian reaches for a second test. The pharmacist smiles kindly, unaware of the gravity of the situation facing Vivian Johnson and her niece. Vivian returns the pharmacist's smile. "I hope you get the answer you're looking for, ma'am," the pharmacist says.

Vivian gazes at the pharmacist with a tired look, "Lord knows I hope so, too. Thank you again for your time. Go finish your food, baby."

The pharmacist waves as Vivian goes up and down a few more aisles to find a few more items and take some time to clear her head.

After several minutes of needless browsing, Vivian heads toward the cashier. However, she stops abruptly when she sees the long lines. She goes to the self-checkout area and proceeds to scan her items. Just as she is about to plug in her reward card information, someone taps her on the shoulder. Vivian turns around and is surprised to see Pastor Chisholm. Vivian feels a girlish flutter in her chest as he smiles warmly at her, "Hello, Pastor Chisholm. What are you doing here?"

Pastor Chisholm's gaze lingers over Vivian before he replies, "I live in the area, and I needed to pick up some vitals." He lifts his bag to show off his purchases, "How about you, Vivian? What brings you here?"

Vivian feels her mood shift as she converses with her charming pastor while completing her purchase, "I really love shopping at Peats Market next door so I make a dedicated run out here once a month."

The pastor looks at her and lights up when she turns to him as she waits for her receipts. He reaches over to help her pack her bags as the self-checkout line had gotten much longer since she started her purchase. "Oh, yes. I love to shop at Peats myself. It seems we have more than our love for God in common," Pastor Chisholm notices. They both smile flirtatiously.

"Well, it seems we do, Pastor," Vivian looks deeply into his eyes. The pastor looks at his watch and then toward the door where they both were headed.

"Well, it was great seeing you, Vivian." Pausing, he asks, "Can I call you Vivian?"

"Yes, you can, Pastor. I look forward to seeing you in church on Sunday."

"Amen. And hey, you can call me Rich," the pastor says as he waves to her. Just before he turns in the opposite direction to find his car, the pastor sees Vivian's purchases and notices the two pregnancy tests sitting at the top of her bag. After gesturing for her to get out of the way of a car backing up and with a concerned look on his face, the pastor lowers his voice, "You know you can talk to me about anything, right?"

Vivian is a bit confused, "Yes, Pastor, thank you. It's just been a hard day, and I need to start heading home to prepare dinner." He smiles at her, and they bid each other goodbye for the second time.

Vivian walks to her car and wonders what would make him express such concern. Opening the trunk, she notices that the pregnancy tests she purchased are sitting on the top of the bags and were likely visible for the pastor to see. She mutters to herself, "Oh, Lord! He probably thinks the tests were for me!" Cognizant of the silliness of the situation, Vivian laughs for the tears that are yet to fall, for the love her niece needs, and for herself and to herself. It is a laugh she truly needed.

The ride home is eerily quiet. After a blur of streets, lights, and passersby, Vivian pulls into her driveway. They unfasten their seatbelts, and Vivian hops out to go unlock the front door. "Sheila, after we get these groceries put away, I'm going to prepare some dinner. Anything you had in mind?"

Sheila, still an empty shell, drags herself to the trunk and starts removing the bags. She replies to her aunt in a low voice, "I'm not hungry." Her aunt looks at Sheila as she approaches the steps and takes the first set of bags from Sheila's hands.

"Well, you have to eat something. Why don't we keep it simple and split a ham sandwich with some vegetable chips?"

In the same dejected tone, Sheila replies with a shrug, "Okay. Thank you." Sheila and Vivian continue to unpack the groceries. Finished with this task, Sheila closes the trunk and stands on the porch, hugging herself tightly. She looks toward the direction of Damien's house for a while before going inside to wash her hands and put the food away.

Vivian stands in the quiet kitchen preparing a ham sandwich for her and her niece to share. She slices it in half and places each half on separate plates, then she opens up a fresh bag of vegetable chips to accent each of their plates.

Sheila looks up from her phone while in the living room to see that her aunt is nearly done preparing their meal. Despite saying she wasn't hungry, Sheila doesn't hesitate to go into the kitchen. She opens the refrigerator before sitting down, "Auntie, what would you like to drink?"

Vivian lets out a deep sigh, "After a day like today, sweetie, I think I'll get myself a glass of wine in a bit."

"Okay. I think I'll have some ginger ale," Sheila closes the fridge, thanks her aunt for the meal, and takes the plate to her seat at the table. Her aunt follows close behind and they eat in silence, stealing occasional glances at each other.

As they finish up their chips, Vivian breaks the silence, "As soon as we're done eating, we can head upstairs and I'll help you with the test."

Sheila tosses her napkin on her plate and waits for her aunt to finish so she can clear the table. "I don't really need your help with the test, Auntie."

Vivian smiles half-heartedly, "I guess I used the wrong words, sweetie. I won't actually be helping you. I'll be more like a witness to the test. I bought two pregnancy tests, so if the first test comes back positive, we can have you take the second test a few hours later to be sure."

She then tosses her napkin on her plate and gets up to pour herself a much-needed glass of wine. Sheila moves to clear the table, a blank look on her face, "Okay. That makes sense."

After Sheila finishes cleaning up, she and Vivian head upstairs. Sheila, preparing for the worst, just stares at the bathroom. Her aunt, sensing the muddled feelings in her niece's heart and mind, reaches out to comfort her.

"There are a few things we need to discuss before taking the test. First of all, I want you to be prepared if the test comes back positive. You need to be ready for the potential backlash from your mother, and possibly even Sharon." She takes a sip of the wine and contemplates getting another glass before they see the results.

In a voice just above a whisper, Sheila replies, "Yes, I know." They stand in the doorway of the bathroom, bracing themselves for the first test.

Vivian is halfway through her first glass of wine when she says, "I want you to know that there were some poor choices made by both you and Damien. So, if there is backlash from your mom and Sharon, because they are your parents, it is warranted. But I need you to remain calm and restrain yourself from being argumentative. In other words, please don't go off on anyone. I heard from your mother in the past about how you can react when you get angry."

Turning away from her aunt, Sheila rolls her eyes and puts her head in her hands, ready to get on with the test. "I can't promise you, Auntie, but I'll try my best."

"Sweetie, that's all I ever ask of you," her aunt says, eyes glittery as the wine calms her jittery nerves. Vivian reaches out to hug her tense niece and continues speaking as Sheila rests her head on her aunt's shoulder. "I want you to know that I understand that all protection is not one-hundred percent safe or reliable, but because you and Damien let the heat of the moment take over without trying to figure out a safer solution than relying on your birth control pill, you risked the chance of not only getting an STD but also of getting pregnant. But what's done is done, and we must deal with it head on. Regardless of the outcome, I find it necessary to say that the only way to ensure an unwanted pregnancy or an STD is by abstinence. It's by choosing not to have any sexual contact until you are ready to plan a family."

Sheila takes a deep breath as she slowly releases herself from her aunt's embrace. "Yes, Auntie, I've heard that millions of times. But I have to say that despite my choice not to remain abstinent, I know the main reason we are in this position today is our lack of judgment."

Her aunt widens her eyes. Having barely heard anything from Sheila all day, she is grateful for her niece's insight and willingness to be held accountable. "Yes honey, that's absolutely right! The best you can do is learn from your mistakes, so that you can do better next time. Understand?"

"Yes, I really do." Sheila sits on the closed toilet seat. Seeing her aunt is still determined to talk to her about her poor judgment, Sheila simply sits there and listens.

Sheila's aunt places her wine glass on a nearby bookshelf and continues to lean in on the doorway. "And I need you to know that your mother and Sharon may be upset, but I know they both only want the best for their children. And, regardless of how the world may look at it, a child is a blessing from God. But that blessing is easier to appreciate when you're an adult and there's a lot less stress for both the mother and the father when the pregnancy is planned. I'm sure you've seen the struggles that your own mother had to go through raising you as a single parent. I've watched my baby sister make so many sacrifices in her life to provide the best for you. And she does it! But it hasn't been easy. I'm definitely not saying that raising a child as a single parent can't be done, because single parents, women and men, are raising children all over the world. It requires a lot of strength and support, and it certainly requires a lot of sacrificing. So please, if the test comes back positive, don't expect for everything to be all peaches and cream, baby. I can't lie to you. It just isn't going to be easy," she looks at her niece who is sitting, absorbing her aunt's guidance.

With her own mom constantly tied up at work, mother and daughter never had much time for in-depth, heavy conversations. For the most part, Sheila felt that she had to do a lot of learning on her own. Despite her disappointment and fears, she was grateful that her aunt took the time to be real with her. Sheila reaches for a tissue as more tears well up in her eyes.

Her aunt continues, "Sheila, I also have to say that it's always best when the child is raised by both parents. Several university studies have shown that having both parents actively involved in a child's life can provide significant social, psychological, and health benefits. Most importantly, the stability of having and seeing a healthy relationship with both parents can provide greater opportunities for children to find their path to success. I know that you never knew your dad, so if the test comes back positive, I'm sure that you would love for Damien to be involved in the child's life."

Sheila shrugs. "I guess I would love for all three of us to be a family, but if that doesn't happen, then I would at least want him to be involved in our child's upbringing," Sheila says as tears fall down her cheeks, "It really, really hurt growing up without my father. I don't even know what he looks like."

Vivian rubs Sheila's back to comfort her sobbing niece. "Yes, sweetie. I know, let it out." She reaches for a piece of toilet paper and blots her niece's tear-stained face. Vivian gives Sheila a few moments to collect herself, then she continues, "I'll try to wrap it up here by saying that regardless of a couple planning on being together or not, it's very important that they both work together for the good of the unborn child. The two may not agree on everything, but for the child's sake, there has to be less name calling and blame throwing and more coming together. This is not always possible, but this is part of the sacrifices I spoke of earlier. You will really have to grow up and mature to manage all of this. It's just as simple as that."

Sheila sobs, and her aunt continues to rub her back. Vivian finds a ray of hope, "It won't be easy, but together with our family and the love of God, you can make it through any difficult times that may lie ahead. Even those plans you mentioned to me about attending Spellman college and Harvard University? Those plans are still attainable! If you don't remember anything else today, no matter how hard the road looks ahead, don't ever give up on your dreams."

Sniffling and sitting up straighter, Sheila looks at her aunt, who holds Sheila's face in her hands, and says, "No, Auntie I never will, I'm not a quitter."

Vivian embraces her, "That's my girl, that's my girl!"

Sheila reaches for the test and thanks her aunt, "I truly understood everything you said, and I'm truly grateful to have someone like you to talk to. I'd be lying if I told you I'm not scared about the results, and how Damien will react. But I can honestly say because of our conversation and my own sense of self, I know I got this." She smiles a genuine smile for the first time that day.

Vivian kisses her niece before going to refill her wineglass one last time. Sheila closes the bathroom door and proceeds to take the first test. Minutes later, Vivian returns. Just before she knocks on the door, Vivian hears Sheila's upset and knocks frantically on the bathroom door, "What's going on in there?"

Sheila opens the door and hands her aunt the test which she's placed on a tissue. Vivian sees that the test is, in fact, positive. Sheila's aunt remains calm, handing the test back to Sheila. "With everything you told me from when you failed to use a condom, to five weeks later having a missed period, nausea, and vomiting, this result is actually of no surprise to me. Why don't you wait another four hours or so to take the second test?"

With a defeated look on her face, Sheila nods her head and excuses herself to go to her bedroom. As she walks by, her aunt says one more thing, "We'll have to come up with a plan to share the news with Damien and Sharon in case the second test reads positive, too."

Thinking about how to break this life-changing news to Damien's family, Vivian follows Sheila to her room, where she sits in a desk chair to face her niece and brainstorms, "Well, I had promised Sharon that I would call her tonight. She mentioned that she had some good news to share with me. I think I will invite her over so that she can share her news with me and then we can share ours with her."

Looking flustered, Sheila groans, "I'll go along with whatever you think, Auntie. I would like a moment to myself, though, to prepare for it all and take everything in. I feel very overwhelmed."

Her aunt kisses her on the head and leaves Sheila's room, closing the door behind her. Sheila lays on her bed for a moment, drowning under the weight of everything that has unfolded that day. After several minutes trying to calm her body, Sheila tiptoes downstairs to retrieve her laptop so she can go watch Netflix before taking the final pregnancy test. A few hours pass, and unable to bear the uncertainty, Sheila rushes into the bathroom, hoping her previous results were just a false alarm. To her shock, Sheila sees that the second test is also positive. Sheila calls out for her aunt who is downstairs sorting through family photos. "I'll be right up!" she responds.

Vivian walks into the bathroom to find Sheila sitting on the floor with her head in her hands, holding both positive pregnancy tests in her lap. Knowing that her aunt is there, Sheila speaks without even looking up, "There's our answer."

Her aunt stoops down immediately to rub Sheila's back and says, "Let's take a snapshot of both tests and then bag and date them. I'll call now to set you up a doctor's appointment with my doctor. Hopefully she can see you before you go back to New York." Immediately, Vivian goes back downstairs to make the call. Rummaging through her purse to find her cellphone, she starts to cry. Placing the bag beside her, she stops for a moment to release her own tears. How could this baby be so careless? And what of her father's failure to give her the guidance and love that she deserves?

She wouldn't be going about life like this, looking for these boys to give her the approval that her father should've been there to give from the beginning.

Knowing that the situation is well beyond blaming or pointing fingers, Vivian dries her eyes and calls her doctor. On the first ring, she reaches a nurse to whom she explains the situation. The nurse checks to see what dates and times are available for Dr. Patterson. After keeping Vivian on hold for some time, the nurse returns with a potential date, "Mrs. Johnson, the earliest appointment that I can set up for your niece is on Friday, July 31st at one p.m."

"Three weeks from now? There's nothing sooner?" Vivian remembers that Sheila is scheduled to fly back to N.Y on August 5th and continues, "Are you sure that's the earliest date available?"

"Unfortunately, yes, Mrs. Johnson. The doctor just went on vacation and won't be back until that week. The best I can do is make a note to call you in case there's a cancellation."

With an exasperated sigh, Vivian thanks the nurse, "Thank you so much. I'll keep the July 31st appointment then."

"You're so welcome, Mrs. Johnson. I hope everything turns out well for you and your niece. Until then, we're all set. Take care!"

"You, too, and thank you again." Hanging up the phone, Vivian hears her niece crying upstairs. She goes into the kitchen to make another call. Dialing Sharon Jackson's number, she waits for her friend to pick up.

Sharon Jackson dashes from the kitchen to the backyard where she left her phone sitting in her chair. Seeing that it's Vivian, she picks it up immediately, still brimming with joy from the good news that her children shared earlier. "Hello, my dear. How are you?"

Vivian winces at the complete joy she hears in her friend's voice. "I'm fine, but I have some news for you, Sharon."

Hearing the gravity in her friend's voice, Sharon's tone becomes serious, "I have some news for you, too. We're all sitting in the backyard, and I was just getting ready to heat up some supper for everyone. Why don't you and Sheila come on over and join us, so we both can share our news?"

"Are you sure?"

"Oh yes, Viv! You know we love you and Sheila like our own blood. Plus, there's plenty of leftovers if you all haven't eaten yet."

"Okay, Sharon. Thank you. I'll go tell Sheila and we'll head right over." She looks toward the stairs, where she can hear Sheila sobbing. Vivian places her hand on her head and rubs. She feels a migraine coming on. The two friends say their goodbyes, and Vivian prepares to go and gather her niece to break the news to the Jackson family.

Sharon informs her children that Vivian and Sheila are on their way to share the family's good news and that they have some news to share of their own.

Tanya looks up from her phone, "I wonder what it is?" She goes on to joke, nudging her brother's arm playfully, "Hey, Damien, maybe Sheila's getting married and they wanna break it to us that you've lost your Boo to another man!" She cracks up laughing as Vivian rolls her eyes and goes back inside.

Damien glances over at Tanya, "How many times do I have to tell you that she's just a friend and not my Boo before you believe me?"

"Well, from the looks of how you two get along, maybe you need to try to figure out how long it'll take to convince *yourself* that she actually *is* your Boo. Then you can get back to me, big head."

Damien swats at his sister playfully and shakes his head, unable to deny that she may be on to something. Luckily, it isn't her business anyway.

Mrs. Johnson tells Sheila to freshen up so that they can head over to Mrs. Jackson's house.

Sitting upright in her bed, Sheila nearly screams, "Are you serious?"

"Yes, sweetie. Very serious," Vivian replies, "We need to have this discussion today."

Sheila feels several waves of anxiety and then nausea coursing through her body. She has never experienced so many back-to-back blows as she has this day. "Can't we wait until tomorrow? I'm really not ready," she begs.

"No, Sheila, the longer we wait, the more stress it will cause us both, and I don't like stress in my life. Plus, you will learn that it's not good for you or the baby." Vivian is standing at the bottom of the stairs shocked and in disbelief thinking about the day she and Sheila have shared.

"Okay, I'll be right down," Sheila whimpers. She stands in front of the mirror to straighten out her clothes. She notices that she hasn't gotten any bigger. She thinks that maybe it's too soon. Making sure that her hair looks good, Sheila applies a little bit of makeup to distract from the puffiness under her eyes from crying all day. Once done, she slowly makes her way downstairs and sits beside her aunt in the living room.

"Auntie, I'm scared," Sheila admits.

Wrapping her niece in another warm embrace, Vivian says, "I can't help but say that I'm pretty scared, too. But I told you, baby, everything will be okay." Releasing each other, Sheila opens the door. She looks at the setting sun and wonders what could possibly come next.

Chapter 15

Breaking News

As the sun lowers in the sky, Vivian and Sheila walk down the street to Sharon's house. Once they arrive, Vivian rings the bell, and Tanya runs to the door with a large smile, "Welcome to the Jackson Family Residence."

Sheila cracks a little smile while Vivian laughs lightheartedly and replies, "Well thank you, Ms. Tanya Jackson! Where is everybody?"

"We are sitting in the backyard. Come on in," Tanya says, gesturing toward the back of the house. Sheila and Tanya exchange small talk.

"Here we are! The gang's all here," says a beaming Sharon Jackson. She gets up and gives her best friend, Vivian, a much-needed hug. She looks over at Sheila and greets her with a small peck on the cheek. "How are you doing dear? You know, every time I see you, you always look so adorable," Sharon says.

Grateful for Sharon's kindness, Sheila flashes a heartfelt smile. But deep in the pit of her stomach, she can feel her dinner churning as she braces herself for the Jackson family response to the difficult news she and her aunt came to deliver. She musters out, "Thank you, Mrs. Jackson."

Damien finishes sending a text and puts his phone in his pocket as he stands up to give both Sheila and her aunt a hug. Heading back toward the house, he looks at Sheila and Vivian as they continue making small talk, "Would either of you like anything to drink?"

Looking at Damien and remembering the reason for the impromptu visit, Vivian feels her blood start to boil. She takes a deep breath to calm her nerves, "A glass of water would be fine, thank you."

Sheila can hardly look Damien in the eyes, "I'll have a glass of water, too, please."

Oblivious to Sheila's changed demeanor, Damien simply smiles and jokes, "Sounds like a plan."

Despite their inside joke about her catchphrase, Sheila is too nervous to return Damien's smile. Damien shakes his head, unsure of what was causing Sheila to be so standoffish.

Vivian continues to drag out the conversation. In the back of her mind, she thinks that maybe Sheila was right and they should have at least waited until the following day to deal with such a heavy topic. "Your flowers look absolutely beautiful, Sharon. I see you've really got the hang of this gardening thing now," Vivian says.

"Thank you so much, dear. Every summer it seems like I have to work twice as hard to keep them looking like that," Sharon beams, taking a sip of a fresh glass of lemonade.

Still looking over the flowers, Vivian nods her head and looks at her friend. She's so grateful to finally see her reclaiming her peace again. "Well, whatever you are doing, it's definitely working. So, if you get some free time, please come over and help me with mine."

The two women laugh. Vivian's wit is always enough to wipe the frown off the Grinch's face.

Shaking her head, Sharon continues, "What is free time?"

Vivian shakes her head and reaches out to high-five her friend, "Child, isn't that the truth!? What was I thinking?" They share another laugh as Damien emerges with two glasses of water. Vivian looks around for anything else to comment on before breaking the news.

Damien hands her a glass, and she thanks him kindly.

"So how have you all been doing today?" Vivian asks as she glances at Tanya, who is reclining to her left, "Tanya, you are getting so big. It seems as if you grew six inches since I saw you in church last Sunday."

Tanya smiles, grateful that someone has noticed her rapidly changing body, "I'm doing great Mrs. Johnson. I'm almost as tall as Damien."

"Yes, I see!" Vivian acknowledges. Damien shakes his head and rolls his eyes as he hands Sheila her glass.

She barely whispers, "Thanks."

Vivian takes a sip and figures that it's time to face the music. She hopes that the Jacksons will at least go first with their news, "So, Jackson family, what's the good news you wanted to share with us?"

Taking another sip of her lemonade, Sharon says, "No, no. You're our guests after all, why don't you go first?"

Knowing how these things go, Tanya excitedly takes the initiative, shouting, "I'll go first!"

Vivian and Sharon laugh. Vivian takes another sip of water and lets out a sigh of relief, thankful for Tanya's intervention, "Well, I guess that settles it! You go first, sweetie."

Tanya stands to make her wonderful announcement, "Well, I've been invited to appear on *The Voice*! They said that I was picked out of more than 120,000 contestants, and will be performing live on stage in Los Angeles, California on August 4th!" Hearing the news out loud again, Tanya jumps for joy before returning to her seat.

With a genuine look of awe, Vivian reaches out to hug little Tanya, who she has known since before she was born. "Wow that's so fantastic, baby! Congratulations! I'm so happy for you."

Sheila is also moved by the news. She smiles at Tanya before standing up to give her a hug. "That's so dope. I can't wait to see you perform!"

Tanya pretends to take several bows. "Thank you. Thank you!"

Then Sharon looks over at her son, "Mr. Damien over there has some news, too."

Vivian looks at him with a serious expression on her face, "What is it?"

Taking a deep breath, Damien stands up and says, "I received a full, four-year football scholarship, all expenses paid to Ohio State!"

With an incredulous look on her face, Vivian takes another sip of water and continues looking at Damien and then her niece.

"Well, that's truly fantastic news, isn't it Sheila?"

Avoiding her aunt's gaze, Sheila responds in a dry tone, "Yes, Auntie, it really is." Turning to Damien, Sheila perks up. Knowing that Damien truly does deserve such an exciting and promising opportunity, she says, "Congratulations, Damien. I'm so happy for you. I'm sure you worked hard for it."

Raising her hand in praise and placing her glass down on the table, Sharon interjects, "Oh yes, he did. I was thinking that I will throw a party this month. What do you think, Vivian? Maybe we could celebrate our good news together and throw a big bash."

Knowing this is the moment of the rude awakening for the Jackson family, Sheila and Vivian are quiet.

"Vivian, what is your news?" Sharon asks her friend.

Vivian diverts the conversation to Sheila, who hasn't said much, "Well, it's really Sheila's news, so I'll let her tell everyone."

Sheila glares at her aunt, who is too busy taking another sip of water to notice.

Sitting on the edge of her seat, still brimming with excitement from her own news, Tanya leans in with anticipation, "So, what is it? I can't wait to hear it!"

"Me, too," Sharon says looking as relaxed as she could be.

Eager to get it over with, Vivian nudges Sheila in the arm, "Tell them, Sheila."

The smiling faces surrounding them all fall, one by one, as Sheila starts to cry. Hiding her face, she says, "No, Auntie. This is too much, I really can't. Can you please tell them?"

Hoping it wouldn't come to this, Vivian lets out a deep sigh, "Yes, sweetie, I will."

Remembering her mother's teachings and having learned early on that straightforwardness and honesty are the best way to get to the heart of things, Vivian simply turns to Damien and looks him straight in the eyes, "Congratulations, Damien, you are going to be a dad."

Sheila continues crying. With her knees pressed to her chest, she tries even harder to disappear.

Damien's eyes widen, "What!? Nah, tell me this is a joke." He shakes his head in disbelief.

With her eyes still locked on him, Vivian says, "No, Damien. This is no joke. This is what can happen when you have sex without protection."

The sky grew darker as the sun began its descent beyond the horizon. Damien's mother and sister sit with blank expressions on their faces. All the joy and praise they've experienced seemingly came crashing down around them. It is Sharon's turn to inhale deeply before looking over at Tanya, "Tanya, baby, I'm going to need you to go in the house while we talk."

Leaving her front row seat to the unfolding drama, Tanya looks at her mother and brother with a concerned look on her face. Her brother's head rests in his hands and he presses his temples like he always does when he is overwhelmed.

"Okay, Mom," Tanya says and goes inside the house, where she continues to post online about her achievement.

In a harsh, lowered voice, Sharon leans toward Damien, "Is this true, Damien? Have you and Sheila been having sex?"

In a dejected voice, Damien, who is beginning to tear up, reluctantly responds, "Yes, Mom."

Furious but calm with one eyebrow raised as she looks back and forth between the both of them, Sharon says, "And you both mean to tell me that you've been having sex without a condom?"

In the same heavy voice, Damien replies, "Yes, Mom."

Sharon throws her arms in the air, "How could you do that, Damien!?"

Unsure of what to say, Damien mutters the only thing that comes to mind, "It was only once, Mom."

Sharon looks at him. The same tiredness and stress that has weighed on her since her husband passed returns to her face. "Damien, all it takes is one time." Sharon, worried about her only son's future and also the future of her unborn grandchild, shakes her head. She glances at Sheila, who is curled up, sniffling. Despite her concern and anger, Sharon can't help but feel a sense of motherly concern for her.

After several moments of silence, broken up by the occasional sniffles and sighs, Sharon says, "I can't believe that you would do something so dangerous, especially after the conversation you had with your father. Let alone the conversation that you and I just had less than a week ago!" She yells but catches herself before she goes too far. Knowing that despite their carelessness it won't help to push either of them away, Sharon regains her composure, "Son, please tell me why you would risk your health and future like that? It really doesn't make any sense to me."

Before he can try to answer, she turns to Sheila, who has barely been able to face Damien's mom since she arrived with her aunt. Despite her disappointment and anger at the two of them, Vivian felt it necessary to connect with Sheila, woman to woman.

"I personally think that you and Damien are too young to be having sex, but if you are going to have sex, baby, why would you allow a young man to have sex with you without a condom? Will somebody make some sense out of this for me?" Sharon asks.

While Sharon begs for clarity, she knows that her desperate pleas to better understand what she is hearing were futile. She can't help but feel that, despite it being out of everyone's control, she wishes that her husband was still alive. She can't help but think this would have never happened if he were still in the picture.

Sharon shakes her head in an attempt to hold back tears. Sheila looks at Damien's mom with red, puffy eyes. Her cheeks look raw from the constant wiping of tears. "Yes, ma'am. I know that we should have used a condom, but we were just in the heat of the moment," she whispers.

Sharon erupts, nearly jumping out of her seat. "The heat of the moment!?" she shouts.

Sheila, feeling too tired to react, repeats herself, "Yes. Damien couldn't locate the condoms he had brought over to the house, and since I was on the pill, I told him that it was okay to continue without it."

"Unbelievable. The only thing that is one-hundred percent safe is to stay abstinent. Did you know that?" Sharon can barely bring herself to look at Sheila.

"Yes," Sheila mutters.

Sharon turns to her son, "And Damien, isn't that what your father explained to you?"

"Yes, Mom," Damien replies, his head hanging low. He can barely wrap his mind around what is taking place before him. He almost wishes he'd never met Sheila as he's never felt so captivated by someone before.

"So, what made you think that not wearing a condom was safe, or smart or anything other than completely stupid!?" Sharon's eyes nearly glow with rage.

"Mom, it was just that one time I didn't use protection. All the other times I used a condom," Damien admits.

Sharon grips the arms of her chair, trying with all of her might not to jump up and strike him. "Damien, what do you mean by 'all the other times'? How many times have you had sex?"

"At least six times," Damien replies.

"Oh my God, Damien. I am at a loss. Are you hearing all of this, Vivian?" Sharon asks, looking at her friend with a ferocious look. Vivian just shakes her head and stares at the floor before returning her friend's gaze.

"This time around, it's really hitting home, Sharon. I was just as angry as you were, but now I'm just beyond words. I have known both Damien and Sheila to be very responsible and respectable young people, but here we are. What's done is done," Vivian declares.

The lingering birds make their final calls before turning in for the night as the crickets start to sing their evening song. After that emotional rollercoaster ride, they have just shared, everyone sits quietly for a while, still trying to wrap their heads around the entirety of the news they've shared today.

"I'm sorry, Mom," Damien says before turning to Sheila's aunt, "Mrs. Johnson, I'm sorry that I disappointed you." And finally, he looks over at Sheila, who has managed to look at him. There is a pleading look in his eyes, "Are you sure that you're pregnant?"

"Yes, I missed my period last month, and you're the only one that I have been having sex with since I've been here in Chicago. I've been nauseous sometimes, too. Then earlier today, my aunt bought me two pregnancy tests. and they both were positive," Sheila replies with a blank look on her face.

Sheila reaches in her pocket and pulls out her phone to show Damien the pictures of the tests. Sharon leans in to see the picture too. She looks over the photos with a look of disappointment on her face. Leaning forward, Sharon rests her head in her hands.

Then, for further proof, Vivian pulls out the baggie with the two pregnancy tests for all to see. Damien and his mom just look at each other and shake their heads. Vivian continues, "I set up a doctor's appointment for Sheila, but the doctor won't be able to see her for another three weeks."

Unable to bear any more bad news for the day, Sharon stands up. Furious, she inhales and exhales slowly so she doesn't displace her frustration on her friend, Vivian. It's not like this is something they could have kept a secret. Vivian was right to get it over with. "I'm sorry Vivian, but this is honestly just too much for me to take right now. Is it possible we can continue this conversation tomorrow?"

Vivian gives Sharon a halfhearted smile. Vivian, who is equally worn out, feels the need for a long bath and a deep sleep to face the days ahead. She stands up, and Sheila follows suit. "Yes, that's a great idea, Sharon. Sheila and I will head home now."

Sharon responds in a tired voice as she collects the empty drinking glasses and heads inside the house, "I'll walk you two to the door." While Sharon and Vivian take the lead, Sheila and Damien lag behind, too tired to say much else. Sheila looks at Damien, and he quickly gives her the call me sign. She nods her head as Damien moves to hold the door for everyone. Sheila moves past him to join her aunt. Everyone says their goodbyes and Sheila turns to walk back home with Auntie Vivian.

Vivian looks at her niece walking by her side. "Well, it was good that we got it all out in the open tonight," she says.

"Yeah, I guess I do feel a lot better," Sheila says. Then she becomes worried again. "Do you think Mrs. Jackson is mad at me?" Sheila looks at her aunt.

Knowing her friend well, Vivian answers with confidence, "No, I don't think she is mad, but like me, I know she is very disappointed with both you and Damien. This could have definitely been prevented, but you know this now and we need to move forward from here."

Sheila feels grateful for her aunt's much calmer demeanor, and breathes in the cool, night air. She can't imagine what it would be like if her aunt was truly angry. Her disappointment is bad enough, but it is great to at least have her aunt on her and the baby's side.

Once they reach the house, Sheila locks the door as her aunt makes her way to the kitchen, "I'm going to make myself a cup of tea. Would you like a cup?"

Sheila yawns, "No, Auntie, I'm going upstairs and to bed."

Her aunt comes to the doorway, making eye contact with Sheila as she starts up the steps. "Goodnight, sweetie, that sounds like a great idea. I probably won't be too far behind you. We'll talk in the morning."

Sheila smiles slightly, "Okay, Auntie, you have a good night, too. Thanks for everything."

"You're welcome, sweetie. We're gonna get through this happy, healthy, and as a family."

Vivian then pours some water into her tea kettle before looking for a flavor of tea to try. She figures a good old fashion relaxation blend will do wonders right now. As the water comes to a boil, she goes around the house to check that all the doors are locked and the lights are off. The kettle whistles and she re-enters the kitchen, half jogging, not wanting to disturb Sheila upstairs. She pours the steaming water into her cup, adds some honey, and stirs as she inhales the calming aroma emanating from her warm cup. She turns off the kitchen light and heads up the stairs to her room.

As she walks by Sheila's bedroom, Vivian sees the door is cracked and notices that Sheila is on her phone. "Make sure you get a good night's sleep, sweetie," she says.

Jumping at the sound of her aunt's voice, Sheila looks toward the door to see her standing in the bathroom across the hall, washing her face. She speaks loudly enough for her aunt to hear through the door, "I will, Auntie. I'm just calling my mom and checking all my messages."

"Okay, honey." Vivian closes the door. Sheila looks over her messages and calls her mom, who is still unaware of the news. They hang up just as her aunt comes out of the bathroom, turns off the light, and thumps down the hall to her bedroom.

While checking her messages, Sheila notices that there are already several texts from Damien, asking her to call him. Reading over his messages, she can tell he is feeling anxious again, just like when they had finished having sex that first time when they didn't use protection. Knowing that it will likely be an emotional conversation, Sheila realizes that she is too tired, and not at all ready to hear what Damien has to say. Taking her aunt's advice, she decides to simply turn her phone off and get some good rest. Sheila takes a nice warm bath, complete with some quiet music on her speakers. She soaks in the water for what feels like hours and emerges ready for bed.

Damien, upset that Sheila isn't returning his calls and texts, looks at the time and decides to call Celeste instead.

Celeste is watching a reality show when she hears her phone ring. Seeing that it's Damien, she immediately picks up, "Hey, what's up? I'm surprised you are not with Sheila tonight."

Raising his eyebrows, Damien chuckles to himself, knowing that there weren't going to be anymore nights spent sneaking around with Sheila again. "Not tonight, I'm sort of in some serious trouble."

Looking away from her show, Celeste sounds concerned, "What sort of trouble?"

Knowing Celeste has always had his back and his best interests in mind, Damien still needs to be sure that he can trust her. "If I tell you, you've got to promise not to tell anyone."

"You know how we do," Celeste replies. Then she adds quickly, "Unless it's life threatening, in which case I'm obligated by law not to keep it between us."

She and Damien share a hearty laugh, but Damien quickly sobers up and comes back to reality. "I'm serious."

"So am I," Celeste assures him, "So, what's up though?"

He dives right in, "Sheila's pregnant, and she's claiming that I'm the dad."

Celeste's eyes widen incredulously. "Really!? You're bugging, Damien."

"I know it's crazy, but I wouldn't ever joke about this, Celeste. Not with the plans I have for my life right now."

Celeste shakes her head, "Well, did you have sex with Sheila?"

Damien sighs, "Yes, several times, but only once without protection."

"Are you serious! Without protection? Why would you even do that, Damien? I myself would never ever have sex with anyone that refuses to use protection. But everyone's different, I guess," says Celeste, who is clearly disappointed with her childhood friend.

Feeling the weight of his decisions, Damien sighs again, "You're right. This was a very careless mistake. I got caught up in the moment and wasn't thinking straight."

Having heard more than enough stories of her own, Celeste chastises Damien, "Guys are funny. They try to act all big and bad but when they get around girls, they can't even control themselves. I mean, would you even say you love Sheila?"

Damien has to stop and think for a moment. "I never told her I did, and even though we only knew each other for a short time, I really think I do. It's just that I also know for a fact that I don't want children—at least not now."

Celeste feels a pang in her chest when Damien admits his love for Sheila. "How does Sheila know that she's pregnant, anyway?"

Damien runs his hand through his hair. "She missed her period, she's been feeling queasy and she has taken not one, but two pregnancy tests that both came back positive. Sheila came over with her aunt tonight and shared the news with all of us. Oh, and get this, her aunt showed me and my mom the two positive pregnancy tests."

Celeste nearly spits out the handful of chips she'd just put in her mouth. "Seriously?"

"I'm very serious," Damien says flatly, "I'm just not ready to be a father to anyone. I will just have to ask her to have an abortion. I just received a four-year scholarship to Ohio State, and I'm not messing that up for anyone."

Celeste continues to eat her chips while looking aimlessly at the screen. But after hearing the a-word, she sits upright in her chair and lets Damien have it.

"Okay, I'ma have to stop you right there, Damien. I know we're cool and all, but as your friend, I have to be honest with you. You should have really thought about not wanting a child or messing up your scholarship when you decided not to wear protection. And that's the bottom line. There's no one to blame, and that child is not going to pay the price for you getting so caught up in your hormones that your brain stopped working, apparently. You have instantly made your life more difficult, and for what Damien, a few minutes of pleasure? You were right when you said earlier that not wearing protection was a really careless decision, almost stupid, in fact."

Celeste takes a moment to catch her breath. Damien feels completely beaten down by everyone coming at him all night.

Celeste, still fuming, realizes that she did just go off on him and tries to think of a way to help him find his strength in this situation. "At least being a dad at your age won't mean the end of your life. There are plenty of successful young mothers and fathers who have a ton of support and determination to make something of themselves. You can definitely do that, Damien, I know you. Plus, there are a ton of different agencies in-person and online that offer counseling and assistance to teenage parents. I'm sure that your families will help out and of course, you know I'm here for you as well. I've always wanted to be an Auntie."

Damien brushes off all possibility of struggling to care for a child at his and Sheila's age, "That may be true, Celeste, but like I said earlier, I don't want to be a father, at least not now."

"But Damien, it's really not your choice any longer. What's done is done."

"I know, but I still don't think it'll hurt to at least ask Sheila if she'll consider having an abortion."

Celeste winces as if she's in pain, "Please stop saying that, you know how I feel about abortions." She looks at the cable box to see the time. "I have to go, but regardless of what happens, I'm here for you. Just don't do anything else reckless."

"I won't," Damien says, getting ready to lie down himself. Before hanging up, he continues, "Even though you just chewed me out, thanks for being honest with me, Celeste."

She smiles, "Isn't that what true friends are for?"

Damien agrees, "Yeah. And I truly appreciate it. Have a good night."

"Stay strong, D. I love you, and we'll talk soon."

"I love you, too," Damien says.

After ending his call with Celeste, Damien decides to head down to the kitchen and get something to drink. When he enters the kitchen, he's surprised to see his mom and Tanya sitting down at the kitchen table talking. Damien opens the refrigerator and hears his mom say, "You must have heard us talking about you." Damien closes the fridge and sees his mother and sister looking in his direction. "We are a family, right, Damien?" she asks.

He takes a long, refreshing sip of water, which makes him realize how thirsty he truly is. "Of course."

His mom continues, "And do you remember what our motto is?"

"Yes, Mom," Damien says, taking another sip. He already knows where this is going.

His mom is still eyeing him. "Well, what is it?"

With no energy behind his words, Damien utters the family motto, "Our motto is that we are Jackson Strong." He finishes his iced tea and washes out the cup.

Sternly raising her voice, Sharon gets Damien's attention immediately, "Is that how you would say it if your father were sitting here? Is that how a son of an awarded military captain would say it? And lastly, is that how the man of the house would say it?"

"No, Mom," Damien replies, remembering the other times when they were all there, reciting that motto with his late father.

"Then, son, say it like you mean it!"

Damien puts some bass in his voice and shouts, "We are Jackson Strong!"

His mom and sister smile, "You know, son, you're starting to sound more and more like your dad every day." She closes her eyes and reminisces for a while before continuing, "And yes, we are Jackson Strong, baby. You know the Jackson family sticks together no matter what the circumstances. Keep your head held high. We will make a way. Do you understand me?"

"Yes, Mom," Damien says, unsure of what the future is going to hold.

"Now come over here and give your mom a big hug."

Damien goes over to his mom, who extends her other arm for Tanya to join, and they all share a huge Jackson family hug. As they hug, tears well up in his eyes. His voice cracks as he says, "I love you both so much."

"We love you, too," Sharon and Tanya respond in unison.

His mom continues, "And we will always be here for you."

Tanya chimes in, "Yes, always."

Damien decides to get another glass of iced tea and join his family at the kitchen table, where they all continue the conversation.

Damien's mom looks at Damien, "So, what's your plan?"

Damien sighs, "I assume that you are talking about Sheila being pregnant?"

"Yes, son. That is one of our hottest topics right now."

Damien shrugs and leans back in his chair, "Honestly, Mom, I don't have a plan."

His mom leans forward, resting her elbows on the table as she gazes at her son, "Well, let me give you some advice."

Damien adjusts his posture. A tired look on his face, he listens to his mom. "I'm all ears."

"Assuming that the test is correct, and that the doctors confirm that Sheila is in fact pregnant, you will need to immediately request a DNA test."

Having kept her two cents to herself for much longer than usual, Tanya interjects, "Maybe you can call the Maury Povich show."

Damien glances at his sister, his hands resting behind his head as he shakes his head and closes his eyes. "I see you got jokes, Tanya."

Looking at her children, Sharon gives them both a stern look and they compose themselves. "Listen up, this is no joking matter. If the DNA comes back and the test reads that you are the father, you will have to face some serious obstacles. First you need to be aware that Sheila is only sixteen and is considered a minor. I really don't know what you were thinking, Damien. I don't want to scare you or get too ahead of ourselves, but it's possible that you could do jail time for being with a minor, if Sheila or her family decide to file charges."

Damien puts his head in his hands and sighs deeply. His mom continues as Tanya sits quietly, looking back and forth at her mother and brother. She continues, "Put that aside. Sheila and the baby will both need you to live up to your responsibilities. Even if you and Sheila don't decide to stay together as a couple, you will *still* need to be involved in the child's life. Then there will be the huge financial responsibility you will have to address."

Damien flops back in his chair again as he takes in the weight of his mother's advice. He stares at the ceiling, calculating all the things that she's presented to him.

"And you will have to pay child support until the child is eighteen. Then if the child attends college, you will have to continue to pay support until the child is twenty-two. Whatever amount the court decides that you will have to pay will definitely be enforced by the State. If you don't pay your child support, you will face some serious consequences, which may include losing your driver's license, your passport, jail time, and other severe penalties and fees. Then in most cases, child support is taken directly out of your paycheck, and that's before you even receive a cent. So yes, son, this is a very serious matter, and I can't emphasize how important it is that you have a plan."

"I just found out about the pregnancy a few hours ago, so there wasn't much time to have a thorough plan," Damien says. He also realizes that he wouldn't have to worry about any of this if he hadn't allowed lust to get the best of him.

His mom continues, "I also assume that you don't want to lose your full four-year scholarship from Ohio State, right?"

Damien's eyes fly open, and he sits bolt upright. "No, I can't lose that scholarship, Mom; I earned it."

His mom softens her gaze, looking at her son who has come so far. "Yes, son you certainly did earn that, and I am still so proud of you. That's another reason why we will need a plan. And I make it a point to use the word we, because we are a family."

Suddenly, Damien remembers something that could make things easier for everybody, especially for him and maybe even Sheila. "Mom, I know I told you that I didn't have a plan, but actually, I have an idea."

Damien watches as his sister raises her eyebrows in wonder. His mom looks curious, "What is it, son?"

Damien states his master plan, "I was thinking that if Sheila is confirmed pregnant, I will ask her to have an abortion."

A disappointed Sharon looks at Tanya and places a loving hand on her head, "Sweetheart, I really need you to leave the room."

Knowing their mom is about to let Damien have it, Tanya wishes she could stay. But, knowing better, she gets up from her seat and walks toward the stairs. "Okay, I figured that was coming. Good night, Mom. Good night, Damien," Tanya replies disappointedly. She looks back at her brother before darting up the stairs. "You in trouble!" she says as Damien glares at her.

Once Tanya is out of earshot, Damien's mom looks him straight in the eyes. "Don't you ever use that word loosely in this house. Although I will never condemn a woman for making a personal choice to have an abortion, I personally don't believe in abortion and would never ask a woman who was having a grandchild of mine to have one, let alone encourage my son to ask that of a young woman," she chastises, shaking her head in utter disbelief, "Making the decision to have an abortion is a very serious and personal decision. Using that word is a cop-out, like it's just a matter of flipping a coin. It is very irresponsible of you and goes against our family faith."

Damien is firm in his stance and ready to defend his wishes with gusto. But he continues to hear his mother out.

"I admit that there are times when an abortion is necessary—a major one being to save the life of the birth mother," Sharon says, "I pray that if Sheila is confirmed pregnant, she doesn't have to deal with any of these serious issues. And I absolutely hope she won't be forced into an abortion by you. Your father and I raised you better than that."

Damien tries to interject his opinion, but his mom continues talking. Though Damien tries not to show it, he is getting really tired of all the long talks, but wisely, he remains quiet.

"See, Damien, if you would have just used protection, or even better, not had sex with Sheila in the first place, we would not even be having this conversation."

There is a long enough pause where Damien tries to state his case again, but his mom beats him to it, "So again, Damien, although you are still a child yourself, if Sheila is confirmed pregnant by the doctor, I would want and I know that your father would have wanted you to stand up and face your responsibility like a man should."

There she goes mentioning Dad again, Damien thinks. He can't help but feel all of his bravado wash away as his eyes well with tears. "Yes, Mom. You're so right, I'll talk to Sheila and see where her head is at and take it from there. Then I guess I'll just have to wait for her doctor's appointment to confirm the pregnancy. Then if it's confirmed, I'll request a DNA test. Then from there, I just don't know, Mom." He looks at the ceiling again, sniffling loudly as he tries to stop crying.

His mom looks at him, and reaching out to her son, she offers Damien a tender hand. "Now you know we've also raised you to express your emotions, baby, especially the difficult ones. You know you can't keep that stuff bottled up, son. Let it out. I know you've gotten a lot of harsh criticism today, and I know that's never easy for anybody. But I love you, son. And I told you already, we are going to get through this as a family. That's the bottom line."

Damien sits there crying and holding his mom's hand for several minutes. After he composes himself, Damien lets out a long sigh, feeling much better after letting those tears fall.

"Mom, I'm truly sorry. And I am so grateful that you won't give up on me despite my careless and brazen behavior with Sheila. I never wanted to disappoint you," he gratefully remarks as looks down and clutches at the necklace containing an image of his father. Damien kisses it before looking up to the heavens and closing his eyes. "You too, Dad," he thanks.

Damien's mom opens her arms to hug her son. Damien kneels by her side and hugs her. They stay there for a while, crying silently together. His mom gets a napkin for her eyes and meets her son's red-eyed gaze, "I love you, Damien. And I can't tell you enough that while I may have my feelings about all of this, I am one hundred percent here for you, and we will make it through this situation together as a family—Jackson Strong."

Damien squeezes his mom and says in a low, firm voice, "Jackson Strong."

His mom looks at the clock. "Wow, it's getting late. I guess I couldn't tell how much time has passed since we stepped into this twilight zone situation today. Whew, chile," she jokes as she dots at her eyes again, "I think it's a good time for us to go get some rest."

Damien yawns loudly and covers his mouth before agree with his mother. Damien stays behind as his mom walks up the stairs, reminding him to check the doors. He hears his mom readying herself for bed upstairs, then he turns off the kitchen light and heads upstairs.

Chapter 16

Searching for a Resolution

The next morning, Sharon Jackson wakes up, still feeling mentally exhausted by yesterday's events. She looks at her calendar and decides that today will be an impromptu spa day. She calls Vivian to see if her best friend would like to join her.

Unable to sleep much with her mind racing a mile a minute, Vivian has been awake for several hours. She hears her phone ring and sees that it's Sharon. "Hey, my love. How are you feeling today?" Vivian says sweetly.

Sharon sounds tired but cheerful, "Hey, Viv, I hope I didn't wake you. I'm doing all right, but I have a question for you."

"I've been awake, honey," Vivian assures her, then raises an eyebrow. "It doesn't involve any more news, does it?" she teases.

Sharon chuckles, "No, silly. It'll definitely help us deal with our news though. How would you like to come to the spa with me, say in an hour or two?"

Vivian's eyes beam with joy and excitement, "Are you kidding!? That sounds perfect, I would love to join you. How are we getting there?"

"I'll swing by and pick you up at eleven."

"I'll be ready."

"Okay, I'll see you then."

Vivian knocks on Sheila's door. She enters the room and tells Sheila about her plans with Sharon. "And what do you have planned today? Shoot, I should ground you," she teases.

Rolling her eyes and with a small smile on her face, Sheila replies, "I have an appointment with Celine African Hair Braiding on

Ashland Ave. I got to get my hair redone, especially after that mess yesterday. It'll feel really refreshing."

Her aunt admires her niece, "You know, I'm very impressed by how fast you were able to learn your way around Chicago on your own."

Sheila gets out of her bed and walks over to her closet so she can pick out an outfit to wear to the salon. "Well, it wasn't really on my own. Damien was a big help," she admits.

Now it was Sheila's aunt's turn to roll her eyes. "Yes, I'm sure he was very helpful, but I'm talking about you. And you learned pretty fast." She sits on the bed, watching Sheila rummage through her clothes before another thought strikes her, "I know you're from New York and all, but please be extremely careful traveling around here by yourself."

Looking back at her aunt, Sheila flashes her a smile. She returns the expression, happy to see that her niece seems to be coming back around to her usual self. "I will, Auntie," Sheila replies.

Vivian stands up to leave the room. She stretches and yawns with emphasis. "Well, I'm about to fix myself some eggs and maybe some toast. Would you like some?" she offers.

Sheila eyes two potential outfits closely. "No, I just had a bowl of cereal."

"Okay, sweetie, I'm glad you ate something. Especially now that you're eating for two," she teases.

Sheila chuckles, "Thank you so much for reminding me, Auntie."

After deciding on an outfit, Sheila washes up, gets dressed, and walks downstairs. Greeted by the smell of her aunt's cooking, she's tempted to take her aunt up on the offer for some more breakfast. However, knowing that she could make herself feel queasy if she overindulged so early in the day, she continues to the patio, sits in her favorite loveseat, and turns on her phone.

Sheila puts it down, waiting for it to load and is startled by the loud, repeated buzzing coming from her phone. She checks the screen and sees that she has received more than ten texts from Damien asking her to call him. The last text was at six-thirty in the morning. Her stomach feels nervous just thinking about talking to

Damien again. She figures she can compose herself better if she confirms her hair appointment first.

Sheila dials up the salon, and the stylist answers on the first ring. "Hello this is Tammi at Celine African Hair Braiding. How may I help you?"

Sheila puts on her grown woman voice, "Yes, my name is Sheila, and I'm just calling to confirm my appointment at eleven."

Tammi asks her to hold as she looks through the calendar to check for Sheila's name.

Sheila sits staring up at the big, blue sky while she waits for Tammi to finish. "Yes, we have you scheduled for today at eleven, hon."

"Great," Sheila says, looking at the time, "I'll see you then." Realizing that it is almost ten a.m., Sheila decides that she better start getting ready if she wants to get there on time.

"Okay, see you soon," Tammi says graciously.

Sheila ends the call and immediately dials Damien's number.

Damien sees that it's Sheila and picks up on the first ring, "Well, well, well, it's about time. Why haven't you been returning my texts? Are you all right?"

Sheila is relieved to hear that Damien isn't angry with her. "Yes, I'm fine, I was very tired last night, and I decided to shut off my phone so I could go to bed early," she explains, "So tell me, what's so important that you had to blow up my phone?"

"We need to talk," Damien says plainly.

"Um, about what?" Sheila asks, now pacing around the patio.

Bewildered by Sheila's ignorance, Damien makes a face. She has to be joking. "We need to talk about this baby situation, Sheila," his tone getting slightly harsher.

"What about our baby situation do we need to talk about?" Sheila can feel herself getting nervous again.

Damien carelessly blurts out his question, still oblivious to the intense feelings it evokes, "Have you considered having an abortion?"

Sheila is amazed by how nonchalant Damien could be by asking such a question so easily. She stands up, prepared to go off on him, "Before you say another word..." She stops herself, remembering her aunt's advice about keeping her cool. She doesn't want to start the bickering and dysfunction before the baby even arrives, with a calmer demeanor, she says, "You know what, scratch that. I'm going to tell you something that only my mom and my best friend Melanie know."

Damien is silent as he listens. He lies in his bed and tosses a ball in the air. "Damien, do you remember the first time we had sex and you kept asking me if I was one hundred percent sure that I had been taking my birth control pill regularly?" Sheila asks.

"Yes, I remember," Damien says in a dry tone, recalling that was why they felt confident with their carelessness. He doesn't know what that had to do with his initial question either, but he continues to let Sheila speak.

"Well, that was true," Sheila assures him, "I also told you that I wouldn't lie to you about taking the birth control pill regularly because I didn't want to go through that same crap again. Do you remember that as well?"

Damien sounds confused, "Yes?"

Sheila continues, "And at that time, you asked me what crap was I talking about. Do you remember that, too?"

Damien, trying to understand where she's going with this, answers, "Yes, go on."

"And at that time, my answer to you was that's a conversation for another day—a conversation that I hope you and I will personally never have to have."

Damien barely remembers the conversation, but Sheila's careful recounting awakens his memory, "Yeah, Sheila. I remember that, too."

Sheila sighs. "Well, Damien, that day has unfortunately arrived," she continues, "See, Damien, I was only 15 years old and a virgin when I first met my ex-boyfriend, Tory, who at the time was 19. We ended up fooling around for a while. He was very forceful and very cruel to me. I'm just coming back around after all that situation did to me. So, Damien, if you are calling to ask me to consider having an abortion, I'm telling you right now that it's not going to happen. I refuse to put myself through that again."

Damien sits in silence. Sheila says, "After dating for a few months, Tory convinced me to have sex with him without any protection at all and said that everything would be okay as long as he pulled out when the time comes. Being naïve, I trusted him until I found out that he never did pull out. When I questioned him about it, he just laughed and said, 'My bad.' Six weeks later when he found out that I had gotten pregnant, he threatened me. And I quote: 'Sheila, because you are considered a minor, if anyone finds out that you are pregnant, I could do some serious jail time and will have to register as a sex offender. If that happens, someone will seriously get hurt.'

"Then he shouted and shook me. 'Do you understand what I'm saying, Sheila?'" She pauses, trying to shake the memory, "I was so scared, and even more scared to tell my mom, and since my dad was nowhere to be found to protect me or my mom, I just nodded yes. Less than a week later, I had an abortion that was set up by Tory's mother. Although I was definitely not ready to be a mother, it was the worst personal decision I've ever had to make. I've been regretting it every day since. I promised myself that if I found myself in that predicament again, I would definitely keep the baby. I've also learned since having the abortion, that there were several other choices that I could have made other than to just terminate my pregnancy."

Damien sighs, feeling some type of way about everything he is hearing. He clenches his teeth as Sheila continues telling her story, "Anyways, it wasn't until several months later that my mom found out about the abortion. Of course, she was very upset, but we had a long talk about many things, and I've learned that my mom is not just my mom, but she's also my best friend, and I can talk to her about anything."

Damien thinks to himself that if Sheila had so many lessons and conversations in such a similar instance, how could they be in this situation today? He shakes his head but continues listening. "Immediately after our talk, my mom set up an appointment for me with my doctor and requested that she perform a full medical exam and prescribe birth control pills for me. Because of all that had happened, I've only had sex with one other person, and I have strictly relied on my birth control pills as a means of protection. Since I hadn't gotten pregnant just using the birth control pills, I thought it would be safe to continue having sex with you without a condom. So, it sucks, but I guess we'll be the poster kids for the fact that all protection, even birth control pills, is not one hundred percent safe!"

"You think?" Damien says sarcastically and begins speaking his piece, "Look, Sheila, I'm very sorry to hear what happened to you. But I really don't want a child—not now. I'm only seventeen. I haven't even graduated from high school, yet. I don't have a real job, and most importantly, I have a four-year scholarship to go to my top school and I can't afford to mess that up."

Sheila is bewildered by Damien's response. How could he selfishly continue to press the issue after all she has just shared? She keeps her cool, "I'm sorry too. I'll take responsibility for telling you that it was okay to continue having sex without protection because I was on birth control pills. But we all know it takes two to make a baby, and my being the only one taking any responsibility here won't change anything now. Whether you like it or not, Damien, you just need to step up and be a man."

"That's the point, Sheila. I'm not a man. I'm a teenager. Maybe you should have acted as if you were one, too, instead of trying to run around acting like you're grown."

Sheila raises her voice, "Well, now you will be a teenager with a baby. And get this, Damien, I really loved chilling with you, and I think you are an awesome person. But see, the reality is I'm only a minor, you hear that, Damien? A minor. Me and your baby will need your help, and lots of it. It's as simple as that."

Damien shakes his head, "Speaking of the baby, are you sure it's even mine?"

Sheila rolls her eyes and answers in a curt tone, "Yes, how many times do I have to tell you that I'm sure it's your baby? You are the only person I've had sex with since I've been in Chicago, and prior to that I hadn't had sex for three months, so for the hundredth time, I'm one hundred percent sure."

"Yeah, well you were one hundred percent sure about your birth control, and here we are," Damien snaps. Sheila sits on the loveseat and stares at the phone in disbelief. Damien continues to let her have it, "And you know what, Sheila? I'm really just tired of you, I'm not going to stay on the phone and go back and forth with you any longer."

Before they hang up angrily, Sheila interjects, "The bottom line is that I'm not going to have an abortion. Don't ask me again. So, if you don't want to be part of your baby's life, take it from someone who knows that it will be extremely painful for me and the child. But we will be all right regardless, Damien. Just be prepared to pay child support for the next twenty-two years."

Damien begins to speak. Sheila cuts him off, "Say no more, I'm done with this conversation. You can text me again when you are ready to have a more mature conversation."

"Yo, Sheila. Why are you going off on me like that?" Damien, in his own way, is still trying to wrap his head around everything. But wrapped up in his own head, he fails to see the bigger picture.

Sheila paints a vivid picture. "Because I'm pregnant, Damien," she shouts, "and all you are concerned about is yourself and your four-year scholarship to Ohio State. You're not concerned about me, not the baby. Just yourself." Sheila abruptly ends the call.

Damien looks at his phone and wonders what just happened. Then he goes to the front porch to let off some steam and get some much-needed fresh air.

Chapter 17

A (Well-Deserved) Day of Relaxation

Moments later, Tanya is awakened by the sound of a door closing loudly. She runs downstairs and hears Damien talking.

"Who are you talking to?" she asks.

Startled at first, Damien is relieved to see his little sis. "Just myself," he lies. He stares into the distance somberly.

"Well, if you need someone to talk to, big brother, you can always talk to me," Tanya offers. She taps him on the shoulder, and he looks at his sister, who smiles at him.

Damien smiles back, "Yeah, I know little sis, thanks so much! What are you doing today?"

"I was hoping that Mom would take me to the mall so that I can pick out an outfit for *The Voice*," Tanya says.

"I'll take you. That way you and I can spend the day together," Damien says with a genuine smile.

"Are you serious?" Tanya asks, her voice filled with excitement. She looks at Damien in awe.

He smiles and looks at her, "Yeah, sis." He nudges her playfully.

"So, what, Sheila, your Boo, is not around today?"

Damien smiles and shakes his head. "I told you a million times, Sheila is not my Boo. But yeah, she's around," he mutters to himself, "She's just talking crazy." Damien rolls his eyes and clenches his jaw. Seeing the look on Tanya's face, Damien calms down, "Besides, we haven't had a brother and sister day together in a while."

"Okay, Damien. I would really love that. I'll go upstairs and get ready." She turns toward the door. "Big head," she yells and runs to the house.

"Make sure to tell Mom," Damien shouts.

"I will," Tanya shouts back.

Tanya is giddy with excitement about spending the day with her brother. She runs upstairs to tell their mom, who she sees at the top of the stairs. "Didn't I tell you not to run up these stairs with those socks on?" Sharon scolds.

Tanya stops short and walks slower, "Yes, Mom, sorry, my fault. It won't happen again."

"What are you so excited about?" Sharon asks.

"Damien and I are going to spend the day together, and he says that if it's okay with you, he'll take me to the mall, so I can pick out an outfit for *The Voice*. Is that okay with you, Mom?" Tanya asks.

"Of course, that's very sweet of him. Where is your brother now?" their mom asks.

"He's out on the front porch."

"Okay. I wonder if he ate yet. Well, give me a hug, baby. I'm not sure if I'll be here when you come back down. I'm leaving soon to pick up Vivian for a spa day," she says excitedly. Her mom shimmies happily before reaching into the fruit bowl for a crisp Bartlett pear.

Glad to see her enjoying herself, Tanya smiles at her mother, "Have a lot of fun, Mom."

"Yes, baby. I'm really looking forward to it," Sharon says as she scoops her daughter into her arms. They stand by the stairs and hug for a long time.

"I was thinking I'd give Damien my credit card so you can treat yourself to whatever outfit you want. And because it's a special occasion and my baby will be on national TV, I think a $2,000 limit is fair. Don't you think?"

Tanya squeals so loudly that Damien can hear her outside. He smiles and shakes his head.

Knowing that was her happy squeal, he can't wait to hear what it was about.

Tanya jumps up and down, exclaiming, "Oh, really, Mom!? Really?" She hugs her mom tightly, nearly knocking her over, "Thank you so much, Mom!"

Sharon rubs her daughter's head and reminds her, "Now, Tanya, just because you have a $2,000 spending limit, that doesn't mean you have to spend every cent of it."

Tanya looks up at her, "Yes, Mom, I understand." Then Tanya makes a beeline upstairs to find an outfit for her special day with her big brother.

Moments later, Sharon heads out to the front porch, where she finds Damien standing and looking into the distance. She gives a half smile before stepping toward him and putting her arms around him. "Tanya tells me that you two will be spending the day together. That's marvelous son," she says with a genuine smile. They stand hugging before she reaches into her bag. "Here's my American Express card. You can use this for Tanya's outfit for The Voice. I told her that she has a limit of $2,000, but please use the card wisely. You two might as well treat yourself to a nice lunch."

Damien looks at his mom and flashes a smile, "Thanks, Mom."

Examining her son's face, she can see that something is troubling him, "Is everything okay? You seem a little down."

Damien sighs, "I'm good. I just got off the phone with Sheila a little earlier, and she's talking really crazy, Mom."

"That's understandable. You two have endured a lot in the last twenty-four hours. What you really need is a break from each other."

Damien smiles at the thought, "I guess you're right."

Donning her sunglasses, Sharon looks at the skyline, grateful for another beautiful and sunny day in Chicago. With a smile of her own, she replies, "Well, son, I have a good feeling everything will work out fine."

Damien looks at her curiously, "Really, Mom?"

She replies with confidence, "Yes, son."

Damien exhales loudly., exclaiming, "Well, I truly hope so." He shakes his head and runs his hand through his hair. He watches as his mother descends the stairs and walks toward the car.

"Well, you and Tanya have lots of fun. I'm heading out to pick up Vivian for a day at the spa." She does another excited shimmy, making Damien turn away as he pretends to be disgusted. Damien knows that his mom not only deserves the spa day, but also the good feelings she was expressing. It is wonderful to see her feeling so happy.

"Enjoy yourself. You truly deserve it," Damien calls to his mom, who is about to sit down in the driver's seat, "Oh, Mom! Please let Mrs. Johnson know how bad I feel for all I'm putting her through."

His mom looks at Damien and gives him a half smile. She is definitely ready to get moving. "Okay, son, I sure will. Now go have some fun with your sister!" she calls back.

"Will do! Love you, Mom." He salutes her.

"Love you more, son," Sharon replies and blows a kiss. Then she sits emphatically in her seat, turns the radio up, and makes her way to Vivian's house. She rolls the windows down and readies herself for a much-needed fun and relaxing day with her best friend.

Damien goes back inside the house to get ready to spend the day with his little sister. Feeling a buzz, he checks for his phone and sees that he received a text from his teammate, Chris.

Chris: Are you going to the party @ Thomas' house this Friday?

Damien: Hey bro. Yea I'll be there.

Chris: Are you bringing that fine honey, Sheila?

<Chris inserts a smirking emoji>

Damien: Not sure. It looks like I'll be bringing Celeste, if anybody.

Chris: What's up with Sheila?

Damien: Nothing really, she's just talking crazy.

You know what, maybe I'll just show up by myself. Knowing Thomas, there will be plenty of fine honeys there anyway.

<Damien inserts his own smirking emoji.>

Chris: Very true.

<Chris adds the thinking emoji and the 100 emoji.>

Damien: I've got to go, but I'll see you @ football practice on Thursday morning.

Chris: Where are you going?

Damien: Right now, I'm heading to the mall with my little sis, I'll be free later tonight to do whatever.

Chris: Ok! That's what's up, big brother of the year!

<Damien inserts a laughing emoji.>

Chris: Well, stay safe and I'll text you later.

Damien: Sounds like a plan.

Realizing what he just texted, Damien shakes his head and smiles before putting his phone back in his pocket.

Just then, Tanya walks downstairs with a mini backpack in hand. She pulls out a pair of sunglasses that match the ones their mom was wearing earlier. "I'm ready, big brother," she says with a smile.

Damien smirks at his little sister, who is growing up before his eyes. "Did you shut off all the lights upstairs?"

Tanya looks at her sunglasses and wipes off a few smudges. "Yes."

Damien then ensures everything on the first floor is secured. Once done, he faces his sister, "Looks like we're all set, little sis." He gestures for her to lead the way, then he locks the door and high-fives Tanya. "Now, let's go have some fun!"

On the way to the mall, Tanya and Damien go back and forth about their exciting news. She talks about how exciting it is that she will be performing on *The Voice,* and Damien talks about how excited he is to be attending Ohio State next year.

Looking at her brother, Tanya gets serious for a moment, "Do you plan on coming with me and mom to see me sing on *The Voice?*"

Damien looks at his sister in disbelief, "Is that a joke? Of course, I am. I wouldn't miss it for anything in the world." He laughs, "Well maybe I'll miss it, if someone gives me tickets to a Bears game."

Tanya playfully punches Damien's arm. Damien laughs and rubs his arm. "Wow, you really throw a mean punch, girl! Besides, I was just kidding."

Tanya waves her fist, pretending to threaten him again. "Yeah, you better be," she says and laughs.

"You have any idea about what you wanna buy at the mall today? Any stores you wanna check out?"

"Yes! See, I would like to purchase a pair of Amari ripped blue jeans and a navy blue YSL clutch bag to go along with my white leather blazer, my Ivy Park blue, high-top sneakers, and my light blue T-shirt with white lettering that reads, 'Work Hard and Your Dreams Will Come True.'"

Damien nods his head in approval. "That sounds fire," he says, "Did you put this outfit together by yourself?"

"No, not really," says Tanya, "I got some of my ideas from following @styleyourthreads on Instagram."

Damien nods, "Awesome. Text me the handle. I'll have to check it out sometime."

Pulling out her phone, Tanya sends the Instagram address to her brother.

Meanwhile, at Celine African Hair Braiding, Sheila is scrolling through her contacts when she suddenly comes across Travis's number. She smiles as she reminisces about the moment she met Travis at the convenience store a little over seven weeks ago. It was the same day that Damien took her sight-seeing.

Sheila told Damien that she would never call Travis; however, Sheila is still extremely angry with Damien. Besides, giving Travis a call would be a nice change of pace. Without another moment's hesitation, Sheila dials Travis's number.

Travis sees an unfamiliar number pop up with an area code he's never seen before. He answers in a gruff voice, "Who's this?"

"Guess?" Sheila says, moving her head as the braider tugs on a tangled bit of hair. Sheila winces a bit, looking at the braider, who relaxes her combing slightly.

Relieved to hear a feminine voice, Travis relaxes, "Kim?"

Sheila rolls her eyes, "No. Before you start naming all these other girls, it's Sheila, the girl you met at the convenience store on Lincoln Ave about seven weeks ago."

Travis pauses for a minute, trying to think back to seven weeks ago. "Shorty with the braids and a boyfriend? The fine shorty with the pink phone with the letters N.Y.C.?" he recalls.

Sheila smiles, "Yeah, that's me. I don't know about that whole boyfriend thing. He's just a friend."

Travis raises an eyebrow, "Oh, now he's just a friend?"

"That's what I just said," Sheila says with a hint of aggravation in her voice.

Travis chuckles, "Okay, okay, I hear you. That's what's up. Well, where are you now? I was just getting ready to plan my day."

"I'm at Celine African Hair Braiding salon on Ashland Ave getting my hair did," Sheila replies with a silly voice.

"Oh word? I know exactly where that place is. My sister's been going there for a while. I don't live too far from there. What time are you out of there? And I do mean approximately, because having a sister, I already know that you can be there all day depending on the style."

Sheila laughs, "Isn't that the truth. Hold on, I'll ask my stylist."

Sheila puts the phone on mute and turns to her hairdresser, "Hey, Tammi, how much longer do you think we'll be?"

Tammi continues braiding, glances over Sheila's head, and answers, "Two hours."

Sheila unmutes her call and relays the information to Travis, "She said two hours."

Travis checks the time. *Okay, that's what's up*, he thinks to himself. "Well, do you have plans after your appointment?"

"No, did you have something in mind?" Sheila asks expectantly.

Travis smiles, brimming with excitement, "If you're hungry, we can hit this great soul food joint nearby. If your 'friend' hasn't taken you there already."

There's a pause, and Travis can faintly hear people talking and popping gum in the background, but nothing from Sheila. Nervous, he asks, "Why the silence? You don't like soul food?"

Sheila catches herself, "No, I love me some soul food. I was just texting my aunt with some updates. But I would definitely love to check out that soul food joint. I've never been."

Travis grins, "Okay, then we're on. I'll see you in a couple of hours."

Sheila is excited and recites her catch phrase: "Sounds like a plan."

They exchange goodbyes before hanging up. Sheila looks in the mirror as her stylist breezes through her intricate braids. Sheila closes her eyes and relaxes.

Meanwhile, Vivian and Sharon are both getting pedicures at the One Stop Spa when Vivian notices a text from Sheila. Vivian reads the text and responds by thanking her niece for the update.

Auntie: That means we'll be both getting back home around the same time. Please plan to grab yourself something to eat. I will not be cooking tonight. Getting early dinner with Mrs. Jackson.

Sheila: Ok, enjoy, I love you and I'll see you @ home.

Auntie: Love you, too, sweetie and please stay safe.

Vivian turns to Sharon, who is reclining in her massage chair, "Now, what was I saying before I was kindly interrupted by my niece?"

Without looking up, Sharon responds, "You were explaining why you never mentioned Sheila to me before."

"How ironic. Yes, that's right, like I told you before, it's complicated. I'll try to explain it the best way I can."

Sharon still sits peacefully, the massage chair rumbling beneath her and soothing all of her problems and worries away. "I'm all ears."

"See Sharon, when my sister Anita visited me here in Chicago a little over sixteen years ago, she and a friend decided to visit a local dance club where they met some men. I was told that one thing led to another. I think you know what I mean by that," Vivian eyes her friend.

Sharon glances at her friend and smirks knowingly, "Yes, I have a good idea."

Vivian continues, "Anyways, a month later, I got a call from Anita, crying and telling me that she's pregnant. She went on to say the man that she is sure is the father is denying it. I asked for his name, but she never told me."

Vivian shrugs and winces as the nail technician cuts her cuticles. She gestures for the lady to be gentler before continuing, "Then without letting me know she was back in town, Anita made arrangements to meet the same young man at a coffee shop in downtown Chicago. This time, she was prepared to face him with an ultrasound. It was during that conversation that they had a huge argument. She told me that she stood up, slammed the ultrasound on the table, and yelled at the top of her lungs. She still remembers all the startled onlookers looking in their direction. 'This ultrasound of your daughter will be the last picture of her that you will ever see. Please don't come looking for us. Have a terrible life.' Then, she stormed out of the café, never to see or hear from him again. Anita believes that Sheila's father most likely lives somewhere in Atlanta or in Chicago."

Sharon looks at her friend and is at a loss for words, Vivian continues, "I have always kept this story between Anita and myself. She's since regretted her actions at the café and prays that one day Sheila will have an opportunity to meet her dad. Anita works extremely hard, so I thought this year the least I could do would be to give her a break and have Sheila visit me. It also gives Sheila an opportunity to take a vacation away from the hustle and bustle of New York City."

Vivian and Sharon sit in silence for some time. Sharon breaks the silence, shaking her head, "What a story, Viv. I don't even know what to say."

Admiring the nail technician's work, Vivian continues, "As you can see from the recent events, Sheila is by no means a saint. But she really is an amazing girl. She's definitely made mistakes that could have been avoided. Shoot, as everyone on earth has at some point. It's part of life. I believe Sheila's growing up in a household without a father figure has certainly affected her decision-making. I'm in no way excusing her for her poor choices, but not having a balanced home most definitely played a factor."

Sharon nods in agreement, then looks at two shades of nail polish with intensity, "Sure has. As it would in any home where a parent is just completely out of the picture. Raising a child to be healthy and safe, well-rounded, let alone stable, successful and so on, is no easy feat. Lord have mercy, it is such a fragile job, requiring a delicate balance and by all means, every little thing matters."

Deciding on a light pink and gold accented French manicure, Sharon continues, "I really don't know what will happen with Damien or Sheila. If Sheila is confirmed pregnant by your doctor, we just have to stick together and guide them the best we can."

"The kids will definitely be leaning on us, and we will need to remain strong for them," Vivian says sincerely.

Sharon nods. Feeling the Spirit come over her, she affirms, "Absolutely, absolutely. And for each other, girl." They reach out and clasp hands with fervor. It takes all of their strength to keep from crying. They laugh instead. Sharon is grateful that, once again, through it all, her best friend is right by her side.

After they calm down, Sharon continues, "When is Sheila's appointment with your doctor, exactly?"

"July 31st."

"Well, until that time, we will assume that the two tests that Sheila took are indeed correct, and she's pregnant. So, to avoid putting any additional stress on the kids or ourselves, we shouldn't play the blame game."

Vivian nods fervently, "I agree one hundred percent." Vivian scans the nail polish selection and settles on a vibrant orange that pops next to her skin tone. Vivian then decides to change the conversation, feeling that both of them are as at peace as they can be with the situation. "This pedicure really feels amazing, what a fantastic idea, Sharon. Your timing is impeccable," Vivian says.

Sharon looks at her longtime friend, "Yes, this was way overdue. But we're not even done yet." She goes over their itinerary, "See, we've had a massage, a mani-pedi, and now, I have a surprise for you." Sharon wiggles her eyebrows mysteriously.

Vivian laughs, glad to see Sharon returning to her usual self. Sharon continues, "I know I told you I was treating you to lunch, but I didn't tell you which restaurant we'll be dining at."

Vivian is charmed. "Where are you taking me?" she asks excitedly.

"I made reservations at our favorite steak house," Sharon looks at her friend, her eyes glittering with excitement.

Vivian beams in awe, "Are you telling me that you made reservations at the RPM on West Kinzie St.?"

"Yes, girl. Are you good with that?" Sharon asks curiously.

Vivian looks shocked, "Am I good with that? I'm great with that. This day is getting better by the minute." The pair exchange a freshly manicured high-five.

Sharon looks over her nearly complete pedicure then pulls her phone out of her purse.

"Well, let me just check up on the kids, then we'll be on our way."

"Sounds great," Vivian says as she looks over her own nails. Handing the nail technician a tip, she stands up and gathers her belongings.

Sharon decides to call Damien.

Damien is waiting for Tanya when he feels his phone buzzing. He almost hopes it is Sheila, as he finds himself flooded by memories of their conversation. He sees it's actually his mom calling and picks up promptly, "Hello, Mom. How's your fabulous day at the spa going?"

His mom smiles, feeling as if she were floating on cloud nine, "Vivian and I are having a wonderful time. How are things going with you and Tanya? Is she driving you crazy?"

Damien answers honestly, looking at his spunky little sister, who is weeks away from lighting up television sets across the nation. He smiles, "Absolutely not, Mom. I'm really enjoying our brother and sister time together."

Sharon smiles, "That's great. I'm so glad that you two are enjoying each other's company. Was Tanya able to find an outfit?"

"Yeah, Mom, she had it all planned out before we even got here. It's pretty smooth though, I think that you will definitely like it. Here's Tanya now, I'll let her tell you more about it."

Damien hands the phone to his sister, but he pulls back as he still hears his mom talking, "Before you put Tanya on the phone, I wanted to tell you that Vivian and I will be going to the RPM steakhouse for dinner. I should be home around six o'clock."

Damien smiles, "Oh, you fancy, huh?"

His mom laughs, "Oh yes, son. I am. Plus, I didn't want to mess up my manicure eating at Mother's Kitchen."

Damien's mouth waters at the thought of their favorite barbeque rib joint. "Ugh, I love that place," he says, getting an idea, "You know, Mom, maybe that's where Tanya and I will go."

His mom nods in agreement, "That sounds like a great idea."

Eager to get going to Mother's Kitchen, Damien wraps up the call, "Well, enjoy the rest of your spa day, Mom. I'll call you when we arrive back home. Here's Tanya." He hands his sister the phone.

"Hey, Mom," Tanya says sweetly.

"Hello, sweetie, how are you?"

"I'm doing great, Mom. I found a sweet pair of Amari ripped blue Jeans and a YSL navy clutch bag like Sheila's to go with my outfit."

Sharon nods approvingly, "That sounds awesome. I can't wait to see it. How are you and Damien getting along?"

"We are having a great time, lots of laughs. I think I have the best brother in the world."

Their mom beams proudly, "Yes, you do. I've never met one like him."

Then Tanya pauses, wondering if there is anything else she needs to say, "Mom, thanks again for everything. You are the best mom ever."

With all of the heartfelt smiles she's shared today, Sharon Jackson is feeling refreshed, "Thanks, dear. And it looks like it's official. You, Tanya Jackson, are the best daughter ever!"

Tanya giggles. Their mom continues, "I love you and Damien to the moon and back."

"We love you, too," Tanya says.

Damien points to the bus, and Tanya looks up to see one waiting at the red light. Her mom says one last thing, "Now you and Damien, please stay safe and I'll see you when I get home."

Tanya hurries off the phone, "Okay, Mom. Gotta catch this bus. Goodbye!" They end the call, and she gives the phone back to Damien. The two of them run for the bus and make it just in time.

Back at Celine African Hair Braiding, Sheila texts Travis.

Sheila: Hey, I'll be done in 15

Travis: Omw, just got in the car. I'll be sitting outside in a blue BMW with white stripes, and vanity plates that read: "that's what's up."

Sheila: Sweet. I can't wait to see you! It's been a while.

Tammi finishes up the final braid and swoops down some baby hairs, which is Sheila's favorite way to rock her braids. Sheila stands in the mirror, swinging her braids before taking a few selfies to show them off. Then she has to get some pictures with her stylist, Tammi, who's a few years older than her. Finally, Sheila gives Tammi a generous tip and thanks her for her incredible work.

Tammi looks at the crisp twenty-dollar bill from Sheila and thanks her. Beaming, Tammi says, "I really like the way the braids turned out on you, babe. You look stunning, and oh yes, don't forget to enjoy the rest of your vacation."

Sheila smiles, waves, and flips her braids as she walks toward the door. She thinks she sees a BMW pull up outside. "Thanks again, Tammi," she shouts on the way out. A bell chimes as Sheila steps out onto the sidewalk in the muggy afternoon. She stays in front of the shop as she scans the street for Travis, and finally pulls out her phone to check in with him.

Sheila: I don't see you.

Travis: My bad. I had to stop for gas.

Sheila: No problem. I'm waiting right outside of the salon.

Travis: How will I recognize you? What are you wearing?

Sheila: I'm wearing black denim shorts, a yellow crop top, black flats, with yellow and black earrings.

<Sheila inserts a smiley face and bumblebee.>

Travis: Ok cool, black and yellow. you should be really easy to find.

Travis looks up from texting to see the light turn green. He tosses the cell phone to the side for safety and steps on the gas as he scans the block for Sheila. He zeroes in on her standing in front of the salon.

Sheila looks up from her phone, realizing she shouldn't have texted him since he was driving. While putting her phone back into her purse, Sheila notices a blue BMW with white stripes pull up in front of her. She tries to look into the car to ensure that it is indeed Travis; however, the windows are tinted. Just as she tries to make sure that it's him, she sees Travis roll the window down. He steps out of the car and walks over to the passenger side, opening the door kindly. "Hello, Sheila," Travis says with a smile.

Sheila, swept up in the moment and all the fine material things Travis seems to come with, embraces him warmly. Then, without thinking, she reaches up and kisses him.

Travis squeezes her, feeling the softness of her body next to his. He smells her sweet perfume and becomes intoxicated by her. She brushes past him to get into the seat. He closes the door, and they fasten their seatbelts before he pulls off. Sheila can see Tammi and her co-worker standing in the window, watching her. She waves goodbye before rolling the tinted window up again.

Tammi, Sheila's stylist, looks at the pictures she had sneakily taken of the two teens embracing outside. She turns to her co-worker, Rene, and shows her the picture.

"Isn't that Travis' car?" Tammi asks.

"It sure is," Rene says after taking a careful look at the picture.

"That boy is such a player. Maybe he'll change, though, now that he is going to be a dad," Tammi says.

"What do you mean by that?" Rene asks as she files her nails while waiting for a client.

Tammi fills Rene in on the latest gossip about Travis, "Remember my client, Sheila, who was just in here?"

"Yes," Rene replies eagerly.

Tammi, who is the best at spilling the tea and serving it hot, shares Sheila's business like it is hers, "Well, she was telling me that she's just here for the summer visiting family. But then she went on to say that she did something stupid and got herself pregnant by someone here in Chicago. I'm just putting two and two together, but I just saw her kissing Travis."

Rene's eyes widen with shock and concern, "Wow, I can't believe Travis is going to be a father." Rene just shakes her head and continues filing her nails before they hear the bells chime over the door. It is Rene's next client. Rene greets her warmly, and the two walk to the back to start on this new head of hair.

Chapter 18

Living My Best Life

O nce in the car, Sheila glances in Travis's direction. She's impressed by the way he's maintained his car. She attempts to make conversation, "So what's up?"

Travis glances at Sheila and returns his eyes to the road in order to keep the two of them safe. He smirks, "You're what's up. You are seriously looking as if you belong in *Fire Girls Only Magazine.*"

Sheila gives him a quizzical look, "Um, is that even a real magazine?"

Travis shrugs and laughs, "Well, it is now, and you just made the cover with a full-page spread."

Sheila blushes, "Well, thank you very much. I love compliments. Speaking of compliments, this is one fly car."

Travis beams proudly, "Thanks, I must admit that this is my baby." He caresses the steering wheel.

What a choice of words, Sheila thinks as her mind drifts to Damien. Those were the words she wished she could've heard him say. She looks over at Travis and feels her stomach fill with butterflies as she smiles at him and reaches for his hand.

Travis looks down at her hand, repeating his catch phrase, "That's what's up." He smiles as he glances at her, "Well, are you hungry?"

Sheila rubs her belly, "I'm starving." They continue driving in silence. Sheila looks out the window to see if there's anything familiar that they have passed. Her aunt was right; she really is learning the city pretty quickly.

"So, you're not from Chicago, huh?" Travis says, interrupting her wandering thoughts.

"How did you know?"

"Your accent." They both laugh. "So where are you from?" Travis asks.

"I'm from New York, baby bay-beh!" Sheila answers with pride, mimicking Notorious B.I.G.

Impressed by her sense of humor, Travis chuckles, "That's what's up." He attempts to slip in another compliment, "Do all the women in New York look as good as you?" he asks, looking Sheila over hungrily.

Sheila gives him a daring look, "You'll have to go to New York and see for yourself. Besides, I'm the only New York fly girl that you need to be thinking about at this moment. But I can guarantee by the end of the night, you won't even care to see the rest."

Travis smiles, admiring her again, "You're a feisty little thing. I like that!"

Before Sheila knows it, Travis pulls up to the 6978 Soul Food restaurant where he parks his car and cuts the ignition. "We're here," he announces.

Travis gets out of the car, goes to the passenger side, and opens the door for Sheila. She flashes a bright smile, her hair still shining from the fresh oil sheen Tammi sprayed earlier. "Thanks," she says, keeping her eyes on him, "Are you always a gentleman, or is this special treatment just for me?"

Travis smirks and extends his arm for Sheila to hook hers into. "Let's just say that when it comes to treating a lady with respect, my father taught me well," he brags. Sheila's braids swing as they head into the restaurant. Travis grabs the door and holds it open for her.

Once inside, Sheila is seriously impressed. Her mouth starts to water as the classic, down-home smells of mac and cheese, collard greens, fried chicken, and so many other soul food dishes reach her nose, making her smile, "This place smells so good."

Sheila stands in amazement, taking everything in. Travis looks at her as they stand in the entrance together, "That's just the smell, wait until you actually taste the food." He nods his head and rubs his hands together, "It's awesome." Travis leads the way and selects a table, pulling out a chair for Sheila. Sheila smiles again and sits down.

Travis looks at her. He's feeling grateful to see her after those seven long weeks. "I can get used to this. If you were my shorty, I'd spoil you every day."

Sheila replies with a huge smile, "And I'd definitely let you." She fans out a napkin to place over her legs.

As Sheila looks over the 6978 menu, she is transported back to New York. "Mmm, this menu looks very similar to Sylvia's. I sure hope it tastes as good as Sylvia's."

"What's Sylvia's?" Travis asks curiously.

Sheila's eyes light up, "Sylvia's is a very famous soul food restaurant back in my hometown of Harlem, New York. I eat there at least once a week, especially because mad celebrities eat there all the time, so you never know who you'll see."

Travis nods his approval, "That's what's up."

The waitress, Tina, approaches the table and instantly recognizes Travis. They exchange flirtatious looks and greet each other warmly. "How are you today, Travis?" she asks.

Travis smiles politely, "Fantastic, do they ever give you a day off?"

She responds, "Yeah, they do, but I always try to take extra shifts so that I can pay my bills."

Travis nods, "That's what's up." He pauses for a moment then looks at Sheila, who is finalizing her order, "Well, Tina, this is Sheila."

Tina and Sheila meet each other's gaze and smile sweetly at each other. "Hello, Sheila, it's so nice to meet you. Are you ready to order?" Tina asks.

Sheila dances in her seat, "I sure am. This place really smells great."

Tina looks at her with interest, "Is this your first time eating here, hon?"

"Yeah, I'm visiting from New York."

Tina nods. "Well, welcome! I'm sure you will enjoy the food. We have a five-star rating," she says proudly. Looking at Travis with a smile, Tina adds, "We have many repeat customers." Turning back to Sheila, she asks, "But what can I get you, sweetie?"

Sheila replies excitedly, "I'll have the catfish, mac'n cheese, black-eyed peas and red rice, collard greens, and cornbread."

Hearing his stomach grumble, Travis nods approvingly, "Good choice, make that two, Tina. Thanks."

Tina scribbles their order on a notepad. "Any drinks?"

Sheila eyes the menu briefly before answering, "I'll have a root beer." She closes the menu, and Tina places it under her arm.

Travis hands Tina his menu as well, "Great choice. Make that two."

The waitress looks at Travis and Sheila, "You two are so cute. Do you always agree on everything?"

Sheila replies with a smirk, "We'll see."

Tina goes to put in their order then returns minutes later with their root beers. "Your order will be ready in about fifteen minutes," she announces.

"Thanks," Sheila says as she bangs her straw on the table to open it and takes a sip of the fizzy drink.

Travis leans over the table and looks deeply into Sheila's eyes, "So, why did you really call me?"

Sheila thinks up an answer, "Well, I've been in Chicago for a little while, and I'll be heading back to New York soon. So basically, I just wanted to socialize with some new people."

Travis sits back and relaxes in his seat. Sheila mutters bitterly and takes another sip of her root beer, "And besides, I'm upset at Damien."

Travis looks intrigued, "Who's Damien? Is he that guy I saw with you at the convenience store?"

"Yeah," Sheila rolls her eyes.

"Well, why are you upset with Damien?" Travis takes a sip of his soda.

Sheila swirls her drink a bit and starts to vent, "Well, if you really want to know, I'll be straight up with you."

"That's what's up. I'm all ears," Travis says, finishing his drink and leaning back in his chair.

Sheila tells Travis about her relationship with Damien over the last seven weeks—from how her aunt introduced her to Damien all the way up to their argument right before her hair appointment.

Travis sits with his hands in front of his mouth, listening intently.

"Now that there's a possibility that I may be pregnant, he's asking me to consider having an abortion," she lowers her voice, then feels herself getting hot, "I've tried to convince myself that I don't love Damien, I even tried to convince my aunt. But who am I kidding? I realize that I really do love that boy."

Travis is still stuck on an earlier part of the conversation, "Hold up, you're what?"

Sheila circles back and brings Travis up to date, "I'm pregnant." She looks at his face but can't tell what he's thinking. So she adds, "If you have a problem with that, you can just drop me home or I'll take the bus. I know my way now."

Travis tries to calm Sheila down, "No, no. I mean, it is what it is. And you don't even look pregnant, yet." He thinks to himself for a moment, "And you did just say that it's a possibility that you're pregnant. So, are you pregnant or not?"

Sheila continues telling her business, "I've missed my period, and I have proof from not one, but two positive pregnancy tests. I'm just waiting for my doctor's appointment on the 31st of this month to confirm it."

Travis nods slowly, "Now I understand." He looks around to see whether Tina is bringing their food but sees that she is assisting another couple. He asks, "How do your parents feel about you being pregnant?"

"Well, I never knew my dad," Sheila says and shrugs.

"I'm really sorry to hear that," Travis says, shaking his head.

"Hopefully one day I'll meet him," Sheila continues optimistically. "Then as for my mom, we really haven't spoken about all of this yet."

They sit quietly for a few moments, looking around for the food before Travis interjects, "Damien really is blessed. I wish I were Damien."

Just then, Tina finally returns with their food. She places a steaming platter in front of each of them as she jokes, "For once, it's not going to be hard knowing who ordered what."

Sheila and Travis laugh and unwrap their utensils so they can dig in. Tina looks at the couple before asking, "Need anything else?"

Already chewing on a piece of cornbread, Travis scans the table, "Oh yes, please, I'll have some hot sauce."

Tina smiles, "I'll bring it right out."

Somewhat embarrassed, Travis watches as Sheila takes the time to pray over her meal. Then she takes a few bites and chews slowly, savoring the food. "You're right Travis, this food is very tasty."

"I never lie," Travis assures.

Sheila rolls her eyes and snorts, "Yeah, at least not this time. I know how guys can be."

Travis laughs, knowing she is right. They enjoy their food in silence. Sheila seems to really be enjoying herself as she hops around her plate, completely loving the meal. Sheila looks up at him and sees Travis admiring her.

"So, before we were interrupted, you were telling me that you wish you were Damien. Why would you say something like that?"

Travis readies himself to give his own background story, "I don't share this with too many people but, you seem mad chill, and I love the way you've been honest with me. Now that's what's up. But when I was fifteen, I stupidly competed in a karate tournament in Detroit, Michigan without my protective cup. During the match, I was kicked extremely hard in my genitals, and was severely injured. I needed several operations after the fact."

Sheila stops mid-chew and covers her mouth. She winces in pain as she imagines the pain he felt, "Ouch."

"Ouch doesn't even cut it. I can almost feel it now if I think about it too much. But after a series of operations, the doctors told me and my parents that I would never be able to have children. I remember my parents were crying, but at the time I didn't care. I really just needed that pain to go away. But as I've gotten older watching my niece and nephews grow up, I've regretted that dumb decision to compete without a protective cup ever since. Now I really wish I could have children of my own." Travis looks pretty sad. It is a topic he rarely shares because of how emotional it makes him. He takes a breath to compose himself, and Sheila reaches out to touch his hand. He looks into her eyes, "Looking back, the pain back then was nothing compared to the pain I feel now."

Sheila is amazed by everything she's hearing. She has since stopped eating in order to comfort Travis.

"I know several individuals who are in the same position as me who would love to have children. So, I'm serious when I say, I wish I were Damien," he says, "If Damien continues to push you toward having an abortion, and it's not what you want, I'm truly here for you!"

"Thanks so much, Travis." Sheila reaches across the table and gives Travis a kiss.

Sitting back down, Sheila hesitates before asking another question, "And just curious but, is everything okay down there now?"

Travis chews eagerly, "Down where?"

"You know," she points with her fork in the direction of Travis' genitals.

Travis looks down, "Oh yes, very much so." They both laugh loudly. Some people turn to see what's going on at their table, but Sheila and Travis are in their own little world.

Sheila is more than halfway done with her plate before she realizes something else. She shakes her head as she picks up a forkful of mac and cheese. "That's so strange."

Travis is nearly done with his plate. He answers with a mouthful of food before catching himself, "What's so strange?"

Sheila looks toward the ceiling as she tries to explain her dilemma, "It's just strange that here we have two guys that didn't use protection. One created a child by not using protection and doesn't want the child. Then the other will never be able to create a child due to the fact that he didn't use protection, yet he would love to create one. I guess it's so true that someone else's pain and agony can be another person's blessing."

Travis nods in agreement, "For sure. What's up, though, is that you realized that. You must be really smart, putting stuff together like that."

Sheila shows him how aware she really is, "So anyways, Travis, why did you go to prison?"

Travis nearly chokes on his food, "How did you know I went to prison?"

Looking at Travis with a knowing, flirtatious smile, she says, "Your tattoos."

Travis looks at his scratch and poke tattoos and smiles to himself. "Really, I see that you're pretty street smart, too. That's what's up." Answering her question, Travis continues, "I did two years for assault and weapons violations, and I'll be done with my parole next month."

Just then, Tina comes back to refresh their drinks on the house. The pair express their gratitude and continue talking.

"So, are you from Chicago?" Sheila asks. "You sound a little different from everyone else I've met," she observes.

Travis looks intrigued, "You're really observant, huh? No, I'm actually from Los Angeles. My parents moved here when I was two."

Sheila takes a sip of her drink, "Do you like living here in Chicago instead of sunny L.A? I've always wanted to visit L.A."

Travis takes a moment to think, "Yes, I love Chicago. Besides, it's all I've known. I really never had a chance to visit other cities."

Sheila smiles as she contemplates whether she should save or finish the remaining food in front of her, "Well, maybe someday you can visit me in New York."

Travis smiles back, revealing pearly white teeth.

"That's what's up. I would love to take you up on that sometime."

Sheila looks at Travis' empty plate and back at her own. Seeing the time, she decides to get a to-go box and save the rest for later, "Well, the food was delicious. But now I think I'm ready for dessert."

Travis scans the room looking for Tina and waves her over to the table. When Tina arrives, Travis orders one of the best desserts in town.

"Can you please bring us two peach cobblers?"

Sheila is shocked. It's as if Travis read her mind. She was eyeing the peach cobbler on the menu earlier. She flashes a magical grin. "Great choice," she says. The two continue getting to know each other in the dimly lit atmosphere. They are greeted by Tina's warm smile and two even warmer fresh slices of peach cobbler. Sheila's eyes dance at the sight of the caramelized sugar, sweet, fresh peaches, and the buttery crust, topped off with some homemade vanilla ice cream.

It isn't long before Travis and Sheila finish their delicious desserts. After sweeping the crumbs from her area, Sheila looks out the window and sees that it's nearing dusk. She begins to gather her belongings, "It looks like it's getting pretty late, and I promised my aunt that I'd be home by 5:30."

Travis wipes his mouth and places his napkin on the empty plate. "Do you need a ride home?"

"No, I know how to get to the bus stop from here. I looked it up while I was at the salon."

Travis nods sadly, wishing she would've accepted his offer, "That's what is up." He looks around, thinking of something to say, "Will you at least let me walk you to the bus stop? It can be a bit dangerous in these parts."

Sheila looks at him as if he's clueless. "I'm a big girl, Travis," Sheila says, "Besides, I grew up in Harlem."

Travis nods knowingly. "You're so right. You did mention that. Just promise me you'll be careful," he says with a deep sense of concern in his voice.

"Yeah, I will," Sheila picks up the check, "Would you like to split the bill?"

"Please, don't ever insult me like that again." Travis gives Sheila a look of distaste. "Anytime that we go out together, you don't ever have to pay for anything." Travis proceeds to put twenty dollars in the checkbook along with his credit card.

Sheila smiles sweetly, "Thanks, I'll have to remember that." Then Sheila walks over to Travis and gives him a hug and kiss. "Thank you so much for the meal and for being such a great listener. I really enjoyed myself."

Travis feels himself getting woozy with affection for Sheila. "Yeah, we must do this again, and soon."

"I agree," Sheila whispers in a sultry voice Travis finds hard to resist.

Tina returns with Travis's credit card, and he puts it in his wallet. Then Travis assumes full protector mode as he stands up to lead Sheila out the door. He gently helps her out of her seat and places his hand on her waist as they walk toward the entrance. "I'm going to need you to text me when you get home, so that I know you've made it home safely," Travis tells Sheila.

Sheila feels a tingle up her spine as Travis' hand lingers on her back. She keeps it cool. "Sounds like a plan," she responds.

Travis wonders if Sheila is as enticed as he is. "That's what's up."

As Sheila walks out of the restaurant, Travis goes back in, thinking he'd forgotten his keys. He passes by Tina. "Back so soon?" she asks.

Travis gives her an exasperated smile before checking around the table. He taps his pockets and realizes the keys were in there all along. He catches Tina again, realizing she's the only waitress on duty. He reaches for a one-hundred-dollar bill, folds it up, and hands it to her on his way out.

When Tina goes back to the kitchen, she takes a moment to investigate what Travis placed in her hand. Her eyes widen with shock and excitement when as she sees a crisp one-hundred-dollar bill. Holding it up to the light, she smiles and says to herself, "That's what's up."

After a slower than normal ride on the CTA, Sheila arrives home to find her aunt sitting in the backyard, enjoying a glass of wine and listening to some smooth jazz. Sheila stands in the threshold, watching her aunt. "I see you're having a relaxing time out here."

Her aunt's eyes flutter open. "Yes, sweetie, I am."

Sheila flops down into her favorite loveseat and examines her aunt, who looks as if she's still at the spa. "Well, how was your spa day?" she asks.

"It was excellent. Everything about today was excellent. That is the best way for me to explain it." She takes a sip of her wine. "Can you believe Sharon treated me to lunch at my favorite steakhouse, the RPM?" She pauses, still savoring the succulent meal they shared. She smiles, remembering that she still has some food wrapped up in the fridge for tomorrow.

"I tell you Sheila, I thought I was in heaven."

"I'm glad you enjoyed it, you deserved it," Sheila smiles, grabbing her braids to move them before reclining in the loveseat.

Her aunt sits up and glances in her direction. "That's enough about me, sweetie. I know you just sat down, but I'm going to need you to turn around and let me see those beautiful braids."

Sheila swings her braids. Vivian's face registers approval, "Wow, Sheila, they did an awesome job. That must have been expensive."

Sheila sits back down and shakes her head no, "Not really. It was around the same price I pay for them in New York. I'm thinking I need to start doing them myself more often though, then I won't have to pay for anything but the hair."

"Okay, please remind me to give you some money tomorrow. I don't want you to be broke out here in the Midwest."

Grateful for the offer of more money, Sheila laughs, "Thanks, Auntie, but I still have a little money, and my mother will be depositing more into my account sometime next week."

"Well, sweetie, you will need more money until then. Aren't you the one who told me that you always need money?"

Sheila can't believe her ears. Her aunt is convincing her to accept even more free money. Aside for helping around the house, Sheila really doesn't feel like she deserves or needs her aunt's money. But how could she resist? "I did, I did," Sheila replies, giving in.

"Well, it's settled, you are my niece, and I can spoil my niece if I want to."

Sheila laughs, "Yes, you can, Auntie."

"Now come over here and give your Auntie a big hug." They embrace warmly. Her aunt looks her over and pokes Sheila's belly. "Did you eat?"

Sheila giggles, "Yes, I did. I went over to the 6978 Soul food restaurant close to the Celine African Hair Braiding salon."

"Oh, yes. I know that place well. Who told you about it? They really have excellent food."

"A friend," Sheila responds mysteriously.

Curious, Vivian asks, "What friend?"

Sheila rolls her eyes, "My friend, Travis."

"I didn't know you knew people here in Chicago." Her aunt looks surprised.

"No, Auntie, I don't. I met Travis when I was with Damien."

Her aunt relaxes a bit, "Okay, honey, as long as Damien knows him."

Unwilling to explain to her aunt that Damien really doesn't know Travis and has just seen him once, Sheila weasels her way out of the conversation. Standing up, she says, "Well, I'm going to go upstairs and take a shower then catch up on my Netflix series."

"Okay, honey. I'm going to sit out here for a while longer, then I think I'll call it an early night."

"Sounds like a plan," says Sheila as she heads inside and goes upstairs to her room.

Vivian Johnson picks up the phone to call Sharon and ensure that Damien and Tanya have gotten home safely. Vivian smiles when she hears her friend sounding just as tranquil as she feels. "Hello, sweetie. I just wanted to call and check on Tanya and Damien. Did they get home safely?" Vivian asks.

Sharon feels as if she's still floating and sounds like she's moments away from falling asleep, "Yes, they did, hon. They got back home about an hour ago. Next time you come over I'll have Tanya show you the outfit she purchased today to wear on *The Voice*. My baby is going to really shine on that stage."

Vivian smiles, her eyes glassy and her body warm from the wine, "I can't wait to see it."

"Damien says that they had a great time, and after they finished shopping, they went to Pearl's Kitchen over on Michigan Ave. for some soul food."

"That sounds like a great time, but I see that they decided not to go to yours and Damien's favorite place, Mother's Kitchen."

"Yes, child. Damien says that was Tanya's idea."

"How cute. It's so good that they were able to spend some time together."

"God is good," Sharon says, grateful for her loving children.

"Well, how's Damien feeling?"

Sharon lets out a sigh of relief. "He seems to be feeling much better than he did twenty-four hours ago, and that's definitely a good thing. And how about Sheila? How is she feeling?"

Vivian leans back in her chair and looks in the house to make sure Sheila's upstairs before answering, "She seems to be doing well. She just went upstairs to take a shower and catch up on her Netflix. You should see her braids. They look so good! I swear my baby could be a model, chile."

Sharon shakes her head. Smiling contently, she says, "God is great, what a wonderful day for everyone."

"Amen, Sharon. Amen. And seriously, honey, thank you for treating me to such an incredible and relaxing day."

"Oh, Viv, you're so welcome. You know better than anybody that we both deserved that. As always, it was lots of fun spending time with you today. But honey, that masseuse hit the spot earlier, and I have been needing some sleep since before we left RPM."

Sharon laughs with her friend, "Well, you have a good night, and we'll talk tomorrow."

"Okay, my dear. You too," Sharon smiles, and they both end the call.

Vivian, still in the backyard, leans back in her favorite lounge chair and sips her wine without a care in the world, exclaiming, "I'm living my best life today."

Chapter 19

Crazy in Love

It's a Thursday morning, and Damien is just waking up. Knowing instantly that he has football practice that day, he looks outside to check on the weather. It's pouring rain, so he reaches for his phone to check on the weather forecast for the day. Oddly enough, the forecast reads that the rain will stop shortly, and that it will actually be a nice and sunny day. Damien smiles. He's excited to get out and play some football with the boys. He checks his text messages to see that he has several calls and texts from Celeste.

The messages that Celeste left seemed urgent. After checking one of the many voicemails she left, it sounds like she had some good news for him. He feels relieved, unable to bear anymore heavy news for the rest of his teenage years.

Damien immediately dials Celeste's number. She answers impatiently, "Finally! Where have you been?"

Damien can only imagine her demeanor, knowing she would definitely be giving him the stank eye if she were there. He laughs at the thought. "My bad, my bad. I fell asleep early and didn't even realize the volume on my phone was down. But what's up, though? What's so important?"

Celeste sounds giddy with excitement, "Well, remember a few weeks ago, I told you I have friends everywhere? Well, Boo, I literally have a friend everywhere."

Damien readies himself for the news, figuring it's just the usual gossip he eventually will tune out. "Continue..."

Celeste paces back and forth in her room, feeling as if she would pop open with this juicy information. "So, I know you told me you love Sheila—or whatever—even though you've only known her for a short time. But I think what I have to tell you may change how you feel about her."

Damien sighs, tired of the conversation already, "Just go ahead, Celeste. Say what you have to say."

Celeste spills it all, "Okay, so see, what had happened was that I have a friend who works as a stylist at Celine African Hair Braiding. She told me that she had a client the other day named Sheila, and that she and Sheila got to talking. That's when Sheila mentioned to her that she's from New York visiting her aunt, and that she had met this guy that she likes a lot, and that they got intimate, and now it's a possibility that she may be pregnant."

Damien shakes his head, completely stunned by the way women tend to share their business with anyone who will listen.

"Then she said when Sheila left the shop, she saw her get into a car with a young man known in the neighborhood to be a big-time player, named Travis. I know Travis, and he's definitely a player. He tried to get with me not long ago."

Damien can't help but ask, "How do you know it's the same Sheila?"

"I know it's the same Sheila because my friend sent me a picture of her and Sheila and a picture of Sheila kissing Travis before getting into his car."

Damien sits up in his bed, feeling his heart race. "No way, can you please forward me the pictures?"

Celeste is one step ahead of him. "Sending them as we speak. Hold on."

A few seconds later, Damien receives a text, and his jaw drops when he sees the selfies of Tammi and Sheila at the salon. He scrolls down to a photo of Sheila hugging and kissing Travis, along with a picture of Sheila getting into Travis's car.

Damien is completely engulfed in the drama Celeste has eagerly brought to him, he asks, "Do you have a clearer picture of Travis?"

Celeste smiles hungrily, happy to know that things were coming together so beautifully—or rather, falling apart. "I sure do. Give me a second and I'll forward it to you, too."

When Damien receives the picture of Travis, he shouts through the phone, "No way! That's the guy she was exchanging numbers with at the convenience store. I can't believe that she keeps lying to me and telling me that I was the only one she was having sex with in Chicago."

Furious, Damien stands up and paces his room.

Celeste chimes in, "So, I believe this is proof that there's a possibility that another guy may be the father."

"Yeah, for sure. I'm definitely getting a DNA test," he declares. He sits in silence, scrolling through the picture in disbelief. But he reminds himself that he should've known better. "Thanks so much, Celeste, I owe you big time."

Celeste pats herself on the back, feeling proud of her detective work. "No problem, D. You know I love you, and after all that's what friends do for each other. But like I said, be careful! Because I have friends everywhere!"

"Well, I guess this is proof of that as well," Damien says. He's still in shock. Although he's feeling a little disheartened, Damien shakes off those down feelings.

Saying their goodbyes, Damien and Celeste hang up so they can go about their day.

Damien puts his phone down on the bed. Lying down and staring at the ceiling, Damien sighs. Realizing that aside from his connection with Sheila, this news could mean that he's a free man, Damien decides to confront Sheila, so he texts her.

Damien: I want a DNA test, ASAP. You been lying to me all this time. First u tell me that u weren't going to call that guy, Travis, from the store, then telling me I was the only person u had sex with in Chicago. Now ur telling me that I'm the father of your baby! U know, I thought u were mad cool; and although I don't want any children right now, I had mad love for you. But I see ur nothing but a liar; and before u start lying to me again, I've attached some pictures for u to look at.

Sheila returns to her room and unties her braids after emerging from a refreshing shower. Hearing her phone chime several times,

Sheila grabs her towel and dashes into her room. Taking the phone off the charger, she sees the long text from Damien and thinks bitterly to herself, "Oh my God, what a moron, I can't believe the things he is saying to me." Seeing the pictures, she feels like her stomach will drop. 'How did he even get these pictures? Does he have someone following me? What a weirdo." She walks in circles around her room, rereading all of the harsh things he spat through the phone and begins to cry, just then Travis calls. Sheila wipes her eyes.

"Hello?" Her voice cracks slightly.

Travis feels relieved, though he can hear the pain in Sheila's voice. "Hey, I didn't hear from you last night so I'm calling to make sure that you got home safely." He pauses when he hears Sheila sniffling faintly. "Are you okay? You sound as if you're crying."

"No, I'm not." Sheila wipes her face again, trying to sound as if she's not crying. "I fell asleep early last night, and I was just about to text you that I arrived home safely. But then I noticed that I received several long, nasty texts from Damien calling me all sorts of names, and saying that I was lying to him all along. He even accused me of having sex with you and told me that he wants a DNA test immediately. He also said that he believes the baby is yours. Then to top that off, he sent me pictures of us at the salon, embracing and me kissing you by the car."

Travis is disgusted. "Nah, are you joking?"

"No," Sheila cries, unable to hold back her tears.

Concerned, Travis paces his room as he wonders how he can help Sheila.

"Was he following you?"

Sheila shrugs, feeling a little freaked out by Damien's behavior. "I don't know. I don't know how he got these pictures. It's really weird."

Travis shakes his head. "Forward me the texts and the photos."

While texting Travis, Sheila unwittingly mutters to herself angrily, "I hope Damien loses his little four-year scholarship to Ohio State. Even better, I wish he were dead."

Travis pauses and looks over the messages. In a low voice, he mentions something to Sheila, "If you really want that, I can make it happen."

Sheila is half listening, still wrapped up in her rage. Out of anger, she continues, "I can't stand him." Then she realizes what Travis was telling her. "You'd really do that for me?" she asks.

Travis looks out the window, looking somber and serious. "Yeah, I would do anything for you. Just give me the word."

Sheila thinks to herself and assumes that Travis is just talking and trying to impress her. She doesn't think that this was something he'd ever really do. Playing along, Sheila says, "Yeah, that's what I want."

"Then consider him dead."

Ignoring Travis's threat against Damien's life, Sheila starts crying again.

"I have to go. I'll talk to you later."

She hangs up before Travis says, "I love you."

Travis stays in the window for a while, listening to the sirens, passing cars, people talking, and sounds of the summer singing below him. He closes the curtain angrily.

Realizing he needs to calm down, Travis goes to the local basketball court to play a game of pickup with some of his friends from the neighborhood. He takes off his shirt, puts on a red T-shirt, and removes his pants to reveal basketball shorts underneath.

After the game, Travis is sitting on a bench, taking a long sip from a water bottle. His friend, Raymond, sits beside him. Travis shares his frustrations about Damien when Raymond, looking curious, interrupts Travis, "I think I know the Damien you're talking about. He's the kid that plays on the Morgan Park Stallions football team."

Travis's eyes bug out as he makes the connection, "Yeah, that's got to be the same dude."

Raymond sits there for a moment and turns to Travis, "He's also the same kid that received a four-year scholarship to attend Ohio State."

Travis nods in agreement, finishing his bottle of water. "Yeah, I definitely know him. Hold on," Raymond takes his phone out of his pocket, goes to his Instagram, and shows Travis a picture of Damien along with their mutual friend, Jarvis, standing on the football field together. "Is this the Damien you talking about?" he asks.

Travis looks at the picture with disgust, "Yeah, that's the deadbeat." He tosses the water bottle into a distant recycling bin.

Raymond looks confused, "Well, from what I hear, he's a cool kid. And all the girls love him." Checking the time on his phone, he stands up and grabs his bag. "Well. I have to go. I promised Jarvis that I'd pick him up after practice and give him a ride to his girl, Theresa's, house. If you want, you can ride with me. Damien will probably still be at the practice field," he suggests.

"Nah, I'm good. I'll get with you later." They execute their special hand shake and go in opposite directions.

Suddenly, Travis looks back and shouts at Raymond, "Yo, what time is practice over?"

Raymond yells back, "Usually at seven."

Travis gives him a thumbs up symbol. "Good looking out." He continues walking back toward his house.

As he unlocks the front door, Travis decides to confront Damien that night as he's leaving football practice. He quickly changes his clothes and checks the time. Seeing that it's just before six-thirty, Travis hurries down the stairs, out the door to his car, and drives to the Morgan Park Stallions' practice field.

Travis pulls up about two blocks away from the practice field. He sits there calmly, scanning the crowd of teenage faces for Damien. Travis looks into his rearview mirror and sees a group of football players walking in his direction. Once they get near his car, Travis, wearing a mask, rolls his tinted window down slowly. The players seem on edge; some of them walk away quickly while others stay behind, trying to check Travis out. He keeps his mask on and proceeds to politely ask one of the unsuspecting players a question, "Yo, have you seen Damien?"

One of Damien's teammates answers before anyone can stop him, "Yeah, over there." He points in Damien's direction. Damien is standing on the sidewalk a little less than a block away and appears to be distracted by his phone.

Travis smiles underneath his mask, "Oh, word. I see him, thanks."

Travis checks his black mask, making sure he's well covered. He then creeps up the block slowly with the window still rolled down. "Yo, Damien!"

Damien turns to see who's calling him and realizes there's a car in front of him.

Before he can speak, Travis pulls out a 45-caliber gun and immediately fires three bullets in Damien's direction. The last thing Damien hears through the gunfire is Travis's eerie words, "These bullets are from me, Sheila, and your unborn baby."

Damien falls into the street. His teammates, hearing the gunshots, run to Damien just as Travis pulls off. Damien is losing consciousness, and he can hear a muddle of voices calling out for him and asking him if he's okay. Some of his other teammates attempt to chase down the car to get its license plate number.

The scene quickly becomes chaotic. Everyone stands around with their phones out. Several people call 911, while others videotape the scene around them. The football players kneel over Damien, using their football jerseys to try and stop the blood pouring from his wounds. Despite all of the action, the sounds of crying, wailing teens echo throughout the practice field. The streetlights flicker on overhead, and his friends all stay by Damien's side, encouraging him and lifting him in prayer. Damien hears their loving words before fading out, "We are here with you, Damien. You are a Morgan Park Stallion, man! We love you, and we won't let you die."

Moments later, the sounds of crying and sniffling people are drowned out by wailing police sirens. Police surround the practice field. A few ambulances follow close behind. Police officers and EMTs rush out of their cars and kneel over Damien to administer help. The remaining officers start securing the scene with yellow tape and try talking to any remaining onlookers. Then an intimidating officer yells into the crowd, "Has anyone else been shot or injured?"

Several people shake their heads, and a distant voice cries out, "No, just help Damien, please!"

Then the officer asks another question of the disgruntled crowd, "Did anyone see the shooter?"

At first, everyone says no. But then, one of Damien's teammates steps forward, saying, "I was filming some of my teammates goofing around just before the shooting. I may have captured the whole thing on my phone."

The officer asks to see the video. As the officer watches, a small crowd hovers by trying to get a glimpse of the video. The officer notices a Blue BMW with white stripes, tinted windows, and vanity plates that read, "That's What's Up," slowly pull up beside Damien. Then he sees Damien quickly turn and suddenly fall to the ground. The tinted windows make it very difficult to get a clear view of the shooter.

The car was very distinct, so the officer immediately calls in the description of the vehicle and the direction in which it was traveling. He turns back to Damien's teammate and tells him that he will have to confiscate his phone. The teammate looks pretty disappointed about giving his phone up indefinitely, he asks, "Can I just email or text you the video?"

The officer shakes his head, "I'm sorry, what you have on your phone is now considered evidence, and we need to make sure we have our forensics unit take the video directly off your phone. You can stop by and pick your phone up at State Street station before the end of the day tomorrow."

Although Damien's teammate is willing to cooperate, he certainly doesn't want to give up his phone. But it's for Damien's sake, and if he can help identify his shooter, then anything is worth it. After exchanging information with the officer, he hands the officer his phone.

Suddenly, an unmarked dark blue Ford pulls up to the scene, and two distinguished men head right over to the ambulance where Damien receives care. One of the men introduces himself as Detective Williams. Then he introduces his partner as Detective Matthews. "Who is our victim tonight?" Detective Williams asks, taking out a notepad.

One of the EMTs stands up as the other remains with Damien, he shouts, "His name is Damien Jackson, and he's alive. He's in very serious condition with a lot of blood loss."

The detective scribbles the information, he asks, "How many times was Damien shot?"

The same EMT responds, "We've found three gunshot wounds. It looks as if he's been shot at least three times."

"Where are you taking him?" Detective Williams asks, still writing in his notepad.

The EMTs prepare to drive off. One EMT remains with Damien while the one who's been corresponding with the detective turns to face him, "We will be taking him to Chicago Medical Center." The EMT then turns to open the driver side door and hops in the seat. Sirens blaring, they rush Damien to Chicago Medical Center.

The detectives stand around, going over everything and comparing notes. All of the officers on the scene know Detective Williams and his colleague, Detective Matthews, so there is no need for a formal introduction. The officers explain to Detective Williams what they saw when they arrived on the scene. They show him the three shells they have confiscated from the scene. The detective eyes the shells, gauging that they were from a. 45-caliber weapon that is yet to be confiscated. The Detective Williams pats the nearest officer on the back, "Great job, everyone."

Then an officer points indiscreetly toward Damien's teammate that he spoke to earlier, "I confiscated a phone from that gentleman. The young man captured the whole shooting on video."

The detective is impressed, "Did you bag and tag it?"

"Yes sir, I did." The officer hands the teen's phone to Detective Williams, who hands the phone over to Detective Matthews. "Please take this to the car, Matthews."

"Thank you all for your good work. Let's clean this up," Detective Williams shouts as he joins the officers in their investigative search around the practice field.

The two detectives walk around the entire perimeter of the field before walking in the direction of a group of Damien's teammates standing in the middle of the street. As the detectives get closer, they pick up their pace, realizing that several of them are covered in Damien's blood.

Detective Williams walks up to the group hurriedly. "I'm Detective Williams and this is my partner, Detective Matthews. Did anyone see the shooter?"

Looking at the detective with blank, terrorized stares, everyone shakes their heads no. Disturbed by the sight of these poor scared kids standing before him, Detective Matthews turns away.

Detective Williams follows up with more questions, jotting the answers in his notepad, "Is there any reason that someone would want to shoot Damien?"

They all shake their heads no. Another young man elaborates, "Everyone who knows Damien loves him and would never want to harm him."

Detective Williams continues taking notes. "Did Damien have a girlfriend?"

Someone answers, "No but, he definitely had plenty of female friends." Some of the kids laugh, feeling grateful for a chance to lighten the experience they've just had.

On a mission to find the shooter, Detective Williams takes copious notes.

"Are there any girls that he hung around with more than others?"

Chris, Damien's teammate and friend, has been silent and numb until this moment. He pipes up, "Yeah, this girl, Celeste, and this new chick visiting from New York named Sheila."

Detectives Williams and Matthews face Chris, "Do you happen to have Celeste's or Sheila's number?"

Chris shakes his head, "I don't, but I do have Damien's mother's and sister's numbers. They should know. Would you like one of their numbers, instead?"

Grateful to be heading in the right direction, Detective Williams says, "Yes, please. Thank you, young man." Detective Matthews takes the information down as Detective Williams addresses the uneasy crowd. He makes eye contact with each of them as the sun sets in the distance. "I'm very, very sorry about what happened to your teammate and friend. Thanks for your cooperation, and I promise you that we will find the shooter. If any of you would like to go to the hospital, let one of us know and we will help you get there. Here is our information in case you need or hear anything else."

The crowd at the scene continues growing as several local news station vans pull up one by one. The crowd parts for Monica, a well-known reporter for 7 News Chicago as she quickly exits her van and immediately goes live. She flies over to Damien's teammates and shoots them with questions, "So, what is the name of the player who was shot?" She blurts out, failing to realize that Damien's family has not yet been notified. Someone says, "Our friend's name is Damien Jackson."

Monica goes on to ask, "Is that same Damien Jackson who is the popular Morgan Park Stallions player that recently received a four-year football scholarship to Ohio State?"

The teammates crowd in front of the camera talking all over each other. "Yeah, that's him," someone says.

"Is there anything you would like to say to the shooter?" Monica holds the mic in the teammates' direction.

Coming to the front, Chris grips the mic angrily, fighting back tears, "Yeah, I would. I would like to say that this was truly a senseless shooting. My teammate and friend, Damien Jackson, represents all that is good about our city, our school, and our team. I feel that the politicians in Chicago, including our mayor, are not doing enough to get weapons off our streets. Too many people, young and old, have been seriously injured or even killed due to this senseless gun violence." Chris wipes the angry, hot tears that have spilled down his cheeks. He remains confident and articulate in his message, "We have to do something now. I mean today. We've got to show more love and compassion than evil and hate." Finished speaking, Chris hands Monica the mic and starts to leave. The remaining onlookers applaud and chant: "Damien Strong! Stop the violence! Stop the violence! Damien Strong!"

Sharon lies in bed, grateful that there are leftovers for whenever the kids get hungry. She hears Tanya practicing for *The Voice* in her room while they wait for Damien to come home. She turns to watch the evening news when suddenly there's a breaking news flash. She rolls her eyes, wondering what could possibly be going wrong in the city now.

"Lord have mercy, these kids with this violence today. Lord help them." She sits up abruptly when she sees that there has been a shooting of a popular local Morgan Park Stallions football player who has been rushed to Chicago Medical Center. The news flash is followed by Monica's interview with the Morgan Park Stallion teammates.

Holding her hand over her heart, Sharon screams, "Tanya! Tanya, baby, Damien has been shot! Oh, please come here. Hurry, hurry!"

Tanya runs frantically into her mother's room and sees her crying uncontrollably.

Tanya looks horrified, "What's going on!?"

Sharon begins hyperventilating. Unable to get the words out of her mouth, she points to the television that's mounted on the wall. Tanya reads the news ticker detailing the shooting at the bottom of the screen. It reads:

"A member of the Morgan Park Stallions football team has been shot and remains in critical condition. The player has been identified as Damien Jackson, who is being treated for multiple gunshot wounds at Chicago Medical."

Tanya breaks down and joins her mom in a tight huddle on the bed. Their mom is inconsolable, "They shot my Damien, they shot my Damien! Who could have done this!?"

Tanya squeezes her mom as they cry in each other's arms. Tanya, still in denial, grabs her phone and dials Damien's number. There's no answer. Tanya, becoming almost angry, decides to dial Chris's number.

Chris sits crouched by a tree, crying alone while the crowd and the reporters remain active in the distance. Feeling his phone buzzing, he sees Tanya's name pop up. They greet each other with sniffles and tears.

"Is it true?" Tanya asks, sobbing, "Did someone shoot my brother!?"

"Yeah. I'm so sorry I didn't call you. It's just been so chaotic here," Chris says while trying to fight the tears.

"Is he okay?" Tanya sounds hopeful.

Chris sounds drained, "I'm not sure. To be honest with you, he didn't look too good when they put him in the ambulance. The whole football team is heading to the hospital now."

Tanya, still crying, nods her head, "Okay, thank you. Me and my mom are on our way to Chicago Medical. That is where they've taken him, right?" They couldn't afford to go to the wrong hospital.

"Yeah, that's what I'm hearing."

Tanya sniffles, "Thanks, I'll see you soon."

Meanwhile, Sharon has since gotten up and grabbed her keys, "I'm heading to the car now, Tanya. Let's go! Let's go!"

Tanya, still crying, runs downstairs. Suddenly realizing that she has to be strong for her mom, she takes a deep breath and stands in the doorway for a brief moment. This is the same doorway where she got the news of her father's passing. But something tells her this time is different. She regains her composure and heads for the car. "Mom, Damien is going to be okay," she says with as much confidence as she can muster.

Her mom turns the key and puts her foot on the gas. "Yeah, I know. I prayed while you were on the phone." They drive for a while before her mom whispers, "Please God, hear my prayer."

As they approach the hospital, their mom asks Tanya to call Vivian and let her know what happened, "Please tell her to meet us at the hospital, if she can."

"Yes, Mom," Tanya says, dialing Vivian's number. It goes straight to voicemail, so she leaves a message, "Hey Mrs. Johnson, Damien..." Her voice trails off as she bursts into tears, "Damien has just been shot. We are heading to Chicago Medical Center. Please meet us there." She hangs up and takes a deep breath, exhaling loudly as Sharon rubs her knee. Tanya puts an arm on her mom's shoulder as they approach the hospital.

Chapter 20

The Power of Love and Prayer

When Sharon and Tanya arrive at the Chicago Medical Center, they race to the reception area. Ignoring the people idling near the desk, Sharon hurriedly introduces herself, "Hello, I'm Sharon Jackson. My son, Damien Jackson, was shot earlier tonight and was brought here. Where is he?"

The security officer at the front desk looks up at Sharon with very little emotion and says, "Mrs. Jackson, I'm going to need you to file a few papers before you can see your son."

Sharon's eyes nearly pop out of her head, "I don't care about your papers. My son could be dying and you're asking me about some paperwork? Where is my son? My son has been shot, and I need to see him right now."

The security officer loses all color from his face. He quickly stands up and points toward the elevators down the hall, "Ma'am, your son is on the fifth floor. Forgive my ignorance. You can file the papers later since this is an urgent matter."

"Thank you," Tanya says as Sharon rushes past them both to get on the elevator. Tanya runs to catch up.

On the elevator to the fifth floor, Sharon and Tanya continue praying and holding each other. They both wonder who could have done such an evil thing.

Once the elevator doors finally open, Sharon and Tanya are greeted by Damien's teammates sitting in the waiting area. Many of them stand, recognizing Damien's mom as well as Tanya, who runs up to them. Everyone stands crying and embracing each other as Chris makes his way to them. He puts an arm on Sharon's shoulder, saying, "Good evening, Mrs. Jackson. Come with me. I'll walk you over to the nurse's station."

Once at the nurse's station, Chris introduces Sharon and Tanya as Damien's family. Sharon leans on the desk as she talks to the nurse.

"How's my son? Is he okay?" Tears stream down her face.

The nurse tries to muster a smile. Despite having seen so many crying mothers in Mrs. Jackson's situation, she still doesn't know how to alleviate their unbearable pain.

"The doctors are working on him now. Your son has been shot three times and has lost a lot of blood. The doctors will be out to talk with you as soon as they get him out of the operating room."

Sharon looks disheveled. Filled with so many raging emotions, all she can do is to lean on the wall and feel its coolness against her skin. The nurse follows up with another question in a calm tone so as not to overwhelm her, "Ms. Jackson, will you be able to answer some important questions for us regarding your son? These questions are very crucial for Damien's treatment."

Sharon nods fervently, "Yes, and my daughter, Tanya, can help me."

The nurse stands up and points to three chairs in a quieter part of the waiting area. "Let's sit over here," she suggests. Grabbing a box of tissues, Sharon follows the nurse and Tanya to the quieter area with a clipboard in hand.

She begins her questioning as soon as she's seated, "I'll start by asking if Damien has medical insurance?"

"Yes, we all do, and we have the best, so we want the best doctors working on Damien. Do you understand?" Sharon asks rather harshly.

The nurse is unmoved by her demeanor, knowing that it is just a natural response to something as heinous as this.

"Yes, I do. Absolutely. Doctor Thompson is the operating doctor, and he and his assistant, Doctor Miller, are tending to your son as we speak. You can rest assured that your son is getting only the best care Chicago has to offer," she smiles tiredly.

"Thanks," Sharon mutters. Tanya rubs her mother's tense back as she leans forward in the chair, resting her forehead in her hands.

Celeste, who was on the phone with Damien when he got shot, is frantic and desperately trying to find out what went down. Celeste nervously dials Tanya's number.

Tanya, still rubbing her mother's back, feels her phone buzz and pulls it out to see that it's Celeste calling. She picks up in a somber tone, "Celeste, Damien has been shot."

Celeste gasps, "So, it's true, oh my God! No, he's not dead, please tell me he's not dead."

"No, but he's in critical condition," Tanya informs her.

Celeste's voice becomes shaky, "Tanya, I was on the phone with Damien when he got shot."

Tanya stands up, "You were!?"

"Yes, he had just called me, and we were making arrangements to meet up to get some ice cream."

Tanya remains silent. Stricken by the innocence of her big brother, she wonders how could anyone do this to him.

Celeste becomes frantic, "Oh my God, what hospital are y'all at?" Hurriedly, she gathers up her things.

Tanya looks out the window at the bustling street below. The glow of the racing headlights and the buildings and the streetlights blend into a haze as more tears fall silently from her eyes. "He's here at Chicago Medical Center," she replies.

Celeste wishes she could hug Tanya but she settles for talking, "How's your mom?"

"She's in terrible shape, Celeste. This is all so terrible," she cries.

"I'll be there soon, little sis," says Celeste,

"Everyone is here: the Morgan Park Stallions, their coaches, and some of our neighbors."

"Wow, I promise I'll be there soon," Celeste says her goodbyes and heads out the door.

She runs outside where an Uber driver is waiting, she almost forgets to confirm the license plate before hopping in the car. Once she confirms, she slams the door shut.

Meanwhile, Sheila is in her room watching Netflix. Unaware of the tragedy that has just occurred, Sheila pauses her show to run downstairs and get something to drink. She quickly looks at her phone and realizes that she has received an eerie text from Travis.

Travis: It's been done.

Sheila: What's been done???

Travis. Damien is gone.

Sheila. Nah, you buggin.

Travis: Go turn on the news.

<He adds three handgun emojis.>

Travis: I did it for you.

Sheila runs to the television. Fumbling with the remote, she searches anxiously for the channel, ABC Chicago Seven News. She's greeted by a breaking news flash that reads across the screen: "A young man and star member of the Morgan Park Stallions football team has been shot three times on his way home from football practice. He is in critical condition. The police are still searching for a male shooter. Although the victim has not been confirmed, we are learning from his teammates that his name is Damien Jackson, and the shooter is driving a blue BMW with white stripes, tinted windows, and vanity plates that read 'That's What's Up.'"

Sheila screams and drops the remote to the floor, which lands with a thud, "Oh no, oh my God! Oh my God!" Sheila recognizes several of Damien's teammates she met at the Block Mall. They are all visibly shaken, standing there in the blinding lights of the latest, tragic news report. There were clips of some teammates and others speaking out and shouting: "Stop the gun violence!" and "We need to stop the gun violence in the city today, not tomorrow."

The final clip before the weather is of one showing everyone chanting Damien Strong as they disperse.

Sheila can barely see the screen through the blur of tears, but she manages to text Travis.

Sheila: I thought you were joking.

Travis: I asked if you really wanted him dead and you said yes.

Sheila: But Travis, I was mad. I just thought you were joking, I just thought you were trying to make me feel better. Travis I was just mad I didn't mean it! What have you done?

Travis: I did it for you. I love you. I did it for us so that we can be together. I'll take care of the baby and it can just be us three.

Sheila: No Travis, that's not what I wanted. I just only really met you today. How can you say you love me?

Travis: Well, let's put it this way, I have mad feelings for you and that's what's up. Where are you now? I really need to see you.

Sheila: I can't see you right now.

Travis: Then when?

Sheila: I don't know Travis! I don't know.

Sheila tosses her phone into a pile of clothes, flops onto the bed, and sobs into her pillow.

Returning home, Vivian calls out for Sheila, "Sheila, sweetie. You awake?"

Hearing her aunt coming home from her hair appointment, Sheila runs down the stairs and into her aunt's arms, crying inconsolably.

Sharon is taken aback and alarmed by Sheila's behavior. "What's wrong, baby? What's wrong?"

"Auntie, something really terrible has happened," Sheila cries.

"What is it sweetie!? Tell me."

A sobbing Sheila says, "Damien got shot and he's in critical condition at Chicago Medical Center."

Vivian leans back and clutches her chest, "No, that can't be true! How did you hear this? Did Sharon or Tanya call you?"

Sheila answers in a heavy tone, "It's all over the news and social media."

Still in denial, Vivian picks up her phone to find that she has a new voice message from Tanya. Listening to it, Vivian immediately starts crying, her hands shaking as she uses one to cover her mouth before she screams in horror. She stumbles back to the couch and immediately calls her dear friend Sharon.

Sharon sits staring blankly at the neutral toned hospital wall—the same one where she sat when her husband passed. Sharon stands up straight and looks to the sky. "Please don't take my baby boy from us, too, God. And honey, please watch out for our son. Dear Lord, we need you."

Covered in prayer, Sharon sees her phone light up on the chair. Realizing that it's Vivian calling, Sharon rushes to answer the phone. Both are crying as they talk. Sharon is as relieved as she could possibly be, but the tears continue to flow.

She picks up and cuts straight to the point, "Damien has been shot several times and they aren't sure if he will make it, Viv."

"Lord, help us," Vivian cries, "Lord help us!" They continue crying and consoling each other.

"He'll make it. He's a strong young man, and God's not done with him yet," Vivian asserts. Excusing her absence at the hospital, Vivian says, "I'm just getting in now. I was at the hairdresser, and my phone died. I left the charger at home again. I saw Sheila crying and talking about Damien, then I just heard Tanya's message." Her voice breaks as she lets out a deep, heavy sob.

Sharon holds her hand over her mouth as she sits in the plastic hospital chair, praying for the best outcome for her son.

Vivian goes on to say, "I can't understand why someone would shoot Damien."

In a gruff voice, Sharon replies, "No one can."

Vivian, at a loss for words, gathers her things and runs to the car, taking her portable charger with her, "I'm getting in the car now and heading to the hospital. Which one are you at?"

"We're at Chicago Medical Center. Please hurry, Vivian, I don't know what I will do if he doesn't make it."

Vivian, unwavering in her faith, shakes her head, "We won't even start thinking like that, Sharon. God is not done with that boy. I'll be there shortly, and I'll call pastor Chisholm and our prayer group so they can begin praying for Damien."

Sharon cries, "Thank you so much." Tanya returns to her side and continues rubbing her back.

"I love you all, and I'll see you soon," Vivian promises.

They hang up, and Vivian yells upstairs to Sheila, "I'm going to the hospital to be with the Jacksons right now. Are you coming?"

"No," Sheila says as she lies face down in a pool of her own tears, "No."

Her aunt frowns as she hears and feels Sheila's pain echoing down the stairs. "Are you going to be okay, sweetie?"

"Yes, I'll be okay. I've already caused enough trouble. You just go be with Mrs. Jackson and Tanya, but please keep me updated. And please let Mrs. Jackson know that I'm so very sorry for what happened to Damien. I'm so, so sorry," Sheila pleads, crying louder as she throws herself on the bed.

Just as Vivian turns to lock the door, something tells her to go back inside. Her voice takes on a somber tone, "Sheila, you don't have anything to do with Damien being shot, right? Please tell me that you have nothing to do with this."

Sheila presses the pillow to her ears, wishing her aunt would just go. "I can't. I truly think he may have gotten shot because of me," she confesses.

"What are you saying, Sheila?" Her aunt's eyes fly open, and her heart pounds in her chest as she flies upstairs and shoves Sheila's door wide open.

"I'll have to explain to you later, Auntie. I really can't do this right now." Sheila looks broken. Vivian goes over to her niece and rubs her shoulder.

"Well, we'll definitely have to talk more about this when I get home. Don't say anything to anyone. And I mean no one," Vivian says emphatically.

"I won't."

Vivian leaves the room, and Sheila lies sobbing in her bed. She hears her aunt's heels click and clack down the stairs, listens to the door slamming shut, and hears her aunt's car start and pull off in the direction of the hospital. Sheila turns and looks up at the ceiling, muttering a gentle prayer before drifting into a tear-stained sleep.

Meanwhile, Travis is going crazy texting Sheila back-to-back. Sheila has silenced her phone so she won't have to see his texts. Disturbed by the day's events, Sheila tosses and turns in her light sleep. Travis then texts Sheila in anger and confusion.

Travis: Yo, if you don't want what happen to Damien to happen to you, you need to text me back right away.

Sheila wakes up shortly after Travis sends his cryptic texts. She reads through every one that he sent very slowly. She's terrified of this dude and what he could truly be capable of doing. Reluctantly, she texts back.

Sheila: I'm with my Auntie. I can't text you now. I'll text you later.

Travis: Ok, but don't forget.

<Travis sends a heart and kiss emoji.>

Sheila throws her phone on the bed and goes downstairs for a cool drink. She sends up a prayer, thanking God that she didn't let Travis bring her home the other night.

By the time Vivian reaches the hospital, she is breathing heavily. She sees Tanya standing by the front entrance talking on her phone as she stares out the window. As soon as Tanya looks up, she sees Vivian. Tanya ends her call, promising to keep her friend updated. Tanya puts her phone away and runs over to Vivian with open arms. She starts crying, "Thank you for coming, Mrs. Johnson."

Vivian Johnson squeezes her best friend's baby as if she's her own. "I'm so sorry, Tanya. What a terrible tragedy. Who could have done such a thing? How is Damien?"

Releasing from their long, heartfelt embrace, Tanya wipes her eyes. "All we know is that he's in critical condition and the doctors are operating on him now."

Vivian puts a hand on Tanya's shoulder as they walk toward the elevators together. "I called Pastor Chisholm and told him to inform our prayer group. As sad as all of this has been, I truly believe that's he's going to come through all right," Vivian declares, "We truly serve an awesome and powerful God, and he always makes a way. Damien has always been in his right spirit, and whoever did this to him clearly was not aligned with God. They'll get theirs, baby, believe that."

"Amen. Thank you so much for all of your prayers," Tanya replies. "My mom said she felt he would be okay, too. That does make me feel a lot better," Tanya smiles halfheartedly.

They step into the elevator. "You're welcome, baby. You know God got us."

As they're the only ones in the elevator, Tanya turns to Vivian to prepare her for the scene upstairs, "Mom is in bad shape. No one can wrap their heads around why anyone would try to kill Damien."

The elevator rises to the fifth floor, where it seems that half of Chicago is awaiting news about Damien. Tanya begins to cry again.

Vivian holds Tanya's hands and caresses them. "It's gonna be okay, honey. We're going to get through this as a family," Vivian assures. Suddenly, the elevator dings, and the doors fly open as they reach the fifth floor. Vivian and Tanya make their way to the waiting room.

As if by a sixth sense, Sharon looks up and spots Vivian walking in with her daughter. She runs up to Vivian and hugs her, then reaches her hand for Tanya to join. They are all overcome with emotion.

"My son. Someone shot my son," Sharon cries, "I haven't been able to answer any of these phone calls coming in. I just can't believe this could happen to my baby."

Tanya hands her mom a tissue, which Sharon graciously accepts.

Dabbing at her tear-stained face, Sharon says, "Thank you dear." Then she blows her nose and takes a deep breath, and looking deeply into her daughter's loving eyes, Sharon says, "I am just so grateful for you—for both you and Damien. But right now, baby, I'm so proud of how strong you are being for yourself and truly for all of us. What an example." Sharon hugs her daughter tenderly.

"Thanks. After all, we are Jackson Strong!" Tanya says.

For the first time that night, Sharon flashes a genuine smile, "Yes, we are, sweetheart."

They squeeze each other again. Then her mom turns to Vivian, feeling a little more hopeful.

"And the nurse did say that they have the best doctors working on him. They should be updating us any minute now."

Vivian, Sharon, and Tanya stand holding each other. They begin to hum and pray. The entire room joins in, forming a powerful symphony to uplift Damien and all of Chicago in love and healing.

Something in the air shines and glitters throughout the room, giving everyone a sense of hope.

"We got a lot of people praying for Damien tonight, y'all," Vivian says.

Suddenly, Sharon looks to her right, and notices two men in white coats and a nurse walking in her direction. "Oh, this is it, Viv," Sharon says as she squeezes Tanya and Vivian's hands with all her might.

The doctors stand a few feet from Sharon, one asks, "Which one of you ladies is Damien's mom?"

Sharon walks toward them, "I am. Where is he?"

The doctor faces her with somewhat of a blank stare, but the other two doctors seem hopeful despite being tired from their intense work. "Well, Mrs. Jackson, I'm Doctor Thompson, the operating doctor, and this is Doctor Miller to my left, and to my right is your son's nurse, Ms. Roberts. All three of us will be taking care of Damien during his stay here at Chicago Medical Center."

Sharon's eyes widen passionately, "Did you just say during my son's stay here at the hospital?"

The lead doctor smiles. Grateful to be able to see the smile on Damien's mother's face, he says, "Yes ma'am."

"So you're telling me he's alive?"

"Yes, Mrs. Jackson. Your son Damien is alive." The crowd around them claps and rejoices.

"Thank you, Jesus." Sharon jumps around with Tanya and Vivian, then they stand and cry tears of joy. Overcome with joy, the crowd joins in a big group hug as Damien's teammates high-five and embrace each other.

"Is it okay if we talk here or would you like me to find a room where we can talk in private?" Dr. Thompson asks.

Noticeably shaken, Sharon says, "No, it's all right, you can speak with me here. This here is my family, so I don't mind them hearing what you have to say. Thank you for asking, though, Doctor."

Dr. Thompson steps forward. "Okay, Sharon, as you already know, your son is alive. To add to that good news, the operation was a complete success."

Sharon puts her trembling hand over her heart. "Oh, thank you, Jesus. Thank you, Jesus for watching over my son." She smiles and thanks the operating team. Reaching for their hands in deep gratitude, she says, "And thank you to both of you incredible doctors as well as to Nurse Roberts."

Doctor Thompson continues, "Damien was shot three times. Twice in the right shoulder and once in his right torso. Fortunately, no bones or main organs were struck. However, Damien did lose a lot of blood, and will need to stay with us at least two to three months so that we can keep a close eye on his vitals." The doctor gives a half smile, knowing this will still pose challenges to the family moving forward. "Also, I understand that Damien plays on his high school football team. Is that true?"

Tanya proudly pipes in, "Yes, he plays wide receiver for the Morgan Park Stallions."

Doctor Thompson looks at Damien's proud little sister and smiles. "Well, sadly, I don't see him playing football this season. But with lots of hard work and dedication through his rehabilitation process, he can definitely return to the game in a year if not sooner." He continues, filling the family with hope and possibility, "I know for a fact that Chicago has some of the best rehab hospitals in the country. So again, with lots of hard work, commitment, and support from his large and loving support system, Damien should make a full recovery in no time."

Despite the upcoming challenges, Sharon is beyond grateful that her son is still with them. She beams as she clasps her hands together in front of her chest.

"Thank you so much. That is fantastic news. When can we see him?"

"Damien is still under heavy anesthesia. He should be waking up in a couple of hours," Nurse Roberts responds.

Dr. Thompson adds, "I can imagine how badly you want to see your son, but it is my recommendation that you let him rest."

Nurse Roberts sees Tanya's and Sharon's faces fall again. She puts a hand on each of their shoulders and smiles gently, "If you'd like, I can put two cots in Damien's room, and you can spend the night."

They nod their heads readily. Vivian looks at the medical team with gratitude, knowing how much it will mean for all of them to be together when Damien wakes up.

Dr. Thompson looks up at the clock on the wall. "Well, I have to go now, but Nurse Roberts will share all of our information with you. Please feel free to contact me at any time."

Sharon gives both doctors and the nurse a large hug. "Thank you so very much, from the bottom of my heart. You all are saints," she says, truly grateful for them.

"We are all glad we could help," Dr. Thompson says as the medical team wave off her compliments, knowing that it was so much more than them that spared Damien's life.

Dr. Miller adds as the others turn to leave, "You know, the fact that Damien is in great shape really came into play. I just know he'll recover in no time."

As the two doctors leave the waiting area, Nurse Roberts puts a hand on Sharon's arm. "Why don't you all stay here while I have your room set up?" she offers.

"We'll be ready and waiting, Nurse Roberts. Thank you." Sharon is all smiles.

Sharon embraces her daughter and Vivian.

Vivian shakes her head in awe, "He did it again, baby. You see the power of prayer? Oh, do you see it!?"

Sharon and Tanya rejoice. Sharon rocks back and forth with tears of joy dotting her eyes as she clasps her hands again. "I sure do, Thank you Jesus. Thank you, God," Sharon shouts.

They hug and praise God for some time before Vivian pulls away to check the time. She remembers Sheila is still home and unaware that Damien is okay. She turns to Sharon, holding her hand, "I have to head back home, honey. Please keep me updated." She stands up and gathers her purse.

Sharon looks up at her departing friend. She and Tanya stand up and walk Vivian to the elevator. "We will," Sharon promises.

Sharon remembers Sheila as well, "How's Sheila doing?"

Vivian shakes her head, remembering her niece's hysteria. "She's devastated," says Vivian, "She was crying uncontrollably and said that she really needed to talk to me."

"Well, I'm sure she'll be relieved to hear that Damien's all right." They hug one more time. "Thank you so much for coming."

Vivian waves as the elevator doors open in front of her. "After all, that's what family's for." They share one last hug before Vivian scurries into the elevator. Sharon and Tanya return to the waiting area and open their phones to share the good news about Damien.

Chapter 21

More Confessions

Vivian exits the elevator and walks through the parking garage to her vehicle. She gets in and starts her drive back home, feeling much happier than she did when she left. But then her stomach drops as she braces herself for what Sheila has to say about her potential involvement in Damien's shooting. She turns up the volume on the radio and tries not to overwhelm herself with more worry. She's had more than her fair share for the rest of the year.

Pulling into the driveway, Vivian is surprised to see Sheila crouched in the front doorway. Vivian parks the car and before she can get out, Sheila runs to her. Vivian gets out of the car and faces her niece. "How's Damien? Is he still alive?" Sheila questions.

Her aunt looks at her coolly, she calmy replies, "Yes, he's still alive and he's expected to make a full recovery."

Sheila jumps around in the driveway, "Thank you. Oh, thank you, God!"

"Sheila, we need to go in the house and have a serious discussion. And I need you to tell me everything," Vivian says, looking at Sheila with a frozen gaze.

Sheila feels her face grow hot. "Okay." The two women go inside, locking the door behind them. Vivian kicks her shoes off and leaves them by the door. Sheila follows as her aunt and gets a cup of water. "Start talking," Vivian demands.

Sheila gulps and stammers, "Auntie, I told Travis that I hated Damien and wished that he was dead."

"Why would you say that, Sheila!?" Vivian practically slams the cup on the table.

"Because Damien was saying bad things about me and denying that he was the father of my baby, as well as suggesting several times that I should go and have an abortion." To solidify her case, Sheila takes out her phone and shows her aunt the nasty texts Damien sent a few hours before he was shot.

Although Vivian is completely disgusted with all of it, she remains quiet. Sheila continues, "When I told Travis that I wished Damien was dead, I didn't mean it. I was just angry." She shrugs. Sheila is shocked that so much has stemmed from her unbearable moment of anger.

Her aunt cuts her eyes at her niece. "First of all, Sheila, who is this Travis guy?" she questions.

Sheila comes clean, "He's someone I met on the first day I met Damien."

Her aunt sips her water slowly. "Does Damien know Travis?"

Sheila shakes her head, "Not really, Auntie. He's seen him round but he doesn't really know him."

Sharon is completely disturbed. "Well, go on." She rubs her head as if to prevent a migraine.

Sheila looks up, trying to remember where she left off, "Oh, so like I said, I told Travis that I wished Damien was dead and then this evening I received a text that said it was done."

Her aunt gives her niece a stern look, "What was done?"

"Damien was shot. Then he texts me to turn on the news. I turned on the news, and that is when I learned that Damien had actually been shot. I felt so terrible." Sheila starts crying, wiping her eyes so she can continue her story, "I never wanted anything bad to happen to Damien. I can't believe this happened."

Sharon ignores Sheila's tears. She raises an eyebrow, feeling very concerned about this Travis person. "When was the last time you heard from Travis?" she asks.

"About an hour ago, and he keeps texting me," Sheila answers, "I told him that I couldn't talk because I was busy with you. But then he said that if I didn't text him back, he'll make sure that what happened to Damien will happen to me."

Vivian grips the table, she shouts, "Oh my God, Sheila! What? Does he know where you live?"

Sheila shakes her head, "No."

"And do you know where he lives?"

Sheila shakes her head and looks down, "No."

"I just have to ask, have you ever been intimate with him?"

"Other than a few kisses on the cheek, no, I've never been intimate with him." Sheila looks at her aunt with pleading eyes, feeling a deep sense of fear and anxiety wash over her. "But he's been saying that he loves me and wants us to be together. And by us, he means the baby too."

Her aunt raises a brow, "How does he know you are pregnant?"

Sheila answers, "Because I told him about Damien wanting me to have an abortion."

Her aunt continues to rub her tired head. She responds in a disappointed voice, "Why do you keep making one bad decision after another? See how you've gotten yourself into this serious hot water, right after jumping into the pot just over a week ago."

Sheila hangs her head shamefully, "I know, Auntie. I'm really, really scared."

Vivian lifts up her niece's drooping head and gazes into her eyes, "You have every reason to be scared. I'll call my attorney tomorrow morning and ask him what he suggests that we do. Then I think it's about time I call your mother and explain it all to her."

Sheila reluctantly agrees, "I understand."

Her aunt yawns and shakes her head again, "Well, I'm getting tired after this long whirlwind of a day. Let's go upstairs and get some rest."

Sheila stands. "Okay, Auntie. I just feel so terrible for what happened to Damien."

"I know your own anguish will be enough of a lesson for you, but remember when I told you not to let your anger get the best of you? Do you see how far we can go and what can happen because of such fleeting emotions?"

Sheila nods in agreement.

Her aunt puts an arm on her shoulder. "We just need to continue to trust in God and that everything will be okay. Everything will continue to work out according to His plans even if they feel painful, scary, or hard. We just need to trust. Remember that."

Sheila sniffles. "Okay, Auntie. I will." She turns to go upstairs. Then she remembers something and turns to her aunt, who has gone to the sink to wash out her cup. "Can we at least hold off on calling my mother until after you've spoken to your attorney?"

Her aunt turns slightly, "Yes, we can definitely do that."

"Thanks, Auntie. And what should I do about Travis? He expects me to text or call him."

Vivian turns off the faucet and puts the cup in the dishrack to dry. "I think I have a plan. Let's try to buy some time. Text him and tell him that all is good, but you can't talk right now because of all the people around you. Tell him you'll try to meet up with him later tonight, then shut off your phone."

"Okay, Auntie. I'm so sorry for everything," she sighs.

Her aunt lets out a deep sigh as well, turning off the kitchen light. "I know you are, Sheila." They both go their rooms. Sheila spends most of the night tossing and turning as her conscience keeps her restless and awake. Vivian lays wide awake. She looks at the clock and decides to go back downstairs.

Vivian reaches for her phone and calls her attorney, Otis Bradley. He picks up on the second ring. "Hello, Otis, I hope all has been going well with you and your family. I know it's late but I have a bit of an emergency."

Otis chuckles politely, "Good evening, Mrs. Johnson. All is just fine, and I hope the same for you."

Vivian sighs, pacing her room expectantly. "That's great, but I wish I could say the same. I'm actually calling about a family crisis."

Otis sits down, ready to hear his client's detailed account. "Mhm, I'm all ears, Mrs. Johnson."

"I have my niece staying with me for the summer, and she got herself into some serious trouble which I need your advice on."

Otis is curious, "What kind of trouble, Mrs. Johnson? I hope you are okay and I'm so sorry to hear that."

Vivian smiles. "Yes, I'm okay, thank you," she says and goes on to detail Sheila's chaotic situation.

"Although it's late, all three of us should meet at the police station in one hour," Otis states flatly.

Vivian whimpers. Finally feeling tired after all that has transpired, she says, "Can we meet in the morning? We have been through a lot, and I'm extremely tired. I'm sure my niece is exhausted, too."

Feeling tired himself, Otis responds, "I'm sorry. But we can't put it off. Right now, we have leverage, and tomorrow, we may not. Plus, the sooner we go, the sooner we all can get to bed."

"I understand. After all, you are the attorney." Vivian readies herself to get off the phone before Otis interrupts her.

"Oh, and Mrs. Johnson, if you arrive at the police station before I do, please don't say anything to anyone—and I mean absolutely no one."

She promises, "I won't, and thank you, Otis, for your sense of urgency. You are the best."

Otis smiles warmly. "You're welcome. After all, you've always been like a mother to me. And just like parents should be there for their children, children should be there for their parents," he gushes.

Vivian smiles at his kind words. Having known him since he was in the crib and having taught him in school, she knows Otis and his family very well. "That is so sweet, and so true," Vivian says, "Thanks again, and I'll see you soon, baby."

"See you soon, Mrs. Johnson," Otis says, hanging up the phone and stepping into his dress shoes by the door.

Vivian goes upstairs and knocks on Sheila's door. Sheila sits up in the dark having barely been able to keep her eyes closed for more than thirty seconds. She hears her aunt whisper, "Can I come in?"

"Yes, Auntie." Sheila sits on the edge of her bed as her aunt walks into her bedroom.

"I just wanted to explain what my attorney suggested. Now, Attorney Otis Bradley has been my attorney for more than ten years and is known as one of the best attorneys in Chicago. He suggested that we all head down to the police station immediately while we still have leverage. Sheila, you will need to explain everything you know to the detectives. Do you understand?"

Feeling herself getting scared again, Sheila asks, "What will I have to do?"

Her aunt speaks in a calm voice, "Just repeat exactly what you told me to Attorney Bradley, and then to the detectives."

Sheila braces herself, "I can do that, Auntie. Let's go." She stands up and goes to the closet to find something quick to throw on.

Vivian walks toward the door. "Fantastic. I'll go fix us a quick snack and then we can head right out."

Vivian heads down to the kitchen and prepares a couple of turkey sandwiches with chips and two glasses of iced tea. Sheila comes downstairs ready to go. Her aunt hands her the bag with her snack. Snack in hand, Vivian turns off the lights and meets Sheila on the porch. She locks the door, and they get in the car to go to the police station.

Once at the police station, Vivian walks up to the officer at the front desk and smiles, "Excuse me, will it be okay if we wait in the lobby for our attorney?"

Still looking down at a newspaper, the officer replies, "That's okay. Who are you here to see?"

Vivian, remembering her attorney's careful advice says, "My attorney will explain when he arrives. He should be here in less than half an hour."

The officer nods, "I understand." Pointing down the hall, he says, "If you need to use the restroom, it's over in that direction."

Vivian thanks the officer and then turns to Sheila, who is standing by a bench.

"You have a seat there. I'm going to use the ladies' room. Remember, don't say anything to anyone. I'll be right back," Vivian says.

Sheila nods and sits as still as a statue.

While waiting, several officers pass by Sheila and ask if she needs any help. She just shakes her head each time, refusing to make much eye contact. Then a plain-clothes gentleman with two coffees stops by and looks at Sheila.

"Oh, hello, Pam. Are you waiting for your dad? I'll let him know that you're here."

Sheila looks at the officer as if he's crazy, "No, sir. My name is not Pam, and I don't even know my dad."

Feeling foolish, the officer's face reddens. "Oh, I'm so sorry. Well, I'm Detective Matthews, and you are truly the spitting image of my partner's daughter. His name is Detective Williams." Before leaving, he looks at Sheila. Still amazed by the resemblance, he asks, "Is there anything I can help you with?"

Sheila shakes her head, wishing she could just be left alone. "No, thank you," she says and yawns, "I'm just waiting for my aunt. She's in the restroom."

"Okay, have a great evening." Detective Matthews walks in the other direction, leaving Sheila in peace.

Detective Matthews goes upstairs to his office. Hands full, he uses his hip to open the door and pass his partner a steaming cup of coffee. Still amazed, he walks over to his desk and says, "You know, there's a young lady in the lobby that looks like she could be your daughter's twin."

Detective Williams looks intrigued, "No kidding? Well, what did she want?"

Detective Matthews has a puzzled look on his face. "I'm not quite sure. I asked if I could help her, and she said no. But her name is Sheila and she's waiting for her aunt to come back from the ladies' room."

Detective Williams stops before taking the next sip. Looking at his colleague over the rim of his cup, he asks, "Did you say her name was Sheila? Why does that name sound so familiar to me?" Detective Williams reaches for his notes and flips through them feverishly. He turns to Detective Matthews.

"Sheila is the girl from New York who was friends with Damien. There's only one reason why she would be here at this time."

Detective Williams picks up the phone and dials the front desk. He asks the officer who answers the phone if there is still a young woman sitting in the lobby.

The officer lazily spins in his chair to see Sheila sitting there as her aunt hurries back to her from the ladies' room. "She's sitting here with an older woman," the officer says.

"Great, I'll be right there." Both detectives get up and head to the lobby. As soon as Detective Williams lays eyes on Sheila, he is immediately reminded of his daughter. He tries not to seem to awestruck as he walks over to Vivian and Sheila. "Hello, I'm Detective Williams, and this is my partner, Detective Matthews. Is there anything we can help you with?"

"Not right now," Vivian says. Sitting next to Sheila as though she is guarding her, Vivian says, "We are waiting for our attorney."

Just as she finishes speaking, Attorney Otis Bradley walks in and greets Mrs. Johnson. In turn, Vivian introduces an overwhelmed Sheila to him. Attorney Bradley bends down next to Sheila and places a hand over hers. "It's nice to meet you, Sheila. I'm going to see to it that everything is going to be okay," he smiles weakly.

Sheila just looks at him as a flood of tears cascade down her tired face. Her aunt pulls out a tissue from her handbag and hands it to her niece. "Thanks, Auntie," Sheila says and blows her nose.

Detective Williams introduces himself to Attorney Bradley. "Now that your attorney is here, how can we help you?" Detective Williams asks. Attorney Bradley quickly reaches in his jacket pocket and pulls out two business cards. He hands one to each of the detectives.

"As I'm sure you have already heard, I am Attorney Otis Bradley, and I'm representing this young lady here." He puts his hand on Sheila's shoulder. "May I speak with the detective handling the Damien Jackson case?"

Detective Matthews raises an eyebrow and glances at Sheila. "Are you talking about the gentleman from the Morgan Park Stallions football team that was shot earlier this evening?" he asks.

Attorney Bradley nods, "Yes, that exact gentleman."

Detective Williams steps a little closer. "You are speaking with him directly. I'm the lead detective on the case along with my partner Detective Matthews."

Attorney Bradley adjusts his briefcase. "Well, we have some important information for you. I just need to speak to my client first. Is there a private place where we can talk?"

Gesturing and walking in the direction of the area, Detective Williams says, "Yes, why don't you all follow me upstairs and you can use my office."

Attorney Bradley nods and waits for the ladies to get ready to leave the lobby. "That will be just fine."

After a few minutes, they reach the office, and Detective Williams clears his desk. "Please make yourself at home. We will be right down the hall. Please let us know when you are ready to speak with us."

"We will. Thank you," Attorney Bradley says as the detectives exit the room. Sitting down at the desk, he gestures at the two seats before him. Vivian and Sheila sit down hastily. Attorney Bradley takes out his iPad and looks at Sheila while he waits for it to load, "How are you feeling?"

Sheila looks at him with pleading eyes. "I'm really nervous, but I'll be okay." She shrugs.

"That's understandable, but I'm going to need you to try and calm down as much as you possibly can. I'm going to have to ask you some very important questions, and I will need you to be completely honest with me. Do you understand?" He looks at her over the glow of his iPad.

"Yes," Sheila affirms.

Attorney Bradley begins his interrogation, "First, I need you to explain to me everything you know about this young man named Travis that your aunt mentioned to me. What was his and your involvement in Damien's shooting?"

Sheila nearly jumps out of her seat. "I had nothing to do with Damien's shooting!"

With an agitated look on her face, Vivian gestures for Sheila to lower her voice. Attorney Bradley remains calm, "Okay, that's excellent. I just need you to explain to me what happened."

They sit for several moments while a crying Sheila goes over the tragic story ending in a shower of tears. Attorney Bradley, who typed her statement, is not finished with his interrogation.

"I have a few more questions for you, Sheila. Was there anyone else in your company that witnessed you saying you wished Damien was dead?"

Sheila shakes her head, wiping her face with a damp sleeve, "No sir, I was alone in my room."

"Did you ever see or touch a gun while in the company of Travis?"

Sheila shakes her head again, "No, sir."

Attorney Bradley continues, "Well, with the information that you gave me, and the story that you told me, which I presume is true, I feel that we may be able to share this information with the detectives and the prosecutor and possibly strike a deal. That would all be based on two important things."

Sheila sits up eagerly. "What are they?"

He looks at Sheila while her aunt sits dozing off in the seat by her side. "Number one is that Travis has not yet been captured, and you can assist in said capture. Number two is that if and when they capture Travis, you'll have to cooperate with them fully, which could possibly mean wearing a wire or even testifying against Travis."

Sheila looks serious. "I'll do whatever it takes to get Damien and his family justice and to prove my own innocence."

Attorney Bradley smiles faintly, "That's a great start." Then he excuses himself to step outside and speak with the detectives.

Vivian rubs Sheila's tight back while they wait for the men to return. "Great job, Sheila." Then they both take out their phones to check their messages.

Sheila sees more messages from Travis and decides to put her phone down. She looks around the detective's office, yawning exaggeratedly. Suddenly, she notices a photo sitting on the mantel behind Detective Williams's desk. Upon further inspection, she sees that it looks like a family photo of his wife, son and daughter. She stares at the picture and realizes that she does have a strong resemblance to the detective's daughter. Then, as she glances over to her left, she notices what looks like a framed picture of an ultrasound. Sheila thinks it is unusual, but she has too much on her mind to think any more about it.

Just as Sheila and Vivian begin dozing off, the door opens, and both detectives enter the room, followed by Attorney Bradley. Detective Matthews speaks first, "We are waiting on the prosecutor to come in before we get started. We are fortunate that she was still in the building going over her other cases."

Detective Matthews jokes, "We're a regular bunch of night owls around here." Everyone chuckles, thankful for the lighthearted attempt to lighten the heaviness in the room.

As they continue waiting, Attorney Bradley leans over to Vivian. "I'd like to talk with Sheila a little more outside the office. And just so you're both aware, a female officer will be coming up shortly to take Sheila's DNA sample. It will just be a swab, and I'll be with her. So, there is no need to worry."

Vivian raises an eyebrow and expresses her deep concern, "And why do they need her DNA?"

"Because Prosecutor Martin will need to ensure that Sheila didn't touch the weapon before offering her any deals. In the meantime, Detective Williams has a few questions for you. Please feel free to answer them if you wish."

As Detective Matthews looks on, Detective Williams sits down to ask Vivian some questions, "So where is Sheila's hometown?"

"Harlem, New York."

"And what is her mother's name?"

Vivian starts to look irritated. "Sheila's mother's name is Anita Robinson."

Detective Williams looks up from his notes. "Did you just say Anita Robinson?"

"Yes, sir," Vivian says.

A wide-eyed Detective Williams continues with a bewildered look on his face, "And what is Sheila's father's name?"

"Sheila never knew her father. He left her mother when she was pregnant."

Detective Williams's face starts to flush, "Do you know where we can possibly locate Sheila's dad?"

"No," says Vivian, "Anita thinks that Sheila's dad probably lives here in Chicago or in Atlanta. The last time Anita saw or spoke to Sheila's dad was at a local café here in Chicago. At that time, they got into a heated argument because Sheila's dad continued to deny being the father of her child. Anita said that during that argument, she slammed down an ultrasound of his daughter in front of him and said, 'This is the only picture of your daughter that you will ever see. Please don't come looking for us.' Then she left the café, and shortly after, she left Chicago altogether, never to see or hear from him again."

Detective Williams wipes his forehead with a handkerchief from his pocket. "One last question, Vivian. Do you have a picture of Sheila's mother?"

Vivian starts to reach for her phone. "Yes, here's a picture of Sheila's mother," Vivian says, pointing to a picture of her, Anita, and Sheila as a toddler.

Detective Williams drops his pen. Hands trembling visibly, he regains his composure by sitting at his desk. "Thanks, Mrs. Johnson. I'm sure Sheila not knowing her father must have really affected her."

Vivian shakes her head disapprovingly, "Yes, it really is a shame. It's such a sad story. I truly hope that they can find each other someday."

Detective Williams looks as if he could cry. "Yes. So do I."

After another large yawn, Vivian poses a question of her own, "So, Detective Williams, what do these questions have to do with the case?"

"Great question. The prosecutor will need this information as we move forward."

"I understand," Vivian says.

"Thank you, Mrs. Johnson. You have answered all of my questions," Detective Williams says. Vivian stands up and stretches before leaving the room to locate Sheila and Attorney Bradley.

Vivian spots Attorney Bradley leaning against a wall a few doors down from the restroom. "How did everything go in there?" he asks.

"Just fine, just fine," Vivian says as she remains standing with a pins and needles sensation in her legs from sitting so long. Tired, she yawns again.

Attorney Bradley smiles, "Great, I just have a few more things to discuss with Sheila, then we'll head back inside. Please join us. Hopefully after that, we can all go home to our beds."

Vivian cracks a smile, "I know that's right."

Back in the office, Detective Williams paces the floor. Feeling overwhelmed by the circumstances, he excuses himself, "I'll be right back. I'm going to the men's room."

Detective Matthews is curious as Detective Williams rushes out the office. Scrolling aimlessly on his computer, he prays that Williams doesn't have that stomach bug that's been going around.

Detective Williams enters the men's room, locks the door and bursts into tears. He sits on a stool, sobbing to himself. He stands up, splashes cold water on his face, and looks at himself in the mirror. "I still need a DNA test, and I must deal with the serious issue at hand without getting carried away," he tells himself before walking out the bathroom and returning to the office. He's greeted by the prosecutor, Ms. Martin, who is already acquainted with everyone else. Detective Williams looks at his fellow detective and the prosecutor and asks, "Could you two step out with me into the hallway for a moment? Attorney Bradley, Vivian, and Sheila, please forgive us, but we will return shortly. Thank you for your patience." His eyes linger on Sheila for a moment, and it takes all of his might to keep from shedding more tears right there. Once outside the room, Detective Williams breaks the news to his colleague.

"I can no longer work on this case due to personal reasons."

The prosecutor looks agitated. "Could you elaborate a little further, Williams?"

Detective Williams looks at her and proceeds to explain, "I know it may be difficult for you to understand at this moment, but I have good reason to believe that Sheila is my daughter. As a matter of fact, I know she's my daughter. She's the daughter I've been trying to find for over sixteen years." The tears well up in his eyes again.

Since he's the one that brought it to Detective Williams's attention, Detective Matthews is not fazed. Prosecutor Martin's stiff demeanor melts away, and she looks surprised. "Well, I have no choice other than to grant your wishes." Then she glances at her phone to check the time. "You'll have to explain this to me in depth at another time. Just please don't say anything to Sheila or her aunt until after she has given her written statement. Can we agree on that?"

Detective Williams is crushed and disappointed because he has to wait. He gives a quiet thanks and heads down the hallway.

Detective Matthews and Prosecutor Martin re-enter the room to update everyone. "So, it looks like Detective Williams had to withdraw from the case for personal reasons that will be discussed with you at another time."

Everyone looks concerned. "Is he okay?" Vivian asks.

Detective Matthews and Prosecutor Martin chime in at the same time, "Yes, thanks for asking."

Prosecutor Martin turns to Sheila, "I know it's getting late, and you are probably very tired of repeating your story over and over again. It's just that it's extremely important that you repeat your story to me one more time tonight and be completely honest about everything. I also want you to know that everything that you say will be recorded. Do you understand?"

Sheila looks at her attorney and her aunt, who give her the nod of approval. Then she looks back at Prosecutor Martin, who's nodding her own head. "Yes, ma'am," Sheila replies softly.

Ms. Martin puts her finger on the play button on a digital recorder. "You can begin," she says. She presses the button, and Sheila recounts the story.

Forty-five minutes later, a crying Sheila ends her story by saying, "I really didn't mean for anything to happen to Damien."

Ms. Martin shakes her head in disgust. "I understand, but it did happen, and unless you can get Travis to testify as the shooter other than the texts you showed me, you will be charged with attempted murder. I have no other choice," she continues, "Hopefully, if he does confess, and we find that it was not your intent for Travis to actually act on your conversation with him, and you agree to testify against him, then we are ready to offer you immunity. At the least, you'll probably serve very little if no time at all."

Sheila sits in disbelief. To top it all off, now she's facing jail time!? Talk about a cruel summer.

The prosecutor looks disappointedly at Sheila. "You are sitting here with luck on your side. It's a good thing that that he didn't die and he's looking at a full recovery. Otherwise, your circumstances would be completely different."

Prosecutor Martin looks at Detective Matthews, "Well, let's get started, Matthews. From Sheila's story alone, it's a possibility that we can make an arrest tonight."

The detective looks at Sheila, "Didn't you mention that he was expecting a text from you tonight?"

Sheila nods, "Yes, sir."

Detective Matthews continues, "Well, send him a text and try to get him to confess. We will be keeping tabs on the entire conversation."

Sheila calls Travis and he picks up almost immediately. "Where are you?" he sounds panicked.

Sheila lies, "I'm still at the hospital with my aunt; I told her I was going downstairs to get some fresh air, but I only said that so I could call you."

She goes on, trying to soften him up, "Thank God Damien isn't dead. The doctor told my aunt that he will make a full recovery."

Travis sounds agitated, "Are you serious?"

"Yeah. I didn't want you to hurt him, Travis. I was really just joking."

"Well, it's done now, Sheila. Maybe next time you'll stop playing so much," he says, chastising her. Completely shocked that Damien is still breathing, Travis says, "There's nothing we can do now. I shot him three times. I don't know how I missed killing him."

Just then the prosecutor gives a thumbs up. "We got him," she declares.

Feeling hot tears well up in her eyes again, Sheila says, "I'm just glad he didn't die."

Travis, oblivious to the severity of it all, continues, "Well, anyways, forget Damien. I miss you and I need to see you tonight."

Sheila feels herself getting nervous. "With everything going on? I really don't know if I can see you tonight, Travis. Plus, it's mad late, and I don't have a car."

Travis pushes, "I'll come pick you up. What's your address?"

"I can't have you pick me up at my house. When we leave here, my aunt will be having a late prayer group coming over to pray for Damien. There will be way too many people there."

Travis is desperate, "Okay, then where?"

Sheila, drooping with exhaustion, thinks of an answer. She looks at the prosecutor, and remembering their deal, she comes up with a response, "Why don't you meet me at the bodega where we first met in about an hour?"

Travis sounds confused, "Huh? Where?"

Sheila catches herself, "I mean the convenience store on N. Lincoln St. I just won't be able to stay long."

Travis looks at his phone. "I'll be there at eleven-thirty."

Sheila gives the prosecutor a thumbs up. "I'll see you there." Before hanging up, she hears Travis say, "I love you."

Sheila winces, and for the sake of keeping Travis calm, she responds, "Love you, too."

Wishing she had never even met him, Sheila hangs up.

When Sheila hangs up the phone, she's greeted by a smiling group of people. The prosecutor, along with Detective Matthews, congratulate her, "You did a fantastic job."

Vivian chimes in defiantly, "I don't want my niece to be anywhere near that young man."

Detective Matthews turns to Vivian, who is sitting in a chair, "I can understand your worries, but Sheila will be safe. If we don't make the arrest tonight, he may hurt someone else."

Vivian gives the detective a stern look, "Okay, as long as you will be there." Then she looks at Sheila, "Are you okay with all of this, sweetie?"

Sheila gives her aunt a hug. "Yes, Auntie. It's the only way to right my wrong."

Detective Matthews hands Sheila a set of keys. "Now, as soon as you are sure it's him, drop these set of keys that I'm giving you and clear out the way. Do you understand?"

"Yes," Sheila says, nodding nervously.

"Your aunt has already confirmed the address of the convenience store on N. Lincoln Street, and I have instructed her to call me as soon as you leave the house," the detective continues, "Trust us, everything will be just fine. Why don't you all head home for a bit and try to relax before this all goes down?"

Stretching again, Vivian stands up slowly and gathers her things. "That's a great idea. I can't wait until you take this young man off the streets."

Detective Matthews opens the door. "I'll walk you to your car."

Vivian flashes a tired smile. "Thank you, sir." They all head downstairs as Detective Matthews confirms that everything will go just fine. He sees the two women off before heading back to his office.

Opening the door to his office, he sees the prosecutor and his partner, Detective Williams, talking. Detective Williams has red, tired eyes. He goes to put a hand on his normally very rigid colleague and feels the intensity of his emotions.

"What a day this turned out to be," Detective Matthews sighs.

The prosecutor rests her feet in an empty chair. "Yes, but it's not done yet. We have to get Travis off the street tonight and return Sheila home safely."

Detective Matthews nods, "Yes, indeed." Detective Williams looks up at Matthews, who continues, "Sheila is definitely your daughter. I know you will still have to get a DNA test, but she's the spitting image of Pam, man."

They both shake their heads in disbelief. "She sure is. And when Sheila's aunt showed me that picture of Sheila's mom, that sealed the deal," Matthews admits.

Detective Matthews claps his buddy on the back. "I'm so happy for you. When are you planning on telling Sheila?"

Detective Williams thinks deeply. "I'll definitely tell my family tonight, then I'll make arrangements with Sheila and her aunt to meet soon."

"I wish you well, man. It's time for me to go downstairs to go over the details with the other officers helping us to get this kid, Travis, off the street."

"Sounds like a plan. Keep my daughter safe."

Detective Matthews points at his friend before heading out the door. "You got it, Williams."

Once everyone receives their assignment, several squad cars head toward the convenience store on N. Lincoln Ave. where Travis's arrest will take place. Detective Matthews calls to notify Vivian and Sheila that everyone is in place. He reminds Vivian to call again as soon as Sheila leaves the house. Then Detective Matthews goes on to mention something new in the plan, "Just know that Sheila will have to be handcuffed and arrested to protect her from any backlash from possible gang activity that Travis may be involved in. There's also a great possibility that the local and national media will also be there."

Vivian sighs, ready for all of it to be over. "This new news concerns me. Is it possible to hold off until the families have been properly notified?"

"No. We have to move forward, and this is our best shot to get Travis off the street."

Although both Sheila and Vivian are upset by the updated plan, they also know the importance of moving forward with Travis's arrest. They turn off the lights, lock the doors, and make their way to the convenience store.

Chapter 22

Coming Clean

S heila prepares to meet Travis at the convenience store, and Vivian reassures her as they sit talking in the living room for a few minutes before making the call to the detective and heading to the store, "Sheila, God knows your heart, and he will see you through this night, baby. You're doing the right thing."

Unsure of what to say, Sheila nods quietly.

Her aunt continues, "Now, I'll have to call your mother and Sharon to explain things to them and to let them know that they may be hearing some untrue stories in the media before we get a chance to talk in depth."

Sheila, feeling exhausted and drained by it all, just shrugs as she looks out the window. She opens it to get some cool night air on her hot, tear-stained skin. "Do what you have to do, Auntie. I trust you," Sheila says. They sit quietly for a moment, and Sheila closes her eyes, feeling the cool air calming her. "I know my mom. She's going to be extremely upset and scared. And Mrs. Jackson, Damien, and Tanya will hate me forever."

Vivian glances at her, "Well, honey, that's understandable. But now we have no choice but to weather the storm and trust God."

Sheila starts to cry again, "Okay, Auntie." They sit and cry together. Sheila looks at her aunt and wipes the tears from her eyes. "Stay strong, Auntie." Then she gets ready to leave the house. Sheila locks the door and stands on the porch, texting Travis.

Sheila: I'm on my way. Walking now.

Travis: I'm already in the parking lot by the convenience store. How long will you be?

Sheila: About five minutes.

Then Sheila texts Detective Matthews as she walks to the store.

Sheila: Travis is already in the parking lot sitting in a blue BMW with white stripes and tinted windows. I'll be arriving shortly.

Detective Matthews: Once you see that it is indeed Travis in the car, drop the keys I gave you and pretend to pick them up. The cashier is also a police officer. You are safe.

Sheila is close enough to the convenience store to see Travis's car. She crosses the street with her hands stuffed in her pockets. Feeling for the keys and trying not to look nervous, she walks up to the driver's side. Travis rolls the window down. "Get in," he demands with a smile.

As she walks around the front of the car, Travis sees that Sheila dropped something that she has bent over to pick up. Before he can look up, his car is surrounded by a swarm of flashing lights and sirens blasting. Several shadowy figures step out one by one and have their weapons pointed at Travis. He hears the muffled sound of loud, angry voices, "Get out of the car! Now!"

Travis gets out of the car with his hands up. To his surprise, he looks to his left and sees that Sheila is being handcuffed as well. He notices a female officer is patting Sheila down while another one is searching through her purse. After searching her, Travis notices an officer reading Sheila her Miranda Rights before shoving her into the back seat of a squad car.

Travis can hear Sheila screaming, "I didn't shoot anyone! Why am I being arrested!?"

Travis is so absorbed in Sheila's situation that he barely notices the officers searching his car. Suddenly, one of them yells, "I got something!"

He pulls out a weapon from Travis's car and hands it to Detective Matthews. The detective looks over the weapon and smiles, declaring, "That's the same caliber weapon used to shoot Damien."

The second officer moves to Travis's trunk and shouts, "I found a second weapon."

Detective Mathew yells back, "Bag and tag both weapons, read Travis his Miranda Rights, and bring him in to be processed." Then he turns to the officer near him and mutters, "Looks as if Travis will be going away for a long time. Looking at his file, he's still on parole as we speak."

With the window of the patrol car rolled down, Sheila turns to look out the window when she notices two local news trucks pulling up to the scene: NBC5 and ABC7 news. They quickly jump out of their vehicles and point their cameras at Travis. They run toward the vehicle that Sheila's sitting in, pointing the camera directly at her and firing off questions, "Did you have anything to do with Damien Jackson being shot earlier tonight?"

Sheila responds angrily, tears lining her cheeks, "Absolutely not. I love Damien."

"Are you his girlfriend?" the reporter inquires.

"No. But I'm the mother of his child," she replies defiantly and rolls her window up.

Just in time, two officers get into the cars Sheila and Travis are in and drive back to the station. Upon arrival, Sheila sees even more news vehicles, most notably an affiliate of CNN, a station her mother watches every evening. She gulps nervously. Then she hears a door open and sees Travis being forcibly removed from the police vehicle.

Travis can't even see her through the commotion in front of him. He's surrounded by cameras, microphones, and bright lights. They continue to question his involvement in Damien's shooting until he gets into the station. He remains silent, scowling angrily.

Once Travis and Sheila are inside the police station, they are put into separate interrogation rooms. Detective Matthews swings the door open and walks in. "Travis, you're in a lot of trouble, and you'll make this easier for everyone if you just admit to your involvement."

Travis scowls ferociously at the detective. He clenches his jaw as the detective continues, "We believe that once we test both weapons found in your car, one of the weapons will match the bullets taken out of Damien's body. If you don't help us out right now, the prosecutor will recommend the maximum sentence for attempted murder—life in prison without parole. Then you will still be facing a number of other charges including not one, but two weapon charges."

The detective removes Travis's handcuffs, sits in front of him, and says, "Now the ball is in your court. How would you like to play this?" He turns on the tape recorder that is sitting on the table in front of Travis and smiles.

Travis sighs and just comes straight out with it, "I shot him. But Sheila said she wanted him dead."

Detective Matthews nods, "Did she pay you money or give you the weapon?"

Travis shakes his head, "Nah." He runs his hand through his hair, realizing how badly he's screwed up.

The detective continues, "So what makes you think she was serious?"

Travis just sighs, feeling defeated, he answers, "I didn't know for sure. I just assumed that she meant it. I mean, the truth is that I love her. I mean, I really care about her. And when she told me her story, I just knew I had to be there for her. I wanted to be with her, and for us to be a family."

The detective looks curious, he asks, "What do you mean that you wanted to be a family?"

Travis shares the details, "Sheila is pregnant by Damien, and Damien says that he wants nothing to do with the child. He kept insisting that Sheila have an abortion, and see, I can't have kids because of an accident I had, so I thought if I got rid of Damien, we could be a family."

Detective Matthews looks at Travis, pitying the young man with such great illusions. "Did Sheila say that she wanted you, her, and her baby to be a family?"

Travis catches himself, feeling foolish. "No." He looks at the detective, completely convinced by his own reasoning. "But she didn't have to. A child needs a father." He continues, a look of disgust smeared across his face, "Damien isn't even a real man. A real man would take care of his child. So, yes, I shot him. And you know what, I'd do it again. I would do anything to be with Sheila and her baby!"

Detective Matthews stands up, amazed at how easy the entire process has turned out to be. "Well, you are under arrest for the attempted murder of Damien Jackson," he announces. He looks at Travis, who is still fuming from his rant. He continues, "You are actually lucky he's alive, otherwise you would be booked for first degree murder." He stands and walks toward the door. "I'm going to let the prosecutor know that you cooperated, and we'll see what happens from there."

Travis stops the detective as he walks out the door. "What will happen to Sheila?"

The detective turns to him, "What do you think should happen to Sheila?"

Travis sighs, wanting to do anything he can to at least absolve her and her unborn child of this burden. "Nothing. To be honest, I knew she really didn't want him dead and that she said it out of anger, but it gave me an excuse to make those moves." He recalls one of their last conversations, "Well, she told me that she loved Damien and just wanted him to stop saying those mean things to her. As for me, like I said earlier, I just wanted him out of the picture."

The detective looks at the recorder on the table. "Well, again I'll share this information with the prosecutor. Maybe they'll give Sheila a break." He reaches for the door and turns back to Travis again. "Travis, is what you have been telling me the truth?"

Travis meets the detective's gaze, looking unbothered. "Yeah."

The detective continues, "Okay, well before I shut off the tape, is there anything else you would like to say?"

"Yeah," Travis admits.

"Go on. The tape is rolling."

Travis moves his mouth closer to the recorder, "I love you, Sheila, and I would do it all again. That's what's up." He moves away.

The detective maintains his composure, "Is that all?"

Travis nods, "That's all I have to say."

Detective Matthews shuts off the recorder then leaves the officers in the room to begin processing Travis.

Detective Matthews walks toward the room where Sheila is waiting, dozing off in her seat. He notices that Sheila's aunt is sitting outside the room with one of his fellow officers. Detective Matthews motions for Vivian to enter the room with him.

Sheila snaps awake, hearing the door open. She looks up to see her aunt and Detective Matthews, they both commend her for doing a great job assisting him and his officers in the arrest.

Detective Mathews follows up with some good news, "Well, Travis admitted to the shooting, and he confirmed your story that he acted alone and that you did not want anything to happen to Damien, that you actually told him that you love Damien, and that he acted out of his love for you and your unborn child."

Vivian shakes Sheila's shoulder. "That's great news for you, Sheila!"

Sheila still looks concerned. "What will happen to Travis?" she asks.

The detective answers her, "Well, I will talk to the prosecutor and let her know that he has cooperated. He may get a reduced sentence, but he will be locked up for a long time."

Sheila yawns. "Well, can I go home now?"

Detective Matthews chuckles, having seen his share of bleary-eyed teens sitting before him, "Yes, I will release you in your aunt's custody, but we will need to speak to you again sometime tomorrow."

Sheila stands up and stretches. "Thanks, sir."

Vivian stands as well, swinging her purse onto her shoulder. "Yes, thank you, Detective Matthews."

Detective Matthews smiles, "You're welcome, now go home and get some of that well-deserved rest."

Sheila and Vivian can't get out of there fast enough. Vivian checks the time and sees that it's approaching midnight. Once in the parking lot, Sheila confides in her aunt, "There were a ton of reporters there when me and Travis were getting arrested."

Her aunt glances at her as they approach the car, "I know, honey. I've received several voicemails and texts that I have not answered. And before you ask, yes, they were calls from your mother and from

Sharon. I will answer when I get a chance to catch my breath! My head is still spinning from all of this, Sheila."

Sheila gives her aunt a tired smile as her aunt unlocks the car. "Thanks, Auntie, for being here for me."

Vivian sits in the driver's seat and puts the key in the ignition. "You're welcome, sweetie. Just remember, you're not out of the woods yet."

Sheila rolls down a window, grateful for the cool night air on her tired body. "I know." She sighs, and they ride back in silence—both feeling wired from the chaotic day that is finally behind them.

Sheila and her aunt step onto the porch. "I feel like having some ice cream. How about you?" Vivian asks.

Feeling like ice cream was worth the extra half hour without sleep, Sheila smiles, "I would love some ice cream, Auntie."

"Great." Her aunt puts her purse down in a nearby chair and goes to the kitchen. She washes her hands before turning to open the freezer. "We're having three, no four big scoops of vanilla ice cream with chocolate fudge on top, then I'll take a warm bath and return the calls to both your mother and Sharon."

Sheila washes her hands at the sink and decides to sit in the living room with the TV. Her aunt calls out to her, "Also, Sheila if you've received any messages from your mother or Sharon, which I'm sure you have, please don't return their calls until I have spoken to them. I truly think it's for the best."

Sheila looks out the window while waiting for the ice cream. "Sure."

Her aunt approaches carrying heaping bowls of ice cream. They find something on TV to watch while they snack.

About halfway through her ice cream, Sheila mentions something to her aunt, "You know, I saw something pretty weird today at the detective's office."

Her aunt raises an eyebrow, "What was that, sweetie?"

Sheila elaborates, "Well, I saw a picture of Detective Williams' family and…"

Vivian interrupts her, "Yeah, what's so weird about that?" She can feel herself getting hot with anxiety.

"Auntie, let me finish. Beside that picture was a framed picture of an ultrasound."

Vivian drops her spoon on her lap. "I must be more tired than I thought. Excuse me, sweetie, pass the towel, please." As she cleans up the mess, she looks over at Sheila, "Sweetie, are you sure?"

"Yes, Auntie, I'm sure. Why do you have that strange look on your face?"

Her aunt, having opened enough cans of worms in the past week, decides it isn't the time to get into that. "I can't explain, honey, but that does explain why Detective Williams was asking me all those questions. And why he removed himself from the case."

Sheila is the one with a strange look on her face now. "What questions? And why did he remove himself from the case?"

"Oh my God. Oh my God. Oh my God!" Vivian exclaims. She moves her bowl of ice cream so it won't spill. "Sheila, this is fantastic news. Thank you so much for that important information!"

Feeling confused, Sheila shrugs her shoulders, "I really have no idea how I helped, but I'm glad I did."

Vivian rejoices. "Hopefully I can explain everything to you in the very near future. But right now, let's just enjoy our ice cream and each other's company," she says, smiling, "Oh, Sheila, it's so very true that one doesn't know when or how God will pour his blessings upon us."

Chapter 23

Have a Talk with God

Meanwhile, back at Chicago Medical Center, all of Damien's teammates and friends have left the hospital, leaving Tanya and her mother resting as comfortably as they can on the cots in Damien's room.

Damien is in a deep sleep. His right arm and shoulder are in a cast. His right torso is heavily bandaged, and his face is so swollen that he is unrecognizable. But to his mom and sister, Damien looks as handsome as ever. They can't help but feel blessed that Damien is alive.

Each time Nurse Roberts makes her half-hour rounds to check on Damien, Sharon asks about her son, and each time Nurse Roberts gives a promising report. This time as she does her rounds, she uplifts Sharon and Tanya with her report, "Your son is doing very well, and his vitals are excellent, Mrs. Jackson. Also, it's a very good sign that Damien is resting longer than expected. So don't be alarmed if he sleeps through the night."

Although Sharon and Tanya desperately want to see Damien open his eyes and speak, they understand the importance of his rest and recovery. Sharon nods, "Yes, I certainly agree."

Nurse Roberts continues, "Well, I'm going to be heading home now, but Nurse Rebeca Green will be taking over until I return tomorrow."

Sharon flashes a smile at the kind nurse, "And is Nurse Green as good as you?"

Flattered, Nurse Roberts smiles, "Yes, I wouldn't leave you in anything but good hands. Nurse Green has actually been here longer than I have. She was the head nurse when I first began working here.

Rest assured, all the nurses here at Chicago Medical Center are excellent, so I leave you in excellent hands."

"How long have you worked at this hospital?" asks Tanya, who is fighting sleep.

Nurse Roberts replies, "Funny you ask. Next month will be 21 years."

Tanya's eyes widen. "That's a long time."

Nurse Roberts laughs and sighs, "Yes, indeed. Yes, indeed."

As Nurse Roberts approaches the door, she turns to face the Jacksons once more, "I know it doesn't look that way now, but Damien will be just fine. I'll see you good folks tomorrow."

Tanya and Sharon echo each other, "Thank you so much for everything."

"You are so welcome." Nurse Roberts waves as she closes the door.

While waiting for Damien to wake up, Tanya and Sharon spend their time praying and discussing the day's events, including what they heard on the news regarding Sheila's possible involvement in Damien's shooting. They receive even more strange news from Celeste, including pictures of Sheila kissing Travis Brown, the young man identified as the person who shot Damien.

Overwhelmed with all the bad news and confusion, Vivian and Tanya can't even bring themselves to go to sleep. Sharon remembers Vivian's choice advice and decides to honor it. Vivian had told Sharon not to draw any conclusions based on what they saw or heard regarding Sheila's involvement in Damien's shooting until they were able to talk.

Sharon decides to rest on the cot beside Damien's bed and to continue reading the Bible. Tanya is busy scrolling through a number of songs her brother enjoyed hearing her sing. She's considering singing one of them on *The Voice*.

"Mom," Tanya says, seeing her mom reading the Bible and nodding off although trying her best to stay awake. "Mom," she repeats.

Sharon lifts her head up and smiles at Tanya, who smiles back, "Ma, I think you need to get some rest. I'll stay up and keep watch over Damien."

Sharon closes her Bible. "I think I'll take you up on that. How about I try to get a few hours of sleep then we can switch off?"

Tanya agrees, "Okay, Mom." She walks over and puts a light blanket over her mom and kisses her on her forehead. "It'll all be okay, because we are Jackson Strong."

Sharon squeezes her daughter's hand. "Yes, sweetheart, we are." She finally lays her tired head down on the pillow and immediately drifts off to sleep.

It's early on Friday morning, and Sharon is watching over Damien while Tanya rests in her cot. As she flips through her Bible, Sharon hears mumbling sounds coming from Damien's direction. She jumps up and stands over Damien and holds his hand. She puts an ear close to Damien's mouth to hear what he's saying.

Damien's eyes are still shut, and his voice sounds gruff, "Mom, is that you?"

With excitement in her voice and tears of joy streaming down her face, Sharon replies, "Yes, baby, it's me. I'm here."

Damien's eyes flutter open slowly. "Where's Tanya?"

His mom brushes her hand through his hair. "Tanya's here, too, son. I'm so glad to hear your voice." The tears flow down her cheeks.

The noise and excitement wake up Tanya, who turns in her cot and sees Damien moving around. Tanya rushes over to the other side of Damien's bed and immediately starts tearing up as she squeezes his free hand. "I love you so much, big brother, I love you so much."

Moments later, Nurse Green enters the room to check Damien's vitals. She introduces herself to the family and Damien, then she turns to Sharon, "How long has Damien been awake?"

Sharon sniffles, wiping her eyes. "He just woke up about five minutes ago."

The nurse smiles, making her notes, "Well, I guess that was good timing by me."

"Yes, indeed," Sharon chuckles.

Nurse Green gives Sharon and Tanya a huge smile. "Forgive me, could you move away from the bed for a moment so that I can check Damien's vitals?"

Reluctantly, they both back away from the bed while closely watching Nurse Green as she checks his vitals.

"So how are you feeling?" Nurse Green asks, looking down at him.

Damien, still feeling tired, gives her a thumbs up.

Nurse Green continues, "And where do you feel the most pain?" Damien immediately points to his right shoulder.

"That's understandable. From one to ten, how bad is the pain?"

"An eight," Damien replies, wincing as he tries to adjust himself in bed.

Nurse Green fiddles with his IV. "I'll adjust the morphine to lower your pain."

Trying not to alarm his family about the amount of pain he is in, Damien whispers, "Thanks."

Nurse Green moves around the bed, clearing the way for Sharon and Tanya to return to Damien's side. "Do you feel like you can eat something?"

With a slight smile, Damien whispers, "Definitely." Bubbling over with gratitude, everyone laughs.

Nurse Green turns to Sharon and Tanya, "I'm going to send breakfast up for all three of you. Would you like for me to send one of our aides to feed Damien?"

Sharon smiles warmly, "No, I got this. After all, I've been feeding my son since the day he was conceived." They all laugh again.

Nurse Green smiles, "Okay, I truly understand."

Then Sharon remembers something as Nurse Green steps out the door. "Could you please have them bring me a cup of hot tea?"

Nurse Green looks at her, "You got it." Then she turns to Tanya, "Any special requests from the young lady?"

Tanya beams, "Yes, may I please have a glass of orange juice?"

The nurse nods, "No problem." She looks at Damien, with a slightly hapless look on her face, "Unfortunately, you are on a strict diet, so we can't grant you any special requests at this time."

Damien smiles and mutters, "I'm just glad to be here."

Nurse Green turns back to Sharon and gestures toward the door. "May I speak with you for a moment outside?"

Sharon moves toward the door, with her tender hand lingering on Damien's head before pulling away. "Yes, you can." She turns to Damien and Tanya, promising to be back soon.

Once the door to Damien's room closes, the nurse talks to Sharon, "So, Damien is scheduled for a full day of testing and x-rays. Although he is awake now, we would like for him to get as much rest as possible. I know it'll be hard, but what I'm recommending to you is that after breakfast, you and your daughter go home and get some well-deserved rest yourselves. Then you can return later this evening." Sharon looks at her as she continues, "Also, prior to you leaving this morning I will arrange for Damien's doctors to meet with you to discuss Damien's vitals, as well as the tests and x-rays that we will be administering today."

Still feeling groggy from the light sleep she had in the hospital, Sharon feels relieved. "That sounds like a great idea. Then Tanya and I will have the time we need to freshen up and pick up some essentials for Damien's hospital stay."

Thankful for her understanding, the nurse smiles, "Great, I'm glad you agree. I'll have breakfast sent right up to you now."

Sharon puts a hand on the door. "Thanks so much."

As Sharon re-enters the room, Tanya meets her mom's gaze, "Is everything okay?"

Sharon has a softened look on her face. Feeling content, she responds, "Yes, sweetheart. Everything is just fine." She moves over to the other side of Damien's bed to continue comforting her son.

Back at the Johnson household, Vivian is just getting out of bed. As always, she starts her day with a prayer. Today's prayer is somewhat longer than her usual morning prayers. She reads her favorite Bible verse, finishing her morning talk with God with tears streaming down her face.

Anticipating a long day ahead, Vivian decides to make herself a hearty breakfast consisting of an English muffin with almond butter, oatmeal, and a cup of coffee. As she wraps up her breakfast, Vivian begins planning her day, which includes making some heavy phone calls to Sharon, Anita, Attorney Bradley, and both detectives.

Before making her calls, Vivian closes her eyes and asks the Lord for a verse for strength and courage. She opens her eyes as the book of Exodus comes to mind. She types 'Exodus' into Google, and the first verse that pops up is Exodus 14:14. It reads:

The Lord shall fight for you, and ye shall hold your peace.

Vivian looks to the heavens. "Thank you, Lord. Those are perfect words for me to follow today." She takes a deep breath, picks up the phone, and begins making her phone calls, starting with Sheila's mom.

After five minutes of trying to calm Anita down, Vivian mentions to her sister that she believes there may be some good news regarding Sheila in the near future.

Anita sounds excited, she shouts, "What is it? Did you find Sheila's father?"

Vivian is amazed. "Not sure, but I'm on it, sis." Maybe Anita could've been a detective herself as quick as she was to guess that, Sharon thinks.

"If it's true, that would be such a blessing; Vivian please don't tease me like that," Anita continues.

Vivian gets serious, "I know what this would mean not only for you, but also for that baby upstairs. I just have to wait a while longer before confirming things."

"Okay, Vivian. My Lord, what a roller-coaster ride Sheila is having there in Chicago!"

Vivian clucks her tongue. "Chile, who you telling? God must have a serious plan for all of this."

"Would He have it any other way?" Anita asks, and they both laugh.

The conversation winds down. "Well, I'll speak with you later after all of these calls I have to make today," Vivian says.

Reviewing her own to-do list for the day, Anita says, "All right, we'll talk soon, Viv."

They hang up, and Vivian makes her next call to Sharon.

Sharon picks up the phone, sounding notably more cheerful, "Hello Vivian, I was just thinking about you."

Although her friend's demeanor is answer enough, she can't help but ask, "How's Damien?"

Vivian can hear the smile in Sharon's voice. "Damien is doing fine. I just got done feeding him. The doctors are on their way now to go over his tests and x-rays. Is it possible I could call you back in a few hours?" she requests.

Vivian feels somewhat relieved. "For sure, I'm so glad to hear that Damien is doing much better."

"I know you are, and I'll keep you updated," Sharon promises.

Vivian bids her goodbye. "Okay, have a great day." They hang up, and Vivian gets a glass of water before calling Attorney Bradley.

He picks up promptly. "Hello, Vivian."

Vivian smiles, taking a sip of her water. "How are you, Otis?"

"Your ears must be ringing. I was *just* reaching for my phone to call you," Otis replies, shaking his head.

Vivian looks shocked. "Really?"

"Yes, I literally just got off the phone with Prosecutor Martin, and she informed me that Travis's attorney has struck a deal with the state."

Vivian leans on the table. She is eager to hear the rest of the details. Otis continues, "Travis signed a sworn statement saying that he acted alone in the attempted murder of Damien, and because of his sworn statement, there will be no trial. Travis will receive a maximum of nine years for the attempted murder of Damien, plus two years for the weapons charges, for a total of eleven years."

He clears his throat and continues, "As for Sheila, she will receive three months of house arrest for simple assault which is a class C misdemeanor here in Chicago." Vivian listens intently. "If she completes the three months' house arrest without any further incident, she will have her record expunged. This means that her criminal records will be sealed and no longer available to the public."

Vivian smiles and looks to the heavens. She remembers her Bible verse. "Is it possible that she can be exempt from house arrest since Travis admitted that he acted alone and because she didn't fire the weapon?"

Attorney Bradley sighs. "No, I'm very sorry. But she's got the best deal anyone could've gotten her."

Vivian is grateful. "I think it's an excellent deal, considering the circumstances."

"You know, Sheila is very lucky that Damien did not die, and that Travis is taking the blame. Otherwise, her circumstances would be drastically different."

"I really hope that these young people can learn that words matter and the consequences can be serious when we aren't careful. And that's especially when they're fueled by positive or negative emotions," Attorney Bradley says, "Although Sheila said she didn't truly mean that she wanted Damien dead, and I truly believe her, someone who claims to love her and wants to protect her took her words seriously."

Vivian voices her agreement, "Yes, I understand completely. I'll discuss all of this with Sheila later today." She continues, "By the way, what is simple assault?"

"It varies from state to state. Here in Chicago, it's when a person without lawful authority knowingly engages in conduct which places another person in reasonable apprehension of receiving a battery. That is exactly what Sheila did." He pauses. "You know, I think you should know that Prosecutor Martin called Mrs. Jackson and explained the whole deal to her. She signed off on it. We couldn't have gone ahead with this deal without Mrs. Jackson's consent."

Vivian is thankful but concerned. "When did the prosecutor speak to Sharon?"

"I believe they had a conversation early this morning," he replies, "Prosecutor Martin told me that Sharon was eager to just move on from all of this. She felt that two good people, meaning Damien and Sheila, have both suffered dearly. She doesn't want either of them to suffer anymore."

Attorney Bradley hears Vivian crying on the other end and shakes his head in amazement. "You must be living right, because it seems as if God is fighting your battle for you, Vivian."

Vivian excuses herself to blow her nose. "I can't believe you just said what you said."

"Did I say something wrong?"

Vivian chuckles and dots her tears away. "No, everything you said today was right, absolutely everything," she continues, "And oh yes, son, I do have God fighting my battles for me. So, with you and God on my side, I've couldn't have asked for a better team."

Flattered, Attorney Bradley chuckles heartily, "Thank you so much. I really appreciate those words."

"Okay, Otis, just send me the bill and I'll handle it shortly."

"There's no charge." Attorney Bradley waves a hand, playing with an abacus on his desk. "This one is on me."

Vivian is on the verge of tears again. "Thank you, son. I think I'll at least bake you that chocolate cake you love so much."

"Now you talking," he says, "I'll be looking forward to it. In the meantime, I'll email you the paperwork regarding Sheila's house arrest. You can have her mother sign and notarize the papers. I'll pick them up when I pick up my cake."

Vivian looks at her calendar. "Why don't we say Tuesday?"

Attorney Bradley looks over his calendar and nods, "Tuesday it is." They say their goodbyes before he interjects, "Oh, before I forget, I have a message for you from Prosecutor Martin. She wanted me to let you know that Detective Williams would like for you to call him. I wonder what that's about." He thinks for a moment. "Would you like for me to call him for you?"

Vivian waves her hand in the air and thanks the Lord. "No, no. It's fine, I think I know what this is about."

"Okay, Mrs. Johnson. I'll see you on Tuesday."

She smiles, "Thank you so much for everything, Otis. Tell your mom I said hello."

"Will do," he says, "And you are always so welcome."

Vivian decides to go upstairs and share Attorney Bradley's updates with Sheila. She approaches Sheila's bedroom and finds that the door is still closed. Vivian knocks, but there is no response. Vivian feels herself beginning to panic, and a look of concern sweeps across her face when there's no response. She knocks again. "Sheila, sweetie, are you okay? Can I come in?" Vivian asks. She knocks a third time, and still there's no response.

Even though she's used to Sheila sleeping late, Sheila is also a light sleeper. It is truly unlike Sheila not to at least answer. Vivian slowly opens the door and finds Sheila passed out on the floor and bleeding from her mouth.

"Lord, it's one thing after another this summer! Oh no, Jesus help us." She falls to her knees to check for Sheila's pulse and is grateful to find that Sheila does have one. She immediately reaches for Sheila's phone lying on the bed and dials 911. When the operator picks up, Vivian details her situation clearly.

"Hello, my name is Vivian Johnson, and I found my niece unresponsive on her bedroom floor, and bleeding from her mouth."

"Okay, ma'am does she have a pulse?" the operator inquires.

Vivian checks Sheila's pulse again. "She's not moving, but she does have a pulse. Please hurry, please have them hurry," Vivian shouts frantically at the operator, "She's also pregnant. Please tell them to hurry!"

The operator drily explains that the ambulance is on its way and should be there any moment now. To Vivian's relief and joy, she hears an ambulance approaching her home and hurries downstairs to open the door. She's greeted by two EMTs and eagerly leads them up the stairs. "Thank you and please, please hurry!"

They run up the stairs. Vivian dashes into Sheila's room and sees that her niece is still unresponsive on the bedroom floor. One technician quickly follows and checks her pulse and blood pressure.

"Her pulse is very faint, and her blood pressure is dangerously low," one EMT tells his colleague. He wipes the blood from Sheila's mouth as tears stream down her aunt's tired face. She stands in the doorway watching the tragedy unfold. "I don't know if they told you but, Sheila is also pregnant," Vivian tells the EMTs, "Please don't let anything happen to her or the baby. Oh Lord, please don't let any more trouble come to this child."

The EMTs prepare to put Sheila on a stretcher. "Ma'am, we have to rush her to the hospital."

Vivian nods and makes space for the EMTs to carry Sheila through the doorway and down the stairs. "Do whatever you need to do. Please just don't let anything happen to her or the baby."

The technicians are preoccupied with getting Sheila the care she needs. "Because of your niece's critical condition, we will need to take her to the closest hospital. It looks like that'll be Chicago Medical Center."

"Okay, I'll follow you."

The EMTs load Sheila into the waiting ambulance as Vivian flies around the house getting her things before leaving. Vivian picks up her Bible and scurries toward the door. Just as she locks it, it crosses her mind that Sheila will be at the same hospital as Damien. She takes a moment to pray before buckling up and driving over to Chicago Medical Center.

Vivian prays all the way there. As they approach the hospital, she looks to the sky as if speaking directly to the Lord, "Lord, you are really testing me. But guess what, I still trust in you, and I trust in your plan."

Chapter 24

Here We Go Again

Vivian runs into the hospital looking like a wildfire and makes a beeline for the front desk.

"Hello, I'm Vivian Johnson, and my niece was just brought here," she says gravely.

The receptionist looks at her, "What's your niece's name?"

She stammers, "Sheila. Sheila Robinson."

The receptionist scans the computer. "Yes, Mrs. Johnson, we do have a Sheila Robinson who was just admitted here." He stands up and points down the hall. "You see the woman with the long, bright red nails? Please see her for further assistance."

Vivian mutters a thank you and half jogs to the desk at the end of the hall, where she is greeted by a kind nurse, "I've been informed that you are Vivian Johnson, and your niece is Sheila Robinson?"

Vivian nods eagerly, "Yes."

"Follow me. The doctor has been waiting for you." The nurse turns and walks toward an open doorway. They walk swiftly.

"How's my niece?" Vivian asks, quickening her pace to keep up with the nurse.

The nurse looks back at her, "I can't say, but we're heading to her now. Then, I'll go and get Dr. Miranda Peters, who is the doctor in charge today."

Vivian can make out her niece's braids and recognizes her in a nearby room. She runs ahead of the nurse to reach Sheila's bedside. There are two nurses in the room. One is taking her vitals, and the other is setting up to do the blood workup. When Mrs. Johnson sees Sheila breathing through a tube, she looks away, trying to catch her breath.

The nurse monitoring Sheila's vitals looks at her aunt, "Are you Sheila's mother?"

Vivian's face looks pale in the harsh hospital lighting. "No, I'm her aunt, Vivian Johnson."

"Nice to meet you. My name is Christina Hernandez. I will be Sheila's nurse today. We will need yours or Sheila's parents' consent before we administer the bloodwork."

Vivian looks down at Sheila, whose breathing is shallow. Her skin looks gray from the lack of oxygen. "How is she doing?" Vivian asks as she runs her hand through Sheila's hair.

The nurse glances at her vitals again. "Well, right now, she is in stable condition. She's just running an extremely high fever, and Dr. Peters believes that she likely has a serious infection. We'll need to take a blood test ASAP."

"Okay, can you give me a moment? I will get her mother on the phone right now."

Nurse Hernandez nods, "Yes, please go right ahead."

Vivian goes to a corner, pulls out her phone, and calls Anita. Thankfully she answers immediately, "Hey, Anita. I am so glad you picked up. But baby, I need you to sit down for a minute."

Feeling nervous about her sister's call, Anita gets comfortable.

"Anita, I found Sheila unconscious in her room, and she has been admitted to Chicago Medical Center."

Anita feels dizzy. "Oh, no. Please tell me that she's okay. How bad is it, Vivian?"

"I'm with her now, and at the moment, she's breathing through a tube. The nurse said that the doctor requested Sheila's bloodwork immediately. She has an extremely high fever, which the doctor believes is being caused by a serious infection." Anita listens in complete shock.

"Can I speak to the doctor?" Anita asks hopefully.

"No, she's not here right now," Vivian says, shaking her head as she looks toward the door where someone is knocking urgently. "Oh wait, I think this is her coming in now. Hold on."

Dr. Peters walks into the room and turns to look at Vivian, "Hello, I hear you are Sheila's aunt."

Vivian nods, "Yes, I am. But I actually have Sheila's mother on the phone now. She's a registered nurse at Harlem City Hospital in New York."

The nurse approaches her. "What is her name?"

Vivian puts the phone on speaker, Anita replies, "Anita Robinson."

Dr. Peters mouths a *thank you.*

"Hello, Anita. I'm Doctor Miranda Peters, the emergency room doctor here at Chicago Medical Center. As I'm sure you know, your daughter has been admitted here. Right now, she is in stable condition, but she is running an extremely high fever, and we will need to start her blood work immediately. It is my professional opinion that Sheila has a very serious infection, and that we will need to get to the bottom of the infection much sooner than later. We need your consent before following through on any of this."

"Yes, Doctor Peters, I agree. For Sheila's sake, I'm giving my sister proxy rights, and I'll be taking the first flight out. Please call me once you get the results of the bloodwork." They exchange numbers, each taking a moment to scribble the digits down.

"I will call you personally," the doctor promises.

Anita thanks her, and the doctor gives Vivian her phone back. Walking over to Nurse Hernandez, Dr. Peter tells her that they can proceed with the bloodwork.

Vivian turns off the speaker and puts the phone to her ear. "Hello?"

"I just wanted to let you know that I'll be taking the first flight to Chicago. Is it okay if I stay with you for a few days?"

"Chile, please. That's not even a question. Stay as long as you need."

"Thank you so much. I told the doctor that you can sign off on anything that has to do with Sheila until I arrive. Just keep me updated please," says Anita, who attempts a smile as she swiftly focuses on getting to Chicago as fast as she can.

"Okay, sis. I will be praying for you and Sheila."

They make kissing sounds, then both rush back to their duties. "See you this evening, Viv."

"Okay, dear. Please call me when you arrive at the airport," Vivian says.

"Oh, don't worry about picking me up," Anita responds, "You just stay with Sheila, and I'll take an Uber over to the hospital."

"Are you sure?"

"Yes, Mom," Anita teases.

Vivian laughs, grateful for the release. "Okay, I'm going to go now, but have a safe flight, Anita. Love you!"

"Love you more!" Anita exclaims. She hangs up and zips around her room, packing for her urgent trip to Chicago.

As soon as Vivian hangs up, the nurse comes over and gives her a handful of documents to sign. It takes her about thirty minutes to read and sign the documents before she returns them to Nurse Hernandez.

As Vivian awaits the results of Sheila's blood work, she pulls out her Bible and reads it intently. Suddenly, she feels her phone vibrating and is amazed to see it's a call from Detective Williams.

"Hello, Detective Williams. I was going to call you earlier, but I ended up having to rush Sheila to Chicago Medical Center."

Detective Williams' smiling face turns into a horrified frown. "Is she okay? What's going on?"

"This morning I was trying to follow up with everyone regarding Damien, and I found Sheila unconscious in her room bleeding from the mouth. I was just told that the doctor believes she has a serious infection. They just took her back to complete the bloodwork, and I'm here waiting for the results now."

Detective Williams bites at a cuticle and stares at the ultrasound photo in his office. "Is Sheila awake?"

Vivian shakes her head, "No, Detective, but thankfully, she is alive. They have her breathing through a tube, but they say she is in stable condition. And they can't do anything further until her bloodwork comes back."

"Detective, what's your first name?" Vivian asks.

He stares at the picture. "John. Detective John Williams."

Vivian nods as she peers down the hall in hopes of seeing Dr. Peters. "Would you mind if I call you John?"

The detective shakes his head. "Not at all."

"So, John, are you calling to tell me that you believe you are Sheila's father?"

His voice begins to crack, "No." He pauses for a while. Vivian can hear sniffling sounds. "I'm actually calling to tell you that I *am* Sheila's father."

"Oh, my Lord. Thank you, Jesus! That's the best news I've heard in a while. I can't believe it." She nearly jumps out of her chair. Detective Williams smiles as he takes in her excitement. "So, John, you say that you know you are Sheila's father. How do you know for sure?"

"Well, Vivian, I was one-hundred percent sure after talking with you at the station, especially after you showed me Anita's picture. That sealed the deal. However, I still ran Sheila's DNA against mine, and it came back 99.9 percent positive that Sheila is my daughter." Curious, he asks, "How did you know that I was Sheila's father?"

"I didn't know for sure, but my sister told me that story about her being at a café and slamming an ultrasound down on the table in front of the guy who had gotten her pregnant. She was telling him that would be the last photo of his daughter that he'd ever see."

Detective Williams chuckles as he brushes back his hair with his hand. Years of guilt well up in the pit of his stomach. "Yes, that was me. What else confirmed my fatherhood to you?"

"Oh yes, when Sheila and I got home from the station, Sheila told me that she saw something weird at your office."

John looks around his office, which is pretty average looking. "And what was that?"

"Sheila said that she saw a framed ultrasound sitting on your office mantel."

Staring at the framed ultrasound, he responds, "That's true."

Vivian proceeds, "And then I combined the ultrasound picture with the questions you asked me at the station regarding Sheila's mother, and the look on your face when I told you her name and showed you her pictures. And last but not least, the fact that you suddenly pulled out of Damien's case."

Detective Williams chuckles again, "Well, great job." He claps dramatically. "I'm going to have to make you an honorary detective."

Vivian laughs, "Oh no, I've got more than enough on my plate right now." Just then she looks up to see Dr. Peters turning the corner. "Oh, John, I see the doctor heading in this direction. Are you planning on coming to see your daughter?"

He looks at his watch. "Yes, I'll be there this evening. Please keep me updated. This is my personal phone I'm calling you from. Please feel free to call me at any time."

Vivian nods as she stands to greet the doctor. "Okay, John, I will." Just before hanging up, she remembers something important. "Oh, and John, I just have to say that I'm so very happy and thankful that you and Sheila found each other. Congratulations!"

He smiles warmly, "Thank you so much, Vivian! I'll see you later."

Just as Vivian hangs up, Doctor Peters says, "Hello, Mrs. Johnson, is it possible that you can get Sheila's mother back on the phone? I promised her that I would update her, and I have some very urgent news regarding Sheila that requires her immediate attention."

Vivian dials Anita again. "Yes. Just a moment. I'm calling her now."

Dr. Peters gestures for Vivian to follow her as they walk to another area. "Let's take this call to that empty room next door. The nurses will watch over Sheila."

"Hey, Viv. What's going on?"

"Hello, Anita. I have you on speaker phone, and I have Dr. Peters here with me. She says she has the results from Sheila's bloodwork and needs to speak with you immediately."

Dr. Peters leans toward the phone. "Hello, Anita, this is Dr. Peters again. The bloodwork came back, and the results show that Sheila has a serious kidney infection which requires the surgical removal of a large abscess."

"Oh, my Lord," Anita cries. She clutches her chest and glances at the clock, counting the seconds until she boards her flight to be by her baby's side.

With a voice filled with concern, Dr. Peters says, "Yes, unfortunately we have no time to waste, and we'll have to operate on her immediately before the abscess bursts. But once we remove the abscess, your daughter's fever should begin to reduce rapidly. Her body will be going through a lot, and she will need plenty of rest, so you may not be able to see her awake until tomorrow."

"Can we first treat it with an antibiotic?" Anita asks.

The doctor shakes her head. "I'm sorry, Anita. We are way past that point. If we would have caught it weeks in advance, maybe that would have been an option. Now, I'm afraid that if we don't take action immediately, the abscess will burst, and that could possibly kill her."

Running a hand through her hair, Anita tries to remain calm. "Yes, Dr. Peters, I understand."

"I believe that in three to four weeks, Sheila will fully recover. She just needs to stay with us here at the hospital so we can monitor her. Time is running out on us, so why don't I have my nurse send you the results of the bloodwork and x-rays to a secure portal, and you can get a second opinion? In the meantime, I'll have an operating room and our best doctors on standby."

Anita checks the time again. "That sounds like an excellent idea. Can you please send it immediately? I have a flight leaving in three hours."

Dr. Peters also checks the time on her end. "Yes, Anita, I'll put the nurse on now and you can give her your secure portal information."

"Okay, and before you go, how's the baby?" Anita asks eagerly.

Doctor Peters looks over her clipboard. "Yes, we were informed by the EMTs that Sheila was pregnant. But it looks like the test came back negative for a pregnancy."

Anita and Vivian each put a hand over their mouth. "No way!" Vivian says. "But Sheila took not one, but two pregnancy tests, and they both came back positive."

"Well, when a woman has an infection, especially one as serious as Sheila's, it can cause blood or white blood cells to show up in her urine," Dr. Peters explains, "This can create a false positive reading when taking an over-the-counter pregnancy test."

Anita nods her head, thinking over the information she is hearing. "That's so true. Sheila shared with me earlier this week that she didn't feel as if she were actually pregnant. She noticed that she hasn't gained any weight or had any morning sickness."

Looking at the clock and then toward Sheila's room, the doctor says, "Well, I'm not sure whether your daughter not being pregnant was good or bad news, but we really need to focus on the infection. So, Anita, please get back to me no later than an hour from now."

"Yes, Dr. Peters. I'll make sure I have an answer for you then."

As Dr. Peters and Nurse Hernandez leave the room, Vivian continues talking with her sister.

"Oh, Anita, I'm so sorry."

"For what, Viv?" Anita removes the phone from her ear to check the portal for Sheila's results.

"I really thought that Sheila was pregnant," Vivian says, running a hand through her hair.

"Don't be so hard on yourself. Besides we have to be strong for Sheila. That's all that matters now," Anita says.

They say their goodbyes so Anita can focus. When Vivian returns to Sheila's room, she starts to hyperventilate at the sight of the tubes all over her niece's body. Looking at Sheila, Vivian blames herself for all that's unfolded since the pregnancy test which she insisted that Sheila take. *If I hadn't told Damien that he was a dad, and just waited until the doctor confirmed Sheila's pregnancy, maybe he would not have even gotten shot.* Crying, Vivian speaks to God, "Lives were changed and nearly destroyed by things that I said. My Lord, what have I done?"

Vivian sits in the empty room, feeling defeated and ashamed, with her head in her hands. "I should've waited until after the doctor's appointment and an accurate urine or blood test to confirm her results. What was I thinking?" Vivian imagines a plethora of awful scenarios and feels responsible for all that has gone wrong with Sheila's stay in Chicago.

Crying quietly in the empty room by herself, Vivian calls on Sheila for forgiveness, "Oh, I'm so sorry, sweetie, I'm so sorry. I should have known better, Sheila." Vivian is crying uncontrollably when suddenly she receives a call from Sharon. Vivian wipes her face and picks up the phone.

"Hello, dear, how are you?" Sharon says, sounding hopeful.

Vivian lies through her tears, "I'm fine." Then she catches a glimpse of her reflection in the window and shakes her head. "Oh, Sharon, who am I'm fooling? I feel terrible."

Sharon, concerned for her friend, who was so strong for her just a few hours before, asks, "Do you have a few minutes to talk?"

Vivian takes out a tissue and gently dabs at her face. "Well, yes, but I'm back at Chicago Medical."

Sharon is shocked. "Really? I should have told you that I went home to freshen up and grab some essentials for Damien. Did they let you see Damien. How is he?"

At that moment, Vivian bursts into tears. Sharon sits down, ready to listen to her distressed friend. "What's wrong? Is everything okay with my Damien? Why are you crying, Viv?"

"I'm sorry, but my crying has nothing to do with Damien," Vivian explains, "I'm actually not here to visit Damien right now. But I pray he's doing fine." She cries softly. "I'm here because Sheila was just admitted to the hospital a couple of hours ago." Feeling the unbearable weight of the situation, Vivian sobs loudly.

"Oh no, what happened to Sheila?" Sharon clasps her hand over her mouth. "Please tell me that she and the baby are going to be okay."

"I certainly hope Sheila is going to be okay. This is all getting to be too much for me, Sharon," Vivian says, voicing her distress. "However, I have no choice but to continue to lean on my faith."

Sharon raises a hand in praise. "Amen, Viv. And if you feel up to it Vivian, please tell me what happened to Sheila. Are she and the baby okay?"

Vivian explains everything to Sharon, who nearly drops the phone in disbelief. "Now, after everything we went through, a series of blood tests confirmed that Sheila was never pregnant."

Sharon is silent for a while. "Say that again?"

"Yes, you heard me right. Sheila was never pregnant. The doctor explained that Sheila's kidney infection caused white blood cells to enter her urine, thus creating the two false positives."

"Sheila must have been unaware of this infection, but I can only imagine it must have been causing her pain," Sharon speculates.

"Yeah, pain that she never mentioned to me." Vivian shakes her head in disbelief.

Sharon gets up to finish packing things for Damien. Vivian continues crying over the phone. "I'm so sorry, Sharon. Look at this mess that I've gotten everyone into."

"I'm just speechless, and if your doctor hadn't been on vacation, maybe they could have seen Sheila sooner," Sharon says, "That was completely out of everyone's control, Viv. You can't blame yourself for this. It was Sheila and Damien who had no business fooling around like that in the first place."

Vivian is grateful for Sharon's broader perspective. "Yes, that's true, but I've made some harsh judgments about Sheila and Damien for which I'm so sorry."

Sharon continues comforting Vivian, "Please, don't be so hard on yourself. I was selfish in thinking that it would be lovely to have a grandchild, but Sheila not being pregnant actually gives the kids a fresh start. Hopefully they will learn from their poor choices, and in the future make better ones." She looks out the window and checks the time. "You need to concentrate on Sheila. We have a lot of work to do to get these kids back on their feet."

Vivian agrees while Sharon continues to share her words of encouragement, "So, let's please stay strong and continue to trust God's plan."

Vivian feels a little better. Wiping her eyes, she says, "I will. Thanks so much, Sharon—for everything."

Sharon smiles, "Well, I'll be there soon. Don't you worry about Damien. I've got him while you concentrate on Sheila. Then we will meet somewhere in the middle."

"You are a beautiful woman, Sharon. You are an angel. I truly love you. You have always been an amazing friend," Vivian says sincerely.

Sharon's heart warms. "Thank you, Vivian, and so are you. We got this, girl. I love you."

As both women prepare to end the call, Sharon remembers something, "Oh, before I go, the reason why I was calling was to explain to you that, although Tanya and I were initially very angry about what happened to Damien, especially because of Sheila's involvement in it, we have decided to forgive both Sheila and Travis."

Vivian sits in awe. "I told Detective Williams that Damien and Sheila have suffered enough, and I truly believe that Sheila was talking out of anger. From how we've all gotten along, I know she really didn't want to hurt Damien. I also believe that Travis acted out of what we used to call puppy love. He just wanted to prove himself to Sheila, but unfortunately, now he has to pay a steep price for trying to play the macho man."

Vivian is overwhelmed with gratitude for her kind friend. Sharon continues, "I'm just so glad that Damien survived the shooting; because although I'm a Christian woman, if Damien did not survive the shooting, I don't know if I would be as forgiving."

Vivian nods in agreement, completely amazed that Sharon is so forgiving. "I understand, and I truly thank you and Tanya so much for your kindness and grace. There are so many lessons to be learned from all of this."

"And believe it or not, we're not even done yet," Sharon interjects. "It looks like this is just the beginning of a long road to recovery for the kids. Shoot, for all of us."

Vivian agrees. "Oh yes, but before I forget, there was actually another sprinkle of hallelujah/good news that happened today."

"I'm all ears for this." Sharon sits down at the dining room table with the essentials for Damien packed and ready to go. "Please tell me."

Vivian sits up straighter, feeling renewed in her faith. "In the midst of all of this, Sheila's father has been identified."

Sharon sits back in her seat. "Are you serious, Vivian?"

Vivian nods, "Yes, I am."

Sharon is reminded of her gratitude earlier when she saw Damien open his eyes. Things were looking up, and it was all thanks to God, she thought. Smiling, she says, "That is absolutely fantastic news. Does Sheila know?"

Vivian shakes her head and begins to stretch. "Not yet, but we've got to tell her as soon as she wakes up. She will think it's a dream."

"I know. I'm so excited for her," Sharon says enthusiastically. "I have to ask you, though, who is her father?"

"Detective John Williams, girl."

Sharon leans forward on the table. "No!? Not the same Detective Williams that was working on Damien's case?"

Vivian paces the floor, feeling lighter. "Yes. That's him."

Sharon looks at her arms and watches the goose bumps rise. "I'm feeling chills. It's so true that you never know which direction God's blessings are coming from."

Vivian agrees as Sharon goes on, "Before I tell Tanya the good news, was Detective Williams able to take a DNA test?"

Vivian giggles, "Yes, and it came back 99.9 percent positive that Detective Williams is Sheila's father."

Sharon sits in disbelief. Reaching for a crisp pear, she stands up to wash it and sandwiches the phone between her ear and her shoulder. "I can't get over it. That is such wonderful news. You will have to tell me the whole story when things settle down."

"Girl, we're going to have to do this over another spa day at least. Shoot, I need a vacation to the Bahamas after this. My treat either way," Vivian says.

Sharon cracks up. She bites her pear, feeling much more relaxed.

Looking at the time, Vivian makes a mental note of the rest of her day. She looks toward the door and gets ready to go check on Sheila. "Well, Sharon, I've got to get going, but I'll be seeing you soon."

Sharon finishes her pear and puts it in her compost bin. "We've got this. I'll see you soon."

"We sure do," Vivian smiles as she ends the conversation with her dear friend, Sharon.

Chapter 25

A Race Against Time

A nita stares at the tarmac as she calls Dr. Peters. "Hey again, Dr. Peters. After consulting with a urologist and other medical staff at Harlem City Hospital, they have confirmed that the operation is vital," Anita affirms.

"Well, Ms. Robinson, everything is ready to go, and I'll have the nurses prepare Sheila for the operation," says Doctor Peters.

Wishing she were already in Chicago so she could make sure everything was all right, Anita says, "Please take care of my little girl. I should be arriving around seven-thirty."

"No worries. We'll take very good care of Sheila," says Dr. Peters, who smiles as she moves toward the door to get ready.

Anita flashes a half smile, "Thanks." She picks up the phone and calls Vivian, who is sitting a few feet away from Sheila when the phone rings. "Hey, sis."

Sounding a little panicked, Anita asks, "Viv, how is Sheila?"

"Sheila is still in stable condition, but the nurses say that she's still running a high temperature."

"Okay, I just called Dr. Peters and agreed to move forward with the operation."

"Oh dear," Vivian gasps.

Sighing deeply, Anita says, "Don't worry, it will all turn out fine. I researched the urologist performing the operation and he is one of, if not, the best in his field."

"Great, you know I'll be praying for sure."

Sighing deeply, Anita smiles as she watches another flight take off in the distance. "Thanks, I'm gonna go find something to do here before my flight. I'm due to land in Chicago at 6:30 and will head directly there."

"Be safe, Anita. I'll see you soon," Vivian responds.

Anita hangs up and continues staring out the window for a while before taking a walk around the airport, hoping to find something special to bring for her sister and daughter. She stops to get a soft cinnamon sugar pretzel. The stress of the last few hours melts away with each powdery bite.

A short while later, Nurse Hernandez enters Sheila's room and tells Vivian that they will be prepping Sheila for surgery. "The estimated time for everything to be completed will be at five p.m. If you'd like, you can stay in the waiting area, and someone can come get you when Sheila awakens from the anesthesia."

Vivian stands up and kisses her niece on the forehead. "That sounds great. Maybe I'll get something to eat and visit my friend's son who was also admitted to this hospital. Then I'll be in the waiting room until I hear from you."

Nurse Hernandez nods as she preps Sheila for the operation. "That's fine. The waiting room is where we will look for you once Sheila is back in her room."

Vivian walks toward the door. "Thanks again and please take good care of my niece."

Nurse Hernandez meets her gaze and smiles, "Without a doubt. Sheila's in good hands."

Meanwhile, Sharon and her daughter, Tanya, are on their way back to the hospital with Damien's essentials. Stopped at a light, mother and daughter review Tanya's performance on *The Voice*. "So have you decided which song you are going to sing yet?"

Tanya looks up from her phone and replies, "I've selected some songs that Damien loves to hear me sing. So out of those songs, I want Damien to make the final decision."

Sharon tears up as she drives. "That's so sweet, baby. I am truly so proud of the relationship you have with your brother." Sharon glances at her daughter. "With all that's going on back here, I may have to ask Thomas to go with you to Los Angeles. Is that okay with you, dear?"

Tanya shrugs nonchalantly, "Yeah. I know you need to stay here and take care of Damien."

Feeling relieved, Sharon smiles, "I knew you'd understand." She rubs Tanya's hand. "I was going to ask Vivian, but she needs to stay at the hospital with Sheila." She shakes her head in complete disbelief.

Tanya looks shocked. Putting her phone down, she looks at her mom, "What do you mean? Why is Sheila in the hospital? Is the baby okay?"

Sharon looks conflicted. "I'm sorry sweetheart. I didn't want to tell you all of this at the house with everything that has happened as of late. I wanted you to get some rest, and I knew that telling you what I'm about to tell you would have interrupted that. But yes, Sheila was rushed to Chicago Medical earlier today. Vivian found her on the floor unconscious and bleeding from her mouth. When she arrived at the hospital, they discovered that she had a dangerously high fever. The doctor diagnosed her with a serious kidney infection that requires an emergency operation to remove an abscess. I'm sure they're performing that operation as we speak."

"Oh no. Well, I hope that Sheila and the baby will be okay," Tanya says, shaking her head.

Vivian glances at Tanya, "Well, dear, while testing Sheila's blood for the infection, the doctor discovered that Sheila is not even pregnant."

Tanya's mouth drops open. "Sheila is not pregnant?" she says in shock.

Her mom shakes her head, "Nope. Can you believe that?"

Tanya sits in silent awe for a while, then turns to look at her mom, "Are you serious?"

Bewildered and with her head still spinning from the last two dizzying weeks, Sharon says, "Yes, dear. I wouldn't joke about anything like that."

"I know, Ma. I just can't believe that all of this has happened this summer," Tanya notes.

Sharon sigh, "I know. It's a lot to take in. But we just gotta stay strong in our faith for both Damien and Sheila. Especially, we have to continue to remain non-judgmental."

With so much news floating around, Sharon Jackson is reminded of one more silver lining in the chaotic recent events. "You know, there is a bit of good news that came out of all of this."

"Yes, I know. Damien and Sheila have an opportunity for a new beginning now," Tanya notes, oblivious about the remaining news.

Sharon nods, "That's true, but that was not the good news I was speaking of."

Tanya glances at her mom curiously. "Oh boy. What's the good news?"

Her mom looks at Tanya, eyes dazzling with excitement, causing Tanya to appreciate how nice it was to see joy returning to her mom's face.

"Honey, it's my understanding that Sheila's father has been identified!"

Tanya shakes her head and throws her hands up in amazement. "My goodness, Ma! News has been coming fast and furious. Who is he? Do you know?"

Sharon looks at her daughter again as she pulls up to the hospital. "Are you ready for this?" Tanya nods yes. "It's Detective Williams, one of the first detectives who was working on Damien's case," Sharon says.

Tanya's eyes widen. "This whole thing sounds like a movie!" she exclaims.

Her mom agrees, "I know, dear. But if it's true, then that is really good news for Sheila."

Tanya is curious, "Does Sheila know?"

Her mom shrugs, "I don't think so."

Tanya looks out the window and rolls it down for some fresh air. "Wow. This is going to make her so happy."

Sharon shakes her head and smiles, "I know. That girl has been through a lot, and nothing will make her happier than finally meeting her father."

Tanya takes a deep breath. "Well thanks for waiting to tell me all of this, Mom. You were so right. There was no way I would have gotten *any* rest if you had told me all of this earlier." They share a laugh. "When we get to the hospital, can we buy flowers for Damien and Sheila?"

Sharon smiles and runs a free hand through her daughter's hair. "Yes, we definitely can, dear. How thoughtful."

Sharon pulls into the parking garage and finds a spot right on the fifth floor. She and Tanya get out of the car, making sure not to forget Damien's bag. They head toward Damien's room, where they're greeted by Nurse Roberts. She smiles at them, "I hope you two had a chance to get some rest."

"Yes, we did, thank you very much. How about you, were you able to get some rest?"

Nurse Roberts puts a hand on her hip. "Well let's put it this way: It's never as much rest as I'd like, but I do feel refreshed." They chuckle before she continues, "And Damien is doing extremely well. All his tests came back fine. In fact, Damien is even eating very well and has a great sense of humor." She laughs and shakes her head as she recalls something he said, "When asked if he knew what happened to him, he said that his coach probably shot him for fumbling the football."

Both Tanya and her mother laugh. "Well that definitely sounds like our Damien," Sharon says. They both remain smiling as they head for Damien's room.

Before they reach the door, Sharon and Tanya hear what sounds like Damien laughing. They walk in and are greeted by a smiling Vivian and Damien having a jolly ole time. Vivian immediately gets up and gives Sharon and Tanya big hugs. Then Tanya and her mom walk up to Damien and kiss him. Sharon stays by her son's side, playing in his coils.

"How are you feeling, son?"

Damien looks down at his bandaged body. "Well, I've had better days," he jokes. Glancing at Tanya, he asks, "And how are you, little sister?"

Tanya's eyes fill with tears of joy. She smiles as they trickle down her cheeks. "I'm good, big brother."

Damien asks Tanya to come closer to him. He reaches out to hug her as best as he can. "You know what, little sister? I had a dream about you and the crazy thing about the dream was that it seemed so real."

Tanya looks intrigued, "Oh, yeah? What was the dream?"

Damien continues, "I dreamed that you were singing my favorite song."

"Is it 'I Wanna Know What Love Is' by Foreigner?"

Damien nods slowly so as not to cause himself too much discomfort. "Yes, and after you sang your heart out, the audience and the judges went wild."

Tanya's eyes continue to well up with tears. "Well, big brother, that's the song I'll sing." She kisses him on his forehead.

Sharon, Vivian, Tanya, and Damien continue talking for another hour before Nurse Roberts knocks at the door. She walks in with a smile on her face and a cart in her hands. "Time for your bandage change," she announces.

Vivian moves toward the door. "Well, it seems that's my cue to leave." She looks up at the clock. "It's about time for me to go check on Sheila."

Damien smiles at Vivian and says, "Please tell Sheila that I said hello, and that I hope she feels better."

"Will do," Vivian promises as she leaves the room. Vivian walks down hall to the elevator, where she goes up one flight to the waiting area where she had agreed to meet Nurse Hernandez. Taking out her phone to check her messages, Vivian sees that she has a missed call from Anita. The message said: "Hey, Viv. I was able to get bumped up to an earlier flight and will be arriving an hour earlier than expected."

Vivian puts a hand to her mouth when she realizes that Anita and Sheila's father are on a collision course to run into each other. To avoid any further drama, she calls John to warn him that he may have to face Anita tonight.

When John picks up, Vivian greets him with a warm, "Hello, John."

He smiles, "Hello, Mrs. Johnson. Is everything okay?"

Vivian glances down the hall to see if she can spot any of Sheila's nurses. "I'm not sure. I'm sitting here in the waiting area so they can let me know when Sheila will be ready for visitors. I'm sure she will be out shortly."

"I'm actually on my way there."

Vivian gulps. "Well, that's actually my reason for calling. I just wanted to let you know that there's a very good chance that you'll be running into Anita tonight."

John feels his stomach drop. "No way."

Vivian nods as she paces in the waiting area. "Yes. She should also be arriving shortly."

John takes a deep breath, bracing himself for two encounters that are sixteen years overdue. "Well, I have no problem with it, if you don't. I'm more than ready to own up to my shortcomings and to move forward on the right foot."

Vivian smiles, "Oh no, I have no problem with it; I just wanted to give you a heads up. It's been hectic enough as it is."

John looks up as he approaches the hospital. "Thanks, and hey, Anita and I can discuss our differences another time. Right now, and in the foreseeable future, it's all about Sheila's health and making up for lost time."

Vivian nods sweetly. "Yes, and knowing my sister, I'm more than one-hundred percent sure that's what Anita wants, too."

John stops at a red light and smiles. Feeling the warmth of the setting sun on his skin, he responds, "Good, then everything should work out fine. I'll see you all soon."

"Okay, John. See you." Vivian hangs up and finds a seat by the window. She watches as the sun casts an orange haze over the city she loves so much and waits for her family to arrive.

After waiting for information about her niece for over an hour, Vivian is relieved when Nurse Hernandez comes out to update her on Sheila's condition. Smiling wholeheartedly, Nurse Hernandez says, "Hello, Mrs. Johnson. So, the operation went well and Sheila's temperature is back to normal. She's been recovering for several hours and now she's awake and lively." Vivian smiles. "As expected, she is in some pain, but we are managing it with low doses of morphine. She will be able to have visitors shortly—probably about an hour from now," says Nurse Hernandez.

Vivian breathes a sigh of relief, "Well, that's good news. Thank you for the update. I'm just so anxious to see her."

"Yes, that's understandable, and Sheila has definitely been asking for you," Nurse Hernandez says.

Vivian adjusts herself in her chair. "Rest assured that I'm not moving. I'll be right here waiting, and you can tell her that."

The nurse chuckles. "Okay, dear, it won't be too much longer," she says before heading back to continue caring for Sheila.

Just as Vivian begins checking her phone, she notices John walking toward her. Standing to greet him, she wraps him in a warm hug. "Hello, John. I just spoke to Sheila's nurse, and she told me that the procedure went well. Sheila is conscious and talking, but she may still be in a lot of pain."

Looking somewhat sad, John says, "That's expected. Can we go in and see her yet?"

Vivian shakes her head. "No, John. Not yet. Nurse Hernandez says we will have to wait another thirty minutes or so."

John follows Vivian back to the area where she was sitting. "Well, I waited sixteen years, I guess another thirty minutes won't kill me."

Vivian turns to him as they sit comfortably in the seats by the window. "See, about that, John, it may be a little longer for you because I don't want to put too much on Sheila at once. I would like to go in and speak with her prior to you seeing her. You can wait out here for Anita and you both can get reacquainted then come in together."

John beams. "Now that sounds like a plan. Imagine her seeing both of her parents walk in at the same time. That could cheer her right up," John says, feeling optimistic and excited about reuniting with his daughter.

With all that's unfolded recently, Vivian is determined to remain cautious. "But it could also workout negatively. That's why I would like to speak to her first."

"You got it, boss." He looks around and stands again. "By the way, can you point me in the direction of the cafeteria? I can sure use a cup of coffee."

Vivian stands and points toward the elevators. "Sure. It's on the second floor, right where the doors open up."

John smiles before turning toward the elevators. "Thanks, I'll see you in a few, Vivian."

Alone again while waiting to hear from Nurse Hernandez, Vivian begins to pray that it will all work out well between Anita and John. She says prayers for Sheila and the entire Jackson family and lastly for herself.

Just as she wraps up her "word" with God, John walks out of the elevator with his coffee cup in hand and goes to join Vivian. "It's pretty busy down there."

Vivian nods in agreement, "Wow, still? It was busy when I was down there, too."

Turning her head to look at the dusky skyline, Vivian notices Nurse Hernandez walking toward her and sits up eagerly. Nurse Hernandez bustles over to Vivian and John. "Hello, dear. It looks like Sheila is ready to see you."

With tears in her eyes, Vivian stands up with a sigh of relief, "Please take me to her." As they walk away, Vivian stops in her tracks and turns to John, "Excuse me. I'm so sorry. Nurse Hernandez, meet Sheila's dad, Detective John Williams."

"Hello, John, I'm Nurse Hernandez, and I've been taking care of Sheila since she arrived."

John extends a hand, and they greet each other somewhat formally. "Thank you so much, Mrs. Hernandez. I've been hearing from Vivian that everyone has been so wonderful in caring for my daughter."

Nurse Hernandez pauses. Looking a bit puzzled, she asks, "Did I hear it right? Is it true that you are Sheila's father?"

"Yes, I am," John says.

Nurse Hernandez is puzzled. "I'm a little confused. Sheila told me that she never knew her dad. Maybe I've adjusted the morphine a little too much."

They all laugh while Vivian clarifies, "No, you didn't. It's truly a long story. I'm sure you will hear more about it prior to Sheila leaving here. But right now, I'm ready to see my niece."

"Yes, ma'am, come right with me." Vivian follows behind the nurse as John takes a seat and waits for Anita. He sips his coffee calmly, feeling the dark roast warming him up in the cool hospital room.

Not knowing what to expect from Sheila's mother, John braces himself to handle whatever comes his way with strength and understanding. Confrontation comes with the job of being a detective anyway. It's nothing he isn't used to.

Chapter 26

Reunited (And It Feels So Good)

Nurse Hernandez brings Vivian to room 602 where Sheila is recovering. Vivian is greeted by Sheila's dazzling smile. "Hello, Auntie," Sheila's voice cracks, and she is groggy with sleep.

Vivian rushes to her side. "Hello, my sweetie. How are you feeling?"

Wincing due to the pain, Sheila speaks in a croaky voice, "I'm feeling some pain, but other than that, I feel okay."

Vivian rubs her niece's arm as Sheila's eyes dart back and forth.

"You don't know how happy I am to see you," Vivian says, "You really scared me this morning. I walked into your room and found you unconscious and bleeding from the mouth."

"Really, Auntie? I'm so sorry for scaring you," Sheila says.

"No, don't be sorry. I'm just glad that I found you when I did!"

"Auntie, the last thing that I can remember was feeling a pain in my side and I got up to tell you. But I must have passed out. Next thing I know, I'm waking up here in the hospital."

Vivian smiles fleetingly, "Well, you have some good doctors and nurses taking care of you here. Did the doctor explain what happened to you, yet?"

"Yes, both Nurse Hernandez and the doctor, I forgot her name."

"It's Doctor Miranda Peters, dear."

Sheila snaps her fingers in recognition. "Yes! That's her. They told me that I had a serious kidney infection, and that I had an abscess on my left kidney that needed to be removed immediately."

"Yes, sweetie, that's what I understood as well. Were you ever feeling pain in that area prior to going unconscious?"

Sheila smiles sheepishly, "Yes, Auntie, however, it would come and go. I honestly just thought it had to do with the pregnancy. But this morning, it was more painful than before."

Vivian puts a hand on her shoulder. "Honey, any time you feel unexpected pain please tell someone. And with you being sexually active, you need to be getting tested regularly."

Grateful to see her and for her loving understanding, Sheila looks up at Vivian and says, "Yes, Auntie, I promise. And I do get tested, but I guess it has been a while." Sheila's eyes widen as she recalls something rather dream-like. "Then, Auntie, when I asked about the baby, the nurse told me that they tested my blood to confirm my pregnancy and it came back negative. They said the kidney infection was likely the reason I received two positive pregnancy tests."

Vivian smiles, amazed at Sheila's strong, working mind despite a day of deep sleep. "Wow, sweetie, yes. That's what the doctor told me and your mom, too."

Sheila lights up. "My mom is here!?"

Vivian smiles brightly as she brushes Sheila's hair with her hand. "Well, not yet, baby, but any minute now, she'll be walking through that door."

Sheila feebly points toward the foot of the bed. "Auntie, please pass me that water."

Vivian picks up the water and hands it to Sheila. She watches as Sheila tries to position herself to drink the water but ends up moaning in pain. Startled, Vivian says, "Oh, baby. Would you like for me to call the nurse?"

Sheila takes a breath. "No, I'm fine," she assures her aunt. She closes her eyes and takes several deeper breaths as her aunt looks on with concern.

"Are you sure, sweetie?"

Sheila shakes her head, "Seriously, Auntie, I'm fine."

"Well, if you need the nurse, please let me know. Did they show you where the button is?"

Sheila slowly sips water and enjoys the cool liquid flowing down her dry throat. She sighs with satisfaction. "How's Damien doing?"

Vivian, realizing that she's still gripping her purse, goes to a nearby chair and puts her things there. "Damien is doing just fine. In fact, he told me to tell you hello, and that he hopes you get well soon."

Sheila's face lights up again. "Really? He told you to tell me that?"

Vivian walks back to her side and pulls up a chair. "Yes, sweetie, the whole Jackson family has forgiven you for your part in Damien's shooting. And because of Travis's written testimony that Damien's shooting was all his doing, combined with the courts being tied up and Sharon and Tanya signing off on a deal, you will not be locked up. You will have to serve three months of house arrest for a misdemeanor charge of simple assault, and your house arrest will take place at your home in New York. If you have no further incidents during your house arrest, your records will be expunged, which means that your records will no longer be available for the public to see."

Sheila tries to take in everything her aunt just shared. "What is simple assault?"

"In short, it's when a person threatens to commit bodily harm to another person. And Sheila, I want you to know that you were very blessed that it didn't turn out worse for you. We can discuss the rest of this at another time," Vivian says, "There's just so much for you to catch up on!"

They laugh. Both are unsure of what else to do in response to the rollercoaster ride of an experience they've all shared. Vivian considers bringing up more news for Sheila to digest. "How are you feeling overall? Because believe it or not, what I'm about to tell you may shake you up a little."

Sheila smiles again, "I'm fine, Auntie."

Vivian inspects her closely. "Are you sure?"

Sheila nods, and Vivian proceeds with the greatest twist of all on their rollercoaster ride in Chicago. "Well, Sheila, I have some more news for you. I told you that your mother will be arriving, right?"

"Yes, is she okay?" Sheila asks.

"She's fine, sweetie, and she will be arriving shortly." She pauses for a moment and breathes slowly. "But what I didn't tell you is that your father is sitting outside your room as we speak."

Sheila sits up with a confused look on her face. "My what?" She tears up suddenly. "Did you say that my father is out there?"

Vivian rubs her niece's shoulder. "Yes, sweetie." Vivian feels herself tearing up as well.

Sheila can't believe what she's hearing. "Is this some sort of joke? Because if it is, it's not funny."

Vivian wipes Sheila's tears. "Not at all. Your dad is sitting outside and is ready to come in."

Sheila lies back down and looks up at the ceiling, shaking her head. "This must be some sort of dream," she says in disbelief.

Vivian shakes her head. "No, sweetie. This is all very real, though very magical. See how mysterious and glorious our God is?"

Sheila wipes her eyes and takes another sip of water. Vivian removes the empty cup from Sheila's hand. "Do you want to meet him?"

Sheila nods excitedly, "Of course, I want to meet him. How do you know that he's my dad, though?"

"Because he matched his DNA with yours, and it came back 99.9 percent positive that he's your father. I know you have a lot of questions, sweetheart, so before your parents come in, I'm going to try to answer a few of them for you."

Sheila tries to piece everything together as her aunt continues recounting the latest series of events involving her father. Vivian explains how her mother gave the ultrasound to her father, who remained in denial. "Ever since that day, that young man has been holding on to the ultrasound, praying that one day he finds you. When he became a detective, he had the ultrasound framed and placed it on the mantel in his office beside the framed photo of his family. It's so beautiful to see that your dad has never forgotten you. He saw you every day when he walked into his office."

Sheila, propped up as comfortably as possible, cries silently. She looks up, stricken by a sudden revelation, she asks, "Are you saying that Detective Williams is my father?"

Vivian nods excitedly, "Yes, dear, that's exactly what I'm saying."

Sheila continues to sit in a stupor as tears stream down her face. "Now it's all coming together. His partner, Detective Matthews, thinking that I was Detective Williams' daughter, Pam, and me looking at his family photo, seeing that I do resemble his daughter, seeing the strange ultrasound framed on the mantel, and you spilling your ice cream when I mentioned it to you." She looks at her aunt suspiciously. "Auntie, how long have you known?"

"Oh, sweetie I only had my suspicions when you told me about the picture of the ultrasound, and then I put that together with the questions he was asking me about you and your mom. Plus, the fact that he pulled out of the case so suddenly."

"Yeah, he pulled out of the case within hours of meeting me."

Vivian feels some regret for not being straightforward about it sooner. She sighs, "Yes, sweetie, I wanted to tell you my thoughts. I just wanted to be sure before telling you. But just earlier today, Detective Williams called and told me about the DNA test results." She looks out the window, and seeing that the sky has long since turned dark, she imagines that her sister must have arrived by now. Vivian begins preparing herself for their big moment with Sheila's father.

Sheila, still in a daze, lies gently on the bed and speaks with her eyes closed, "Wow, this is truly unbelievable. And you're telling me that he's out there right now with my mom?"

"Yes, sweetheart. Would you like to see him?"

Sheila turns her head slowly and nods, "Yes, it would be great to see him and my mother together."

"Okay, sweetie, I'm going to go see where they are."

When Vivian reaches the waiting room, she finds John watching television. She sits beside him quietly. He feels Vivian's presence and turns to her, smiling. She updates him on Sheila. "So, Sheila is doing fine, and she was very happy to find out that you are her father and that you are here. She just needs a little more time."

John's face falls before Vivian continues, "She wants to see both you and her mom at the same time. And that won't be long, because Anita just called me and said that she's on her way to the hospital.

"I'm going downstairs to get some essentials for Sheila. Do you want to take a walk with me? We'll likely be back up before Anita gets here."

John stands up and finishes his coffee. "Sure. I need to pick up some flowers."

When Vivian and John arrive at the gift shop downstairs, they run into Tanya at the register purchasing flowers. Vivian sneaks up to Tanya. "Those are some beautiful flowers," she observes.

Tanya turns around with a quizzical look, then she breaks into a marvelous smile. "Oh, hey, Mrs. Johnson." They hug warmly, and Tanya continues, "I bought them for Damien and Sheila." She inches closer to the register.

Vivian looks at Tanya in awe, "That is so sweet of you, Tanya. You have really been so admirable through this whole thing."

"Thank you so much. So when can I visit Sheila?"

Thinking that her sister, Anita, could be arriving any moment, she says, "Hmm, let's check in about that in two hours? Just in case she gets tired."

Tanya nods as she hands the cashier her money. "That will be fine. I'll tell Mom."

Vivian looks at John and says, "By the way, Tanya, meet Sheila's father, Detective John Williams."

Tanya turns away from the register. "Hello, Mr. Williams. It's so nice to finally meet you."

"It's nice to meet you, too."

Tanya looks toward the door and checks the time. "Well, I have to head back upstairs now. I'll see you soon."

"Okay, sweetie," Vivian says. She looks around to see where the flowers are and heads in that direction while stopping to get little snacks and items to keep Sheila fed and entertained.

John walks over and selects a card and a bouquet of flowers. Vivian picks up the essentials that Sheila requested along with more flowers and a couple of cards—one for Sheila and one for Damien. Vivian and John meet somewhere in the middle and walk up to the register to pay for their purchases.

They wait in line, and John turns to Vivian with a question, "May I pay for your items?"

Vivian flashes a dramatic look, making them both giggle. "Yes, please. You only have to ask once." She places her items alongside his and leans in. "Thank you very much."

John flashes a smile, "My pleasure. Thank you for all you've done."

The cashier rings up the items, and John asks for a separate bag for Sheila's gifts. As they exit the gift shop, Vivian starts to walk in the opposite direction. She turns to John. "Be right back. I'm going to drop these items off to Sheila."

John continues walking toward the waiting area. "Okay, take as much time as you need."

John goes to the patient information desk, where he is greeted by a woman, looking bored, and sitting behind the desk. She looks up and smiles.

"Excuse me, could you copy a document for me?" John asks.

She reaches for the document. "Sure, sir. Just a moment." Detective Williams waits patiently until the receptionist returns with two copies of his DNA results. He looks over them, feeling proud, and smiles, "Thank you. That was so kind of you."

Detective Williams walks back to the waiting area, where he finds a comfortable seat and pulls out the card he purchased for his daughter. He writes:

To my dear daughter Sheila,

I wish you a quick recovery, I also want you to know that there is no bigger blessing than to have found you. From this day on, I pray that you will allow me the opportunity to spend the rest of my life being the father to you that I should have been and that I promise to be moving forward.

I've also included in the card a copy of the DNA test results that prove that you are indeed my daughter.

Love,

Dad!

John reviews what he has written before folding up the DNA results and placing the paper neatly into the card. He seals the card and crosses one leg over the other as he sits and waits to meet his daughter.

Sheila's father checks his watch and notes that thirty minutes have passed and Vivian is still in the room with Sheila. He stands and stretches before deciding to walk a little and exercise his legs. As he walks to the elevator, the doors open, and Detective Williams is standing face to face with Anita.

Her eyes widen. "Oh my God! John? Is that really you?"

He looks at her and is suddenly flooded with a rush of conflicting memories. "Yes, Anita. It's me."

Anita can't help but run up and give him a big hug. "It's so great to see you. I'm so, so sorry." She starts crying.

John comforts her as they stand in the hallway. The pair move to the side to clear space for passersby. "No, don't cry. I'm sorry, Anita. I was young and dumb and too immature to handle what was in front of me."

Anita smiles slightly while wiping her tears, "Yes, you were." He shakes his head, accepting the jab. "Well, I assume that you are here to see Sheila."

John nods, "Yes."

"How is Sheila? Did you get an opportunity to see her?" Anita asks.

John shakes his head, "No, I was waiting for you. Sheila wanted to see us together. Your sister is in the room with her now."

"Well, let's go see her! Will this be your first time seeing her?" Anita asks, glancing in his direction as she bustles over to the help desk.

"No, I actually met her during the investigation of Damien's shooting," John responds.

Anita's eyes widen, remembering the wild summer that played out in Chicago. "Oh, okay wow! Now, I understand. We will have to get together to catch up."

John smiles, "Sounds like a plan. Let's just try to avoid that café we went to last time you were here."

Anita laughs heartily, "Man, you haven't changed a bit."

Anita and John are standing by a window when he suggests that they check in with Vivian. John decides to call Vivian, who is talking with Sheila and clearing her niece's tray. As the phone rings, Anita whispers to John, "I'm gonna go look for the bathrooms." John points her in the direction of the restrooms just as Vivian picks up.

"Hey, John. How's everything?"

"Great. In fact, better than expected." He smiles, "Anita's in the bathroom now. She should be back soon."

Vivian feels her heart flutter with joy. "Well, that's beautiful," she says, "That's very good news." She tells John that she'll be right out. Vivian finishes clearing up Sheila's space so she can be ready to see her parents. "Hey, baby, it looks like your parents are out in the waiting room. I'm going to get them—if you're ready?"

Sheila looks excited, though her aunt can see in her face that she is tired. "My parents?" She feels the tears come on again. "Auntie, I thought I would never hear those words or see this day."

Vivian wipes Sheila's tears away and smiles down at her niece. "Well, sweetie, it's been a long time coming, but that moment is finally here. It's here." She rubs her niece's shoulder. "So, are you ready to see them?"

Sheila fidgets with her hair and cranes her neck to see her reflection in the window. "How do I look?"

Vivian looks her over and replies, "Hmm, your cheeks look a little swollen, but you look absolutely beautiful. So beautiful." She runs her hand through her niece's crisp braids, adjusting them slightly before heading toward the door.

Sheila tries to prop herself up as much as she can, and her aunt comes over to help her. Then Sheila takes a deep breath and smiles, "Well, Auntie, I'm ready."

Vivian opens the door. "Okay, Sheila. I'll be right back," she says, overflowing with excitement.

Vivian walks as fast as she can to the waiting room where Anita and Detective Williams sit chatting quietly. Anita looks up and meets her sister's gaze, then runs over to give her a huge hug. "Thank you, Vivian. For all you've done. You are a saint."

Vivian smiles, feeling all of the turmoil she felt earlier dissipate from her being. "You are so welcome, Anita. It's wonderful to see you." Vivian looks at Anita and John and does a happy dance to express her joy. "So, Sheila is doing very well. She's in some pain, but she just needs to take it easy. Then of course she's a little nervous about meeting her dad." Vivian nudges John's arm.

Anita looks around. "When will I be able to speak with the doctor or head nurse?"

Vivian responds, "I'll check into it! But first, let me get you two in to see Sheila. We know John's been waiting long enough."

John chuckles, holding his gifts for Sheila in his hands. "Isn't that the truth?" They all make their way to Sheila's room. Anita feels more tears coming on, and she looks up to see John who already has one rolling down his cheek.

Anita is the first to enter the room, with John close behind her. Vivian comes in and closes the door.

Sheila looks at everyone in awe. "Hello, Mom." She reaches for her mother with wide open arms.

Anita scoops her up in a tender embrace. "Hello, sweetie, how are you feeling?"

Anita gives her daughter a kiss as she looks her over. Sheila winces. "I'm in some pain, but I'll be okay."

Then she looks at Detective Williams, who seems a little standoffish. Jumping for joy on the inside, Sheila anticipates that first hug from her father. "Is it true that you are my dad?"

John steps forward. "Yes, it's true." Tears continue running down his cheek. John, by her bedside, kneels next to her. He holds her hand and passes her the card with the DNA test results.

Her mom joins them, putting one hand on John's shoulder and the other over his hand covering Sheila's. "Yes, it's true, baby."

Sheila excuses herself from their loving touch in order to open the card. Seeing the DNA results fall out, she unfolds the document and looks it over intently. "I don't even know what to say."

John stands up and brushes a tear from Sheila's cheek. "You don't have to say anything, dear." He rubs her arm as she sits there crying silently. He looks Sheila in the eye. "We will have plenty of time to talk everything over and do our best to make up for lost time. I'm truly interested in moving forward with everyone as a family. I know it'll take time, but I am more than willing to do the work." He kisses her forehead softly and places the vibrant flowers on Sheila's bedside table.

Then John flashes another smile at Sheila before he takes a seat at the end of the bed. Sheila's mom, being an registered nurse, begins to explain the recovery process to Sheila.

Back in Damien's room, Sharon looks up from a random magazine and notices that Damien is nodding off to sleep. She stands up and abandons the magazine to straighten out the pillow underneath his head. She whispers in his ear, "Hey, son. Tanya and I will be going for a walk. We'll be back shortly."

Damien sounds groggy, "Okay, Mom."

Tanya walks over and kisses her brother on his cheek. "See you soon, big brother." Damien has already nodded off to sleep by the time Tanya leaves the room. She quietly reaches for the flowers she bought for Sheila and exits.

Mrs. Jackson is waiting just outside the door for her and falls in line beside Tanya, she says, "I thought we'd let him get some rest."

Tanya agrees, "Yeah, he looked very tired." Then she looks in her mom's direction, "Can we go see Sheila?"

Her mom smiles, "Sure, there's no better time than now."

Suddenly, Tanya remembers her encounter with Vivian and the detective earlier. "Oh, mom, I forgot to tell you that I met Sheila's dad when I was in the gift shop."

Her mom looks surprised. "Really? I wonder if Detective Williams is still here."

Tanya shrugs, "That was a couple of hours ago. I'm not sure if he is."

Sharon and Tanya arrive at Sheila's room and are greeted not only by Vivian but also by Sheila's father and another woman who they believe to be Anita, Sheila's mom.

Sharon enters the room first while Tanya stands sheepishly to the side. Vivian makes the introductions, "Hello, Tanya and Sharon. You've already met Sheila's father, Detective Williams, and this is my sister Anita, Sheila's mother." Vivian turns to her sister. "Anita, this is my dearest friend, Sharon, and her lovely daughter, Tanya."

Anita smiles brightly, "Great to meet you all."

Tanya and Sharon greet her in unison, "Great to meet you, too."

Sharon steps toward Sheila, wearing a genuine smile. Sheila is moved to tears, seeing that Damien's mom has truly forgiven her for her foolish mistakes. They squeeze each other's hands.

"So how are you feeling, darling?" Sharon asks.

Sheila looks up at her. "I'm feeling okay. How's Damien?" she asks eagerly.

Sharon nods her head, "He's doing much better."

Sheila sobs and gestures for Tanya and Sharon to come to her. She holds both of their hands. "I want to let you, Tanya, and Damien know that I'm so sorry for the trouble I've caused. I never wanted anyone to get hurt."

Sharon rubs Sheila's cold hand. "We know, sweetheart. We have chosen to look past that and are only here to check up on you and your health."

Tanya nods in agreement, "Yes, we all love you. We have brought these flowers for you. I hope you like them." Tanya hands Sheila the flowers and smiles.

Sheila opens her arms to hug Tanya, feeling so amazed by this sweet young girl and all that she is destined for. She feels grateful to know her. "They are beautiful. Can you place them near the flowers my dad brought for me?"

Detective Williams flashes a proud smile. He is overjoyed to hear Sheila call him Dad.

Still holding her hand, Sheila brags about Tanya's upcoming performance, "Mom, Tanya will be singing on *The Voice*."

Anita looks at Tanya and grins brightly, "That's wonderful!"

Sheila's father chimes in as well, "Wow, yes! My family watches that show all the time." Then he turns to Tanya, "When will you be performing?"

Tanya gets excited thinking about it all. "Actually, in two days!"

Vivian looks at her curiously. "Wow, really? That happened so fast! Who's taking you?"

Sharon sighs, "I still don't know, honestly."

Vivian chimes in confidently, "Well, now that Sheila's parents are here, I can take her, Sharon."

Sharon waves her off, not wanting to be a burden. "No, I can't ask you to do that."

"Well, you didn't. I offered." They all laugh at Vivian's endless wit. She places a loving arm on her friend's shoulder. "You just concentrate on Damien, and I will be just fine."

Despite her protests, Sharon looks visibly relieved to have one less thing on her plate. "Well, thank you so much, Viv. You really just took a load of pressure off me."

Tanya chimes in, hugging Vivian tightly. "Thanks, Mrs. Johnson. We're going to have a lot of fun."

Vivian ruffles Tanya's hair. "Oh, we sure will, baby."

While everyone continues to get acquainted, Detective Williams's emergency phone rings. He excuses himself and steps outside to take the call. Minutes later, he returns to the room and makes an announcement with a sad look on his face. "Well, I have to leave due to an emergency." He walks up to Sheila and gives her a kiss. "I'll be back tomorrow morning." Then he turns to Anita, Vivian, Sharon, and Tanya and gives each of them a hug.

As John turns to leave, Sheila says, "See you tomorrow, Daddy."

He smiles, his hand on the doorknob. "Yes, sweetie. Sounds like a plan."

Smiling to herself, Sheila shakes her head at the magic of coincidence.

After Detective Williams leaves, Sheila enjoys her time with her mom, aunt, Sharon, and Tanya. They all share how happy they are that Sheila is finally reunited with her father. Sheila beams, feeling rejuvenated, "I feel very blessed."

Vivian looks at her phone and gasps at the time. She puts a hand over Sheila's. "Sheila, sweetie, it's getting late, and you need to get some rest. We all do, shoot. But your mom and I will be back tomorrow morning."

Anita, who was dozing off, rubs Sheila's arm and adds, "Yes, baby. Get some rest, and we'll see you tomorrow."

Sheila giggles, "Okay Mom." Sheila gives and receives dozens of hugs and kisses as everyone heads out. She thanks everyone from the bottom of her heart. "I have never felt this much love before. Seriously. Thank you so much."

Sheila is left in her room, smiling, crying tears of joy and thinking that this truly must be what real love feels like.

All of the women walk out together. Anita and Sharon get to know each other a bit, while Tanya and Vivian go over their upcoming trip for Tanya's performance. Suddenly Tanya stops and catches herself as tears roll down her face. "It just gives me the chills to think about all of the events that have happened since Sheila came to Chicago. From finding her dad after sixteen years, to the pregnancy, to the shooting of my brother...." Tanya trails off as Sharon comforts her daughter.

"Yes dear, it's hard to explain why it all had to happen this way," Sharon says as she rubs her daughter's back.

"I've learned never to question God's plan even at the worst of times," Anita chimes in as they all face each other while they wait for the elevator.

Everyone nods in agreement. Vivian adds, "He will always make a way. And what a strong force you have been through all of this, Tanya." She praises Tanya, who smiles through her tears.

As they get on the elevator, Tanya shakes her head and wipes her tears. "You couldn't make up a story like this if you tried." Everyone laughs as they share hugs and say their goodnights before going their separate ways.

When Sharon and Tanya arrive back at Damien's room, he's sitting up, wide awake and flipping through television channels. "Hey, Mom. Hey sis." Damien tries to stretch a bit without causing himself any pain. "I woke up about thirty minutes ago," he offers.

Tanya plops down on her brother's bed. "We just left Sheila's room," she says and bats her eyelashes teasingly.

Damien uses his good hand to nudge his little sister playfully. "Yeah, I heard. I just texted Sheila to see how she was doing. She was telling me how grateful and loved she feels, despite all of the wild adventures we've experienced so far. She also mentioned how much she loves you and Mom, and how you've made her feel so welcome and loved from the first day you met her."

Tanya smiles, "Well, that was so sweet of her." She puts a hand to her heart, feeling the emotions intensely.

Sharon sits on the other side of Damien's bed and rubs his leg. "Damien, I really like Sheila," she says.

"Me, too," Tanya chimes in.

Damien looks at both of them and smiles, "I'm glad. I mean, even though her involvement in what happened to me was completely un-called for, I do think that she's mad cool. I was actually going to ask if it would be okay with you if she visits me tomorrow?"

His mom shrugs, "I wouldn't mind at all."

Damien elaborates on his plans. "I already spoke with Nurse Roberts, and she said that my exams and X-rays are not scheduled until after two p.m. tomorrow. So, if Sheila were to visit me, it would be some time around eleven a.m."

His mom nods, "Okay. Well, Tanya and I planned to stay the night and we'll be up and out of here by nine a.m. Besides, I need to arrange Tanya and Vivian's trip to Los Angeles."

Damien turns to Tanya and looks at her with a smirk, "You got clout, little sis. How did you get Mrs. Johnson to go with you to Los Angeles?"

Tanya laughs, "Yeah, Damien, you didn't know? I got clout!" She giggles at herself. "But to be real, Vivian said since Sheila's parents are here, that she would be happy to go with me."

Damien nods approvingly, "Well, that's great!"

Tanya raves, "Yes, I'm so excited. We are going to have so much fun. Ooh, and I'm going to look *so* fly in my outfit!"

Damien smiles, "Go on' head with your bad self." Sharon laughs as Tanya gets up to boogie down in front of them.

After they calm down, Damien is reminded of something. "You know what? That sounded kind of strange."

"What sounded strange?" Tanya asks as their mom sets up the cots for them.

Damien replies, "I was talking about when you said the words 'Sheila's parents.'"

"I know. I wish you were there because there wasn't a dry eye in the room," Tanya notes.

Damien shakes his head. "I can imagine. It's just an amazing story, a true miracle. And I guess I'm glad that I had a chance to be a part of it." Damien smiles goofily, "Well, you know what I mean."

His mom gives him a stern look, "Yes, we definitely understood what you meant, and you surviving the shooting was also a miracle."

Damien looks at her with a sense of seriousness in his gaze, "For sure, Mom, I thank God every chance I get. I'm grateful."

Yawning and stretching, Sharon stands up and kisses Damien's cheek. "Well, I'm going to get some rest now, y'all."

Tanya stretches and yawns with exaggeration. "So am I."

Damien watches as they begin walking away. He feels called to say one more thing, "Okay, before you two get some rest, I really have to take this moment to thank you both for everything, and I mean absolutely everything."

His mom beams, "You are so welcome. After all, we are Jackson Strong!"

Tanya and Damien chime in together, "Yes, we are!"

"Now, you two sleepyheads get some rest. I'll just send out a few texts then I'll get some more rest, too," Damien says.

Sharon yawns. "Okay, son." She closes her eyes as Damien reaches for his phone.

Damien updates some of his friends before he texts Sheila.

Damien: Hey, I'll b free around 11 tomorrow morning; If u feel up to it, I'd love to see u.

Sheila: Sounds like a plan!

<She includes a heart emoji>

Damien: Dope! I'll see u then.

<He includes a heart eyes emoji >

Meanwhile, Anita and Vivian are a few blocks away from the house as they continue discussing the days' events.

Anita thinks about Sheila and smiles graciously, "I am just so happy with how Sheila is recovering. She was pretty active for all she's dealt with, and the surgery, too."

Vivian is reminded of something. "Oh yes; I forgot to mention that Dr. Peters said that she'd get in touch with you in the morning to update you on Sheila."

Anita looks out the window, trying to see if there was anything familiar from her last visit. "That's excellent."

Vivian glances at her sister while they're stopped at a red light. "So, how did you feel when you first saw John today?"

"Oh Lord, I almost fainted when I saw him. The elevator doors just opened, and there he was!" She nudges her sister playfully. "Girl, why didn't you tell me he was going to be at the hospital?"

Anita shrugs sheepishly, "I had planned to, but my day got so hectic that I truly forgot to mention it to you."

Anita teases her sister, shaking her head, "You have not changed; you still have selective memory. I believe you planned it like that."

Vivian laughs, "I wouldn't do that!"

Then Anita goes on, her eyes darting over the nighttime tableaus they passed by on their way to Vivian's house. "Well, I also forgot to mention something. I agreed to have John arrange for Sheila to do her three months of house arrest here in Chicago with his family."

Vivian glances at her sister, a look of surprise on her face. "Wow, that's fantastic! Have you told Sheila yet?"

Anita shakes her head no, "I'm leaving that up to John."

Vivian nods, "I know Sheila would love that." She pulls into the driveway and sits there for a moment, giving herself a chance to really catch her breath for the first time that day. She sighs with relief and looks at her sister. "Well, here we are—home sweet home!"

Anita and Vivian retrieve Anita's belongings from the trunk. They enter the house; Anita sits down on the couch and looks up at her sister. "Thank you for letting me stay here for a few days."

Vivian looks at her before sitting down in her favorite chair. "I told you once and I'll tell you again you can stay here as long as you need. Please make yourself at home."

After relaxing for a moment by watching a reality show they both enjoy, Vivian stands up to stretch during a commercial break. "I was thinking that you can stay in the bedroom upstairs next to Sheila's. The towel closet is at the end of the hall, babe."

"Thanks," Anita smiles.

"You're welcome," Vivian says, yawning. "And as you can see, I'm exhausted and I'm pretty sure you are, too. I'll see you in the morning." She goes over to the stairs before turning to look back at her sister. "Oh, by the way, if you're hungry, the kitchen hasn't moved."

Anita swats at her sister. "Go to bed. You are getting sillier by the minute."

They laugh until Vivian reaches the bathroom and shuts the door. She lights a candle and runs a warm bath before sneaking into Sheila's room to borrow the speaker she'd been using. Anita remains downstairs. She takes in the space around her. Anita stares at the ceiling before she closes her eyes and calms her body with some deep breaths. Before she knows it, she is fast asleep.

Chapter 27

Turning Over a New Leaf

The next morning, Sheila awakens bright and early and watches the sun rise over the city while she sits in her hospital bed. She sees a text from her father and smiles.

Dad: Hey, Sheila. I'm planning on visiting around 9:00 a.m. Text me back if that's okay.

Sheila looks at the time on her phone. Realizing that it's already 8:00 a.m., she texts her dad back.

Sheila: Hey dad! Yes, 9:00 a.m. is great.

Sheila gets up slowly and goes into the bathroom to freshen up. As she slowly returns to her bed, she remembers to let her aunt and mom know not to visit her until after two p.m. because she will be visiting with Damien.

She picks up the phone and dials her aunt. "Good morning, Auntie. How are you?"

Her aunt raises an eyebrow, "I'm fine, sweetie. Is everything okay?"

Sheila smiles, looking out at the bright sky. "Yes, I just wanted to speak to you and my mom."

"Hold on, dear," Vivian says, "I'll put you on speaker. Your mom and I are sitting here having an early breakfast." Sheila can hear her aunt fidgeting with the phone. "Okay, now what were you saying?"

Sheila smiles. "Good morning, Mom. I just wanted to ask you and Auntie not to come and visit me until after two p.m. because I was planning on visiting Damien this morning."

Her mom gives her sister the look, and they both roll their eyes teasingly. "That's great, dear. But you do know that your dad was planning on visiting you this morning. Have you called him?"

Sheila replies, "Yes, Mom, we texted earlier this morning. He will be here at nine."

Chewing her food, Anita covers her mouth slightly before responding, "Oh, that's great. Just please try not to overdo it. You are a long way from recovery."

Sheila rolls her eyes, knowing her mom's nursing senses were going to be tingling for a while. "I know, Mom, I won't overdo it. I love you both and will see you later today!"

Her aunt and mom reply with smiles, "Okay, honey. We love you too."

Sheila's dad arrives shortly after she gets off the phone with her mom and aunt. He comes in to find her sitting on one of the comfortable chairs in the room. Sheila looks toward the door and is greeted by her dad's smiling face. She smiles back. "Good morning, Dad! And hey, before you say a word, I'd like for us to take a selfie. I want the whole world to know that I found my dad and to see how handsome he is."

Chuckling, John walks over to Sheila and kisses her on the head before crouching down beside her. "Okay, sweetheart. Let's go for it." They flash their brightest smiles, and Sheila snaps several selfies. Sheila looks them over and feels herself getting all warm and fuzzy inside.

"This makes me so happy." She shows one of the images to her dad. "I'm going to make this photo the wallpaper on my phone."

John smiles and peers over her shoulder to see the other photos. "You know what? How about you send it to me and I will do the same."

Sheila starts to send some of the nicer-looking pictures to her dad. "Sounds like a plan."

He looks at her curiously. "Hey, I always say that."

Sheila smiles at him, "Like father, like daughter." They both laugh together.

Her dad puts a hand on her shoulder. "Sheila, I have some good news for you!"

Sheila replies sarcastically, "Oh boy, more news?!" She makes a dramatic face. "What is it, Dad?"

"So, I've arranged for you to do your three months house arrest with my wife and your half brother and sister so you can get to know us better. How do you feel about that?"

Sheila's eyes light up. "Really!? That sounds great. I just have to ask Mom."

John looks at his daughter with love and contentment in his eyes. "Sweetheart, I've already discussed it with your mom, and she is fine with it as long as you are. My wife and the children are excited about spending time with you."

Sheila feels herself getting giddy. "Okay, Dad. I would love that."

John gives her a big hug. "It'll give us a solid start on catching up." He reaches for his phone. "I'll tell the family that you will be arriving in about three weeks. Does that sound like a plan?"

"Yes, Dad. It sounds like a plan." They point at each other and laugh.

He rustles her hair again, admiring her braids. "Did you eat breakfast yet?"

"I drank my breakfast," Sheila replies sarcastically, "The doctors have me on a strict liquid diet until tomorrow, I couldn't even eat the snacks that my aunt got for me. Trust me when I say, I can't *wait* to eat solid food again."

Her dad looks at her sympathetically. "The first opportunity we get, I will take you to a restaurant of your choice."

Sheila beams, "I would love that."

Sheila and her dad continue talking throughout the morning. When he gets up to use the restroom, Sheila checks her phone and sees that it's already a quarter of eleven. Sheila waits for her dad to return. "Hey Dad, I actually promised Damien that I would visit him around eleven a.m. Do you mind taking me to Damien's room?"

Looking at his daughter regretfully, John wishes they had more time. "Okay, well... Will we be walking or would you like to be wheeled to his room?"

"I'd like to go in the wheelchair, please," Sheila says, taking into consideration her mom's advice.

John gets the wheelchair. Breaking out some of his dad jokes, he says, "Don't forget to put Damien's room number into your GPS so we don't get lost."

Sheila gets in the wheelchair and jokingly puts room 511 into the GPS. They both laugh.

Moments later, Sheila arrives at Damien's room and introduces Damien to her father with a huge smile, "This is my father, Detective John Williams."

Damien replies with a smile of his own and reaches out to shake her father's hand, "It's really nice to meet you, sir."

"Nice to meet you too, Damien." He shakes Damien's hand. "I've met your mother and sister. They are very lovely people." He steps back a bit. "How are you feeling?"

Damien nods. "I'm feeling much better. Thanks for asking."

John kisses Sheila on her forehead. "I'll have to get going now, sweetheart."

Sheila gives her dad a big hug. "Well, feel free to call me later," she says.

Her dad smiles and opens the door. "Sounds like a plan."

Just then Damien starts to giggle. John turns around. "Did I say something funny?"

Damien tries to rein in his laughter but can't seem to stop. "It's just that Sheila says that same phrase *all* the time."

John smiles. "Well, like father, like daughter," he says, smiling at Sheila before receiving another notification on his phone. "I really have to go now, but take care, and stay safe, you two." Then he backs out the room, closing the door softly behind him.

Moments later, Sheila walks over to Damien and puts her arms around his neck. "I'm so sorry for everything that happened." She starts to cry and watches as her tears roll into Damien's hair. "I never wanted Travis to hurt you. I was just angry and said some terrible things out of anger. I mean, I never knew that Travis would actually try to kill you."

Damien uses his good hand to gently hold Sheila's arm. "Stop, Sheila. That was the past, and I don't want to go back there. I also said some mean things. Although ,I shouldn't have gotten shot for them, I also need to realize that words carry a lot of weight. They can be very painful to those on the receiving end."

Feeling herself getting tired from standing, Sheila sits on Damien's bed as he looks up at the ceiling and counts his blessings. "I'm so blessed to be alive," he says, "I've looked past getting shot and your misdiagnosed pregnancy, and I ask that you do the same." Sheila nods, feeling some lingering regrets regarding her drastic actions. Damien looks at her and places a hand over hers, hoping to help calm her.

"How are you doing since your operation?"

Sheila gets up and gets some tissues before sitting back down next to Damien. "Like I mentioned in our texts yesterday, I'm still a little sore, but that's not the worst thing." Sheila pauses dramatically.

Damien probes. "What is that?"

Sheila replies sorrowfully, "I haven't had solid food since the operation!" She laughs, "But starting tomorrow, I can eat solid foods again."

Damien laughs with her, "Trust me, you aren't really missing anything. The hospital food is not all that great."

Sheila laughs, "How are you feeling?"

Damien sighs, "I've got a long way to go, but the doctors are saying that I'm healing faster than expected. After I leave the hospital, I will immediately start my rehab."

Sheila is curious, "Where will you start your rehab?"

"I don't know. I honestly haven't thought that far ahead yet."

Sheila gives Damien a sly look, "Well, I know what you need to do to heal even faster."

"What's that?"

Sheila smirks, "You need to look at those pictures that I sent you in my Victoria's Secret outfit."

Damien gives Sheila a very serious look, "Sheila, about those pictures. I've actually deleted them."

Sheila looks shocked, "What? Why?"

Damien sighs and reaches for her hand, "Well, first, I was mad. But I've been thinking, and I would like to approach our friendship in a very different way."

Sheila looks curious, "How so?"

Damien looks her in her eyes, "I would like to approach our friendship with love and not lust. Don't get me wrong. I think you are fire, and I'm very attracted to you. But you and I have way more to offer each other than our bodies. And I would love to learn more about the whole you."

Sheila looks amazed. "Wow! I never had someone tell me that before," she says, "All the other boys that I've dated always seemed to want me just for my body. I appreciate you and respect you even more for what you just said." She squeezes his hand.

Damien smiles, "Well, it's true. When I first met you, I must admit that I had plenty of wild thoughts running through my head. But knowing the way I was brought up, I want to make a change in my life sooner rather than later." Damien takes Sheila by the hand. "I truly want to give us a try."

"What do you mean?"

He pauses for a moment as Sheila looks at him nervously. "Will you be my girl?" he finally musters out.

Sheila is overcome with emotion. "Seriously?" she asks.

Damien gives her a look, "Do I look like I'm joking?"

Sheila laughs at herself, "No, you don't look like you are joking." She pauses for a moment and sighs, "Yes, I'll be your girl." They embrace and kiss.

Sheila is suddenly struck by an interesting thought, "And what if we choose to stay abstinent until further notice? Then we can really focus on building a strong, healthy bond."

Damien sits with that for a moment. He's transported back to that day with his dad when they had 'the talk' in his room. He smiles and looks to the heavens, knowing his dad would approve. "Sounds like a plan." They hug again and sit together for a while.

Just as the two teens unwind from their embrace, Damien's phone rings. Although it's a number he doesn't recognize, Damien chooses to answer anyway. He puts the phone on speaker.

"Hello, is this Damien Jackson?"

Damien looks at Sheila as they both look on with raised eyebrows, "Yes, this is Damien. Who's this?"

"Hello, Damien, this is coach Joe Clark from the Ohio State football team."

Damien's eyes flash with excitement, "Really!?"

The coach chuckles, "Yes, sir. How are you feeling?"

Damien replies, "I've seen better days, but I'm pretty good, all things considered."

The coach replies, "Yes, I've been informed of what happened to you, young man. I called to let you know that our whole facility, including our medical staff and coaches, are available to you during your rehab. We want you on our team, and as long as you continue to work hard on your rehab and keep your grades up, we will have a spot for you on the team."

Damien looks at Sheila with disbelief on his face. "Thank you so much, Coach. I don't know what to say."

The coach smiles, "Don't say anything. Just get well and keep your grades up."

"I will, sir."

Checking his time, Coach says, "I've got to go now, but this is my personal phone number. Feel free to call me any time."

Damien looks at his phone in awe. "Thanks again, Coach."

"You got it," the coach replies before hanging up.

Still buzzing with joy, Damien puts his phone down. "God is so amazing." Damien hugs and kisses Sheila on her forehead. "I feel good about this."

Sheila is curious. "You feel good about what?"

Pulling back, Damien looks at her with a big smile, "About us."

As they separate, Damien pulls his phone out again. "I'm going to call my mom and Tanya to share the good news with them." Sheila sits on the edge of Damien's bed as he dials his mother. "Hey Mom, what are you doing?"

Sharon smiles. She is grateful to hear her son's voice. "Hey, son. I'm here with Vivian and Sheila's mom. Is everything all right?"

"Yes Mom. I just got some good news."

"I'll put you on speaker phone. Say hello to everybody."

Damien greets everyone before asking, "Where's Tanya?"

"I think she's upstairs," Sharon says, "She's probably finishing up packing. I have to take her and Vivian to the airport in a few hours."

Damien gets excited. "That's right, there's been so much happening this morning that I almost forgot that Tanya is going to be on TV tomorrow."

Caught up in her feelings about all of the recent events, Sharon sighs, "Yes, son, and she'll have an early rehearsal. Then she will be performing tomorrow night at eight p.m. our time."

"Well, can you call her down quickly? I have some good news to share with everyone."

Sharon braces herself before calling Tanya to come downstairs. "Okay, hold on." She places the phone down and runs upstairs to get Tanya.

Tanya follows her mom into the kitchen. "Your brother has some good news to share with us, and I have him on speaker phone."

Tanya smiles widely, "Hello, big brother. How are you doing?"

Damien grins. He's happy to hear his sister's sweet voice. "I'm good. I just wanted to share some good news with everyone. But before I do, I want to tell *you* that I'm very proud of you and that I know you will knock it out the park tomorrow. We'll all be rooting for you."

Tanya beams excitedly, "Yes, brother, I got this! When God's on your side, you can't lose."

Damien nods, "That is so true, and it's such a perfect segue for my good news."

"So, what's the good news?"

Damien puts an arm around Sheila. "Well, my Boo, Sheila, is here with me."

Tanya gasps, "Did you actually say your Boo?"

Damien kisses Sheila's head. She smiles and rests her head on his chest. "Yes, Tanya. You spoke it into existence."

Tanya laughs, and Damien continues, "Yes, I asked Sheila to be my girl this morning, and we both have decided to renew our relationship from a place of faith and love, rather than lust."

Grateful to hear how mature they've chosen to be, everyone cheers for them. Vivian chimes in, "Absolutely beautiful. We all will definitely be praying and rooting for you."

Tanya's face is hot with tears. "That's so beautiful. You two are going to make me cry."

"Well, that's only half the good news," Damien continues, "I also got a call from Ohio State's football coach, Mr. Joe Clark. He said that the university facilities, medical staff, and the coaches will be available to me during my rehabilitation."

Sharon looks surprised. Vivian goes over to her friend and hugs her. They all feel gratitude for the blessings being poured over them.

"Wow, let's take a moment to thank God for these countless blessings in the midst of our battles. And let's pray for the safe travels of Vivian and Tanya," Sharon says and begins praying with passion. At the end of her prayer, everyone has tears in their eyes. In unison, they all say passionately, "Amen."

Sharon continues, "Well, son I have to go and get ready to take Vivian and Tanya to the airport. Then I want to prepare a little something for us to share while watching Tanya perform tomorrow."

Damien rubs his stomach. Tired of the hospital food, he is eager for his mom's homemade meals. "Sounds great. I would love that."

Sheila chimes in, "Great. Just in time for me to start eating solid foods again! I'll be getting some good food!" Everyone laughs before saying their goodbyes. Damien and Sheila spend the rest of the morning hanging out and reigniting the flame that brought them together.

Chapter 28

I Wanna Know What Love Is

The next day, Damien wakes up earlier than usual and busies himself posting online about his sister's upcoming performance on *The Voice* and thanking everyone for their support.

Damien's nurses and doctors are also excited about his sister's upcoming performance and have been spreading the excitement throughout the hospital.

Damien doesn't know it, but his mom and the hospital staff are planning a big surprise viewing party for Damien that will take place in the hospital cafeteria. While Sharon told him yesterday that she was preparing something small, in reality, she is preparing a large feast.

Back at their home, Sharon and several church members are busy preparing the feast. There are pots, pans, and dishes all over the kitchen, spilling over into the dining room. The menu includes potato salad, barbecue beef ribs with Sharon's special sweet sauce, mac & cheese, baked chicken, red rice, black-eyed peas, string beans, corn, yams, and so much more. And of course, Sharon is baking her son's favorite biscuits along with a special sweet potato pie just for Sheila. With the entire football team expected to come, Sharon is grateful for the extra help she is getting to prepare the meal. Those boys can eat!

Meanwhile, Sheila wakes up to see some very special visitors who greet her with a smile. Her parents are visiting her along with her dad's wife and children.

Sheila, who is feeling much better, reminds everyone that Tanya will be performing on *The Voice* tonight. "Do you think you all can come back tonight to watch Tanya perform? Please?" She bats her lashes dramatically, making everyone laugh.

Sheila's little brother, John Jr., looks confused. "Who is Tanya?"

Sheila replies with a smirk, "She's my boyfriend's sister."

Her dad and mother smile at each other, "We wouldn't miss it for anything in the world."

"Thanks so much. It really means a lot to me."

Feeling much less discomfort in her body, Sheila scoots over in her bed. "Hey, Pam and John, let's take our first sibling selfie!" They run over to her, feeling grateful for their big sister. "After we take a selfie, I would love to get the whole family, too."

Anita replies, "Sure, honey."

Her father's wife, Brenda, chimes in, "I think that's a great idea." Sheila picks up her phone and takes the selfies. They clown around while taking the pictures. It seems they're all having a wonderful time. But no one is having a better time than Sheila.

Back at the Jackson household, Sharon and her friends are still cooking and laughing together while on the radio Luther Vandross serenades the room. Sharon stops and takes a seat in the dining room when she hears her favorite news anchor, Crystal from Chicago 7 News, on television. She listens to the broadcast. "Coming up next is a heartfelt story about tragedy, love, faith, and forgiveness. And even a father's search for his daughter after sixteen years coming to a happy ending and beginning. You really don't want to miss this story. We'll be right back, with Chicago 7 News."

Sharon returns to the kitchen with her church friends. "Did you hear that?" They all look at her blankly.

Sharon sits down and folds her arms briefly. "They just showed a picture of my little girl Tanya, my son Damien, Sheila, and her dad on the news and then they mentioned that they'll be right back with an amazing story."

Overcome with joy and excitement, Sharon waves for her friends to follow her, and they do but not before tending to their pots and pans.

Moments later, the news comes back on and Crystal returns. "This story is so amazing that it actually made me cry. It is a story full of miracles." Some of her fellow reporters nod and voice their agreement.

Turning back toward the television audience, Crystal delivers her report, "A few weeks ago, we reported on a young Morgan Park Stallion football player who was shot three times while walking home from practice. We are happy to say that Damien Jackson is doing very well and is expected to make a full recovery and should be back on the football field as early as next year."

A montage of Damien flashes upon the screen, followed by pictures of Sheila as Crystal continues, "The young lady who we now know as Miss Sheila Robinson had befriended Damien earlier this summer. She was recently convicted on a misdemeanor charge of simple assault for her involvement in Damien's shooting."

Crystal reaches for a tissue. "Now here is the most amazing and heartfelt part of the story. We have learned here at seven news that Sheila never knew her dad until this shooting. She came to Chicago for the summer and was introduced to Damien by her aunt. One thing led to another before Damien's tragic shooting. Fast forward to Sheila and her aunt at their local police department where a detective was walking through the police lobby. When he sees a young woman, Sheila, who he believed was his partner's daughter, he calls out to her before realizing his mistake. The partner apologizes before returning to the office he shares with his partner, Detective John Williams, and tells him that there was a young lady sitting in the lobby who resembled his daughter."

The photo montage continues, showing pictures of Sheila's father, his staff and family. "After gathering his answers to a series of questions directed at Sheila's aunt, Mrs. Vivian Johnson, and after finding out Sheila's mother's name, he realized that this was, in fact, the child that he had denied so many years ago. Being a young man at the time, he was unable to fathom the responsibility of being a father. The only proof of his creation was an ultrasound left behind by her infuriated mother. After taking a test to confirm his suspicion, it was revealed that Detective John Williams is in fact Sheila Robinson's father. To top it off, both Damien and his family have forgiven Sheila and Travis for their involvement in the shooting." Sharon smiles as the broadcast returns to Crystal's smiling face, dotted by two glittering tears, streaming down her cheeks.

Crystal's co-anchors are shown wiping their eyes as Monica, the newswoman who covered Damien's original story, chimes in, "What a touching story. There is so much to be learned from these two kids. They should write a book! We wish them all the very best."

Crystal follows up, "Oh yes, they are amazing people. We would also like to wish Damien's sister, Tanya Jackson, who is representing the city of Chicago on *The Voice* tonight, the very best as well."

She turns to Monica, "We will have a follow-up on Tanya's performance tonight on the eleven-p.m. news and a Q&A with some of the people who were involved in this story, including the shooter. Stay tuned for my latest segment of 'What Did You Learn?'"

Sharon and her friends are huddled together around the TV with tears of joy streaming down their faces. Her friend, Betty Walker, shakes her head, "What a wonderful story. Your children are so precious."

Wiping her eyes, Sharon turns to her, "Thank you so much. All the glory goes to God. I thank him for all He has done and all He will continue to do." All of the women around her echo their praises as they return to the kitchen.

Sharon packs some of the food in the car. Just as she breezes through her house to get another load of food, she hears her phone ring and smiles when she sees it's Tanya. She picks up the phone and puts it on speaker. "Hey baby, I have my friends here with me in the kitchen preparing the food for your surprise viewing party at the hospital tonight."

"Hello everyone." Tanya smiles. The humid L.A. air blows through her large afro as she sits peacefully on a balcony.

"You looked so good on television, baby," Betty says.

Tanya sounds surprised. "I was on TV?"

Her mom smiles, "Yes, you were on Chicago Seven news. The whole city is talking about your performance tonight."

Excited, Tanya takes a sip of some cool lemonade in the hot sun. "That's exciting! I just called to let you know that we arrived safely, and I won't be available for the next hour or two because I'll be at rehearsals with the rest of the contestants. We aren't allowed to have our phones on."

Sharon nods and watches as her friends finish plating food and removing the final pots and pans from the oven and stove. "Okay, dear. I love you and wish you well. Give me a call the first chance you can."

"I will, Mom. Bye, everyone."

Tanya is blown away by the chorus of women singing her praises and saying their goodbyes over the phone. They all wish her well. Just as Tanya prepares to hang up, her mother calls for her, "Hey, Tanya, are you still there?"

Tanya replies, "Yes, Mom, I'm still here."

"Is Vivian with you?"

"Yes, Mom." Tanya hands Vivian the phone.

"Hello, Sharon."

Sharon smiles, "Hey Vivian. I have you on speaker phone and I'm here with a few friends of ours from church. They were kind enough to help me prepare the food for the party tonight at the hospital."

"Oh, yes, that's right, you are having the surprise viewing party tonight. I wish I were there. How sweet of everyone to help out. Hey, ladies!"

Everyone shouts out their greetings, then Betty gets on the phone, "Hello, Vivian!"

Vivian looks surprised, "Is that you, Betty?"

Betty replies, "You know it, honey!"

Vivian smiles, "I thought that was you."

Betty continues, "So how's the weather in California?"

Vivian looks at the majestic scenery, "It's absolutely beautiful. We will have to plan a church trip out here next year."

Everyone nods and murmurs in agreement. "Well, I have to get back to work. I'll see you when you get home, Viv. You two stay safe," Betty says.

Then Sharon comes back on the phone, "Thank you again for chaperoning Tanya."

Looking at Tanya, Vivian smiles, "You're welcome, Sharon. This is like a vacation to me, and Tanya is such a special young lady. I just love her to pieces."

Sharon smiles, "Well, I'm glad you arrived safely and you're enjoying yourselves."

"I guess Tanya already told you that she won't have her phone, but I'll have mine on me. I'll just have to keep it low and can only text."

Sharon prepares to finish loading her car as she looks at the time. "Okay, sweetie, I'll talk to you after her performance!"

"I look forward to it, God bless," Vivian sings before hanging up.

The women in the kitchen stand around taking sips of water and cleaning up the kitchen. Sharon brings some more pans to the car before she calls out, "Betty, could you pack Damien's biscuits and Sheila's sweet potato pie separately from all the other items?"

"I sure will," Betty replies. The other women help put some food in their cars before running home to change.

Tanya checks the time. Seeing that she has ten minutes before rehearsal, Tanya decides to call Damien.

Damien is dozing off in front of a soccer game on TV when his phone lights up with Tanya's name. "What's up, superstar? How are you?"

Relieved at hearing her brother's voice, Tanya says, "I'm fine. I just really wish you were here."

Missing his sister, Damien says, "I'm with you in spirit."

Tanya rolls her eyes playfully. "That's what Mom said. I know you both are. For real, it would definitely have been more fun if you both were here."

Damien sighs, wishing he could be in Cali too. "Well, you know what, I'll definitely be there for the finals."

Tanya nods, "Now that's what I'm talking about. I'll make sure that I'm definitely participating in them."

Damien smiles, "Knock it out the park tonight, little sister."

Tanya feels proud. "I will. Love you!"

Damien replies, "Love you, too."

"And please let Sheila know that I said hello, and that I love her," Tanya adds.

Damien responds as he flips through television channels, "Will do." He continues flipping through the channels until he sees the movie *You Got Served*, which he watches before slowly drifting into a peaceful sleep, a smile dressing up his face while he naps.

Several hours pass, and Sharon is bustling around her home, getting ready to head to the hospital. As she checks the doors, she receives an unexpected call from Nurse Roberts and answers immediately, "Hello, Mrs. Roberts. How are you? Is everything okay?"

The nurse speaks calmly, "Yes, I was actually calling with some good news for you. The cafeteria is all set up. Members from your son's football team came by and brought in a banner signed by his teammates, coaches, and friends. The hospital staff also brought a banner, and everyone on the floor signed it, so we hung both the banners and some balloons all over the cafeteria."

Sharon takes a seat, unable to withstand the amount of gratitude she feels for what she is hearing. The nurse continues, "Oh, yes, and before I forget, we also brought in some finger food and non-alcoholic beverages along with a big screen TV."

Sharon sighs with a deep sense of satisfaction in her soul. "That is excellent news. We just got done packing up the food and will be leaving for the hospital shortly."

The nurse nods approvingly, "That's great timing, Sharon. When you arrive, please text me, and I will have two volunteers meet you at the cafeteria's back entrance."

Sharon nods, standing up to head out the door. "Sounds good!" Then she thinks of something, "So how will we get Damien to the cafeteria?"

The nurse waves her hand nonchalantly. "I have that all planned out." As she goes over the intricate plans, Sharon is impressed by the elaborate details. After confirming that everything is set, they say their goodbyes.

"Oh, Nurse Roberts, before you go, I just wanted to let you know that I really appreciate everything that you, your staff and the entire hospital have done for me and my family."

The nurse smiles warmly, "No, thank you. You have taught us all here a lesson about faith, love, and forgiveness. You have an amazing family."

Sharon looks up to the heavens. She misses her husband and feels grateful for the role he played in making their family what it is. "Thanks again and see you soon." Before leaving the house, Sharon telephones some of Damien's friends and tells them to get to please arrive at the hospital by six p.m.

Nurse Roberts heads to Damien's room and finds him and Sheila playing cards and laughing. She smiles at them before addressing the matter at hand, "Bandage change, buddy."

Damien glances at the nurse with a pleading look, "Is it okay for Sheila to stay while you change the bandages?"

Nurse Roberts shrugs, preparing an area to place the medical supplies. "It's really up to you."

Damien turns to Sheila, "Will you stay?"

She looks at him shyly, "Yeah, if you want me to."

Damien looks at her with love in his eyes, "I do."

Nurse Roberts looks on joyously at their puppy love. Then she slowly removes Damien's bandages. This is the first time that Sheila has seen Damien's wounds from the shooting. She tears up instantly.

Damien looks at her, "It's okay."

Nurse Roberts sees Sheila crying. "I know you're feeling bad about the shooting, but toughen up, girl! One day, you may have to change these bandages for him."

Sheila smiles through her tears. "Yeah, I guess you're right. I'll do anything for my Boo, and that includes changing his bandages."

The nurse glances at Sheila as she wraps the new bandage, "That's my girl."

Then Nurse Roberts pulls a gold and green marker out of her pocket and draws a stallion on Damien's cast and signs it: *Best Nurse Ever. Nurse Roberts.*

Damien checks out the detailed drawing, and his eyes widen. "Wow, that's fire!"

Shocked and confused, Nurse Roberts asks, "Damien, did you say I should be fired?"

Damien cracks up, "Oh no. I was saying that the stallion you drew is fire. That means it's awesome."

Nurse Roberts pauses for a moment and laughs, shaking her head.

Damien and Sheila join in before Damien continues, "Seriously though, thank you so much for everything, Nurse Roberts."

She squeezes his hand. "You're so welcome."

Feeling her eyes begin to water, the nurse dabs at them quickly, smiles again, and takes a deep breath. "Well, how're you feeling?"

Damien nods, "I feel fine."

Nurse Roberts nods in return, "Great, save your energy because you'll be needing it tonight for your visitors." As if by magic, Nurse Roberts gets a call from Sharon, and she excuses herself and leaves the room.

"Hey, Mrs. Roberts, I've just arrived at the hospital," Sharon says.

Nurse Roberts leans against the wall. "Okay. Go to the cafeteria. The two volunteers will be waiting there to assist with everything." She hangs up and goes back to Damien's room to say goodbye to the kids before heading to the cafeteria.

As soon as Sharon reaches the cafeteria, she is greeted by two members of the cafeteria staff, who follow her back to the car with a few carts. The aroma of the food escapes as she opens the car door.

The volunteers look on in amazement. "Wow, the food smells so amazing."

Sharon smiles graciously and takes out a few pans. "Thank you so much. Wait until you taste it." She tries to hand each of them twenty dollars, but they kindly refuse the money. One volunteer, Rachel, shakes her head, "Please donate it to a worthy cause instead."

Admiring their work ethic and genuine kindness, Sharon nods, "You know what, I definitely will." Once all the food is loaded onto the cart, Sharon parks her car and returns to the volunteers unloading the food in the cafeteria.

Sharon enters the cafeteria and looks in admiration at all that the staff has done. Balloons bearing the Morgan Stallion uniform colors are everywhere. There are three large banners. There is one for Tanya that reads: *Congratulations on The Voice Auditions! Chicago is Rooting for You!*

The banner from Damien's football team reads: *Jackson Strong!! We Love You, Damien Jackson! We Wish You a Full Recovery*. The third banner is from his hospital staff, reading: *Your Smile and Your Family Have Truly Inspired Us All. Stay Strong. We Wish You All the Best!* All of the banners are covered in signatures and doodles. Lining the back wall are two round tables filled with finger food, snacks, and beverages along with two large, empty tables for the food that Sharon and her friends prepared.

As she stands there taking everything in, someone taps her on her shoulder. She is greeted by a grinning Nurse Roberts, "Well, how do you like what we've done to the cafeteria?"

Sharon turns and gives Nurse Roberts a long and heartfelt hug. "I can't thank you enough. You all are amazing." She dabs at the tears falling from her eyes.

The nurse holds Sharon's hands. "We thank you for such a wonderful experience. And we'll continue to give Damien the very best care." They hug again, and Sharon stands back in awe.

Nurse Roberts's pager goes off. "Okay, I've got to go, and I'll leave you all to set up," Nurse Roberts says, "I expect for the crowd to start coming in soon."

Sharon walks in the opposite direction to help set up the food she brought. Nurse Roberts shouts back, "I'm going to go take care of this, then I'll head upstairs to bring Damien down."

Sharon gives an enthusiastic thumbs up. "This is so exciting!"

As Sharon sets up the food, she sees a gentleman wearing a Channel 7 Chicago jacket walk in and begins setting up cameras. She stops when she sees Crystal, her favorite news anchor for Chicago 7 news, walk in. Then one after another, guests start to arrive. She's greeted warmly by Damien's teammates and coaches, Sheila's parents and siblings, Pastor Chisholm and members from the church, some of the hospital staff, and even Tom, the gentleman who, according to her son, is trying to hit on her.

While standing in front of the tables, looking everything over, Sharon hears a voice, "Hello, Mrs. Jackson."

Sharon turns to her right and sees Celeste accompanied by another young woman. They hug briefly.

"Hello, Celeste, how are you? I'm so glad that you could make it. I'm sure that Damien will be happy to see you." She glances at Celeste's friend. "And who's this young lady you're with?"

Celeste introduces her friend. "Please meet Tammi, my friend from the African braiding salon. Tammi, meet Damien's mother, Mrs. Jackson."

They shake hands. "I love your braids," Sharon comments.

Tammi smiles, "Thanks. You should stop by the shop some day and let me braid your hair. It will be my treat."

Sharon is taken aback. "You know, Tammi, I may just take you up on that."

Tammi smiles and hands Sharon her business card. "Feel free to call me any time."

Sharon accepts the card with a smile and puts it in her pocket. "You are so sweet. Thank you both for stopping by."

Suddenly someone claps loudly and makes an announcement. It's a volunteer named David, "May I have your attention, everyone? I just wanted to thank everyone for showing up to show support for Damien's sister, Tanya, tonight. I also wanted to inform you that I've seen some negative postings about Sheila online, so I ask you to please show her some love tonight. She's also recovering from a major surgery here at the hospital." Celeste nudges Tammi and rolls her eyes.

David looks around at the patiently waiting faces. "I just received a text from Nurse Roberts saying Damien should be arriving in the next twenty minutes. There is plenty of food and beverages. I know it smells delicious in here, and that's thanks to Mrs. Jackson's great cooking."

Suddenly, Damien's teammates and friends let out a roar of applause. The volunteer intervenes, "We also ask that you wait before eating until the food has been blessed. Other than that, have fun and I'll let you know when Damien's on his way down." Then, the volunteer positions himself outside of the cafeteria and closes the door.

Upon entering Damien's room, Nurse Roberts sees that Damien is enjoying talking to a few of his friends, including Chris and Sheila. Nurse Roberts checks the time and proceeds with the plan. She has a look of concern on her face. "Hey, Damien, unfortunately there's been an emergency, and we will have to close down this floor to all visitors."

Damien looks at her with disappointment, "Nah, you're not serious."

The nurse shakes her head, "I'm sorry, but this is coming from the chief of staff. But before you get all upset, I've arranged to have a television moved to the cafeteria so you and your friends can watch your sister's performance there. I will have the administrator at the front desk direct your guests to the cafeteria. But we do have to move. Now."

Damien sits up slightly. "Yes, I guess that'll work." Nurse Roberts takes her phone out of her pocket and pretends to correspond with the administrator. Actually, she's talking to David, the volunteer outside of the cafeteria.

The nurse moves quickly to get Damien's wheelchair. "Okay, Damien, we need to go down now. This floor needs to be cleared immediately."

Damien grabs his phone and a jacket. "I understand."

Sheila turns to him after scanning the room. "You got everything?"

Damien checks too. "Yeah."

Chris puts an arm on his friend's shoulder as he steadies himself on his own. "Do you need a wheelchair?"

Damien looks at it and shakes his head as he stands tall. "No thanks. I'm good. I just need to call my mom."

The nurse looks anxious, and Sheila responds, "Let's wait until we get downstairs."

Damien replies, "You're right." The teens follow Nurse Roberts to the elevators where they make their way to the cafeteria.

Closing the doors, the volunteers tell the guests that Damien is on his way. Everyone quiets down, and Sharon nervously moves near the entrance. Nurse Roberts arrives at the cafeteria and pretends to have a tough time getting in. She gestures to Damien. "Let's see how strong your left hand is."

Damien steps forward and pulls down on the handle, swinging the door open. Much to his surprise, he's greeted by a room full of people, shouting, "Surprise!"

Damien looks around in awe. "You got me." He can't help but cry. His mother walks up to him and holds him as he continues to weep. He wipes his eyes as several people come up to him, smiling and wishing him well. Fortunately, his guests are also being kind to Sheila by wishing her well on her recovery and congratulating her on her new relationship with Damien.

Sharon takes to the floor, clapping loudly. "Okay, everyone. Let's quiet down so that Pastor Chisholm can bless the food." Everyone gathers around as the pastor approaches the tables of food while Sharon continues expressing herself.

Looking around with joyful tears in her eyes, Mrs. Jackson says, "I want to thank everyone for their help in making this all possible. I would like to give a special thanks to Nurse Roberts, to all of the doctors who have taken such good care of both Damien and Sheila, and of course, to all the volunteers who have made this night possible. Thanks so much to you all." Sharon leads the room in a loud chorus of applause.

Pastor Chisholm smiles expectantly, and seeing the eager faces staring back at him, he makes his blessing short and sweet. "Now I see those mouths watering, let's eat!"

As if approaching the starting block, the entire Morgan Park football team rushes to line up in front of Sharon's famous food. Sharon watches the players racing to get in line. Smiling, she shouts,

"Hey, there's really no need to rush. There is more than enough food to go around."

The coaches start laughing, and one of them comments, "I wish that they rushed like that to practice."

Mrs. Jackson notices Damien watching his teammates as they pile on their food. She places a hand on his and Sheila's shoulders. "I've already made you and Sheila a plate, and I made you both a special treat. So you two take a seat, and I'll bring your plates right out."

Damien and Sheila look up at his mom and respond in unison, "Thank you so much."

She beams at them happily, "You're welcome." As they both get comfortable, she shares some advice. "All I ask of you both is to please take care of each other."

They look at each other and respond at the same time, "We will." Then the teens share a sweet kiss as Damien's mom goes to get their food.

Just then Celeste slides up to Damien and leans on his chair. "Now look at the cute little lovebirds." She reaches out her hand to Sheila and introduces herself, "Hey, I'm Celeste."

Sheila cuts her eyes at her. "So, you're the infamous Celeste. I'm Sheila." She shakes Celeste's hand. "Damien told me so much about you."

Celeste glances at Damien, "I hope it was all good."

Sheila turns to face her, "Well, not quite. He told me that you have friends everywhere, and apparently they're good at spreading misinformation, too."

Before she can respond, Damien bursts out laughing and gives Celeste a big hug. She sneakily rolls her eyes at Sheila. Turning back to Damien, she asks, "How are you feeling?"

Damien smiles, "Much better, honestly." Then he wraps his arm around Sheila's waist. "As soon as me and my Boo are out of this hospital, we should all meet up and go to the movies or something."

Celeste shrugs, and she and Sheila steal glances at each other. "I would love that." Celeste looks over at Tammi, who's fixing their plates. "Well, I wish you all the best," Celeste says, her hand lingering on Damien's shoulder before rejoining Tammi at another table.

The cafeteria is noticeably quieter as everyone sits around enjoying the food. Finished eating, Nurse Roberts turns on the TV. The room suddenly erupts into cheers as *The Voice* appears on the screen while Tanya is being interviewed.

"Well, now that you are in sunny Los Angeles on *The Voice,* what would you like to say to your family and friends back home?" A reporter named Robin points the mic at Tanya, who stands smiling broadly.

Tanya holds the mic and looks directly into the camera with confidence, "I would first like to thank God for this amazing opportunity to be on my favorite show. And of course, I would like to say hello to my mother and my big brother, who I love with all my heart." Tanya takes a moment to think of what else she would want to say. "I also want to give a shout out to First Baptist church on 935 E 50th St., and my brother's football team, the Morgan Park Stallions, and everyone back at home who has shown so much love and support for my family."

Robin, the interviewer teases, "Are you sure there's no one else?"

Tanya chuckles, "Yes, I'm sure."

"So, tell us about the song you'll be singing for us tonight," Robin says.

Tanya answers eagerly, "I will be singing 'I Wanna Know What Love Is' by Foreigner."

Robin peers into the camera with a look of surprise. "How did you decide on this particular song?"

Tanya explains, "See, I had a number of songs that I knew my brother loved to hear me sing. One of those songs was Mariah Carey's version of 'I Wanna Know What Love Is', and we locked that in a few days ago. After my brother, Damien, was shot last month, I told our mom that I would wait for him to wake up from surgery then have him choose the song that I would sing. So, one day, while my mom and I were visiting him at the hospital, he leaned over to me and told me about a dream he had where I was performing 'I Wanna Know What Love Is.' And here we are!"

Robin looks into the camera. "What a great story. I truly love that song. I often find myself singing that song over and over again while I'm in the shower."

They laugh together, and Tanya continues, "I believe you. It's a very meaningful and catchy song."

Then Tanya looks right at the camera and continues, "I would like to dedicate this song to everyone out there who's searching for love. From the newborn babies to the elderly, and everyone in between. A special dedication of this song goes out to my brother's girlfriend, Sheila, who has made a successful reunion with her father after sixteen years without each other."

Encouraged by the Spirit, she continues, "There are so many people in our world that are hurting and that have heard the word love and still never experience being loved."

Robin looks on. "Wow! It's so sad, but it's so true. Well, Tanya, are you ready?"

Tanya looks excited. "Yes!"

Robin then turns to the audience and announces, "Ladies and gentlemen, representing Chicago, Illinois, here is Miss Tanya Jackson."

As Tanya steps on the stage, the music starts up, and everyone can feel the intensity in her voice, growing stronger and stronger with each note. The audience joins in with her as the judges turn around in their chairs, one by one. As she draws out the last melodic note, Tanya finishes the song in tears. The crowd goes wild, and she points to the heavens, "You are an amazing God." Remembering her father, she says, "I love you, Dad."

There isn't a dry eye in the arena. Tanya receives a standing ovation from the judges and the audience. When the judges take their seats, they each reach for tissues to wipe their eyes before competing for her to be on their team.

Natalia, one of the judges, has several number one songs of her own topping the current pop chart. "Well, baby, I'm from Chicago, and my dear, you have an amazing voice. You really lived in that song. Do you know what I mean by that?"

Tanya replies, "Yes, you meant that I truly felt it so you all could feel it, too."

Natalia nods, "Exactly. You are so awesome and extremely mature for your age. I plead with you to please join my team."

Tanya smiles, "Thank you so much. But I'm gonna need some help from the audience." The majority of the audience starts chanting Natalia's name. Tanya nods knowingly, "I don't think that it's a coincidence that my full name is Tanya Natalia Jackson." She looks at Natalia, who is waiting expectantly. "I love all your songs, so I choose you, Natalia."

Natalia, the television audience, and everyone back home in the hospital cafeteria erupt in applause again.

Then everyone in the cafeteria begins to chant, "Tanya Jackson, Tanya Jackson!"

Thirty minutes later. Tanya calls her mom, who waves for everyone to please quiet down. "Tanya's on the phone!"

"Hello, Tanya, I'm here at Damien's surprise party with lots of guests, and I have you on speaker phone. We're all here, and we saw your performance. You were magnificent."

Tanya stands near Vivian. "Thanks, Mom. Hi, everyone!"

"Hello, Tanya," everyone yells and congratulates her. Then they continue chanting her name again.

Tanya laughs as Vivian rubs her back. "Thank you so much, but please stop. You're going to make me cry. But where's my big brother?" Tanya asks.

Damien, standing next to his mom, chimes in, "I'm right here, little sister. I'm so proud of you. You're a superstar in the making."

She smiles, watching the sunset outside. "You know what the Jackson family always says: 'All the glory goes to God.'"

Damien chuckles, "You got it. I love you, little sis."

Tanya replies, "I love you more."

Then Tanya asks for Sheila, "Sheila, are you there?"

Sheila comes closer to the phone. "Yes, congratulations! I loved your outfit. You looked gorgeous, and your performance was awesome."

Tanya beams, "Thanks, I love you so much."

Sheila smiles brightly, "I love you, too."

Tanya looks inside the arena. "I have to do an interview, Mom. But Mrs. Johnson wanted me to let you know that she will call you tonight."

"Okay, sweetie. I'll look out for her call."

Tanya says her goodbyes to everyone as they all start chanting her name again. Tanya says, "I love you guys." Then they end the call.

As everyone finishes up the food, Crystal from Chicago 7 news walks over to Sharon and smiles, "What a performance, an amazing night, amazing food, and an amazing family."

Sharon turns to her and shakes her hand. "That was so kind of you."

Crystal continues, "I also wanted to inform you that the coverage from today's event will be running on the eleven o'clock evening news. I can't wait to share everyone's answers about what they've learned from all of this." She adjusts her purse before looking toward her crew.

Sharon smiles at her again, "It's been an honor to meet you. I love your content. You have a wonderful night."

Crystal flashes a genuine smile, "I already have."

Everyone helps clean up the cafeteria, and Sharon helps pack up leftovers for Damien's teammates. Her friend Tom helps her out as Sharon loads up his car with her pots and pans. "Can you please take these overnight? I'll pick them up in the morning."

Tom smiles at her flirtatiously, "Yes, after such a great meal, that's the least I can do."

Sharon smiles, "You are too kind. Goodnight, Tom. I'll see you tomorrow." She kisses him on his cheek before sending him away.

Sharon then joins her son and Sheila's family at a table, where they sit reminiscing about their incredible night. "Everyone was so lovely," Sharon says.

Sheila's dad nods in agreement, "Yes, and that food!" Feeling quite content, John pats his belly.

"You know mom, the news anchor Crystal asked me if I could change one thing that led up to my shooting, what would it be?"

"And what did you say, son?" Sharon asks, putting an arm around him.

He replies, "I thought about it for a while, and then I said that I wouldn't change a thing."

Everyone looks on, eagerly awaiting an explanation. His mom asks, "And why would you say that?"

Damien responds with a smile, "Because I felt that God used me as a vessel to deliver this gigantic blessing of introducing Sheila and her father. To me, that was worth taking a bullet for." He looks over at Sheila, who is glowing with happiness.

Sharon smiles at Damien and kisses his head. "That is so sweet of you, Damien. I just pray that in the future, God has a simpler way to use you."

Everyone laughs lightheartedly, and then John adds, "In all seriousness, yes, me too, Damien. Thank you so much for those extremely kind words."

Sheila smiles and hugs him. "That was very sweet of you."

Then she takes Damien by the hand and motions for her brother and sister to come with them to take some more selfies. With their stomachs filled with food, her siblings slowly make their way over, yawning as Damien shakes his head. "More selfies?"

Sheila holds up the camera once everyone's settled. "You know it! You can never have enough selfies."

Sheila has convinced Damien to make a video of him and her singing the song as a duet for TikTok. Suddenly everyone in the cafeteria joins Sheila and Damien as they sing, 'I Wanna Know What Love Is' at the top of their lungs.

Sheila's parents look on, admiring the young love blossoming before them. Her father remarks, "Hopefully, they'll get the chance at the love that we missed out on."

Anita looks at him and smiles. Nudging his arm, she says, "It's such a blessing to see that those two young hearts that were jailed by lust have been released by love."

Sheila's father looks at her mother. "Yes, I just pray that I live long enough to enjoy many more of these joyful moments with my daughter."

Anita tears up. "Me, too."

Sharon walks over to Sheila's parents, looking as tired as can be. "I'm beat, everyone, so I'm heading home." Anita and John stand up and hug her. "Thanks for everything. We had an awesome time."

Sharon smiles sleepily. Her face muscles are sore from all of the smiling she has done today. But she is overjoyed by the feelings coursing through her. "You are so welcome." She walks over to her son, who sits with Sheila's head resting on his shoulder.

Tapping him lightly on the shoulder before caressing his head, Sharon says, "I'll call you in the morning, baby."

Damien stands up and gives his mom a hug. "Thank you for such an awesome night. I love you!" He kisses her head.

Sheila makes her way to Damien's mom, giving her a long hug, too. "Yes, Mrs. Johnson, thanks for everything, especially the sweet potato pie."

Sharon smiles, "You're welcome, baby. But about that pie, Sheila, please be sure to check with your nurse before eating it."

Sheila points at her knowingly. "I was going do that, but then I ate it."

Sharon laughs as she backs out. "Let me get out of here, you sillies."

Sheila waves goodbye as Damien walks his mom to the elevator. They kiss goodbye, and Damien stands watching until the elevator closes. He lingers for a moment. Then, looks up to the heavens and smiles at his father. He is met by tears as he stops to thank God for his family, friends, and a second chance at life.

Chapter 29

What Did You Learn?

B y the time Sharon finally reaches her home, it is 11:07 p.m. She remembers the interviews and quickly turns on the news to watch Crystal's latest segment. Unfortunately, Sharon is only able to catch the tail end of the interview. She tunes in as Crystal appears on the screen, she announces, "To conclude this story, I asked one final question to several of the individuals involved. My question is: What have you learned from this whole experience? Let's see their thoughts." A video appears on the screen showing everyone in different settings answering Crystal's trademark question.

Celeste sits on a bench next to Tammi, who says, "I've learned that, although I may have eyes everywhere, I need to confirm the information that I'm given. Sometimes, gossip is just plain gossip."

Tammi chimes in, "I've learned that everything is not always as it seems. When I saw Travis and Sheila kissing outside my salon, I automatically assumed that they were a couple. Then I shared the misinformation with my friends, who immediately shared it with theirs. My assumption almost cost a young man his life and got another to be sentenced to eleven years in prison. It all happened based on my assumption."

The video shifts to a scene of Sheila sitting by a window, the sun casting a bright glow around her. "I've learned so much. First, I learned the difference between love and lust. And that love starts with loving and respecting yourself first. I also learned that there's no shame in practicing abstinence. And if you choose not to be, make it your choice and no one else's. In other words, don't ever be forced into something you don't want to do. I learned to be a trendsetter and a leader, not a follower. I've also learned that miracles really do come true. I mean, being united with my dad for the first time ever while being on vacation in Chicago was a true miracle. Damien surviving after being shot three times was a miracle. And my aunt finding me unconscious when she did was a miracle. Lastly, I learned it's not always about the time you lost, but the time you have in front of you. I plan to utilize my time wisely and cherish each opportunity I get to spend with my dad," Sheila says proudly.

Then, Damien appears on the screen. Sitting in the cafeteria, he says, "Man where do I begin, I've learned so much. The first thing I've learned is that life is so very precious and that as hard as it was for me, I choose to be part of the solution and not the problem. I was so angry when I woke up and was told by my mom that I had gotten shot and that Sheila had played a major role in it."

"My first thought was to get revenge on both Sheila and Travis. However, after praying and expressing what I was feeling with my family, they helped me to realize that I was right to have those feelings. They pointed out that my actions also triggered what went down and that pursuing revenge would not help but would only escalate the anger within me. People make mistakes, and although Sheila's mistake almost cost me my life, I truly know that was not her intention. As for Travis, he's already paying a steep price. So along with my family, I've decided to go ahead and forgive them and not let the anger take over my life. Also, I learned that when parents give you advice, listen closely. Parents usually want the best for their children; I know my dad did. Unprotected sex is extremely risky. It's like playing Russian roulette with you and your partner's life. I also learned that you may have to pay a hefty price for the poor choices that can be made in a split second. And the impact of that same harm can last for generations to come."

Then Damien smiles at the camera and winks, "Finally in renewing my relationship with Sheila I've learned that there is so much more to a young lady than what meets the eyes. A relationship based on love, and not lust truly feels good, and I'm really looking forward to spending a lot more quality time together with my Boo."

Then we see a clip of Tanya, sitting next to her mom. She says, "I've learned that as for me, my faith and family are always first and that I can accomplish anything I put my mind to. All it takes is a little bit of effort on my part, and God will meet me halfway."

The camera pans to Sharon who chimes in, "God is so good all the time, and He's never too late or never too early. He's always right on time." She nods, "And, yes, faith and family first always." She and Tanya look at each other and then pump their fists in the air, shouting: "Jackson Strong!"

We see Vivian sitting on her porch sipping her iced tea. "I learned that love goes a long way, and it always conquers hate," she states. Then, she looks directly into the camera, "And no matter what anyone tells you, prayer really does work I've seen the power in prayer firsthand. Neither one of our families could have survived all that we went through but for the grace of God."

We are taken to a clip of Detective Williams, Sheila's father, sitting in his office with the ultrasound still sitting on his mantel. It's accented by a recent picture of him and Sheila. "I learned that everyone makes poor choices, and we're especially prone when we are young. But all we can do is own it and move forward with grace and inspired action to do better." Then he looks directly at the camera, "And to the young fathers or soon-to-be fathers out there, I've learned that before ever denying that a child is yours, please have a DNA test performed, especially if you're really doubting that the child is yours. And regardless of how angry you may be, always take the time to communicate and listen to one another. If I would have done these important things, I would have never missed out on sixteen years of Sheila's life."

Anita is sitting on the steps of Vivian's house, smiling, "Although you get upset with one another, don't let that stop a parent from having a relationship with their child. Keep the communication open for wonderful possibilities. Forgiveness is a difficult and powerful thing." She looks into the distance. "You will be so free when you let forgiveness into your heart. Not just toward others but also with yourself."

Then we see Travis behind a glass window, wearing a dull orange jumpsuit. "I've learned the hard way that no one is worth throwing your life away for and that I shouldn't have acted too fast on my emotions. There are so many other ways to solve our issues that don't involve violence. Let me be your example that no one wins with violence. After Recently serving two years in prison, I now have been sentenced to eleven years for the crime I committed on Damian, and I could have gotten life if Damien had died. All the time that I am serving in prison is because of the terrible decisions I've made. I don't have anything positive to show for it, not even the family I wanted with Sheila."

"However, from this day on I am committed to working with parents to do everything in my power to help prevent their child from making the same mistakes that I've made. So please, if you are within the reach of my voice, and have been thinking about committing a crime, I beg you to think twice before throwing your life away. It's a fact that your life matters more outside these prison walls, than it ever will inside. The choice is yours."

The broadcast returns to Crystal, who sits shedding tears of joy. "We will be back after these messages."

Sharon turns off the television and sits in the silence for a while. She starts to cry before falling to her knees in front of the couch and rejoicing in prayer.

"Heavenly Father, you have covered all of us in your mercy and light, and I want to thank You, God. For our healing, for our togetherness, for our faith and forgiveness. And thank you so much for all the little miracles hiding in the most mundane things and for keeping us all safe to see another day of your glory."

"Also, Heavenly Father, I want to thank You for opening the eyes and hearts of my son and his girlfriend, Sheila, who have both chosen to turn over a new leaf and begin their new relationship based on love and not lust. Please continue to keep them safe and wrapped in your loving arms. And oh' Lord I forgot to mention, please let my darling husband know that his family remains Jackson strong. Amen!"